Praise for *Suitcase City* by Sterling Watson

"The telling is masterful . . . est. It's better than bourbon on the rocks." starred review

"Hypnotically beautiful novel . . . Paranoia has been defined as 'seeing too much pattern.' Author Watson can make us sweaty victims of that madness, partaking of it, suffering from it, and loving every minute."
—*Booklist*, starred review

"Watson's magic is in pacing and taut prose . . . *Suitcase City* is an absorbing thriller, a vivid adventure in a bright, humid, perilous underworld . . . [A] tense, bloody thriller with a strong sense of place and a soft heart."
—*Shelf Awareness*, starred review

"[A] noir gem . . . A deeply contemplative and darkly poetic prose style complements the well-crafted plot." —*Publishers Weekly*

"A solid revenge tale . . . There is plenty of action to be had in this suspense tale, but it is the examination of the characters' motivations that really makes it shine. For fans of Lee Child and Nicci French." —*Library Journal*

"Gripping . . . As [Watson] spins additional threads within the plot, deepening our interest in even minor characters, his grip remains steady . . . Peeling back the layers of Tampa society to reveal a crosshatching of race and class—the country club scenes are particularly fine—Watson stealthily heightens the suspense." —*Barnes & Noble Review*

"Watson weaves . . . questions about race into a plot that takes one bloody turn after another, a crescendo of violence that ends with a day at sea that might be the most chilling of all." —*Tampa Bay Times*

"[An] irresistible earworm of a novel . . . With its airtight atmosphere of impending, life-sinking doom, and taut language evoking palpable Gulf Coast Florida seediness, *Suitcase City* duly takes its place alongside the best works of former Floridian Pete Dexter, and the brilliant Tampa novels of Dennis Lehane."
—*Paste*

"*Suitcase City* [is] such a damn great book, a too-rare (and sometimes nearly too real) depiction of the wildly different worlds that exist side by side in the city by the bay . . . Events uncoil with an unflashy confidence and understated poetry, drawing in diverse characters whose deep inner lives give the wire-tight plot a thumping, nervous heart." —*Creative Loafing Tampa*

"*Suitcase City* is a beautifully crafted labyrinth of plot and subplot."
—*Florida Book Review*

"The novels of Sterling Watson are to be treasured and passed on to the next generation." —Dennis Lehane, author of *Since We Fell*

"Sterling Watson is an American treasure. If this taut literary crime novel doesn't center him on the map, we should change maps."
—Tom Franklin, author of *Crooked Letter, Crooked Letter*

"I am a huge fan of Sterling Watson's writing, and take it from me: *Suitcase City* is arguably his best novel to date. I began reading and did not look up again until the very last page, so taken was I by its twists and turns, its explorations of race and honor and the love a father has for his daughter. Turn off your phone, lock your door, and dive into *Suitcase City*."
—Ann Hood, author of *The Obituary Writer*

"As Watson reminds us, corruption and cruelty survive through their uncanny ability to take on new shapes."
—Laura Lippman, author of *Sunburn*

Nima Setlur

STERLING WATSON is the author of eight novels, including *Deadly Sweet, Sweet Dream Baby, Fighting in the Shade*, and *Suitcase City*. Watson's short fiction and nonfiction have appeared in *Prairie Schooner*, the *Georgia Review*, the *Los Angeles Times Book Review*, the *Michigan Quarterly Review*, and the *Southern Review*. He was director of the creative writing program at Eckerd College for twenty years and now teaches in the Solstice MFA Program at Pine Manor College in Boston. Of his sixth novel, *Suitcase City*, Tom Franklin said, "If this taut literary crime novel doesn't center Sterling Watson on the map, we should change maps." Watson lives in St. Petersburg, Florida.

THE COMMITTEE

A NOVEL

STERLING WATSON

BROOKLYN, NEW YORK, USA
BALLYDEHOB, CO. CORK, IRELAND

This is a work of fiction. All names, characters, places, and incidents are the product of the author's imagination or are used fictitiously. Any resemblance to real events or persons, living or dead, is entirely coincidental.

Published by Akashic Books

Paperback ISBN: 978-1-61775-768-6
Hardcover ISBN: 978-1-61775-783-9
Library of Congress Control Number: 2019935266

First printing

Akashic Books
Brooklyn, New York, USA
Ballydehob, Co. Cork, Ireland
Twitter: @AkashicBooks
Facebook: AkashicBooks
E-mail: info@akashicbooks.com
Website: www.akashicbooks.com

To Linda, the best sister a guy could ever have

Author's Note

This novel opens in Gainesville, Florida, a university city, in the year 1958 when the infamous Johns Committee of the Florida legislature sought to root out homosexuals, Communists, and advocates for civil rights in public universities across the state, portraying them as a dire threat to the children of Florida.

All writers of fiction based on history struggle with the question: How much latitude may I grant myself in changing the facts to meet the demands of the story? Few historical events of any importance actually arrange themselves as fiction must and does arrange itself. History is often not a story but a mess. Academic historians will find that my greatest sin in this novel is the compression of time. For dramatic purposes, I have made things that took years to unfold happen in months or days.

The facts of history are that in 1953, Florida's governor, Dan McCarty, died of a heart attack and was succeeded by Charley Johns, president of the Senate, who established or at least gave his imprimatur to the Florida Legislative Investigation Committee—the Johns Committee.

When I began graduate school at the University of Florida in 1969, I met professors who had been harassed by the Committee. Some were permanently scarred. I became intrigued by their stories, but I must emphasize that all but one of the characters in *The Committee* are invented. My invented characters are not based on real people, though many are typical—in the sense that people resembling my characters did then and do now populate university cities.

In this novel, I have attempted to portray the thoughts and actions of ordinary people as they would have been in 1958, not as we wish they had been. It is shortsighted and all too easy to write about historical subjects by teleporting our own "enlightened" views back to the past so that fictional characters may resemble us in our more evolved state (which, of course, will seem quaint or worse to our grandchildren). Thus, one of the difficulties of this project was to create characters who are more or less typical of their times but also open to the sympathy of readers who have achieved different or higher levels of consciousness. Of course, I say this in full awareness of the fact that in every age there are people who see far into the future and act as denizens of the future will act when their time comes on the stage. Most of us live and act in the fog and error of our times, to the best of our abilities, sometimes guided by what William Faulkner called "the old verities." If some of those verities have found their way into this book, that is good enough for me. By definition, they never change.

A man lives not only his personal life, as an individual, but also, consciously or unconsciously, the life of his epoch and his contemporaries.
—Thomas Mann, *The Magic Mountain*

The one red leaf, the last of its clan,
That dances as often as dance it can . . .
—Samuel Taylor Coleridge, "Christabel"

ONE

It was a strange sound.

Not a scream, not a shout, not the squealing of brakes, neither obviously human nor clearly mechanical, at least not to Tom Stall's ear.

At three o'clock on an August afternoon, the sound drifted through the open window of Stall's University of Florida office as he sat preparing his recommendations to the English Department chairman for September's graduate assistantships. He sat waiting, thinking the closest thing to that sound he had ever heard was the climactic cry of the French girl he had slept with in Paris, in 1945, his only wartime indiscretion. Such a similarity—the two sounds so much alike, the first imprinted on his memory forever, the second a mystery—struck him as not just strange but ill-omened. The sound resembled love, or if not that, at least passion, and later this seemed to Stall the supreme irony of a day that would change his life forever.

Then a girl screamed and Stall left the stuffy, cluttered office he had inherited when the department had made him assistant chairman and headed down the hall at a pace that would look determined but not hurried to anyone who noticed him. As he passed the offices whose doors were open to catch any breeze that might stir the ancient water oaks that lined both sides of Anderson Hall, he glimpsed the forms of his colleagues (those not traveling during the final days of summer) bent over the articles and books they hoped would get them tenure, or promotion, or the scholarly fame that had thus far fled them like the maiden on Keats's Grecian urn. No one looked up from books, yellow legal pads, clacking typewriters. Apparently, no one but Stall had heard the strange sound. He was moving fast when he passed the office of Sophie Green, the new medievalist, the English graduate faculty's first female professor. In a blue cotton skirt and a white blouse, she stood with her back to Stall, her slender fingers running along the spines of the books he had helped her carry up from a battered DeSoto with New York plates. She was pretty in the dark, intense way of actresses in movies who take off their glasses and shake out their hair declaring themselves not mere vessels of ideas, but human—*human*. She was Jewish, and she was brilliant. (Stall had read her work with what he had to admit was envy.) He considered stopping to ask her if she had heard anything, knew anything, but thought better of it. Better to keep moving.

The girl who had screamed had also vomited. Stall carefully placed his new blazer over the face of the man who lay dead on the sidewalk in front of Murphree Hall and went to the girl. He stood blocking her view of what she had already seen and looked down at the boxwood hedge behind her where her lunch of grilled cheese and french fries steamed into the hot afternoon. The smell of vomit and blood made Stall's own stomach writhe. He patted the girl's shoulder. She wore a sorority pin and seemed to him average for the type, in saddle oxfords, bobby socks, a short-sleeved white blouse, and a tartan skirt that covered her knees. A small crowd had gathered, and Stall thanked his stars for the thin summer-school enrollment. If Jack Leaf had fallen or jumped to his death from a third-floor classroom window a few weeks from now, fifty students might have seen him hit the pavement and a hundred more would have surrounded his broken body before anything could be done to keep them away.

A boy in the crowd looked older than most undergraduates. He wore a light sport coat with leathered elbows and was smoking a pipe. The boy's flattop haircut and erect bearing told Stall he was probably a veteran. Stall guided the sobbing girl to the older boy and whispered, "Would you please take care of her. I've got to . . ." He wasn't sure exactly what he had to do, but he was the only university official here now and had to do something. The boy slipped the pipe into the breast pocket of his sport coat and put his arm around the girl's shoulders.

Tom Stall looked at the shocked faces of the students who had gathered and asked quietly, "Did any of you see him . . . fall?"

Two boys in khakis and button-down shirts shook their heads, unable to take their eyes from the pool of blood that spread from under the canopy of Stall's blazer. Looking at the coat and the growing puddle and hearing the first fly buzz to the smell of blood, Stall thought, *The coat should cover his hands. God, I wish it were big enough to cover his hands.* There was something unbearably sad about Jack Leaf's naked hands lying palms-up on the sidewalk. They were better cared for than most men's hands; save for traces of white chalk dust, they were immaculate. On the third finger of his right hand was a gold ring with a black-and-white insignia. Because he and Jack Leaf had talked about the ring, Stall knew the insignia was the screaming eagle of the 101st Airborne Division. A girl in the circle that surrounded Jack Leaf said, "I, uh, I saw it. Him."

She looked at Stall now as though he should prompt her. Help her tell whatever story she had to offer. The words *official of the university* occurred to Stall again, and he said to her gently, "What did you see?"

"I heard the window go up." Everyone in the crowd looked up at the open third-floor window. The sash had been thrown up all the way and the hole in the building gaped like a wound. The girl, tall and thin with big dark eyes, said, "It was loud. He opened it hard, so I . . . had to look up there. He didn't look down. He looked . . . out that way." She pointed east toward the pine forests where the relentless kudzu vines crept toward University City, gaining a few feet every day. "He stepped out onto the ledge and stood there holding on, and then he just stepped out into the air." The girl's voice diminished to a whisper. "Like he was going for a walk." She peered at Stall, who nodded to encourage her. "And he never did look down. I turned away before he . . . hit. But the sound was . . ." Through wracking sobs the girl said, "It was *horrible*! He made this *noise* . . . just before he . . ."

Stall had to ask the next question: "Did you see anybody else up there?"

The girl shook her head and then put her hand over her mouth.

"Did he . . . say anything?"

She shook her head again, swinging the auburn hair at her cheeks. From under the tent of hair, "Can I please go?"

May, Stall thought, *may* I go, but he said, "Please, stay a little while longer until . . ."

And there he came, Ed McPhail, a campus policeman jogging toward them. McPhail directed traffic at the city's main intersection on football weekends. He was a local character. *Ballet with a Billy Club.* That was what the campus newspaper had called McPhail's gesturing and pirouetting as he guided onrushing steel and rubber to the stadium parking lot for the awesome rite of tailgating. McPhail was anything but balletic now. He had obviously run some distance, and his epauletted white shirt had come loose from his black trousers, revealing a pink rind of belly. He pulled a pad and pencil from his belt and tried to catch his breath. Stall felt his own breathing settle to something approaching normal. His job now was to make sure that the girl who had seen Jack Leaf take his walk into the air gave her name to Ed McPhail.

Stall was passing the baton to a policeman. He was becoming what life had taught him he wanted to be—a spectator. It was a lesson neither pleasant nor unpleasant. It simply was. And Tom Stall would have bet that most men in his profession, whether veterans of the late World War or spectators to it, would agree with him if they were honest about it. What was an English professor if not a spectator?

McPhail went around the circle writing down names and asking questions. Only the tall girl had seen Jack Leaf fall. The others had happened upon Leaf after he had ended his walk in the air, or gravity had ended it for him. But one boy said, "I saw these two guys."

"Mmm-hmm," Ed McPhail said, writing.

Tom Stall took back the baton. "Guys?" He moved to the boy, stood in front of him, waited until the boy looked into his face. "What guys? Students?"

McPhail stopped writing and watched Stall.

"No," the boy said. "Men, you know, in suits. One guy had a briefcase. The other one had . . . I think maybe a badge." The boy touched the front of his shirt. "Here, on his coat pocket."

Stall looked at Ed McPhail, who was writing it down.

"A briefcase and a badge, anything else?"

The boy shuffled his feet and squared the slide rule at his belt. An engineer in the making, Stall thought, or a kid who would fail at the mysteries of aeronautical science and end up haunting the hallways of the English Department. "Yeah," the kid said.

Stall frowned at *Yeah*. It was rude.

The kid said, "I mean, yes sir. They both wore suits and ties, one brown, one blue—"

"You mean the suits, not the ties."

"Yes sir, the suits. Brown and dark blue. I saw them leave Murphree Hall by that door." The boy pointed at the south end of the building about fifty yards from where Stall and the others stood watching flies settle to the pool of Jack Leaf's blood. The insects seemed to skate on the crimson surface, fattening themselves and occasionally stopping to stretch out their wings. The fingers of Leaf's hands had curled a little as though from wherever Leaf was now, he was trying to make fists. Jack Leaf had been a fighter, Stall was certain of that. He had been to parties at Leaf's house and seen in the man's study three Purple Hearts and a Silver Star. And Leaf had been other things that Tom Stall had not understood.

Ed McPhail said, "These two men. Where did they go when they left the building?"

The kid turned and pointed at the quadrangle whose green expanse ended at the steps of the university library. "That way."

"They went into the library?"

The boy shrugged, shook his head.

When the ambulance bumped awkwardly over the curb and rolled across the summer grass to the sidewalk, Tom Stall stepped back to the outer edge of the circle. The rear doors swung open and a man in a white coat and carrying a doctor's satchel hurried out. He ran only a few steps before slowing to a thoughtful amble. The look on his face said it all. It said, *Again I arrive too late*. It said, *I have seen this too many times before.* Tom Stall stayed until Jack Leaf had been carried to the ambulance. He suppressed the impulse, surprisingly strong at the last minute, to grasp the hand that wore the Screaming Eagle ring. To give the man one final press of living flesh.

When Jack Leaf was gone and the students had drifted away murmuring and hugging one another, and the older boy who smoked a pipe had walked away with his arm around the sorority girl, the two talking in a confiding way, Tom Stall and Ed McPhail stood looking at Stall's blazer wadded in the pool of blood. The blood was hard and black now on the hot sidewalk.

Stall said, "Who cleans this up?"

McPhail showed Stall his radio. "I'll get somebody."

"Soon?"

"Yeah." McPhail sighed. "Poor guy. You knew him?"

"I knew him." *A little*, Stall thought. *Too well or not well enough*. It was a mystery.

McPhail touched the sleeve of Stall's blazer with the toe of his shoe. "Yours?"

"Yeah."

"Well, maybe a dry cleaner . . . ?"

"No." Stall picked up the coat by the back of the collar and dropped it into the nearest trash can.

Tom Stall didn't want to go back to work, and he didn't want to go home—though he was already framing the words of the story he would tell Maureen over their first martini. He needed to clear his mind, to think—he wasn't sure about what. He retraced his steps to Anderson Hall, skirted the front entrance, and slipped down the alley between the old redbrick building and Matherly Hall, a newer sandstone structure that housed the College of Business Administration. Across the busy four-lane that divided the campus from the town was a restaurant and general hangout known as the College Inn, CI for short.

Traffic was light in August. In two weeks, it would increase to a temporary madness when hordes of parents arrived to help their sons and daughters carry the trunks and suitcases, the freshly laundered clothes and the desk lamps and electric fans and boxes of books and hotplates and coffee pots for the long nights of cramming that would come in cold November. Stall was in the middle of the street waiting for a Merita Bread truck to pass when he saw the two men come out of the CI. A brown suit and a dark-blue one. No badge that he could see, but the taller man carried a worn brown leather satchel. It was four fifteen and the lowering sun poured its hot light down University Avenue, which ran east and west as true as the flight of a bullet.

The two men stood talking on the sidewalk in front of the CI, only two lanes away from Stall. For some reason, Stall could not make himself walk toward them. He stood on the two yellow lines, a few inches of safety in the middle of the street, watching them until they noticed him. The man in the blue suit, the taller of the two, a man with an athletic build, short blond hair, and a handsome face that reminded Stall of the actor Alan Ladd, nodded to Stall. Then the two men walked east toward the intersection of University Avenue and 13th Street, where the citizens of Gainesville crossed from the town to the campus. University was an avenue of clothing stores, restaurants, bars, and theaters that gave way eventually to the old downtown and the buildings that housed justice, religion, and commerce. Crossing the remaining two lanes in long strides, Stall watched the men go. Before he entered the College Inn, one of the few air-conditioned buildings in the town, he looked down at his shirtsleeves and remembered pulling on the new blazer that morning.

Stall was alone in the place except for the counterman who was stacking silverware in racks for the coming dinner rush. The coffee Stall ordered was a gooey reduction that had sat thickening since lunch. He thought with longing of the glittering bottles that lined the bar at the Gold Coast next door and then noticed the phone booth in the corner. Should he call Amos Harding? Harding, the aging department chairman, was Stall's boss and the man he hoped to replace someday. In late August, Harding vacationed in the mountains of North Carolina, a place he loved for the isolation and the trout fishing, and for the absence of his wife who stayed in Gainesville with her sister. *Why bother the old man with bad news? He'll be back soon . . . soon enough to hear of death.*

TWO

Still in his shirtsleeves and feeling the return of the adrenal energy that had poured through him during that long half hour at Murphree Hall, Stall leaned on the kitchen counter and watched his wife slice tomatoes for their salad. The good smell of roast beef came from the oven. Their first martinis stood crystalline on either side of the sink, Stall's half finished, his wife's untouched. She had stopped crying, but Stall could see the pathways of her tears in the light dusting of powder she had applied for his homecoming. The two things, the makeup she had put on for him and her tears, moved Stall so much that his own eyes burned. He took a long pull of cold gin and turned away to square himself. He had banished their daughter Corey from the kitchen at the first sight of Maureen's tears and without any proper explanation for her exile, and he knew he'd have to make that right with her soon. Maureen put down her knife and rinsed red tomato juice from her hands.

"Jack Leaf. I just can't . . . How do you understand a thing like this?" She looked at Stall out of swollen red eyes as though she meant the question, as though she thought he could tell her how.

He shook his head thoughtfully and took another sip of the good cold gin. *Gin*, he thought, *how I love it. It's one way to deal with the surprising hell of life*. He had not told Maureen that, after he had tried the coffee in the CI and found it to be not enough, not by a long way, he had gone next door to the Gold Coast, a student dive, for two stiff shots of bourbon before taking the city bus home. She'd had the martinis waiting when he walked in the door and he'd taken a long sip of gin to cover the bourbon before giving Maureen her first kiss. Then he'd told her about Jack Leaf's walk in the air.

Maureen drew in a hiss of breath. "Oh my God, did you . . . did anyone call Sarah?"

Oh Christ, Sarah. Jack's wife Sarah.

Bourbon-stunned, Stall had ridden the bus home to their prairie-style house on a hill just up from the construction site for the new law school. They'd bought this house so that he could walk and bus to work and Maureen could keep their Packard at home. She'd told him she'd be a housewife for him, but not housebound like her mother had been. She wouldn't be without a car for anyone. As the bus had labored up the hill past the vast sprawl of married-student housing, Stall had thought through what he had done for Jack Leaf and for the university. When he'd finished the sad inventory of his actions, he'd said to himself, *I did my duty*. Now, standing beside Maureen in their kitchen waiting for a second martini, he had to tell his wife that it hadn't occurred to him to call Sarah Leaf, or even to wonder who would call her. The awful thought hit him that right now Sarah could be standing at her own kitchen sink paring carrots and waiting for Jack to come home.

"God, Mar baby, I didn't think of that, what with all I had to . . ."

Maureen turned and looked at him sharply, and the fear came alight in Stall's brain that she might cry again. A woman's tears had always turned Tom Stall into a standing heap of mush.

His wife's eyes softened but not into tears. She gave him her frailty-thy-name-is-man look, which, considering her options, was at least in the upper third of good outcomes. He gave her his I'm-very-sorry smile, his only option. "Do you think I should call her now?"

It was a day of things occurring to Stall and one came to him now: he, they, Tom Stall and wife, would have to visit Sarah Leaf, and soon. They'd have to go to Sarah's door with food of some kind, probably Maureen's chicken-and-mushroom soup casserole, and they'd have to say and do the right things. Stall dreaded it, not because he found no meaning in such things, and not because he took the fashionable literary view of bourgeois convention (which right now meant a French existentialist view, the harshest of any available), but because he was no damned good at such things. He was just flat bad at offering human comfort to his fellow man. It was an odd thing, irony, because Stall believed that he loved his fellow man, loved Him with a capital H in the way that Whitman had loved the crowds in "Crossing Brooklyn Ferry."

We fathom you not—we love you—there is per-
fection in you also,
You furnish your parts toward eternity,
Great or small, you furnish your parts toward the
Soul.

Stall loved people in the aggregate for their wonderful, messy, preposterous, goofy optimism. Loving his fellow man in his individual, farting, nose-picking, often criminally stupid state was hard, but Stall tried. In the war he'd seen the worst of human doings (blessedly, for a very short time), but he'd come away from that experience with a stronger sense of human goodness. He'd seen incredible valor too. Should he ever realize his dream of returning to Paris with enough money to show Maureen around in style, he knew that Jean-Paul Sartre and his sometime friend Albert Camus would not allow him even to walk past their café, Les Deux Magots, much less have a drink with them. Loving the world was not their cup of absinthe.

After thinking it over through a sip of martini, Maureen said, "No, don't call her now. I think it's better for you to wait until we know more." She looked out through the kitchen window at their backyard where a pair of cardinals, bright red cock and dull hen, splashed in the birdbath. To the window she said, "I'm sure *someone* has told her about Jack. Someone from the hospital or the police. We'll call together tomorrow."

By the tone of her voice and the way she surveyed the backyard, beautiful in the falling summer light, Stall knew that she was composing the image in her mind of exactly how to comfort Sarah Leaf. The right way to do it.

After dinner and after Stall and his wife had told their daughter that something bad had happened at the university and this bad thing, the death of a friend, had made her mother cry, their daughter Corey, a hearty, athletic girl of twelve who had not known Jack Leaf except as a man to say hello to as he came and went at the few departmental gatherings the Stalls had hosted, seemed to take the death of Jack Leaf more as an idea (people die), than as anything personal.

Stall had taken pains to tell her that there was a very good chance that Jack Leaf had accidentally fallen from a window. Corey had asked a few questions, and these matched the logic of accidents, not suicide: Was Mr. Leaf teaching when he fell? Did the students see him fall? Did anyone try to catch him? When Stall could see that she was more or less satisfied with her parents' explanations, he sent her to her room to finish her homework. Her mother said, "Corey, you'll hear about this in school tomorrow. It's better not to say that Daddy had anything to do with it."

"But Mom, isn't that lying?"

"No, lying is saying something that's untrue. Saying nothing is not lying. It's discretion."

Both Stalls knew that their daughter would beat a path to her dictionary, so Stall said to her retreating, pajamaed form, "That's d-i-s, not d-e-s."

After washing and drying the dishes, Stall and his wife sat at the kitchen table, the place of their most serious discussions, with third martinis in front of them and commenced what Stall hoped would be a kind of elegy for Jack Leaf. The best thing they could do tonight, a thing in keeping with what Stall thought of as his love of the world, was to remember Jack Leaf well. Tell stories. Bring him back to life in words.

"Why did he do it?" Maureen sipped and gave Stall a look he saw only rarely. She was what the frat boys called a cheap date; the reference was to capacity for liquor not morals, though the two sometimes became confused. From experience, Stall knew that she was very close to the line that separated earnestly inebriated from stupidly drunk. He had only seen her on the far side of the line a few times, and over there she was not pretty. In that country she was abrupt, far too truthful, sometimes angry, and often inclined to think she had discovered things about her husband that her sober mind would have left alone. Stall had poured the third martini hoping it would be elegiac, lubrication for a Whitmanesque celebration of Jack Leaf. He had led Maureen here to the borderland, or at least he had not stopped her from approaching it. He said, "We'd better take it easy," and reached out to place a hand across her glass.

She slid the glass out of reach. "I asked you why he did it."

Stall shrugged. In the last hour, fatigue had hit him. It was nine o'clock and felt like midnight. He'd had five drinks and was reconnoitering number six. "I don't know," he said. It was the truth, but not all of it.

Maureen gave him the sharp look again, and when her head turned toward him, her glass lurched, spilling some of the crystalline fluid. "Was it the war?"

Jack Leaf, like many men who had fought, had not talked much about the war. He answered questions when asked, but questions were rare and his answers were brief. The English faculty were his social group, and they were, like Stall, mostly born to the role of spectator. Jack Leaf could have said a lot about the war, most people knew that, but he chose not to talk, and people respected his silence.

Stall had gone to the war, had served honorably if briefly, had been wounded, had nearly died of an infection probably resulting from having contaminated the shrapnel wound at the back of his thigh with shit that had exploded from his bowels with the concussion that came milliseconds after the explosion of a German shell. He had returned to consciousness lying in the snow between two dead men. He could not call them buddies, friends, anything like that. In the darkness, confusion, fear, and frenzy they had been shapes, faces safer for him than those of the men shooting at him, but nothing more than that.

When Stall awoke, the battle had moved on. In the distance, rifles rattled and cannons flashed. It was unbearably cold and he had no idea where he was. He assumed that he had been left for dead, covered as he was with blood from the men on either side of him. He waited until morning, shivering in the pathetically light wool greatcoat the army had considered adequate for Europe in the winter of 1945. The bleeding at the back of his thigh had stopped, and when dawn came he found that he could walk well enough leaning on the rifle he had found, and that walking did not cause the bleeding to start again. He never found his platoon (most of the forty had been killed), and never found his company, but he found the army and attached himself to it. He did not report the wound which he considered insignificant. For another week he walked, crouched, starved, shivered, and tried to hack holes in frozen ground until his thigh swelled to the size of his waist and he was sent to the rear with a raging fever, incipient gangrene, and the probability of amputation.

His leg was saved by the first-ever application in wartime of a new drug known as penicillin. His recovery took months, and when he was strong enough to enjoy a weekend pass, he went to Paris. Like Jack Leaf, Tom Stall never talked much about his war. He was proud to have served in what he considered a great cause, but he had seen too much of the chaos that arose from the best intentions to care much for causes again. One cause in a lifetime was enough. Now life, to Stall, was an everyday thing. Goodness was in a wife's kiss and the feel of her breast as you left a warm bed in the morning, a child's smile at the breakfast table. It was in a good cup of coffee at a drugstore counter, it was in talking to friends, and in more complicated ways it was in good books, and that was all there was to it.

If Stall had a regret, it was that his wound was not in the front of his body. He had been lying facedown in the snow when the shell exploded, a German 88 with a proximity fuse. A shell designed to burst above the heads of troops, to kill men crouching in holes in the ground. White-hot fragments rained down and killed what they could find, and it was only a tiny piece of steel that found Stall. He still wore it behind his femur. It hid there telling him nothing, not even when the weather would change. His only regret about his war was literary, or perhaps more accurately, historical. He loved the quotation attributed to Alexander the Great when, after years of conquest, his army mutinied before a battle in India. The men were worn out and demanded to go home. The young king called them to assembly, stepped forth, and stripped naked. "Does any man among you honestly feel that he has suffered more for me than I have suffered for him? Come now—if you are wounded, strip and show your wounds, and I will show mine. There is no part of my body but my back which has not a scar; not a weapon a man may grasp or fling the mark of which I do not carry upon me. Show this man to me and I will yield to your weariness and go home." No one came forward. Instead, the army burst into wild cheering. In tears, the men begged Alexander to forgive their lack of spirit and pleaded with him only to lead them forward.

Stall's wound was in the back of his leg. His war had been brief, and all he knew of life so far, it had taught him. Keep your head down when you can. Be good to others, ask for the same in return, drink the wines of the countryside and eat the good food, and don't overcomplicate simple things. Occasionally people asked Stall about his war, and when they did, he gently tried to change the subject, and if they pressed him, and if he'd had a little bit to drink, sometimes he said, "I was only there for a few months. I was shot in the ass, but I was not running away."

Stall drank some of his unusual third martini and said, "Jack fought all the way from Normandy to the Rhine with the 101st Airborne. He was wounded three times, and he won a medal. One of the big ones. He had a good war, or a bad one, depending on how you look at it." Stall set down the drink and examined it, begging it for the truth he knew it held. *In vino veritas.* Was survival itself enough to justify three wounds and a year of brutal fighting? He'd never asked Jack Leaf that question.

"How did *he* look at it?" Maureen waited. She was very close to the line Stall did not want her to cross.

"He didn't say. At least not to me. I saw his medals mounted in a glass case in his study. I just stuck my head in there one night at a party. You know, curious to see a colleague's lair. His was close to perfect—like an English gentleman's study. Leather chairs, a big rosewood desk, rows of books, a mahogany humidor, and a rack of pipes. Everything neat as a pin. Jack was all about order in life and work." *Until the end*, Stall thought.

"*Where* was he wounded?"

Stall wanted to say, *All over Europe*, but knew that would be the gin talking. He said, "I don't know. I never saw him in anything but his professor outfit."

"You never saw him naked?"

Maureen knew, of course, that Stall had showered with many of his colleagues. Handball was the English professor's game of choice. Played well, it was serious exercise. Several of the younger men played the game at noon, showered, and returned to their offices for sandwiches at their desks. So, yes, Stall had seen a lot of professorial nakedness, some of it ugly, some of it beautiful, none of it Jack Leaf. Stall shook his head.

"Where was he from?"

"Oklahoma, I think. His PhD is from Vanderbilt. I don't know where he got his BA." Of course, Maureen knew about Jack Leaf's Vanderbilt connection. Of such things were pecking orders made, and the English Department hierarchy mattered to Maureen as it did to all of the wives. Possibly even more than it mattered to Stall.

She sipped and set down her glass with great concentration. "Did you know his middle name was Red?"

"Red? You mean a nickname?"

"No. I mean his full name was Jack Red Leaf."

"You're kidding."

Maureen shook her head in a way meant to be decisive. Some of her gin slipped over the rim of her glass.

"Where'd you get that?" Stall slid his chair closer to his wife's at the kitchen table. His knee touched hers.

"From Sarah. She told me."

"When? Why? She just told you, *Oh, by the way, my husband's middle name is Red?*"

"Of course not. Don't be an ass."

There it was. The anger that lived in the heart of Maureen from Across the Border. *Where did it come from?* Stall wondered. The gin only let it out, called it from its hiding place. *What was the source of the anger in Maureen Stall?*

From the land beyond earnestly inebriated, Maureen looked at him and then at her martini as though she were having a hard time deciding which she liked best. Or least.

"Sarah told me one night at a party—maybe it was the same party where you snuck into Jack's study and pronounced it neat as a pin. Anyway, we were talking about marriage, you know, couples and how they meet, what attracts them, makes them want to be together."

Obscurely, Stall saw that he might not like where this was going. With women, it was tit for tat, and just as surely as Jack Leaf's wife had told Maureen about her and Jack, so had Maureen given Sarah Leaf her tit. No, Stall didn't mean that. It was the gin talking and not well, but the idea was clear. Stall feared what Maureen might have told Sarah about the attraction between the Stalls. Not because he knew what she might have revealed, but because he had no idea.

Maureen said, "She said it was his skin."

"His skin?"

"Yes, his skin. Come on, Tom. Think about it. The skin of Jack Red Leaf?"

It came to Stall. "No!"

"Yes, what else could it be?"

"You're saying he was an Indian? You're saying Sarah told you that?"

"Not in so many words. Her exact words were, *From the first time I saw him, I loved his skin. His dark skin. It was so smooth. The man had no wrinkles. It covered him like caramel poured over a cake. You know what I mean, Maureen*, and here she stopped and she sort of winked at me. We were both drinking, of course, and it was late at night in their house and most people were already gone, and you were off snooping in Jack's study, and she winked and said, *You know, Maureen, my husband's full name is Jack Red Leaf*."

"And you knew . . ."

"Not until later. Not until I thought about it. And I started to wonder why she told me and what that wink meant. It was sort of a dirty wink, if you know what I mean."

Stall thought about it. She could only mean one thing. "You mean, uh, *sexy* dirty. That kind of dirty."

"Yeah, that kind. I think I know Sarah well enough to know when she goes sexy dirty late at night in her cups."

"What was she drinking? We, uh, ought to get—"

"Oh, don't be an ass. She was drinking firewater. I don't know, probably bourbon. She likes bourbon. The question is, why did she want me to know what, apparently, nobody else knows or has even cared to think about? Why Jack Leaf's skin was so dark."

"I don't know . . ." Stall ignored the fact that his wife had called him an ass twice, and considered the question. "I just thought—I mean *if* I thought about it—I thought his skin was Mediterranean. Maybe Leaf was the Americanized form of Leafiano or something. You know, a lot of people—"

"Oh God!" Maureen's tone was infinitely weary, but Stall thought she was beginning to see the humor in this. The awful, absurd, but inescapable humor. Jack Leaf had been an underground man. And for some reason, his wife had sprinkled hints about his secret under the nose of the wife of the assistant department chairman. Jack Leaf was a Red Indian, and he was *passing*. Passing was serious business in the South, and Gainesville, Florida, was definitely the South.

The important thing, the sobering thing (and God knew they needed sobering), was that nobody in an English department in a Southern land-grant university had ever even considered the possibility that a member of the graduate faculty might be an Indian. A Red man named Red Leaf. It would have been like asking yourself if a man with a very dark tan that never faded in winter was a Negro. To the bigoted minds that worked the farms and picked the oranges and pumped the gas out where the kudzu crept daily toward University City, there was not one inch of difference between a Negro and an Indian. Even English professors knew this. To the bigoted mind, Negroes and Indians were one and the same, and they were bad.

Stall had grown up Southern and had rid himself to the best of his ability of the racial and social ideas of his parents and grandparents. He considered himself liberal in both the old and the new senses of the word. Maureen had not grown up Southern. She was from Oberlin, Ohio, a college town, and she counted professors among the men of her family going back generations. Stall had met Maureen Wiggins when he was a grad student at the University of Virginia just after the war, and in the process of choosing each other, they'd had many political discussions. It was Maureen who had vetted Stall. Stall believed that she had chosen the famously conservative Randolph-Macon College ("Randy Mac" to the boys of UVA) as the place to earn her BA in education at least partly so that she could spend four years there as a member of the opposition to all things Southern and especially the doctrine of separate-but-equal. She had made it clear to Stall that their relationship could go no further than casual dating (though they were strongly attracted to each other) unless he made sincere declarations to her of his liberal values. Like most young men his age, and especially young men who had been to war, Stall would have done almost anything to get a coed into bed, but with Maureen, sincerity came at no price. He really did hate everything that was small-minded and bigoted about the South. He had broken forever with some of his relatives over segregation, and in those days, in the certainty of youth, he knew that he would never regret these partings of ways.

The phone rang. It was too late at night for polite phone calling, so Stall knew this ringing could be about only one thing, the death of

Jack Leaf. He stood a little unsteadily and said, "I'd better get that."

Maureen stared at the jangling instrument that hung from the kitchen wall as though it might leap across the room and bite her.

Stall said hello to the world outside this kitchen in his most confident voice.

"Hello, Tom. Amos here. I'm sorry to call you so late at night and with such a sad thing to discuss." The long-distance line was windy, and Harding sounded as far away as he was.

Amos Harding, chairman of the English Department. Ancient Amos, whose life's work—studies of the essays of Sir Thomas Browne—was considered by most of the younger graduate faculty so hopelessly out of date that it disqualified Harding as chairman. But Harding hung on, mostly by dint of Southern courtliness and a golfing friendship with Thomas Connor, president of the university. Stall walked a narrow line between Harding, whom honor required him to defend, and the younger faculty, who thought Harding kept the department firmly anchored in the nineteenth century.

"Hello, Chairman Harding."

"Call me Amos, Tom, especially on a night like this. I'm calling to thank you for stepping into the breach when we needed you today."

The boy stood on the burning deck, Stall thought, then shook his head. All he had done was give a dead man the decency of a covered face and ask some students the obvious questions.

"Well, thank you, sir . . . Amos. I only did what anyone would have done."

"Not just anyone, Tom. We both know a situation like that requires grit and judgment. McPhail told me you did well."

McPhail? A dancing policeman. The standard for decisive action. Before Stall could thank the chairman again, Harding said, "President Connor wants to see you. Tomorrow. Among other things, he wants to thank you for acting as you did."

Stall's tired brain selected *among other things* from the flow of language as a bear would snatch a leaping salmon in its jaws. Sweat broke out on his forehead. Maureen sipped unsteadily and looked at him with concern.

"He'll see you at nine o'clock. And Tom, come by my office after you finish with the president."

"Yes sir, of course."

"Amos, Tom. Call me Amos. You've earned it. You may well be my successor, so the two of us ought to know each other better before I shuffle off this mortal coil."

"Surely, sir, only the coil of the job. Not the, uh . . . I'm sorry, I meant to say Amos."

A dry chuckle came over the line. "That's all right, Tom. We're all a bit rattled today."

"Amos," Stall said, "have you spoken to Sarah Leaf?"

Harding sighed. "Yes, Tom. I spoke to her earlier this evening. She's in a pretty bad way. I sent my wife over to stay with her until other arrangements can be made."

Stall thought about the appalling awkwardness of Harding's elderly wife appearing at Sarah Leaf's door announced but unwanted. Poor Sarah. And then Stall reconsidered, thinking himself the ass his wife had called him twice tonight. Who was he to say what comfort Sarah Leaf might take from the doddering Mrs. Harding? And Stall knew he was getting a glimpse tonight of the greater reach of a chairman's job, the future that lay ahead of him should Harding choose him as his successor. The job, if Stall got it, would involve more than hiring and promoting, deciding which grad students got stipends and teaching assistantships, chairing meetings, and generally herding a flock of exotic birds. It would mean phone calls like this one late at night, and missions of condolence like that of old Mrs. Harding.

Stall assured Amos Harding that he'd be sitting in President Connor's outer office at fifteen minutes to nine the next morning. Harding thanked him and they said good night.

Stall finished his drink and lifted Maureen by the elbow. She took a final defiant sip of gin, then set the half-finished third martini on the kitchen counter. As they walked to the stairs, she said, "Maybe we should have called Sarah."

"Harding called her. He sent his wife over to stay with her."

"Oh no."

"I know."

And with that the Stalls went up to bed.

THREE

In the early hours of morning as he lay next to Maureen's sweetly breathing warmth, Tom Stall remembered sudden deaths. There had never been a departmental suicide before, but an old professor's heart had stopped in the jury box at the courthouse downtown, and another had died of a stroke on a fishing boat far out on Newnans Lake, the professor, not so elderly, found slumped over the tiller of his outboard motor. When these things happened, the junior members of the department were asked to take on the burdens of extra classes. Who would take over Jack Leaf's summer term class in research methodologies? And what about the two classes Leaf was scheduled to teach in the fall? It was probably too late, even in a university town teeming with academic labor, to hire someone new to teach early American lit (all those Puritans). American Romanticism might be easier to cover.

Listening to Maureen's sibilant breathing and watching the dawn grow more certain at the window across the room, Stall resolved to tell Amos Harding that he would cover Leaf's research methodologies class for the remaining two weeks of the summer term. There were only five students in the class. Research Meth, as it was called, was a required course and a thing of withering boredom both to teach and to take. The students who came for the summer term were often tedious themselves: zealots who had gone without the rest and adventure of a vacation before the rigors of grad school, hard-drivers who thought the summer course would put them a few steps ahead of students who arrived in the fall.

Stall had taught the course as a newcomer ten years ago and had considered it a waste of time. Students should either know research methods from their undergraduate studies or should learn them double-time as they grappled with real courses such as the ones he taught in modern British and American poetry and fiction. As he lay watching the shapes of his bedroom resolve themselves out of darkness, a sudden image of Jack Leaf's hands with traces of white chalk dust on them came to Stall. He did not want to visit the classroom where five students would ask him what had happened to Professor Leaf, but he had to do it.

Stall slipped from the bed as quietly as he could, showered with the bathroom door closed, and went downstairs to make himself a cup of coffee. Maureen was letting their daughter sleep late these last few days of summer. Soon enough they'd all be awakened at six o'clock by the crashing sounds of Corey readying for school. There was no sleeping after Corey's first footfalls on her bedroom floor, but Stall wouldn't mind the early mornings. He'd get to his office a good hour before anyone else entered the English building and work on his article about Graham Greene's religious conversion. He was publishing articles one by one and planning to collect them into a not-so-slim volume. A collection wouldn't count as a book to the most stringent of his colleagues, but it, and his administrative skills, and the good opinion of Amos Harding, might be enough to get Stall the chairmanship when Harding retired. And then what?

Stall had not thought much about what came the day after he occupied the old leather chair behind the big Victorian pedestal desk in Amos Harding's office. A good life, he hoped, and a long one. More of his own research and writing—without the pressure of vying for promotion. A chance to demonstrate his leadership skills and his vision for the future of the department. That vision had not yet come into sharp focus, but no matter. As times changed, the department would change naturally with them.

Stall stood at the kitchen sink drinking his coffee and looking at the backyard. The bird feeder, placid in the morning cool, needed cleaning. Perhaps, as chairman, he'd be able to afford a yardman. Corey entered, bleary but cheerful, and began to make herself a breakfast of toast and peanut butter. "Daddy, can I go to Jeannie's house?" Jeannie Mears was the daughter of the sociologist who lived down the block.

"Sure, honey. Drink some milk."

Toast in hand, Corey headed for the door. Her sneakered footsteps were receding down the driveway when Stall realized that she had not given him his ritual peck on the cheek. The peck had gone away with the advent of the "training brassiere," which gave Stall what his grandfather had called "the fantods" every time he hugged his daughter. Not that she let him hug her much anymore. She was moving into that terrain where Daddy's best use was as an ally against Mother, who, as the other woman in the house, had become a blood enemy. Stall had heard about this, seen some of it. He hoped the Stall family version of the old story would be mild.

He waited a while for Maureen to come down, picturing the look on her face, the one they called Hangover Hell, as she groped her way into the kitchen, her nose pulling her forward, homing in on the aroma of coffee. She did not come down, so Stall went up. He wanted to talk to her before he went to President Connor's office in Tigert Hall, a place he had visited only once, when the president's secretary, Mrs. Braithwaite, a miraculous typist, had done some work for him. He had paid her, received from her immaculate hand the manila envelope holding his modest contribution to American Letters, and had watched her type for a few moments before leaving. Never had fingers moved so fast (literally a blur) and never with fewer mistakes. And she did it all with the serenity of a nun at vespers. The look on her face was not concentration and it was far from effort, it was beatitude.

But Stall feared the president's office as any young professor would, and especially he feared Amos Harding's words, *among other things*. What, besides the death of Jack Leaf, could President Connor want to talk to Tom Stall about? Once, a friend of Stall's father had asked Stall why he wanted to be a professor. Without thinking much about it, the young Stall, weary from his service in the European Theater of War, had said, "So I don't have to be a salesman." College presidents were, above all else, salesmen, and this was another reason to fear the administration building. It was the House of Sales. Stall thought of the English Department as the House of Examined Lives.

So Stall wanted to talk to his wife before he went to school. He wanted, he supposed in some vague way, her reassurance, her approval. He wanted her to say, if not by word, then by look or touch, *You'll do fine. You are more than up to this.*

He found Maureen leaning on the bathroom sink for what looked like actual support. She regarded him from sunken, shrouded eyes and said, "I'll never drink again." It was one of their best old jokes, but this time, he could see, she meant it. He knew that she would drink again (he certainly hoped so; he'd rather not do it alone), but he could see that for now this declaration was the only truth she knew. He went to stand behind her and massage her shoulders. She said only, "Mmmmm."

Stall said, "Is that good or . . . ?"

"Or," she said, and so he stopped, though his hands departed her flesh reluctantly.

He had some time, so he contented himself, as he often did, with watching her do what in Victorian novels was called her *toilette*. She brushed her teeth as though even they hurt, and then let her robe drop to the floor around her ankles. On her way to the shower, she stepped on it. Stall watched her legs, especially her ankles, which were slender and at the same time strong. The ankles of a field hockey star. He loved her ankles. She slowly drew the shower curtain shut, Stall supposed, to make as little of its brutal, rattling noise as possible. Then, modestly, she tossed her panties out through the small aperture between the curtain and the wall.

Stall loved this too, but with complications. Maureen was no more modest than most women of her generation, but she was plenty modest. Even in their thirteenth year of marriage, Stall had to ask her if he could look at her. It went like this:

"May I look at you?"

"Well, of course, dear." A look of concern for the state of his intellect, if not his sanity.

"No, I mean *look* at you."

"You mean, without my . . . ? You mean naked?"

"Sure. That's what I mean."

"Oh," a little laugh, a little giddy, "you've done that plenty of times." And sometimes a somewhat lurid wink.

"No, I mean now. May I look at you now? May I see you naked?" This was the gauntlet thrown. There was no ambiguity left here, at least none that Stall could see. They had entered the land of a simple yes or no.

But Maureen could take the conversation from this simple point to any number of complicated places. She could say, "I don't like the way I look." (One of her best.) This had the effect of enlisting Stall on her side in the battle against a woman's low assessment of her own looks, of her beauty.

Maureen's beauty, at least to Stall, was without question. She was, he would say, in the top 5 percent of all possible beauty short of movie stars, which everyone knew was mostly a matter of lighting and makeup. Stall considered himself enormously fortunate because he had married a beautiful woman who had lost none of her beauty after the birth of their only child. He received and Maureen did too, though she never admitted it, almost constant proof of her beauty when other men and women commented on it or, in ways more stealthy, let Stall and his wife know that Mrs. Stall was . . . a goddess.

But pointing this out to her in the sometimes endless conversations that began with "May I look at you" only led to further complications. "That," she would say, "only means there's something about me that's too . . . I don't know, too much *that way*. You know what I mean?"

Stall thought he knew. *That way* meant sexual. Maureen Stall was too sexual, too fetching, too lookable, and this could only, to her mind, be another reason for not letting the world look. Stall was not the world, but he was her world at this moment, here in this bathroom, and he wanted his wife to let him look at her.

He parted the shower curtain.

Maureen screamed.

Stall jumped back and closed the curtain.

Another time, he told himself. *Another time she'll let me have a good long look. The look of a painter, a sculptor, a satyr, a lecher, a fiend.*

FOUR

Stall entered Anderson Hall by the staircase in the alley, hoping to glide silently down the ancient, linseed-smelling oak floor to his small cell without meeting any of his colleagues. His hungover, haggard face would not be a good thing for them to see until later, after time and more coffee had done their healing work. He had just come through the fire door at the end of the hallway when Amos Harding emerged from his office, head down over a piece of paper. *Christ, the old man must have driven all night to get back here from North Carolina.* Harding looked better for his journey than Stall did for his night of gin. Stall took a sharp left turn into the first available open door, Sophie Green's office.

Oddly, she stood now exactly as she had the last time he had seen her—on his way to investigate the noise that had broken from the throat of Jack Leaf before he hit a sidewalk.

The circumstance gave him a moment to look at her—the delicate back, the slender fingers touching the spines of books in a way that made Stall think: *Loving*. And there was more to look at—a small spot of perspiration in the black silk exactly between her shoulder blades, and a lock of curly black hair that had come loose from the comb on the right side of her head. She withdrew her left hand from the bookcase and sent it to the unruly lock, but the hair fought back. She looked a little lopsided and, to Stall, the effect was charming. He stepped back into the hallway, saw that Harding was gone, and decided to knock lightly on Professor Green's door.

Sophie Green took a step toward Stall, which seemed to mean that he was invited to enter her office. She had been hired after the retirement of a very old medievalist named Inigo Frasier, and for some reason her arrival had not triggered the usual shuffle of office space. She had been given Frasier's very fine office rather than the smallest one in the basement, which usually went to a new hire. This departure from tradition had puzzled faculty of greater seniority and angered some of them. Stall had not been privy to any discussions of the office, but he assumed that the decision was of a piece with the fact that Dr. Sophie Green was the first woman to be invited to join the graduate faculty. The powers that were—in this case Harding and probably President Connor—had wisely not wanted to subject their first woman to the usual mild hazing which included basement offices, early-morning and late-afternoon classes, bad classrooms, and the worst committee assignments.

In the awkward silence, he considered simply welcoming her to the faculty, but he had already done that.

On her first day in Gainesville, he had met her in the parking lot where she was struggling with boxes of books. He had called the department secretary, Helen Markham, from a ground-floor office and asked her to send a custodian to help with the books. Then Stall and Sophie Green had chatted a little awkwardly while they waited for a middle-aged Negro to arrive pushing a dolly. The building had no elevator, so when the books had been rolled inside, Stall and the black man carried them up two flights of stairs. Throughout this long and sinew-wrenching process, Sophie Green had protested that there was really no need for all this trouble. She could have done it herself.

She weighed, Stall guessed, ninety pounds soaking wet, and while she probably could have gotten the books up the stairs, he was pretty sure it would have taken her most of the day, with rest periods and trips to an orthopedic surgeon. A Southern woman would have thanked Stall, complimented his strength and virility, and promised to bake him a lemon chiffon cake as soon as she could get to the store for the ingredients. And that would have been that.

When it was all over, Sophie Green opened her purse, a strange little thing made of chain mail that looked like it came from the boudoir of Virginia Woolf. From it she produced a dollar bill for the Negro custodian. This embarrassed the man enormously, and the more emphatically he refused the money, the more adamantly she offered it. Finally, Stall intervened. He knew the custodian from years of saying hello and goodbye in hallways and empty classrooms. He said quietly, "It's all right, Jimmy. We're finished here."

Flustered, Jimmy bowed from the waist to Sophie Green and beat a hasty retreat.

She looked at Stall with all the puzzlement that growing up in Manhattan and earning a PhD at Columbia University could produce. Stall shrugged and smiled in a way he hoped came across as both kindly and worldly. All he said was, "We pay him to do this kind of thing. He'd never take a tip for it."

Sophie Green frowned. The lines that formed across her forehead were as charming as the hank of hair that her grandmother's mother-of-pearl comb could not tame. "You mean I hurt his feelings?"

Christ, woman, didn't you see how he squirmed? "No, I wouldn't say that. He just has his way of doing things." *And you have yours.*

She looked off into the distance at the place where Jimmy Bright had vanished. Stall regretted mildly calling a Negro man older than he was by his first name. But here intervened more of the local custom—Jimmy would not have wanted Professor Stall to call him *Mr. Bright.* Such a pretense at equality would have insulted Jimmy in a way so complicated that Stall did not even want to think about it.

So there Tom Stall and Sophie Green stood in their mutual confusion, and there Stall welcomed her to the English Department. "I hope you have a fine and productive time here with us." He had almost said, *in the sunny South.* "I've read some of your work and I find it to be . . ." *Embarrassingly better than my own?* ". . . first rate. Really wonderful. And I'm sure you're as good a teacher as you are a scholar."

Sophie Green extended her tiny hand and Stall took it in his own big sweaty one. He wouldn't apologize for the moisture: he had just carried her books up two flights of stairs. "Thank you," she said. "I hope we can be friends."

Later, Stall thought about her verb. Not *will be*, but *can be*. Was she saying that this transaction with Jimmy Bright and the books had opened up a cultural chasm they might not be able to bridge?

Now, standing in Sophie Green's enviable office, hiding from Amos Harding and the rest of the English faculty, Stall said, "I guess you heard about what happened yesterday?" Immediately he regretted mentioning the thing that would cast a pall over the opening of the school year.

Sophie Green frowned (and there again was that wonderful furrowed brow) and seemed to think hard about the bad news. "Yes," she said, "I heard. I didn't know Professor Leaf."

Maybe this was why Stall had mentioned the death. Maybe he wanted to talk about it with someone, and maybe a stranger was the right person. Someone who knew nothing about Jack Leaf. He found that he didn't know what to say about Jack Leaf. *Leaf seemed . . .* was the phrase that kept coming to him, not *Leaf was*. Jack Leaf was the kind of man who forced you to interpret. Made you speculate. You kept thinking, *Who* is *this guy*? Stall had to say something.

"I didn't know him well. He was kind of private, if you know what I mean. I liked him, though."

Professor Green's voice was low and shy when she said, "I heard about what you . . . did for him."

She meant, of course, that Stall had sacrificed a sport coat to the privacy of a dead man. Historians had recorded that when Caesar was stabbed twenty-three times in the Senate by men he had considered friends, his last act before dying was to pull his toga over his face. "Yeah, I . . ." was all Stall could think to say.

"Well, it was good of you, Tom. A kind thing."

It was the first time she had used his first name.

Stall thought about Jack Leaf. "Jack was what you might call dapper. He liked good clothes, and he wore them well. None of that professorial shabby gentility for Jack. He wasn't a dandy or anything, but he didn't go out in public looking casual."

"What did that mean, do you think?" Sophie Green folded her arms across her bosom.

"I don't know." Stall looked out over her head at the dark gloom of the ancient water oaks, trees that had been here since the foundation of the building was laid in 1922. "I don't know, but I always had the feeling he was back there behind the clothes, the manners, the easy bonhomie . . . you know, watching. Looking out at the world very carefully, very . . ." Stall couldn't complete the thought, but he was certain now that the word *mysterious* suited Jack Leaf. Stall knew that war removed men from their contemporaries who had not fought. In important and sometimes unfortunate ways it set them apart, and perhaps that remove was part of what defined Jack Leaf, but that distance was not all of it. There was more to the mystery. Stall glanced at his watch. Christ, it was almost nine o'clock, and it was a five-minute walk to the administration building. "Whoops," he said, "I've got to go. Got a meeting," and he turned for the door.

She was behind him in the hallway. "This is for you," she said.

Stall skidded to a stop and took the envelope from her hand. She smiled when he looked into her eyes, and then he was hurrying again.

FIVE

Stall burst through the door of the presidential suite where legendary Margaret Braithwaite, Typist Immaculata, sat doing what she did best. The entire university knew that Margaret Braithwaite ran a lucrative business out of the president's office while also catering to the great man's every need. It was remarkable, Stall thought, and a testament to the times that she could type whole dissertations for grad students and still manage the schedule of a university president. Either the president was not busy enough, or Margaret Braithwaite was the equal of any three mortal women. Stall halted on the carpet in front of her desk, pulling at the collar Maureen had ironed for him. It was drenched with the sweat of his walk from Anderson to Tigert Hall. Mrs. Braithwaite finished a paragraph, her Olivetti making a sound like the German machine gun so feared by the Allies—a ripping sound rather than that of individual explosions, however close together. The German gun had fired an unheard of 1,200 rounds per minute. Unfortunately, Stall had heard the sound.

Compassionately, Mrs. Braithwaite charged for typing on a sliding scale. Grad students, the poorest of the poor, received her services for a mere fifty cents per page. It was said that she occasionally gave sage advice to the writers she typed. ("If I were you, I'd check that reference to Reinhold Niebuhr on page 213.") The manila envelope passed into your sweating hands and a smile sent you out the door. And Stall had never heard anyone say that her interventions were unwelcome.

He looked at his watch.

Without looking up, Mrs. B. said, "He's stuck in a meeting. He'll be here soon."

Stall thought this probably meant that the president was unable to free himself from a grudge round of golf—which, come to think of it, could also be an important meeting with a regent. It was all of a piece, and in Gainesville, President Connor was almost as well respected as his secretary. Like most Southern university presidents, he was more man of action than scholar. His trajectory had been lawyer, soldier (the Great War), businessman, and university president. The soldier had earned the Croix de Guerre at Belleau Wood. The businessman had prospered with the Atlantic Coast Line Railroad. But President Thomas Connor was known best by rank-and-file Floridians for having been an amateur boxer of some renown: he'd won a Golden Gloves title in the welterweight division. Gas station attendants and grove workers knew him as the young man who had passed the bar examination and lasted ten rounds with Benny Leonard in the same week. Connor had lost the exhibition match but had persisted. Neither fighter's knee had touched the canvas. Inevitably, when the newspapers covered Connor's frequent trips to Tallahassee to finagle dollars for the growing university, the headline was something like: "Connor Boxes Pols for Education Lucre."

Stall took the chair that Margaret Braithwaite offered with a nod of her head, listened uncomfortably to the burring sound of the typewriter as she pushed the machine to the limit of its ability to whack words onto paper while avoiding an apocalyptic snarl of steel and inky ribbon, and examined the framed pictures of James Connor on the walls: a young Connor kissing a boxing trophy, a mature Connor shaking hands with Senator Lyndon Baines Johnson, the same grip with Senator Spessard Holland, Connor breaking ground for a new building with a golden shovel in his hand and a steel hard hat raked across his brow, and Connor standing beside a railroad track with his arm slung over the shoulder of Charley Johns, who had risen from railroad conductor on a stretch of track near Starke to president of the Florida Senate. *It all fits*, thought Stall, who was an English professor but no snob. Stall had fled from the House of War to the House of Examined Lives, but he knew that money flowed only in one direction. It was the way of the world, and better to embrace the world as it was than to worry too much about changing it. Stall was proud to have a man like Connor as his president, a man who had rolled up his sleeves and stalked into the arena, as Teddy Roosevelt had famously said, there to be bloodied but unbowed, his face marred by dust and sweat, and from thence to return to the groves of academe with cash in one fist and hard-won worldly knowledge in the other.

While he waited, Stall opened the envelope Sophie Green had given him.

Dear Professor Stall,

I hope you won't think me too forward if I offer to teach one of Professor Leaf's courses in American literature. I wrote my master's thesis on The Leatherstocking Tales, and, though I later moved on to specialize in Chaucer (a lot of distance between those two!), I remember a good bit about American Romanticism, and I will certainly bone up on it if you repose faith in me to take over the course. I'm new and untried, I know, but I want to be helpful if I can in this sad time.

Sincerely,
Sophie Green

Stall watched Mrs. Flying Fingers exercise her calling and considered proposing to Amos Harding that Sophie Green take over Jack Leaf's American Romanticism course. His Bad Angel whispered to him that he could present it as his own idea while holding the ace to his vest, that Professor Green had already agreed to do it. He imagined himself saying to Sophie Green, *Professor Harding is very grateful to you for agreeing to teach the class, and, of course, I am too. I'll be happy to help you with it in any way I can.*

As it usually did, Stall's Good Angel flogged his Bad One back into its dark lair, and he decided to tell Harding the truth: Professor Green had offered, and he, Stall, was merely delivering her message.

President Connor came through the door like a . . . yes, by God, like a boxer answering the bell. Everybody stood, Mrs. B. behind her desk with a look of maternal affection for the president, and Stall in front of his chair and tugging at his sodden collar, with a look, he hoped, of proper respect. Connor tossed an old-fashioned panama at the hat tree in the corner (direct hit), saluted Mrs. Braithwaite smartly, and, as he passed, smacked Stall on the shoulder. Stall took this to mean, *Follow me.*

In the inner room, Connor went to his desk, opened a drawer, and stared down into it thoughtfully. Stall stood at attention, then at parade rest on the carpet in front of the desk. Connor sat, leaned forward with more energy than the move required, and dropped both hands flat onto the blotter with a sound like Stall's mother using a mallet to tenderize a cheap cut of beef. "Whew," Connor huffed, "tough meeting!"

Yes, Stall thought, *that five iron to the tenth green, with the big pine leaning ominously over the bunker, is probably the toughest shot on the entire eighteen.* But he only looked patiently, intelligently, inquisitively at his president.

"Hell of a day for news," Connor muttered. He looked at Stall for confirmation.

Stall assumed he meant Jack Leaf's unfortunate walk in the air, but that was yesterday. *Well,* Stall thought, *we don't hold this man to certain forms of precision. He's busy.* Stall's confusion must have showed.

"What?" Connor said. "You haven't heard?"

Stall could only stare, a new sheen of perspiration breaking out on his forehead.

Connor shook his head slowly, not, Stall hoped, at the English professor's dullness. Then the president rose from his chair and reached into his inside coat pocket. Out came a copy of the *Tallahassee Democrat*. Connor spread the paper on the desktop, turned it to toward Stall, and waved him forward. The banner headline read: "McCarty Dies of Apparent Heart Attack. Johns Sworn in As Governor."

Stall bent over the paper long enough to read a few lines about Charley Johns. The handsome and probably corrupt McCarty was now history. Johns would be a force. The article said:

> *Senate President Charley Johns swore to uphold the laws of the State of Florida and to protect and defend the Constitution of the United States from all enemies foreign and domestic this afternoon at 4:00 in the chambers of Florida Supreme Court Justice John R. Mathews, Sr., in front of legislators from both parties and his wife Thelma. A grief-stricken Mrs. Dan McCarty was also present in a gesture of goodwill to her husband's successor. The State Capitol building was draped with black bunting, and flags hung at half-mast today in honor of the deceased thirty-first governor of Florida.*

There was a grainy photo of Charley Johns, the former railroad conductor, rumored to be almost illiterate, who hailed from Bradford County, one of the most backward in the state. A place where the Klan marched in broad daylight.

When Stall looked up from the paper, Connor sat and folded his beefy arms across his chest. "It's a shock, is it not?"

"Yes sir." Stall backed up until his calves hit a chair and he sat in it.

Connor's voice was suddenly full of emotion: "So, we lose one of our own, Professor Leaf, and the governor of our state in the space of two days."

"Yes sir." Stall shook his head in astonishment and sorrow. Seconds passed while Connor seemed to master his feelings.

"I called you in here this morning to thank you, Tom, for what you did yesterday."

"Oh, well . . ." Christ, why hadn't Stall prepared something to say? He had known there'd be mystery in this visit to the president's office, but he'd also known that a simple thank you would be a part of it. He managed, "I only did what any man would do."

Connor shook his head sadly. "I only wish that were true. What, uh, what caused you to be there just then, Tom?"

Stall told the story of the strange sound drifting through his window and how he had risen to it, as though to a voice calling him, and hurried to the place where the young coed had stood looking down at dead Jack Leaf.

"I understand that you covered the man with your coat?"

"Yes sir."

"We'll, uh, we'll take care of the expense of—"

"Oh, no sir, that won't be—"

Connor waved his hand as though such things were done as gentlemen did them. No need for further discussion. He cleared his throat and made a church and steeple of his hands.

Stall remembered Jack Leaf's fingers curling into fists as though, from across the divide, he wanted to fight someone.

Connor said, "What do you think happened, Tom?"

"I think he jumped. One of the students saw it. She seemed like a credible kid. She said he just stepped out into the air."

Connor shook his head again and his eyes widened as, Stall supposed, he pictured what Jack Leaf had done. He raised a hand to the side of his head and made a vague sign. "Was he . . . ?"

"No sir, I don't think so. We weren't close, but Jack always seemed as balanced as the next guy, if you know what I mean."

Connor looked at Stall with the eyes of an attorney, a judge.

Stall continued: "Jack saw a lot of action in the war."

Connor nodded sagely. "Ah."

"It made him, I think, a little remote, more inclined to observe than to get involved."

"You mean politically?"

"No sir. I mean just life. Jack was a spectator." To say this, here, now, to this man, made Stall feel strange. Did he, Stall, resemble Jack Leaf? Stall had told no one, not even Maureen, about his theory of himself. Tom Stall, observer of life.

"So, Professor Leaf wasn't involved in politics?"

"Not that I knew," Stall said. *Far from it. Jack considered politics the wasteland of scoundrels.*

"We have to be careful about politics, Tom. Especially now." Connor put his hand flat on the *Tallahassee Democrat*. On the grainy picture of Charley Johns's redneck face. Connor looked at Stall for a long moment out of narrowed eyes. Eyes that said, *You understand me, don't you?*

The mystery had commenced, but Stall was certain of three things: Harding and Connor had talked, this meeting was the beginning of Stall's vetting for the chairmanship, and there was something in Connor's mind about Jack Leaf, something he was not telling Tom Stall.

Florida was America's Vacation Land, and her beautiful beaches, the ring of white sand that enclosed her like a necklace of pearls, were cosmopolitan places where North and South mingled and even the races occasionally came within shouting distance of each other. But, oh God, go inland a few miles and Florida was Alabama and Mississippi with a vengeance. She was a land of lynching, convict labor, peonage, and the bare-knuckles politics that had not changed since Confederate general Nathan Bedford Forrest had served as the first grand wizard for the Ku Klux Klan.

People of breeding knew that you talked about politics and religion in polite company at your peril. Stall had no idea what he was free to say to his president about either one in a state where politics and religion went hand in hand if the religion was Protestant. God help you if you were Jewish or Catholic. In the eyes of Charley Johns and his wilderness tribe, disciples of the Church of Rome were only slightly better than Jews.

Stall decided to play it safe. "Sir, I don't involve myself in politics much, except to vote when November comes around. I've got all I can handle with a wife and daughter, and these courses you pay me to teach."

Connor nodded abstractly as though Stall had just delivered a paean to motherhood and apple pie. In a way, Stall supposed he had.

Connor said, "Tom, have you heard anything about the Committee?"

"The Committee, sir?"

Stall had heard about a lot of committees. He had sat on more of them than he liked. The tenure and promotion committee had been the worst, the august body that decided who kept a job and who had to slink off looking for work with the mark of Cain on his forehead. It was a duty that guaranteed enemies. When this committee's decisions were announced, wives snubbed one another in supermarkets. One of Stall's colleagues had pounded on the door of another man's office late one afternoon, screaming, "Come out, Dawson, you gutless, brainless son of a bitch! Come out and fight! I know you voted me down, and the least I can do is knock you on your goddamned fat ass before I leave this godforsaken sump of mediocrity!"

Stall had sat in his office through this rant waiting to hear if Dawson's door opened, in which case, he would have to go out and try to restore order. But who knew? Grimes, the screamer, might have a weapon. And by the sound of him, Grimes was desperate. Desperate men did desperate things. Stall had waited until he heard Grimes stomp away. Dawson, it was later reported, had made his escape by climbing out his window and scrambling down the ivy that grew up the redbrick wall.

President Connor was waiting.

Stall said, "No sir. I have not heard about the Committee." Stall tried to introduce some levity. "I sure serve on a few of them!"

Connor's eyes brooded. He bit the inside of his cheek and sucked his teeth. "You've heard no rumors. Nobody talking in the faculty mail room?"

Stall shook his head, wanted to look at his watch, but knew that would be a gaffe. Where was this going?

Connor sighed, the long breath that preceded climax. "The Florida Legislative Investigation Committee is Charley Johns's brainchild, though I doubt he has one. A brain, I mean. I don't know what Dan McCarty was thinking when he let Charley get this thing up and running. The Committee has police powers, subpoena powers, a team of lawyers and investigators, and they're all hell-bent to root out Communists, homosexuals, and other undesirables in our schools. I've been working against this behind the scenes, talking with friends up in Tallahassee, trying it keep these people out of our business down here in Gainesville, but now that Dan's gone and Charley's sitting in his chair, well, it could be, *Loose the dogs of war.*"

Stall smiled. The president knew his Shakespeare. "With respect, sir," he said, "what does all of this have to do with Jack Leaf?" *And with me?*

"A man came to my office yesterday. I was out. He wanted to talk to me about Professor Leaf." Connor opened the desk drawer into which he had stared hard when he'd first invited Stall into this office. "He told Mrs. Braithwaite he represents the Committee. He left this with her." Connor lifted a manila envelope from the drawer and pushed it across the desk.

Stall looked at the president for permission to open it.

Connor nodded.

The first picture showed a man walking into a bus station men's room. The second showed another man, well-dressed, dark-skinned, slender, with black hair, entering the same men's room. The third shot, taken inside the men's room through the open door of a stall, showed the slender, dark-skinned man standing with his trousers halfway down his thighs and his arm raised to the wall for support. The arm obscured half of the man's face. Another man kneeled in front of the slender man doing what Stall knew some men did. He thanked God he'd never seen it.

Stall knew why there was no fourth photo, one that might have identified the standing man. There was no fourth photo because after the flashbulb had revealed the lurid pose of number three, all hell had broken loose. Stall closed his eyes and imagined the two men running from the bathroom, stampeding right over the photographer who had caught them in the act. He opened his eyes, looked up at President James Connor, and could not stop himself from muttering, "Holy Christ."

"Far from it." Connor's tone was grim. "That's Jack Leaf."

With these words, Stall knew, he and Connor ceased to be master and man.

They became confederates. Comrades in what project, what venture, Stall was not sure, but he knew they were linked now and forever. He tried this: "You can't tell that's Jack Leaf, not really."

"Come on, Tom."

"It could be someone—"

"You liked the man. From what I hear, a lot of people did, but we've got to face facts. And we've got to stop this before it goes any further if we can."

Stall told the president about the student with the slide rule who had seen two men leaving Murphree Hall only minutes before Jack Leaf had taken his walk in the air. And he told about seeing two men in front of the College Inn.

"Yeah," Connor said, "Margaret described the guy who delivered those photos. Apparently, he played football for Miami. She thinks he's good-looking." The president shook his head at the strange discriminations of women. "A linebacker, I'm told. Also an ex-cop and a sometime preacher of the gospel, a real versatile type. Carries a badge now under the aegis of the Committee. I'm coming to the conclusion that the two men went to Leaf's classroom, talked to him, or . . . did *something* to him, and then he jumped."

Stall, who felt now a little more at ease with Connor, said, "So . . . ?"

"Tom, I want you to look into this as discreetly as possible. Find out what you can about Jack Leaf and about anybody else in the department who might be . . ."

Stall couldn't keep the anger out of his eyes, and the surprising thing was that Connor was surprised to see it. "Sir, are you asking me . . . ?"

"Only to help me protect what I know we both love. This university, its integrity. Its founding principles. The values you talk about every day in those classes of yours."

"Sir, what Jack Leaf did in his private life has nothing at all to do with the integrity of this university. No more than what my wife and I do in our own bedroom."

"Tom, nobody's life is completely private. Nobody knows that better than I do. I can't even curse on the golf course without it getting in the newspaper. And Tom . . ." Connor put the flat of his hand on the manila envelope. "Tom, a bus station? A men's room in a bus station? Can you defend that on grounds of privacy?"

Maybe I can, maybe not, Stall thought. My God, what did the man want—Stall to haunt the men's rooms of Anderson Hall with a spy's camera in his lapel? Stall to take ten pisses a day to insure the integrity of the English Department?

The idea of two men kissing, or doing more, turned Stall's stomach. He didn't think he had to defend that reaction any more than a man did whose guts roiled at the thought of eating an oyster. But if some men kissed and more, and if some others liked or didn't like the idea, Stall considered this none of his business as long as reasonable limits were observed. Was a bus station men's room reasonable? No, it wasn't. Not if somebody's ten-year-old son went in there for the usual reasons and saw what was going on. That could scar a kid for life. Stall's head was dizzy with all this. For now he had to make it clear that he would not spy on his colleagues.

"Sir, I won't police the English Department for inappropriate behavior by male faculty members."

"So, you are saying there *are* other men in your department who do what Professor Leaf did?"

"No sir. I'm saying I consider what they do nobody's business but their own."

Connor stood. After a space, so did Stall.

"Well, Tom, if a man who wants to be the next chairman of the department won't look out for its welfare, somebody else will do it. And you and I both know who that somebody could be—a former University of Miami linebacker who preaches the gospel in his spare time." Connor walked in his still-athletic way past Stall and opened the door. "Think about it, Tom."

Stall stopped, thought better of saying anything more, nodded, and moved past Mrs. Braithwaite's machine-gunning typewriter into the world he loved.

SIX

As he walked from Tigert Hall to the English building, Stall could not stop talking to Thomas Connor. He knew that he must look half-mad, muttering to a phantom listener. Students gave him a wide berth.

My God, what do you expect me to do if I find out that some guy who teaches English also likes to . . . do what the ancient Greeks apparently did? Am I supposed to take him aside and tell him to cease and desist or he'll end up like Jack Leaf—with flashbulbs in his face in a men's room? Leaping from a third-floor window? Am I supposed to pass his name along to you who will give him his walking papers for the good of the university? It's preposterous.

As he walked, debating Connor, it occurred to Stall that, indeed, there were men in his department who were what was politely called "confirmed bachelors." And maybe the study of English attracted such types, but to a man, as Stall knew them, these "types" were good, helpful, and honorable colleagues. He'd never heard an unkind word from any of them, though a few were known for rapier wit, and he'd enjoyed hours of searching and earnest conversation with many of them about mutual research interests. The best thing, the thing that held the potential to break a great many hearts, was that for now at least, Stall's English Department, the one he hoped to chair someday, was a harmonious, happy collection of eccentrics whose greatest love was to read books and talk about them with young people. Of course, there were petty rivalries, and the placid surface was sometimes disturbed by academic politics, but this was a group that could gather for Christmas and New Year's Eve parties and have itself a roaring good time. These were men, and now, with the advent of Sophie Green, a woman, who could get drunk as lords and end their evenings with their arms slung over one another's shoulders in someone's backyard singing "On Moonlight Bay." Christ, it would kill Stall to see anything harm the beauty of his English Department.

Stall imagined Connor on the phone with Harding, the president telling the chairman that Stall had not cooperated. At least not fully. Not in the way that a man with the university's best interests at heart should cooperate. Stall would see Harding now—but what should he tell the old man about his talk with Connor? It occurred to Stall as he walked under the tall, turpentine-smelling pines in the midmorning sunshine, that it might serve both his and Connor's purposes to keep their conversation secret from Harding, at least for the time being. If Connor planned to commission Stall as a secret agent, then it made good sense to tell no one about it.

In Anderson Hall, Stall presented himself to Helen Markham, who stood guard over Harding's inner office. Reading glasses precarious at the tip of her long, heavily powdered nose, she looked up at Stall from her memo pad as though this were any summer morning. As though neither a professor nor a governor had died in the last twenty-four hours. She lifted her cup of Earl Grey tea, sipped, and said, "Go on in. He's had his Sanka."

Amos Harding was known for shunning humanity until he'd finished his first cup of instant coffee in the morning. He preferred instant, he said, for digestive reasons. No one asked him to elaborate. Stall thanked Helen Markham and walked on.

Harding was standing at the tall window that looked out over the student ghetto that began abruptly a block beyond the row of restaurants and bars that lined University Avenue. He was a tall man who always wore black or dark-blue suits with narrow lapels and narrower ties. His face was pale, pocked, and gaunt. What hair he retained was white, combed straight back, and matted to his scalp with pomade. Department wits sometimes referred to him as *Funus Director*, the funeral director, and he did look a bit like a cartoon country mortician. Lost in the mists of history were the reasons that Harding had been made chairman.

Stall cleared his throat and Harding turned from the window. "Well, Tom, how did it go with Himself?" Harding sometimes referred to the president this way so that all who heard would know he was on easy terms with the man who signed the checks.

"Fine, sir." *Damn it, he asked you to call him Amos.*

Harding sat behind the big desk that Stall hoped someday would be his and motioned Stall to a chair. "It's happening all over the state now, Tom."

What did Harding mean? People jumping out of windows? An epidemic of suicides?

"Sorry, Amos. I'm not sure what you mean."

Harding reached out, lifted his empty coffee cup, looked into it, frowned. "This damned Committee. They're going after Communists, the NAACP, homosexuals." He spoke the words with obvious distaste. "Agitators, which I take to mean those shaggy kids out in front of the library."

Stall had stopped by these ragged gatherings a few times to watch the kids hand out leaflets about the overthrow of the Mossadegh government in Iran or read aloud from *Howl*. The local free speech movement seemed to be headed by a grad student from Miami, Stephen Levy, who majored in political science. Mostly, students drifted past these self-styled provocateurs, paying no attention. Sleepy Gainesville was always slow to bend to the fashions from California and New York, whatever they were—clothing, politics, Hula-Hoops.

Harding regarded Stall from across the Victorian desk with its matching period decorations, a bronze figure of a man in knee breeches pushing a wheelbarrow piled high with books, a bust of Tennyson. Harding waited.

Stall said, "You think Jack's death has something to do with this Committee?"

"Yes, I do. I just don't know what. Do you?"

Stall decided to work from the premise that Connor had not told Harding about the photos of two men in a bathroom. "President Connor and I talked about Jack. I told him what I knew about his . . . death, which isn't much, really."

As far as Stall knew, there had been no official determination of a cause of death. He supposed it would be suicide or death by misadventure, which, in the novels he read, meant a polite refusal to decide what had happened (with a rather heavy suggestion that something was amiss).

Harding leaned forward, removed an antique scrivener's pen

from an empty crystal inkwell on his desk, examined it, put it back. "Did the president tell you anything *we* should know?"

We meant the English Department. So far, Stall had only told a lie of omission. He recalled Maureen's insistence to Corey that leaving things out was only discretion.

"Only that he's sorry about Jack's death and worried about the effect it might have on the morale of the university." There, that was good. And it was true in a limited way. Jack Leaf's death would have its effects, but Stall knew, and literature taught, that the living remembered the dead only a short time. Morale would rise again with the first football victory of the fall.

Then it occurred to Stall that maybe by taking his walk in the air, Jack Leaf had made a statement. He had responded to the men who had left Murphree Hall seconds before Jack Leaf had left this world. If Jack was the man in the photos, then he had known someone would use them against him. Perhaps he had known all of it, foreseen all that Stall and Connor and Harding could not yet see. For there would be, there must be, more.

Hearing his own words emerge freighted with a weariness that he knew the older man would recognize, Stall said, "I think we're in good hands with Connor. He's an advocate. He'll fight Charley Johns and his lousy committee."

"Yes," said Harding, "I agree with you about that."

Happy to change the subject, Stall told Harding about Sophie Green's offer to teach American Romanticism. Harding considered it for only a few seconds. "I like it. I'll take your word for her qualifications, and it's good of her as a newcomer to do this for the department."

Stall nodded, gave a deferential smile.

Harding returned the smile of the village elder, stood up, looked at the old railroad pocket watch he kept chained to his belt. "All right, Tom. Thank you. We have to go now. I've called a special meeting."

The graduate English faculty held their infrequent meetings in a large classroom in Anderson Hall. Today the room was full to bursting. Even some *professors emeriti* had shown up. Some of them, the oldest and grayest of beards, were men Stall had never seen before.

Harding called the meeting to order and told the assembled faculty what they already knew: Jack Leaf was dead. "We are not entirely sure what happened. We know little of why it happened, but I'm sure we will know more as time passes. For now, we need to conduct business as usual, in so far as that is possible. Tom Stall, who took care of Professor Leaf, of our friend Jack, at that most terrible time, has agreed to finish out the summer term in Jack's research methodologies, a course he has taught before, and Professor Green has proposed that she teach American Romanticism as an overload in the fall."

"But she's a medievalist," called Fred Parsons from the back. Parsons was an aging scholar of American lit and the obvious choice to fall on his sword for Jack Leaf and the department.

Harding raised both hands to suppress the minor uproar that followed Parsons's remark. "She's more than qualified. I'm satisfied that she'll do a fine job."

That seemed to be it until Sophie Green stood up in the front row and looked back at Fred Parsons. Blushing and holding a delicate hand to the base of her throat, she said, "I didn't mean to step on any toes. I'll gladly withdraw if that's the will of the Americanists of the faculty."

She could not know how much her comment would displease Harding, who had said the matter was closed. Stall didn't like it much either, since he had proposed the plan to Harding. Well, perhaps this was the way things were done at Columbia. (And who on God's earth said *Americanists*?)

Harding cleared his throat. "Thank you, Professor Green. I think this is settled." Then to the group, "I will entertain proposals from any who care to tender them for covering Jack's other course. We are all very, very sorry this happened. My wife and I have helped Sarah Leaf as much as we can in this very difficult time, and I know that some of you have reached out to her. I hope others will as well."

Harding waited while heads bowed or eyes looked off into the middle distance where mortality crouched in all its ugliness. No one spoke. Harding said, "If there is no further business, let's go back to our preparations for what I hope will be another fine academic year."

Sophie Green waited for Stall at the end of the third-floor hallway. Stall had figured she'd want to talk, and he did too. When she began to gush an apology, he raised a hand to stop her.

"It's all right. No harm done. I promise."

"But Professor Harding seemed so stern, so offended. All I did was speak."

"You didn't just speak. You challenged. Harding's old school. He doesn't see departmental meetings as conversations. He presides and he pronounces. When he wants discussion, he lets us know."

She looked at him for a long moment with her head tilted slightly to the side in a way that was, well, cute. "When you're chairman, will you *pronounce?*"

Stall felt the heat of a blush rising up the stalk of his neck. "Who said I'll be chairman?"

"Rumor has it you're gunning for it."

"Gunning?" He chuckled in a way he hoped seemed urbane. "A long time since I've held a gun."

"I was speaking metaphorically."

"Of course. That's our business."

She furrowed her brow. Did she think he really wanted to discuss with her his prospects for the chairmanship? Metaphorically or otherwise?

"Well, look," he said, "it's been a long day. For all of us. Let me assure you again, you're in no trouble with Harding. I think he likes you, actually. He's old school, but in his way he's glad we have you. Even *he* knows we've been slow to bring in . . ."

"Women?"

"Yes, sure, what did you think I meant?"

"What about Negroes? Or do we think *down here* all they should do is carry books up the stairs and refuse money from Yankees for their work?" She said it in a voice full of charm and with a smile on her face, but still the words cut Stall. He couldn't tell if she thought he was on her side or somewhere else.

"We move as fast as we can, I guess." He gave her a dip of his head (his father would have tipped a hat real or imaginary) and started for the fire door at the end of the hall. "When I'm chairman," he said over his shoulder, "maybe we'll move a little faster. Get us some more Yankee girls to teach us yokels how to be . . . Americanists."

Opening the door, he heard her sharp little intake of breath.

SEVEN

When Stall walked into their good-smelling kitchen, he threw his coat over the back of a chair and noted the absence of martinis. Maureen turned from the sink with a shimmer of perspiration on her forehead and said in her put-my-foot-down voice, "Tonight we visit Sarah Leaf."

"Sure, okay," Stall said, deflated. Couldn't a man take a load off his feet and make himself a drink (even if his wife would not have one with him) before getting his marching orders for the evening's proprieties?

"Okay, then," Maureen said a little more softly. She walked over and kissed his cheek, depositing there some of the sweat from her upper lip. Stall reached up and wiped it off, then turned away and secretly tasted it. Good. (And for the hundredth time wondered why he couldn't do things like this where his wife could see them.) He loved her sweat but not his own and not these long hot summers. Someday they'd be able to afford air-conditioning. He'd debated with himself about where the first machine should go—their bedroom or the kitchen, which he sometimes called *Vulcan's Forge*, though he did not like to think of his wife as a hulking demigod.

The kitchen smelled good. The chicken casserole, probably. Probably Maureen had made two of them, one for the family and one for Sarah Leaf.

Stall found the gin bottle in the cupboard above the refrigerator and began to build himself a martini. "Where's Corey?"

"Spending the night with Jenny Sprague."

Maureen said this with a practiced lack of inflection. Stall knew she was thinking, as he certainly was, that tonight, with no daughter in the house, he might lift her nightgown. He even allowed himself to wonder if his wife had encouraged their daughter to sleep under the roof of Gerald Sprague, an agronomist who worked for the university's Institute of Food and Agricultural Sciences, for reasons of nightgown-lifting. It was possible, and it occurred to Stall that Jack Leaf's death might have something to do with it. Death, he believed, made people more than ordinarily interested in life.

Maureen left the kitchen and returned with a coat hanger that held a new blazer almost identical to the one Stall had sacrificed to Jack Leaf's mortal dignity. She stood solemnly holding it out to him. The price tag dangled from a pin in the front pocket. "On sale at Wilson's Department Store. I thought this might cheer you up. And you need it, so don't complain about the money."

"Maureen, I—"

"Oh, shut up and come here." She held out her open arms to him.

After the dishes were washed and dried and Maureen had freshened her makeup, she said, "It's time to call Sarah."

Stall said, "Okay." He waited.

"*You* call her."

"Me."

"You. You're going to be the chairman. You need to practice these things."

Stall called Sarah Leaf.

"Sarah, I'm so sorry."

"I know, Tom."

"Maureen and I want to come over and see you, and bring some—"

"God, Tom, please no food."

"Oh, oh, well, Sarah, of course, if you—"

"I'm sorry, Tom, that was rude. It's just that I've done nothing since I heard the news but cry and answer the doorbell, and cry, and thank people for casseroles, and then Maddie Harding came over, and we've done nothing but play gin rummy for a penny a point and drink bourbon and brush our teeth every time the doorbell rings. I'm just sick of it. I know that sounds terrible, but it's the truth, and isn't this a good time for a little truth, Tom?"

"Well, all right, Sarah, we won't bring any food. Is there, uh, is there anything we can do for you? Anything at all? Anything you need done, we'll take care of it for you."

Stall heard a long sigh, then, "Take me to a bar. No, meet me at a bar. The cheapest one we can think of. I know! The bowling alley out on Waldo Road! I want to drink cheap whiskey and not see anybody I know but you two for the rest of the day."

"Sure, Sarah, we'll do that. We can do that." Stall covered the phone with his hand and looked at Maureen, who had only heard his side of the conversation. If her face had been words, it would have said, *What the . . . ?* Stall said, "So we'll pick you up?"

"No, meet me there. I want to drive. And I want to drive drunk. I want to take some goddamn risks."

"Okay, Sarah. We're on the way."

Stall had his hand on the doorknob when the doorbell rang. A young Negro man stood on the front step holding a plastic clothing bag. There was an envelope pinned to the bag. The man said, "Dr. Stall?"

"Uh, yes?"

"This is for you, suh." The man handed him the bag and stepped back. A delivery truck idled in the driveway.

Stall said, "Do I need to sign anything?"

"No, all taken care of."

Stall dug out his wallet and tipped the man a dollar.

"Thank you, suh."

The Stalls went back to their kitchen and Stall handed the bag to Maureen, who unzipped it while he unpinned the note. She removed a blazer from the bag almost identical to the one Stall had placed over Jack Leaf's face. She looked at the label inside the coat. "Fancy," she said.

Stall read the note aloud: "*Dear Tom, With my compliments and my gratitude, Jim Connor.*"

Maureen said, "Jim? That's even fancier. Two coats in one night and this one's better than the one I got you."

"I like yours better. And I'm returning this one."

"Don't do anything rash."

Stall hung the coat in the closet by the front door. "Let us go then, you and I, coatless to a bowling alley."

* * *

On the way to Alley Gatorz Bowling Center, Stall told Maureen about Sarah playing gin rummy and drinking bourbon with Amos Harding's wife. "And she calls her Maddie."

"Must be short for *Madeleine*." Maureen shook her head and looked out the window of the Packard at one of the town's ugliest streets, a strip of junkyards, industrial dry cleaners, and auto body shops.

"Bourbon and gin rummy," Stall said. "Who knew the old lady had it in her?"

"She probably loves getting away from Harding."

To that, Stall said nothing.

"When I'm an old lady, I'll have it in me."

Stall wanted to say, *When I'm an old man, I'll* put *it in you*, but he kept it to himself. He said, "Are you gonna drink, or are you finished with demon rum forever?"

"I'll let you know when I see the demon quivering in a glass."

"Fair enough." Stall pulled into the parking lot.

Bowling alley bars were the same in every city. The liquor was cheap because the owners knew drunks bowled more lines, and the noise was deafening, which either drove you to drink or made you bowl more lines. And maybe the uneasy business of renting shoes made people think of alcohol as a disinfectant. Stall and his wife found a table as far away from the nearest lane as possible, and he went to the bar for Maureen's Coke and his own bourbon and water. Sarah Leaf had said she was drinking whiskey and Stall figured misery loved company. They sat, sipped, and when he could sneak a peek without offending Maureen, Stall watched the ball game on the blurry television above the bar. The Yankees were pole-axing the White Sox, as usual.

"So how do you think she's taking it?" Maureen twirled her glass in its little pool of moisture on the table.

"Based on one phone conversation, I'd say she's taking it pretty strangely, but I don't know. I've never been a widow."

Maureen drank some Coke. "She's not a widow yet, she's in shock. She won't be a widow for a while, and then we'll know how she's taking it."

Sarah Leaf entered the bar blinking her eyes after the harsh August sunlight of the parking lot. The bright smile on her face reminded Stall of the look he had once seen on the face of a distant cousin who had just been discharged from the county asylum for the insane. Sarah waved and walked toward them fast. Stall stood and so did his wife. Maureen hugged Sarah Leaf first. Maureen's hug was hard and close, two women exchanging messages that men could never parse.

Stall hugged Sarah more formally and held a chair for her. "What can I get you?"

"I'm drinking rye now," Sarah Leaf said, her voice crisp, her words not at all slurred. "Maddie and I went right through the bourbon. On the rocks, please, with an ice water back."

Stall headed for the bar. On the way he thought, *Why have we been chosen for this? We didn't know them all that well.*

The Leafs and the Stalls had attended parties at each other's houses and a lot of other houses too. In the ebb and flow of social gatherings, they had washed up together on sofas and in hallways for conversations of all kinds, ranging from kids to real estate to which doctors delved into which human mysteries in this small university town. When Maureen and Sarah had put their heads together, Stall supposed they had talked about the usual womanly, housewifely things. Maureen had never told him what they talked about.

When he and Jack talked, it was about their research, students they shared, and sometimes about their colleagues. *Reserved* was the word Stall would have chosen to describe Jack, reserved in all things, and he supposed others might describe Tom Stall in the same way. Was this one of the reasons that he and Jack had been able to talk easily and enthusiastically about their work and to go no further? Never into anything personal, just a few comments about kids, cars, sports, and wives? Stall had liked Jack Leaf and, had he asked himself about it, he probably would have realized that he'd have liked to get to know the man better. Perhaps his own reserve had made him defer an approach to Jack, put off the day when he might say, *Hey, Jack, let's have lunch and talk some more about that flow you see from poets like Bradstreet and Whittier to Eliot and Stevens.* Waiting for the bartender to pour, Stall shook his head and thought, *It's too late for that now.*

Maureen and Sarah Leaf were deep in conversation when Stall

set Sarah's drinks on the table. "So I told her," Sarah was saying, "she might be able to beat me at gin, but I could drink her under the table. And then, you won't believe this, the old broad winked at me real big and said, *Try me. Just you try me*, and that's when I went for the bottle of Old Overholt."

Maureen put her hand on Sarah's on the tabletop. "Oh my God, the chairman's wife. Who knew?" Stall recognized well the expression on his wife's face. It was, *Get me out of here*.

He sat and took a healthy sip of his bourbon. "So," he said, "Old Lady Harding turns out to be the secret sister of Tugboat Annie?"

"Nothing secret about it," Sarah Leaf said. "She's a daytime drinker."

Stall was thinking, *Maybe just with you, with a recent widow, maybe just in a crisis and very rarely*, but he doubted it. Whole vistas of Amos Harding's hard life opened up to Stall. Suddenly, he felt sorry for the man.

"Maybe," Maureen squeezed Sarah's hand, "she just knew what *you* needed."

"And sacrificed herself to it." Sarah threw back her head and laughed. "I see. I get it. Mrs. Amos Harding is the village voodoo princess who knows exactly what I need to get through my grief. Well, let me tell you something, kids. You don't get *through* a thing like this."

And so the conversation turned from a kind of hysterical levity to grim platitudes. Stall and his wife sat mute while Sarah Leaf talked about how her life had changed forever, about the two boys, off at tennis camp together, still living in blissful ignorance of their father's . . . what was it? A rejection of them? That was how they would see it, Sarah said. And they would spend the rest of their lives wondering what they had done to cause the father they had loved and who had loved them to take his own life. No, to throw it away. Her voice ground on mechanically as she stared straight ahead, occasionally sipping whiskey. Finally, she just stopped. "I hope I'm not boring you two."

Maureen took the plunge that Stall would not even have considered: "Why did he do it, Sarah?" She leaned forward and looked deeply into Sarah Leaf's eyes, and Stall knew that the two women had crossed again to the terrain where men could not follow. His wife was asking a widow what signs to look for in a husband, what signals came from the masculine side of Marriageland, that could tell a woman when her husband might jump out a window.

Sarah finished her rye and took a sip of cold water. "Jack was unhappy. Underneath it all, he was a very troubled man."

Jack Leaf, Underground Man.

Sarah Leaf was a trim, athletic woman who played tennis in a league with faculty wives and served as secretary of the Garden Club. She never looked flustered, never too busy, never anything but in charge. She kept an immaculate house, was a good cook and hostess, and played excellent bridge. She wore slacks (rarely skirts and dresses), flat shoes, and blouses that showed off the lovely arms she had earned from hours on the tennis court. The effect, Stall thought, was a little masculine, a little like the Katharine Hepburn of *Pat and Mike*, but Sarah had a pretty face and there was no mistaking the *come hither* that came into her eyes sometimes late at night at parties when she'd had one too many. She was sexy in a sleek, hard way. Sexy like a fast car or an expensive hunting rifle.

Sarah and Jack had not been what people called a loving couple; they didn't hold hands or stand with their arms linked, or anything like that. Stall could not remember ever seeing them touch, not even the stray drifting of fingers across a shoulder as one passed the other in a narrow hallway. He had said nothing to Maureen about his talk with Connor and the photos of Jack. Now he sat thinking, *What kind of life did this woman have with a man who could go to a bus station men's room, a man who lived double?* They must have talked about Jack's other life. Must have come to some kind of accommodation so that life could go on. Life with its placid surface of kids, tennis, teaching, bridge, and literary criticism.

Stall invaded the feminine front. He entered at his peril, but he needed to know some things, and Sarah Leaf seemed in the mood to talk. "Was Jack in any kind of trouble? Anything with money?" *Were the people who took the pictures blackmailing him?*

That was when Sarah Leaf lied, and Stall knew it and he thought Maureen did too.

Sarah said, "Money? He liked to spend it. Jack liked nice clothes. I'm sure you noticed that. But, uh, no, no, he wasn't in any trouble I knew about."

Maureen leaned forward again. "Were you and Jack in trouble?"

"You mean our marriage? No, I wouldn't say so. Jack wasn't seeing another woman, if that's what you're asking, and I sure wasn't seeing anyone." Showing her liquor a little now, she leaned over and touched Stall's hand. "Although I've always had a secret fancy for you, Tom. Sorry, Maureen. I'm just feeling truthful today."

No, thought Stall, *you're lying*.

Maureen took it well. "That's all right, Sarah. All the girls like Tom. He's cute, is my Tom." Unmistakable emphasis on *my*.

Stall said, "Sarah, let's get you home."

"Home? The party's just getting started." She looked around the bowling alley with the startled eyes of a woman who has just noticed how drunk she is. "Maybe I'll bowl a few . . . what do you call them, a few rubbers, a few strikes, some pars, an inning? It looks like an interesting game."

Stall said to Maureen, "I'll drive Sarah in her car. You follow in ours." He lifted Sarah by her elbow.

She pulled away from him with a dignified flexing of her tennis muscles. She stood looking defiantly at him, then at Maureen, and then a sad gravity took her limbs and her shoulders fell. "All right," she said, "home. More gin rummy with Maddie. The bottle of rye's only half-empty."

Stall walked her to her car where she stood at the driver's door digging into her purse for her keys. When she found them, she said, "I'll drive. I told you I want to drive drunk."

"Not this drunk," Stall said gently, and held out his hand. He was going to stand firm even if she made a scene. She looked into his eyes and there it was, that *come hither* he had seen a few times before, though never aimed at him.

"Okay, Tommy." Her voice was girlish and flirtatious. She handed him the keys. "You drive."

Maureen came out of the bowling alley stuffing money into her purse. She had paid and tipped.

Stall drove the Leaf's Buick to their house in the fashionable Duckpond area of Gainesville. It was an old Florida bungalow from the thirties, with the neat lawn and shrubbery you would expect of Jack and Sarah Leaf. Stall pulled into the driveway, waved his good intentions to Maureen who had pulled in behind him, and got Sarah Leaf out of the car.

On the way to the front door, she said, "I guess Maddie's gone home. I don't see her car."

Well, Stall thought, *somebody's driving drunk*.

He unlocked the front door and followed Sarah Leaf inside. The house was as he remembered it, except for the faint smell of bourbon and the casseroles piled on the kitchen counter. Sarah pointed at them. "Too many for the fridge. I had to leave them out. Would you like to take some home?"

"No, but thanks. Look, Sarah, are you gonna to be all right? Maybe you should come home with us. Spend the night and we can talk more if you want to."

"Talk?" She gave him a bleak look. "What good is talk, Tom? Jack and I talked forever and it never did us any good."

All Stall could do was shrug. English teachers were men of words, and most of them thought talking did some good.

Sarah Leaf opened a drawer beside the kitchen stove and pulled out an envelope. She handed it to him. "The medical examiner's office gave me Jack's clothes. They found this in his coat pocket. Go ahead, open it."

The envelope held a subpoena from the Johns Committee. The document commanded Jack Leaf to appear on August 25, 1958, to testify under oath before the Committee. Stall knew the answer, but he had to ask the question: "Why did they want to talk with Jack?"

"They don't like perverts. Jack was . . . I suppose the common term is *homosexual*. Jack preferred to call himself *gay*. It's a British word, he told me. But really, Jack was . . . hard to define. He liked *me* . . . sometimes." She looked up into Stall's eyes like a little girl would look at her father. "And I loved him."

She went to the dining room table where two gin rummy hands were still laid out beside a pile of pennies. She picked up the bottle of Old Overholt and brought it back to the kitchen where she poured two straight shots and handed one to Stall. He pictured Maureen waiting outside. She was too polite to honk the horn, though she wouldn't hesitate to come inside to see what was keeping her husband in Sarah Leaf's house. When Stall didn't take the glass from

Sarah's hand, she pushed it against his chest and let it go. He caught it, and she touched hers to his and drank. Stall drank with her. She looked into his eyes.

"Jack liked me if I lay on my stomach." She turned around and looked at him over her shoulder. "See this ass? Doesn't it look a bit like a man's?"

Stall could barely choke the words out through the sudden lump in this throat: "It's a very fine ass, Sarah. It's an admirable ass."

"Jack went both ways, Tom. Some men are like that, and some women too, they tell me. His view of it was that the rest of us, who can't go both ways, are missing out on, well, half the good things in life."

She finished her drink and put her fingers gently under the bottom of his glass and raised it to his lips, making him finish too. *Like you'd do with a baby*, Stall thought. *And when it comes to talking like this, that's what I am.*

"After I got used to everything I learned about Jack, I was just glad to have half of him. Oh, I worried about him. Some of the things he did, some of the men he met, were maybe a little dangerous, but I knew he was as careful as he could be, and I knew he wouldn't hurt me if he could absolutely help it."

Careful? Stall's throat burned from the whiskey, his stomach rolled with too much of it. *Careful in a bus station?*

"May I take this with me?" He held up the subpoena between himself and Sarah Leaf, where it had the desired effect. Her eyes closed, and when they opened again, she was finished telling the truth. "Sure," she said. "I don't think it matters to anyone now. Do you?"

Oh, it matters, thought Stall. *If the newspapers get ahold of it, it will matter to you and your children.*

Even if the Committee moved on to other business, the papers would want to know why a man had killed himself. They wouldn't stop spilling ink until they found out. And the reporters would become the tools of the Committee whether they liked it or not. Florida's sodomy laws were clear. A man could go to jail for having sex with another man. He could go to jail for addressing his own wife from behind. But it didn't have to go that far. A committee of the state legislature in open session could ruin a man in minutes and the press would cover every word of it.

Stall said quietly, "Yes, I think it matters." *And you'll think so too, in the morning*. He tucked the subpoena into his pocket. "I'll take good care of this. Don't worry about it."

When he got to the car, Maureen moved from behind the wheel.

"No," he said, "you drive."

This was rare. She raised her eyebrows. "You two were in there for . . . ?"

"She's not in very good shape right now."

"So, did you loosen her clothing or something?"

He gave her their *come off it* look and they both shook their heads.

Maureen started the car. "Jeez, the things that happen when you least expect, right?"

"Right." He leaned his head back on the seat and put his hand on the subpoena in his pocket. He knew who would want to see it.

At home, the *Gainesville Sun* was waiting for them on the doorstep. Wearily, Stall picked it up and went into the kitchen to spread it on the table. He looked at the headline with dread: "UF Professor's Death Thought to Be Suicide."

Another article was headlined: "Committee Subpoenas UF Professors in Classrooms, Students Look On." And another: "Political Science Professor Targeted for Alleged Subversive Statements in Classroom. Students Read *Communist Manifesto*."

Stall sat at his dining room table and let his head fall into his hands. Christ, the world was ending. What were these people doing to the university he loved? Didn't they know they were running through a village of thatched houses waving burning torches? Were they too drunk with power and hatred to know it? They could destroy in a few months something that had taken a thousand years to build. Stall's face burned with anguish and shame when he realized that now he would have to worry about the economic theories and the political affiliations, however whimsical, of the writers he asked students to read. Christ, Wallace Stevens, hadn't he flirted with communism in his youth? If a political science prof was in trouble for teaching Marx—Marx who was wrong about almost everything but whose work was foundational to modern political philosophy—then what might happen to an English teacher who taught D.H. Lawrence?

Stall felt Maureen's hands come to rest on his shoulders. "I'd offer you a drink to relax you, but you've had enough."

Stall muttered, "More than enough." *Of a lot of things*. He reached up and rested a hand on hers. "But not of you," he said. "You're a brick."

"What, you mean I'm hard and red and good for stacking?"

"No, I mean solid. You know what I mean." She knew.

"I'm your Lady Brett," she said, "and you're my Jake. Wait, that doesn't quite work. You've still got your . . ."

"Last time I looked. Let's go upstairs and use it."

"After you, my bullfighter, my man."

EIGHT

The country club had put its boardroom at President Connor's disposal, and that was where Margaret Braithwaite had instructed Stall to wait while Connor finished his morning round. "He should be done by eleven o'clock, but don't worry if he's a little late." Stall didn't mention any plans he might have for the morning.

A white-haired Negro in a starched white jacket showed Stall to the brass-and-mahogany boardroom. The man bowed when Stall sat down at the long table where the club's leaders met to decide such weighty matters as whether or not a ball that came to rest on the far side of a sidewalk behind the ninth green entitled a player to a free drop. The Negro said, "May I serve you a drink, suh?"

"I'll wait and see."

"Yes suh. He'll be heah in a moment. I just seen him in the locker room."

Connor strode in looking tired but happy after his round. His tan was golden and his step springy. He looked like he could still go ten rounds with Benny Leonard. Stall stood and they shook hands. "Mr. President, thank you for the new coat, but I don't think I can—"

"Ah, forget it, Tom. Comes out of petty cash. And it was the right thing for me to do. You wouldn't dispute a man's judgment in such a matter, would you?"

What could Stall say to that? He placed the subpoena on the mahogany table. "Mrs. Leaf found this when they sent her husband's clothes home from the morgue."

Connor read the document with the sharp eye of a country lawyer. When he finished, he shook his head. "The medical examiner decided not to keep this?"

"That's what Mrs. Leaf told me."

"Still a small town, this Gainesville of ours. You could call it shoddy work by a public official or compassion. More likely this was too hot for him to touch. In any case, fortunate for our cause." Connor rubbed his tanned face and Stall heard the sound of whiskers scraped against the grain. "So now we know what happened. Those two goons went to Leaf's classroom and served him."

Stall touched the subpoena on the table. "I meet with Jack's class tomorrow afternoon. I can ask them what they saw."

"I wouldn't do that. If they bring it up, of course you'll listen. And let me know what they say."

"According to what I read in the paper yesterday, the Committee doesn't always show that kind of mercy."

"No, they don't," Connor said. "They served Professor Margolis in his classroom, in front of his students. Big reputation in political science, did you know that?"

Stall was obscurely embarrassed to say that he was not up on the scholarly reputations of the political science faculty. Whatever political scientists did, Stall was pretty sure it was not science. It seemed that more and more academic disciplines these days tried to confer legitimacy upon themselves by embracing numbers. Someday, perhaps, the Department of English Science, but thank God not yet.

Stall put his hand on the subpoena again. "Mr. President, does having this help us?"

"Call me Jim, Tom." Connor reached out and moved the subpoena from Stall's side of the table to his. "We're up to our backsides in the same trouble, so we might as well drop the formalities."

Stall nodded, but it would be hard to comply. Connor was an imposing figure, a man who would have commanded respect in any walk of life.

Connor said, "They're developing their network of lackeys and informants. They wouldn't know who's teaching what or who's been in a bus station if they hadn't already talked to students or their parents. Some kid flunks a quiz and goes home to his tobacco-farming daddy in Sopchoppy, and shows him his copy of *Das Kapital*, and Daddy gets his humors all out of balance and calls his local representative, who gets in touch with our bootless Mr. Johns, and that's how this kind of thing grows from maggot to full-blown blue bottle fly. Somebody knew Jack Leaf would be in that bus station." Connor took a long breath and looked Stall in the eyes. "We can work that side of the street too, if you know what I mean, Tom."

"Mr. President, I think I do, approximately, but I don't see how I fit into this."

"Call me Jim. That's the second time I've asked. You're an exceptional young man with a promising future at this university. And you know what's at stake here as well as I do."

Jim Connor reached into his coat pocket, pulled out a manila envelope, passed it across the table to Stall. *God*, Stall thought, *so many coats and so many envelopes. This is like Restoration drama.* With something like dread, he opened the envelope. It contained a photo of two men who looked like father and son. They stood by a lakeside with boats and some sort of pergola in the background. The younger man whose father's arm was slung across his shoulders looked vaguely familiar to Stall, a slender young man in a light-colored summer suit with the left sleeve folded over and sewn halfway down. An amputee. Connor waited while Stall examined the picture, his mind developing a memory in the same way that a photographer had made this image come into focus in a darkroom.

A dark room. That was how Stall thought of that time. The field hospital in France, the nurses and doctors coming and going, the constant poking and prodding, the raging fever that made him mutter things that made no sense, and finally the needles, the blessed needles with their cargo of the new medicine known as penicillin, the magic potion that had saved Stall's life, and then waking up, coming back to himself, coming out of the dark room and seeing the young man, no more than a boy, lying next to him in the field hospital, a kid with half his arm missing, shot off, Stall supposed, like the bits and pieces of so many men Stall had marched with and crouched in foxholes with for that brief time that was an eternity in the winter of 1945.

And then the boy coming to himself too, and the two of them talking, shyly at first and then more openly, confident that they might both leave this place and go to Paris rather than to a snowy field where the corpses waited for the ground to thaw and the white crosses to multiply row upon row. They talked about their lives and the futures they now believed they would have.

The boy in the photo Connor had given Stall was named Frank Vane. The door of the dark room opened wider and the light poured in and it all came back to Stall. The boy in the photo hailed from Jacksonville, the son of a prominent businessman, scion, as the novels said, of a wealthy family. Vast tracts of timber and pulp mills and shipping and more. The boy had told Stall, as they lay side by side in the field hospital, the story of his young life, speaking in the diffident, modest way of young men who have been reared to the noblesse oblige of the Southern aristocracy. Together, Stall and Frank Vane had caught a convoy of trucks to Paris, and they had stayed in a little pension not far from Sacré-Cœur, and they had drunk the wines and eaten the food of a delirious, liberated Paris, and then one night, out walking alone, Stall had met the young French girl with whom he had spent the first carnal night of his life.

Stall looked up from the photo into the concentrated darkness of James Connor's eyes. Stall said, "He lost the arm, half of it, in the Hürtgen Forest."

"A bad place, I heard."

"That's what he told me." Stall handed the photo back to Connor. "How do you know about it?"

"I know the boy's father. He's a donor. That's how I came by the photograph. The son, this Frank Vane, works for the Committee now. He's one of their lawyers, and the blond goon who came to my office—his name is Cyrus Tate—says Vane told him he knows you and he thinks you'll want to work with the Committee, help them look into the English Department, which, by the way, they think is the likeliest of all departments to harbor homosexuals and radicals." At this, Connor smiled the smile of irony and said, "When I hear such things, I think of Ernest Hemingway and Stephen Crane."

They didn't teach it, Stall thought, *they wrote it.* He said, "Did you know, Jim, that the great poet Ben Jonson fought as the champion of the English army against the champion of the Spanish in Flanders and slew his man?" *And he did teach it, off and on.*

"I did not know that," Connor said, "but I was certain that you would add to my fund of knowledge. I thank you for that vital information."

There was a knock at the door and Connor said, "Enter."

The white-haired Negro in his white jacket with a white towel folded over his forearm said, "May I serve you gentlemen a libation?"

"Yes, Ezra," Connor said, "I'll have a bourbon. Tom?"

"The same."

When the Negro had closed the door, Stall said, "Work with them?"

Connor lifted his chin in confusion.

"You said the Committee thinks I'll work with them. What does that mean?"

"It means do their bidding. Work *for* them." Connor waited, as though an explanation of this should come from Stall.

"Jim, I . . ."

"You can't think of any reason for this?"

"None."

"Well, Tom, it has to do in some fashion with this young man, Vane. His father is rich as Croesus. He's given generously to this institution. I don't know the man well, or his political leanings, but I assume he is, like most north Florida businessmen, conservative."

"You mean he'll like what the Committee wants to do?"

"I mean I don't know, but it seems likely."

"And his son? Frank Vane? I knew him as a boy in a hospital in France. A nineteen-year-old PFC with half his arm shot off."

"I don't know how he fits into this picture." The president tapped his forefinger twice, on the picture and on the subpoena. "The more pressing point is that for some reason this Cyrus Tate thinks the Committee can work your connection to Frank Vane to their advantage, and we need to know why." Connor waited.

God, this is Byzantine. It came to Stall that now he was expected to supply a reason for the murky workings of the diseased minds of the Johns Committee. The Frank Vane he had known for only a few weeks thirteen years ago was a decent, intelligent, and cultured boy, or as much of one as a rich kid from Jacksonville could become before he was shipped out to Germany and the hell of the Hürtgen Forest. Even more astonishing to Stall was that he had been asked by the president of his university to spy on his colleagues, and now, apparently, the Committee which was the brainchild of a semiliterate accidental governor had told that same president that they expected Stall to spy for them.

"So," Connor said, "we have a quandary. We are caught between Scylla and Charybdis, or as the plainer folk I grew up among say, between a rock and a hard place."

Now the entire, awful absurdity of this thing lay plain before Stall. "You're saying I have to work for you or you'll suspect me of working for the Committee?"

"Let's just say I know whose side you're really on, and it wouldn't hurt the right side if you pretended to warm up to the wrong one. If you see what I mean." Connor's smile was droll, and Stall knew that he wouldn't be smiling if he didn't think he had Stall's balls in a vise. The game was joined, and President Connor had more than an ordinary man's avidity for games. In this one, Stall was to be his pawn.

Stall said, more to himself than to Connor, "If my colleagues, my *friends*, get the idea I'm some kind of informer, they'll shun me. I'll have no chance of becoming chairman. Hell, I'll have to leave town under cover of darkness."

"Tom, you have a flair for the dramatic. It won't be as bad as all that. I'll take care of you. What will be bad, what could be a disaster, is what Charley Johns wants to do to this university. He'd like to turn the whole state system into a Baptist seminary with compulsory chapel, a curfew, a dress code, and loyalty oaths. The best faculty we have will leave for places where this kind of stupidity is laughed at. We'll be censured by any number of professional organizations. It could take this state fifty years to recover from the kind of damage Johns can do."

Ezra knocked again, and this time entered without being bidden. He served the two bourbons from a silver tray and left as quietly as he had entered.

Connor raised his glass to Stall. "Well then, to our arrangement?"

Stall lifted his glass in silence and drank the bitter potion.

NINE

Stall arrived early for the meeting with Jack Leaf's class in Murphree Hall armed with the copy of Leaf's syllabus he had obtained from Helen Markham. The syllabus called for a final exam and a research paper to be turned in on the last day of class. Stall had also used the department's passkey to unlock Jack Leaf's office and search for his grade book. The book now lay open on the desk in front of Stall as the first students drifted into the classroom with looks of apprehension and even fear on their faces. It was just human nature, Stall supposed, that these ambitious boys (the Grinds of Summer, he called them) should worry more about their grades than about the death of a professor. There were only five of them, and when they were all seated (all on time, as he had expected), Stall called the roll.

As was his practice when he called a roll, he looked at each face as though memorizing its features. He had found that this pleased the students. *He wants to know me.* The roll finished, he composed his own face in sadness for Jack Leaf and concern for the apprehensions of these students. "Well, I'm pretty sure you've all heard about what happened to Professor Leaf." He waited while some nodded solemnly and a few mumbled, "Yes." A boy in the back said, "Can you tell us any more than what we've read in the papers?" The boy's tone was not solemn.

Stall had come here planning to make short work of this penultimate class of a dreary summer term. To tell them how they'd finish their academic work and then get back to his own more pressing business. "Sorry, what's your name, young man?" Stall looked down at the grade book while the boy said, "Martin Levy." In the book, a row of As flowed from the name. Stall raised his eyes to the class again. "Thank you for the question, Mr. Levy. I don't know any more than what has been reported in the papers. It was either an accident or it was intentional. The medical examiner will make his decision based on the testimony of eyewitnesses, all students."

Stall thought it right to leave the best possible impression of Jack Leaf in the minds of these students. They had spent a summer with the man, and Stall assumed they liked him. Most people did. He said, "Now, let me tell you how I think we should go about finishing this term in the most efficient and equitable way. I'm going to cancel the final." He waited for what he was sure would be expressions of approval—muted, of course, given the circumstances. Canceling the final was the efficient part of his plan. Next came the equitable part. "I will grade your research papers. I've taught this course a number of times, and I believe I'm qualified to evaluate them carefully and fairly. I will—"

"What about the two men who were seen leaving the building just before Professor Leaf jumped?" It was Martin Levy again.

Stall didn't like to be interrupted by anyone and certainly not by a student. He took a long breath to master the annoyance that had lit up his chest. "I've told you all I know, and everything I know has been in the papers. Students reported seeing the two men. Who may or may not have had anything to do with Professor Leaf and what happened."

"I've heard that the English Department knows more about this than the papers are reporting."

Stall was angry now and sure that his face showed it. "Heard from *whom*? Give me a *name*, and I'll speak to this person and let you know what I find out. Will that satisfy you, Mr. Levy?"

One or two students turned and peered back at Martin Levy as though they thought his questions might complicate the very good deal they were getting with a canceled final exam. Levy looked at his classmates and raised his chin an inch. The gesture said, *Make something of it*.

Stall said, "Mr. Levy, may I continue to explain how we will finish our work?"

"By all means, sir. Pardon my interruption."

"As I was saying, I'll grade your research papers, and I'll weight them to offset the elimination of the final. I've checked Professor

Leaf's grade book, and it seems you're all doing very good work, so I don't foresee any problems . . ." Stall tried for some levity: "Unless you bomb the paper."

A few chuckles, but mostly grim silence.

"These are unusual circumstances, so I want to know now if any of you think this arrangement is unfair."

Stall's authority in this matter was absolute. There was nothing any boy could do if he considered the thing unfair, but Stall thought it best to make the statement anyway. He'd have to work with these boys later on. He waited. No one spoke. "All right," he said, "I'll take questions about research methodologies if you have any."

There were no questions.

"Good, then. Show up here next week with your papers in hand and we'll consider the term finished. I'll be available during regular office hours if you think of anything you need to discuss with me. And again, I'm very sorry about Professor Leaf, as I know you are too."

The students filed out, more or less satisfied, Stall thought. He waited as he always did for any double-backs, students who did not want to speak to him in front of their fellows. He was putting on his new coat when Martin Levy came back into the room. Levy was tall and still had some of a boy's adolescent looseness in his joints. His brown hair was curly and close-cropped, and he wore wire-rimmed glasses that made him look a bit like pictures Stall had seen of Leon Trotsky. He wore a white long-sleeved shirt and tan slacks, and carried books under one arm. He was a good-looking boy in an attenuated, ascetic way. His dark-brown eyes burned at Stall.

"Mr. Levy?" Stall expected the boy to apologize again. It did no student any good to get off on the wrong foot with the assistant chairman of the English Department.

"I'm sorry, Dr. Stall . . ."

"Don't worry about—"

". . . but I don't think you were straight with us about what happened to Professor Leaf."

Another interruption. And now an accusation. *Are you calling me a liar?* Stall started for the door. "I'm going to forget you said that, Levy, and I think before we talk again, you'd better reconsider your attitude."

"I only meant—"

"Keep talking, and you'll talk yourself right out of this department."

Stall left Martin Levy standing in the classroom.

The politics of Florida were simple, as Stall understood them. The state was halved, north and south. The north was called *pork chop country* because the counties there were small and their populations were sparse. Pork, of course, carried additional connotations, all of them apt. The state capital was in the north, in Tallahassee, and much of the political power was concentrated among the porkchoppers. The north was conservative, often radically so, and the south was liberal. Miami, with its Jewish population, retirees from the big Northeastern cities, many of them former members of trade unions, was the center of liberal politics. To say that there was warfare between north and south was to understate the case. Unfortunately (at least from Stall's moderately liberal point of view), the north had won elections and had controlled the governor's mansion and the legislature for most of the twentieth century. If any group with any clout would stand against the Johns Committee and for academic freedom and letting the universities govern themselves within reasonable limits, it would be the lambchoppers, the Jewish community of Miami. They, and sometimes the *Miami Herald*, would be the strongest voice against Charley Johns and his porkchopping pals in the legislature. This was only one of the reasons Stall had a soft spot in his heart for the Jewish students who made the 350-mile trip up from Miami to Gainesville. Another was that his Presbyterian minister father had instilled in his son the belief that the Jews were God's chosen people. What they had been chosen for was a matter of endless debate.

As Stall walked from Murphree Hall back to his office in Anderson, tendrils of regret crept into his mind. He'd been too hard on young Martin Levy. By Stall's standards, the boy had been rude, but where Levy came from manners might be different. And it was entirely possible that Levy, a budding young English scholar, was steeped in the Jewish tradition of midrash, the kind of determined, even angry disputation over the finer points of biblical texts that was, arguably, the earliest form of literary criticism, predating even

Aristotle and his *Poetics*. Stall shook his head as he walked and admonished himself: *He's just a boy. You'll have to call him in and make this right.*

A man fell into step with Stall. "Talking to yourself, professor? I guess it's true what they say about you intellectuals. Got your head in the clouds."

The words were mildly insulting, but they were spoken in a jovial, man-to-man tone. Stall turned to see the blond football player looming beside him, at least two inches taller than his six one. Stall stopped walking, and the big man did too. He faced Stall and extended a hand the size of baseball glove. "I'm Cy Tate. Good to meet you, Tom. Frank Vane recommends you highly."

Recommends me for what? Stall shook the big hand. "Well," he said, "next time you see Frank, thank him for me. I'm pleased to have his high opinion . . ." Stall got lost in the syntax, "of me."

Cyrus Tate chuckled warmly. "You and Frank were army buddies, weren't you?" The big man took a few steps, and when Stall didn't follow, he stopped and turned back. His voice went low and serious like he was offering Stall a special deal on merchandise of uncertain provenance: "Let's talk in your office. I think that'd be better, don't you?"

Better than what? Stall was losing patience. "No, let's talk right here. I'm sure this will be brief."

"No, no, it won't be." Tate said the words thoughtfully, even kindly, again as though he were doing some kind of favor.

Stall felt the worm of fear turn over in his stomach. "All right, my office then." He took off striding toward Anderson Hall.

Cyrus Tate caught up quickly and matched him stride for stride until they crossed the threshold of the small office. Stall sat behind his desk, trying to seem at ease. He considered putting his foot up on the lower drawer that he always pulled out for that purpose, but thought better of it.

Tate took the chair in front of the desk that students usually occupied. He moved the chair so that it blocked the doorway. "Shall I close the door? This will be confidential."

Stall held his hands out, palms down in front of him. They were sweating. "I see no reason for that. As I said outside, this will be brief."

Tate was well dressed for an ex-cop. His gray summer suit was cut to fit, though his arms and shoulders stretched the material in ways that left no doubt of the power of his body. His silk tie was bright but conservative and, even Stall knew, expensive. He unbuttoned his suit jacket and carefully spread it open across his broad, flat chest and crossed his legs with a masculine ease that told Stall who owned this small space.

He has the gift of ease, Stall thought. *Few men have it. He's ready for anything.* And then Stall wondered if the man was carrying a weapon, if the powers conferred by the Johns Committee allowed him to strap on a gun. There were no obvious bulges, but an ex-cop would know how to wear a firearm without making it obvious.

"So, you and Frank were pals in the war. He told me about how you two almost died in that field hospital, how you went to Paris later and had yourselves the time of your lives."

We had the time because *we were alive*, Stall thought, remembering how important it had seemed after he had risen from the hospital bed to do something with his youth. Hearing this man talk about that time, reducing it to the clichés a person might use to describe a vacation to the Grand Canyon, Stall felt anger light up his chest again as it had back in the classroom with the kid, Martin Levy. In the winter and spring of 1945, Stall and Frank Vane had been accidentally not killed, accidentally in beds next to each other in a field hospital, and accidentally in the same army truck that hauled fortunate men to Paris on three-day passes. They had been accidental friends for a time, and then they had lost each other. And now this—a big, powerful man named Tate with a badge and possibly a gun, telling Stall that Frank Vane recommended him highly.

Tate took an envelope from his pocket and put it on Stall's desk. *God*, Stall thought, *not another one. This is beyond Byzantine.* His hand leaden, his anger gone, the worm of fear turning again, Stall opened the envelope and removed a photograph.

She had changed, of course, but he recognized her immediately. Brigitte. Her blue eyes seemed smaller, and there were wrinkles at their edges. Her blond hair was thinner and her cheeks were hollow under the high cheekbones that had been part of her beauty in Paris in 1945. Her lips were as wide and full as ever, and they had been what had first caught Stall's eye, and, as he would have said then, and as he told her then, they were what had quickened his heart on a narrow street near Sacré-Cœur.

He put the picture down on his desktop and looked at Tate, gave the man his bleakest stare. "What does this have to do with me? It was a long time ago. I haven't seen the woman since 1945. I've had no contact with her, not a letter, not a postcard. I don't understand why you bother me with this. A woman I met thirteen years ago during the war."

"Well, she wasn't exactly a woman, for one thing," Tate said with the look on his face of a man who is a little embarrassed to be splitting hairs. "She was only fifteen years and, let's see, seven months old. Not even sweet sixteen, as we say here in the States. Did you know that, Mr. Stall, at the time?"

She looked a lot older, Stall's stunned mind told him. *She looked every inch a woman. And I was what, twenty-three?*

"Well, you asked me what this has to do with you. Ordinarily, I'd say not much, except for this." Tate took another photograph from the inside pocket of his tasteful suit coat and put it on the desk in front of Stall.

There was Brigitte, with whom Stall had two of the most glorious nights of his life, standing on a city street holding the hand of a little girl. Again Stall looked up at Cyrus Tate.

Tate said, "It has to do with you if she had your child."

Stall looked back down at the picture. The little girl could have been anybody's child, the offspring of any man in the world, but Stall knew beyond any doubt that she was his. It was as though a beam of light were fired from the innermost chamber of the heart of a Frenchwoman, now almost thirty years old, across six thousand miles of ocean, to pierce the stricken chest of Thomas Stall. To split him open. And for a few seconds it was as though Brigitte lay next to him again in the warm narrow bed in the pension with the piano and accordion music drifting through the window from the *bal musette* across the street, the sad, lovely notes whispering, *The child is yours, Tom. She is your daughter*.

Stall swallowed and put his heart back together and tried to recover his mind from the narrow bed in a small room that smelled of cabbage soup and cheap wine, and of lovely Brigitte. His voice was a croak when he said, "This is a flimsy excuse for a reason to blackmail a man."

"I doubt your wife would say that, professor." Tate reached down and brushed away some invisible lint from the thigh of his gray suit. "Most women would want to know if their little girl had an older sister. By the way, the girl's name is Françoise. I think that's how you pronounce it, but you'd know that better than I would. You speak some French, don't you, professor?"

Cyrus Tate had pronounced the child's name *Frank-wahz*, and coming from his mouth it sounded like something a man would cough up and spit out. And Stall could not help noticing the usage of *Frank*. Was this evangelist investigator, this blackmailer, smart enough, vile enough, to sit here suggesting that Brigitte had named the girl after Frank Vane? Tate's intelligence was open to question: there was no doubt about his vileness.

"So," Stall said, his voice still a croak, "what do you want?"

Cyrus Tate stood up and looked around Stall's little office, the cramped space he hoped soon to leave for the larger domain of the chairman's office. Tate reached over to the bookcase and pulled a volume of William Carlos Williams's poems halfway out of the shelf, shook his head, and pushed it back in. He tapped the spine until the row of books was neat and even. "Poetry" he said, "I never did get it. I always asked myself, *Cyrus, why don't they just say what they mean? Why does everything have to mean six things rather than just one?* Seemed like a waste of time to me." He turned back to Stall. "Maybe I should give it another chance now that I'm older. What do you think?"

"What do you want?" Stall repeated.

Cyrus Tate took a long breath and squared his wide shoulders like a man who had done a good day's work. "I want you to walk across the street to the College Inn and have a cup of coffee with Frank Vane. He's waiting over there for you."

TEN

Stall had graduated from Williams College in 1943 at the age of twenty and finished a year of graduate school at the University of Virginia before his draft board back home in Greenville had decided that a minor spinal curvature should no longer delay his rendezvous with the German 88. Most of the soldiers he had trained with at Fort Dix were eighteen years old. Stall, at twenty-one, was called *Pappy* by the boys of his squad. Frank Vane had been younger than Stall when they'd gone to war. Vane, he later learned, had enlisted at seventeen.

And Stall remembered, as he walked through the blazing August afternoon toward University Avenue and the CI, that during the brief time when he had known Frank Vane, the younger man had seemed to look up to him, seemed to think of him as the more worldly, the more intelligent, of their accidental pair. But Stall hadn't given this much thought. Even then, he had known that young men were creatures of wild enthusiasms and strong passions. They formed easy friendships and fierce loyalties, all of which could be broken at the hint of an insult or the twitch of a skirt. He had considered Vane a good companion, fine company on an exciting journey, nothing more than that. Stall remembered getting drunk with Vane on their first night in Paris and pledging eternal friendship. The Two Friends, they called themselves in broken French. *Les Deux Copains*. At that time, everyone in Paris was drunk and all were friends. The German Army had only been gone from the City of Light for four months. The best wines and cognacs that had been hidden in cellars all over the city had been resurrected and were being served in liberal portions to the American liberators, and every man in an American uniform was a hero.

On that first night in Paris, Stall and Vane had drunk their share, and in the morning, Vane had been too much the worse for his wine to leave his bed. After knocking on Vane's door and hearing the sound of retching, Stall had gone in search of Paris without his young friend, and the Paris he had found was Brigitte. And after that, he had seen very little of Frank Vane. Neither had said much about Stall's sudden departure from their happy twosome, *Les Deux Copains*, but Vane had known, Stall was sure, what was going on. Stall had found a girl. Soldiers did that. In the presence of death, life sought life. For all Stall knew, the army would soon declare him fit to return to the front, to the last bitter fighting that would end the war. The fighting later known as the Battle of the Bulge.

Stall, with four years of an English major behind him, knew the phrase *carpe diem*. Had even read some of Epicurus who had said, *It is impossible to live a pleasant life without living wisely and honorably and justly. And it is impossible to live wisely and honorably and justly without living a pleasant life*. Vane, four years his junior and only a high school graduate, knew little Latin and less Greek, but must have felt as strongly as Stall did what all of the soldiers who crowded the streets of Montmartre felt. They were young, far from home, temporarily unrestrained by sergeants and lieutenants, and surrounded by the pleasantness of wine and women, many of them willing.

Stall opened the door of the CI, felt the blessed blast of air-conditioning, heard the incessant jukebox playing the hit of the moment, "It's Only Make Believe." Conway Twitty. What an unlikely name, Stall thought, too strange to be invented. But a beautiful song, a song full of truth plainly stated. "*My only prayer will be / Someday you'll care for me. / But it's only make believe.*" Stall suddenly saw an image of himself on his knees before Maureen speaking the words of the song. Begging for her forgiveness, pleading with her to take him back.

He stopped just inside the door, smelled hamburger grilling behind the lunch counter to his left, and surveyed the large dining room. A man waved to him from a table in the far corner. A man with one arm.

Frank Vane stood when Stall approached the table, and Stall's eyes could not help but go to the coat sleeve, turned up and sewn. What would Frank Vane be now, Stall asked himself as he tried to fit a smile to his lips? Thirty-two years old? The man who stood waiting for him looked older than that, looked a little weary, a little pinched around the eyes and the corners of the mouth, as though a lot of what he had tasted in the last thirteen years had been bitter. But his light-gray summer suit and regimental tie were fashionable and, Stall could see, expensive, and the look on his face was confident. Frank Vane extended his right hand for Stall to shake, and Stall thought, *Lucky it was the left arm he lost.* Vane's grip was firm and brief.

When they were seated, Vane said, "I took the liberty of ordering coffee for us." Then: "I went back to see her after you were sent home. Actually, not really to see *her*. I just went back to the pension where we spent a couple of days. I bet you don't remember what it was called." Vane waited, lifted his coffee cup to his lips and sipped.

Stall's coffee was untouched on the table in front of him. He could not remember the name of the pension.

"It was Le Petit Cavalier. Like I said, I went back, about a month later, on my next furlough. You were already back in, what was it, Greenville?"

Stall nodded. He had been separated from the army because his fever never fell below 99.5 degrees. Another degree, a normal temperature, would have sent him back to the front. The army doctor who signed the papers that sent him home, a kindly, avuncular man who seemed to consider Stall an intriguing case, said, "I'd send you back to your squad, but your fever might spike and it'd take two men out of the fighting to haul you back here."

The mathematics of war were usually merciless, but for Stall this time the numbers were mercy. He received his honorable discharge and his CIB, and later, in the mail came the black leather box with the blue felt lining that contained his Purple Heart.

He hung around Greenville for a while, staying with his parents and generally considering everything life offered him dreary and meaningless, and then he conquered what he later realized was a deep melancholia, and returned to the University of Virginia to finish his PhD in English. And it was there, in the library carrels and the classrooms, and in his grad student apartment with Maureen, that Stall had made up his mind. Despite all that had happened to him thus far in his young life, he would love the world. The choice was simple, one thing or the other, affirm life or deny it. It was sometimes a dirty world, but he chose to love it.

"Yeah, it was Greenville," he said to Frank Vane, "and then on to UVA, and after that, here."

"An enviable career so far, a good life."

"So far." Stall could not keep the grim note from his voice. "You were telling me about going back to Paris."

"You're thinking I looked for your girl, but I didn't. I just wanted to stay in the place where we stayed. I knew you'd met someone, but I didn't know who she was. I wanted to sleep in the same seedy little flop and see the sights again, see if I could hold my liquor a little better the second time around."

"So how did you . . . ?"

"She came looking for me. Or rather for someone who might know you. The owners of the pension told her you'd been there with another GI. And when I showed up again, they called her. It was about a month after you . . . spent some time with her, and you know what a girl knows after a month goes by."

"She told you she was pregnant with my child?"

Vane looked at Stall for a long time. "Imagine how tough that was for her, Tom. She was only fifteen. Did you know that when you got involved with her that way?"

What could he say? He had not known. She had seemed far older than her fifteen years and seven months. Maybe war, occupation, did that to young girls, made them look and act older than their years. Stall had seen boys in combat become old men in a few days. He said, "No, I didn't know. I suppose I thought she was at least eighteen or nineteen."

"And that would have been all right?"

Vane's face was blank. Stall saw no reproach in his eyes and heard none in his voice. He said, "Yeah, I suppose so. In a foreign country. In wartime. The French were . . ."

"More sophisticated than we were?"

"Sure."

"Not Brigitte."

There it was. The first sign of Frank Vane's anger. Something in his eyes that said he had known the girl well, the girl Stall had known for only two days. The girl Stall had loved for two days.

And yes, he had told Brigitte he loved her, and he had meant it. And when the army had ordered him home, he had promised himself he would see her again, had imagined it like a scene in a movie, getting off the train at the Gare du Nord and walking with his musette bag over his shoulder, the handsome veteran with the slight limp (actually, the only proof of his wound was a scar the size of a dime behind his thigh) making his way up the street to the little pastry shop where her parents toiled for a modest living, and surprising her there, the beautiful girl who had waited for him, had spurned all the blandishments of men to wait for him, and Brigitte looking up from the napoleons she was making and smiling with a dot of flour on her pretty nose.

And what happened then? What happened after the girl with the flour on her nose looked up and smiled? It was the question Stall could never answer. And it was the want of an answer that kept him from going back to find Brigitte, and as the years passed, it was the never going back that made him forget her little by little until the night when he asked himself, as he lay beside the sweetly sleeping Maureen, if he had ever really loved Brigitte, and the answer came whispering out of the darkness: *I don't know*.

Frank Vane said, "Brigitte was not sophisticated. She was a kid trying to act more grown up than she really was, and she was caught up in all that excitement, all that freedom after four years of occupation. Didn't you notice how thin she was, or was that something a man could ignore in the throes of passion?"

Stall felt his fury rising, his neck thickening, his collar becoming tight. He considered a smart reply, something like, *She seemed just right to me*, but killed it before it found his voice. This was no time for anger or sarcasm. If Frank Vane had kept in touch with Brigitte, if he had done right by her in some way that Stall himself had not, then Vane had a right to reproach him. Stall held his tongue.

Vane sighed and pushed back in his chair, moved his coffee cup to the side, and rested his hand on the table in the shape of a fist. "Brigitte and I had a talk, a lot of talks, actually, after she found me at Le Petit Cavalier. I asked her if she wanted me to tell you about the baby. She said no. She said you'd know, somehow you'd know. You'd come back because you'd know."

With this, tears came to Stall's eyes. Tears he could not show to Frank Vane, who would almost certainly consider them cheap. He blinked and kept himself from wiping at his eyes. "Go on," he said.

"I stayed in France for a while. My family has more money than they know what to do with." Vane spoke these words in the tired way of a man who had explained a life of privilege too many times before. "They were so glad to hear I was alive." He held up the stump of his left arm. "At least most of me. They didn't mind it much when I told them I wanted to live in Paris for a while and take some courses at the Sorbonne. I took those courses, and I took care of Brigitte, at least long enough to see her through the worst of it. You can imagine what her parents thought, how they felt about the condition their daughter was in. They're peasants, Tom, one generation out of Normandy, and good Catholics. If she had gotten rid of the child, they would have disowned her for life. I talked with her about that possibility, but she wouldn't hear of it.

"So I paid for her to go live in Deauville with relatives until the baby was born. Actually, she had no relatives in Deauville, but her parents were pleased to recollect a long-lost aunt. I found a hotel there run by a woman of, shall we say, enlightened sensibilities, who, for a price, gave Brigitte room and board and handled her medical needs as things went along. Deauville's a tourist town, lots of sophisticates and foreigners taking the sea air. When Brigitte returned to Paris, she was a widow. Her husband had been a hero of *La Résistance Française*. What a joke! After the last Panzer division decamped for points west, every guy with a Gauloise dangling from his mouth became a hero of the Resistance.

"Anyway, Brigitte came back to Paris with a baby and a wedding ring and a more or less plausible story about her poor dead husband, the hero. Tom, you know what would have happened to her in that little neighborhood of hers in Montmartre if the baby had started to show, and there'd been no ring? They would have shaved her head, painted her breasts with swastikas, and whipped her through the streets screaming, *Putain!* Some of the woman who slept with Germans were raped or beaten to death. Brigitte would have been lucky to get by with public humiliation."

Stall nodded. He had seen the news stories after the war. Of course, then he had not connected any of it to Brigitte. It came to him that he could offer to repay Frank Vane the money he had spent on Brigitte, had spent on Stall's child, a little girl named Françoise, and he could afford to do it, though not without Maureen finding out. And when she found out, the future would be bleak for Stall and his wife, at least for a while. Probably for a long while.

As though he had read Stall's mind, Frank Vane waved his hand between them and said, "Oh, the money was nothing, *is* nothing. I still send her a monthly check. Why not? I've got plenty, and she has, well, almost nothing."

Stall looked at the man bleakly, wishing this over, wondering where it ended.

"Tom, I know most men, seeing what I saw, knowing Brigitte even the little that I did, would not have . . . involved themselves."

"Why did you?"

Frank Vane lifted his wounded arm again. "Well, there's this, of course. I didn't want to go home. I wasn't ready. And Paris was, let's say, a friendlier place than Jacksonville, Florida, for a man with my problem. There were a lot of men around in those days who weren't . . . whole."

Stall waited.

Vane smiled as a man does who looks back with fondness at a younger version of himself. "And remember, Tom, I was only nineteen. You were a worldly twenty-two, but I was only a year out of high school. I was grateful to be alive and Brigitte was *giving* life. I couldn't just walk away from that. Not when it only cost me time . . . and money that was nothing to me."

Stall could see that for Vane this seemed to finish the story, but he knew there was more. Something in Vane's eyes told him so. Something Vane did not want him to see.

"It was kind of you, more than kind, to take care of her like that."

"Of them."

"Of them." There was a little girl. His little girl. His responsibilities, whatever they were, however they were to be discharged, whether publicly or privately, had begun the moment he had learned of the existence of Françoise. If Vane had not been connected to Cyrus Tate and the Committee, Stall would have simply thanked him for doing the things for Brigitte that Stall believed he would have done himself if he had known about the child. Thanked him and offered to pay the debt, and said he would take over the responsibility that Vane had borne as of right now. But there was more, Stall knew, and now Vane would tell him about it.

"What do you want from me, Frank?"

"I think you know that, Tom."

"I want you to say it."

"I, we, want you to work with us."

"As simple as that?"

"I think it's simple. It's a thing I've worked out for myself in the last few years. I started thinking about how simple all this is when I was in law school. Why did we fight that war? We fought it, and we gave up parts of ourselves to it." Vane lifted the half arm again.

Stall nodded in simple acknowledgment. The wound had its own power, was its own imperative. No man could deny it.

Vane said, "We fought to rid the world of the kind of horrible perversion that sent millions to their deaths in camps and ghettos and on battlefields. Those Nazis, Tom, the leadership, the guys at the top, they were all perverts in one way or another." He stopped and looked deeply into Stall's eyes. His gaze was so hot that it hurt.

Christ, Stall thought, *he's serious about this*. "But Frank," he said, "the Nazis sent Communists and homosexuals, people with mental deficiencies, to the gas chambers."

"No, Tom. Don't you see that was just the overt injustice? They said they hated queers and Communists and morons because those people made society dirty and inefficient, but we know why they really hated them."

Stall looked around the big CI dining room. A lot of empty tables at this time of the afternoon, and a few students huddled over books and burgers. The jukebox playing Ricky Nelson's "Poor Little Fool." So far nobody had noticed how loud Vane was talking, how his eyes bore into Stall's. Stall did not like the way Vane had said *we*.

"What we know, Tom, is they hated those people, those ideas, because they *were* those things. A man hates most the bad things he wants to do. He hates the things he fears that he . . . *is*. Plato said the two most important questions are: *Who teaches the children?* and, *What do they teach them?* We can't let our children be taught by homosexuals and Communists. If we do, we'll lose the country we fought for to perverts and radicals just like the Germans did. And who will be here to fight the war that saves our country from them?" Frank Vane raised the wounded arm again. "I won't be able to do it. Will you, Tom? Will you help us?"

God, Stall thought, *where has he gone? The sweet young man who almost died beside me in an army field hospital. What happened to him?* His mind struggled with the logic of what Vane had said. Sure, it was possible, even plausible, that the preacher who sermonized against wanton women wanted one. And it was possible that the cop who beat the hell out of crooks in the back room at the station house was beating the criminal in himself. But how did Vane get from this psychological commonplace to universities and the people who taught in them?

Stall held up a calming hand, and Frank Vane looked at it as though it were the first blow that might be struck in a fight.

"Wait a minute, Frank. Let's assume for a minute you're right. Bormann and Goebbels and Himmler were sick, and Hitler was the sickest of the bunch. And maybe they did go after some people with special viciousness because they were concealing things in themselves that they *thought* they saw in their victims. I don't see how that gets us to the point where we purge our universities of people who are living good public lives, doing good jobs in our classrooms, even if they hold ideas we don't like or do things in private that we think are wrong. Frank, you're a lawyer. This logic just doesn't work."

Stall pushed back in his chair and tried to keep the look of impatience from his face, the look he'd give a slow student in a seminar.

Vane leaned closer to him. "Tom, you're failing to see the brilliance of what these guys are doing. They're hiding behind their blameless middle-class lives while they corrupt our youth in their classrooms. They want our children to become what *they* are, and if they can make that happen, then what they are will become what's right. If what they're hiding comes into the light, becomes acceptable, then it will take our children. These guys are smarter than Hitler and his gang. The Nazis named the perversions they harbored within themselves. These professors you defend live, as you say, good lives and *teach* the perversions in our classrooms. Can't you see that?"

Stall shook his head and smiled thinly. It was a smile of some real mirth because he was thinking: *If this is your argument, the Committee's argument, you won't be hard to beat.* "Where's your proof of this, Frank? All I see going on in my classrooms is Wordsworth, Whitman, Dickens, and Hemingway. Nobody's talking about the violent overthrow of the federal government."

"We've got plenty of proof, Tom. Students reading Marx and Engels in political science classes. Whitman was a queer. You can't read him without seeing that. Dickens hated capitalism because he was forced to work in a blacking factory as a boy. Hemingway made a film supporting the Communists in the Spanish Civil War."

Stall shook his head. Perhaps he had not chosen the best examples of what was going on in English Department classrooms. "But Frank, you don't know what teachers are saying to students about these books. What if a professor says that Marx was an idiot or that Hemingway was wrong and it was a good thing that the Nationalists won the Spanish war?"

"But we do know. In a lot of cases we do."

With this, Stall's stomach twisted. "You're telling me students are spying for you, telling you what professors are saying?"

Frank Vane nodded solemnly. "We have statements of that kind, sworn statements."

Stall stood up, ready to call this talk finished, and then he remembered Brigitte, and he sat down again, and in Frank Vane's eyes, he saw the man's certainty. This talk was not over until Vane said it was.

"What do you want me to do, Frank?"

Vane smiled warmly, like an old friend returned from the long ago to renew the friendship. Like he knew they would have plenty of time now to make fast their connection. "Just keep me informed for now, in a general way, and when I have specific questions, I'll come to you. How does that sound?"

"Fine, Frank. Are we finished?"

"Sure, we're finished for now. I'm sure you've got papers to grade or class preps to do." Vane's earnest eyes burned. "You know, Frank, I read your article on Wallace Stevens. Not sure I understood it all, but I thought it was good, even brilliant in parts. If this old country lawyer is any judge, you've got a future. Hell, you might find your way out of this Southern backwater to parts north someday."

And they might run me out of this town on a rail.

Frank Vane stood and took his wallet from the inside pocket of his suit coat.

Probably difficult, Stall thought, *to get a wallet out of your back pocket with just one hand. The one-handed man arranges things for his comfort.*

Vane said, "I'll take care of this."

"No," Stall said, "the least I can do." *You've given a life to my child.*

Vane offered his hand and Stall shook it.

Outside on University Avenue, watching Frank Vane walk off toward 13th Street, Stall thought, *Let Frank Vane believe I'm with him. For now.*

ELEVEN

Stall's daughter Corey fielded a ground ball hit by a neighbor boy and tossed it underhand to the second baseman, who turned a neat double play. The kids on the field cheered. The kids at bat sulked. Stall noted that Corey kept her head down, somber about the miracle of the double play. Either she was being correctly quiet about the fact that she was the best shortstop in the neighborhood, or she was already looking ahead to the time when serious ballplayers did not cheer their own successes—at least not by jumping up and down and screaming, "Yay!"

He and Maureen sat on a blanket under a tree on the playground behind the elementary school. Two other couples lounged nearby watching their kids play with varying degrees of interest. One man pointedly read the *Wall Street Journal*. Maureen's picnic basket, a wicker relic from some antique store she had found out near Newberry, lay open between them. The basket held apples and pears, ham sandwiches, and a thermos of lemonade, all wrapped in a plaid tea towel. Sequestered underneath it all was Stall's flask, also a relic but with a darker provenance. He'd found it on a roadside in Germany, taken it from a pile of the personal effects of dead German soldiers. The detritus of war left to be picked over by passing troops. The men who had done the actual killing had, of course, taken the best things already—the Luger pistols, the daggers with SS insignias, the swastika armbands, and the Knight's Crosses. The leather-covered flask Stall had plucked from the heap of trophies was engraved with a name, *Oberst Kleist von Rothenburg*. The owner had been the equivalent of an American colonel. Holding the flask for the first time, Stall had looked at the field beyond the road, littered with the dead and pocked with shell holes, and reflected that von Rothenburg was probably out there contributing to the overwhelming stench. Now the flask was full of the Gordon's gin that flavored Stall's lemonade (and occasionally Maureen's) and fueled his speculations about his daughter and other matters.

He said to Maureen, "Do you think Corey's a little . . . unfeminine?"

By the way Maureen slapped his arm, a little harder than could be called playful, he knew the question bothered her.

"Of course not. She's just a tomboy. She'll grow out of it."

"She doesn't want to grow out of it. She wants to grow up to be Phil Rizzuto."

Maureen held out her lemonade cup for a dollop from Stall's ill-concealed flask. "She'll grow up to be a very pretty young woman who will look back fondly on her days of shortstopping. Just be happy we're not dealing with all those girlie things yet."

"Girlie things?"

Maureen gave him the look that said men had it easy in this world. "Yes, girlie things. You know, like the curse."

"Oh, that." Stall grimaced, forcing away from his mind images of two people in his house capable of bearing children.

On the field, Corey, in denim pedal pushers and a short-sleeved white blouse, faded back for a short pop fly, waving her throwing hand to stop the charging left fielder in his sneakered tracks. *Serious* was the word that kept coming to Stall. When she caught the ball and tossed it back to the pitcher, she held up two fingers to the outfield and called, "Two down!"

Stall couldn't help himself. *If she were a boy, I'd love this.*

He loved Corey beyond all reason although it seemed that she hid more of herself from him every day now. And he had examined himself for any hint that he wished he'd had a son. Unless he had capacities for self-deception unknown to him, there was no regret. Perhaps it was just this simple: he could not find it in himself to fully embrace the idea of a daughter who played baseball better than every boy in the neighborhood.

He said, "Mar, I need to tell you something."

Maureen looked at him seriously over the rim of her lemonade. "Yes?"

He told her about his talks with Connor. Gave her the carefully edited version he had worked out for himself earlier that day. He left out the photos of Jack Leaf in the bus station men's room and of course the fact that Cyrus Tate had given the photos to Connor. And he left out any sense that Connor had implied that Stall's promotion to the chairmanship was contingent upon his cooperation. Most importantly, he left out Frank Vane.

"So he wants you to do what, exactly?"

Just like Maureen to pierce the heart of the thing. Her bearing had changed instantly from Sunday in the park to kitchen-table family conference, but this could have been worse.

"It's kind of vague right now."

"Make it kind of specific for me, Tom. Can you do that?"

"I can tell you what I'm *not* going to do."

"Do tell."

"I'm not going to spy on people. For one thing, I wouldn't begin to know how. I mean, what does he expect me to do? Use the passkey to search offices, follow people around when they're not teaching, or not even on campus?"

Stall had no idea how much his wife knew about the activities of homosexuals or radicals. Probably less, and certainly no more than he did. He had not been surprised by the photos of two men in a bus station, only by the fact that Jack Leaf was one of them. He had heard or read that men met in parks and public restrooms, but that was about the extent of what he knew.

He knew that for most of the twentieth century Communists and anarchists had met openly or in secret to plan the coming of the workers' paradise. The CPUSA had even run their leader, Earl Browder, as a presidential candidate in the '36 and '40 elections. None of this had bothered Stall very much. Back in the twenties and thirties, anarchists had thrown bombs and shot people, attempted the assassinations of government officials, but nothing like that had happened in America since the end of the war. They were things gone by. Like most of his fellow moderate Democrats, Stall believed that Joe McCarthy had vastly overdramatized the Communist threat for his own short-lived political gain. And he believed that the best way to deal with bad ideas was to talk about them, not ban them, and if men wanted to love other men, who did it hurt if they were discreet?

He sipped his lemonade and said, "I keep thinking this will just go away when enough people understand how absurd it all is. Reasonable people will see that nobody's corrupting their kids in the universities." *My university*.

"Well," Maureen said, "you've got to do *something* to make the president happy."

Corey's team retired the side and ran in to take their turns at bat. Stall grimaced at the thought that his daughter might also be the best hitter here today. That would be too much for him. Maybe this obvious physical talent of hers could be channeled into ballet or gymnastics, although the latter was a little too redolent of sweaty gyms to please Stall.

"I'll think of something," he said.

"Did Connor say he'd keep what you're doing for him confidential? If he did, then can't you do something for him without getting yourself into trouble?"

Stall tried to remember. If confidentiality had not been promised, it had certainly been implied. And if this all got out—the president pressing a department chairman to spy for him—wouldn't it hurt Connor? At least by one obvious calculus, Connor had more to lose than Stall did. But couldn't a young man whose professional life was just beginning and whose prospects were as yet unknown be said to have more to lose than an older man whose life was full of accomplishment but entering the shade?

Stall heard his own voice go low and cold when he said, "I suppose I could tell him who teaches writers with radical ideas. And I could tell myself I'm only preparing him for the questions the Committee will throw at him."

"He could just send someone to the bookstore to find out what English majors read."

"Yeah, but I know what the faculty say about those books. We've all talked it out a hundred times at cocktail parties. And believe me, Mar, some of what they say *is* actually a little scary. But I never worried about it. Students usually know when a prof is off his rocker. They think it's funny."

"Well, this isn't making me laugh much. None of it, especially not what I read in the papers about professors being . . . homosexual."

She was whispering when she said, "What are you going to do about *that?*"

"As little as possible, Mar. We had no idea what Jack was." What had Sarah Leaf called it? *Gay?* "How am I supposed to know who else might be like that?" Stall wanted to see the lives of his colleagues as Walt Whitman had seen his people crossing Brooklyn Ferry. Points on the vast spectrum of human experience. Before this merciless scrutiny had come down on him, Stall had considered the variety of faculty lives part of the beauty of the world he loved.

He had hoped to have this talk with Maureen in a way that would reassure her, at least for a time, and maybe himself too, but it wasn't working out that way, and there were the things he had left out. She'd have to know some or all of them eventually, and when she did, he doubted she'd remember what she'd told Corey: *Lying is saying something that's untrue. Saying nothing is not lying. It's discretion.*

With a cheer, the last out was written in the nonexistent scorebook of this unnamed and floating neighborhood baseball league, the only one that Stall knew of anywhere that welcomed a girl shortstop. Nearby, parents were rising from their blankets to brush off their clothes. The stockbroker carefully folded his *Wall Street Journal*. Maureen began to pack up the quaint wicker basket. Corey ran toward them flushed with summer heat and victory. Before she got too close, Maureen said, "You'll figure something out. You'll do the right thing."

TWELVE

Stall met with Jack Leaf's research methodologies class. He collected their papers and repeated what he had said about grading them. "I'll post your marks as soon as possible. I doubt that any of you have anything to worry about. Enjoy the break, and I'll see you in September."

With a few thank yous and one or two anxious faces, they filed out. Martin Levy stayed. He sat, *slouched* was a better word, in the back row, and when Stall passed, the boy got up and walked behind him. This annoyed Stall, but he reasoned with himself: *He probably wants to apologize. And he should.* And Stall remembered his own resolve to make things right with Levy because he had been too hard on the kid. In the hallway, they faced each other and Stall waited.

Martin Levy held out a copy of the student newspaper, the *Alligator*. It was the abridged edition, published by staffers who reported the summer news. "Look at this, Professor Stall."

Irritated by the boy's imperative tone, Stall took the paper. The headline read: "Alligator Elects New Editor." The subheadline was: "Stephen Levy Vows to Improve Student Paper."

Stall looked up from the picture of the *Alligator*'s new editor to the face of Martin Levy. The same close-cropped curly hair, wire-rimmed glasses, and smart, determined brown eyes. "Your brother?"

"Yeah," said Levy. "He's a grad student in poli-sci. He's doing his thesis under Professor Margolis."

Levy didn't have to say more. Stan Margolis was under Johns Committee scrutiny for devoting an entire semester to Marxist political theory. And now Martin Levy's brother would be turned loose on the university to editorialize about this and other matters. Stall wanted to say, *Well, I hope he has a level head on his shoulders*. He said, "Congratulations. I suspect your parents are very proud."

Levy shrugged, then squared his shoulders and took a deep breath. "Last time we talked, you asked me to give you a name. You said find someone in the English Department who thinks students didn't get the straight story on Professor Leaf's death." He pointed at the newspaper. "There it is."

In an article below the fold, Levy had bracketed a paragraph.

This correspondent interviewed Professor Sophie Green, new to the English graduate faculty and its first woman member. Professor Green said, "There is considerable speculation in the department about what really happened that day on the third floor of Murphree Hall. Many of us think that the two men seen leaving the south door of the building were agents of the Johns Committee. Their presence in the building and Professor Leaf's death cannot be merely coincidental."

Asked if the faculty of the English Department planned to press university officials for further investigation of Professor Leaf's death, Professor Green said, "There is no organized effort to do that yet."

This correspondent asked Professor Green to elaborate. "Does your use of the word 'yet' indicate that such an effort will be forthcoming?"

Professor Green answered, "I don't know. I hope we will do something. I hope that many people in the university and outside it will ask questions about this. The possibility exists that Professor Leaf met with some kind of foul play, and if that is the case, we all need to know about it."

Handing the newspaper back to Martin Levy, Stall did his best to hide his surprise and, yes, his anger that Sophie Green, the junior member of the English faculty, would speak out so strongly about a matter that, for the good of the department and the good of Sarah Leaf and her children, was best left alone.

Stall said only, "I see that your brother is getting off to an active start."

Martin Levy folded the newspaper under his arm. "You asked me for a name, and I gave it to you. Do you remember what else you said?"

Stall was too shaken and trying too hard not to show it to remember what he had said that day. He shook his head.

"You said, *Give me a name, and I'll do something about it*. Are you going to make good on that now?"

You little shit. The only thing Stall could say was, "I'll look into this. But I'm not a policeman." *A spy maybe, but not a cop*. "If further investigation is necessary, it will be the job of the campus police to do it. I think that should satisfy you." Stall glanced at the newspaper folded under Levy's arm. "And your brother too."

Martin Levy shook his head. There was no mistaking the resolve in the gesture.

Stall said, "I wonder if you realize that stirring this up can hurt people."

"How many will get hurt if we *don't* stir it up?" Levy waited with his chin raised an inch, a gesture that Stall remembered from their last talk. *Make something of it*.

Stall shook his head. "I guess we'll have to wait and see."

Martin Levy said, "Thank you, Professor Stall," and started off down the hallway. He stopped and turned back. "I'm not very good at waiting."

When Stall got back to Anderson Hall, Amos Harding was pacing the hallways, the heels of his black oxfords thudding the old floorboards. The old man didn't look good. His long face was redder than usual and his hands shook when he wiped his forehead with a white handkerchief. "I want to have a talk with her right now, Tom, but I don't want to do it alone. I want you to come with me."

No mistaking who *her* was. Amos Harding had swung his chin toward the stairway that led to the third floor and Sophie Green's office. He started walking that way with the long strides that had put acres of tobacco and peanuts under his feet when he was a boy on a North Carolina farm.

Stall said, "Amos, wait! Let's talk about this before we go up there."

Harding kept walking.

Stall moved fast and put a hand on the old man's bony shoulder. "Amos. Please."

Harding turned, breathing harder than an old man should on a hot August day.

Stall's mind churned for words. "Look, Amos. If we, if *I'm* going up there to talk to Professor Green, I need to understand what, uh, what our objective is here." *Or am I just supposed to stand by as your loyal retainer while you chastise the woman for exercising what are plainly her rights under the Constitution?*

"She shouldn't have done it, Tom. It's bad—no, it's *terrible* judgment. How am I supposed to have any confidence in her now? She should have come to me if she had questions about the way Jack's death was handled. Put yourself in my place on this thing, Tom."

Where you know I hope to be. "Amos, just tell me what you plan to say to her. Give me an idea."

If Harding said something rash or even actionable, Stall would be implicated. He could not say to Harding, *Calm down!* but calm was needed here.

Harding sighed and moved to the wall. Stall almost reached out to steady his boss when the old man put out a trembling hand to ease himself against a doorjamb. "I'm going to tell her she should have spoken to me first. That's the way we do things here."

Down here? Here in the sunny South? "Amos, could you do it in a more . . . I don't know, fatherly way? Could you *ask* her if *maybe* before she talks to the paper again, you two could discuss what she might say and how it might affect the department? I think she'd respond better to that approach. Where she comes from, faculty have unions. They talk all the time; they talk about everything; they talk to anybody." *They're not afraid to talk.*

Harding's breathing had slowed and his face was more gray than red. He shook his head and looked at Stall as though he did not recognize him. Well, maybe this was the new Stall. The man who could no longer follow in his boss's footsteps smiling and nodding thoughtful yeses to whatever the old man said.

Harding looked into his eyes. "Tom, are you telling me I *can't* talk to her the way I want to?"

I'm trying to tell you that if you do, it could be the end of you. "No, Amos, of course not. I'm telling you a softer, more collegial approach might work better with her."

"Catch more flies with honey, is that it, Tom?" It was Harding's country-boy tone. Maybe a little sarcasm there, but nothing deadly. And maybe an acknowledgment that Stall knew Sophie Green better than Amos Harding did.

"Yes, basically that's it."

Harding pushed himself off the doorjamb and looked down the hall at his own open office door where Helen Markham's typewriter clacked. "All right, Tom, *you* talk to her. I delegate you. Take your honeypot up there, and the two of you have some together. But make sure she gets the message. Get it across to her somehow, Tom, that she'll come up for tenure in a few years, and when she does, it won't just be me who didn't like her going to the student fish wrapper with our departmental business."

Harding was off walking down the hallway before Stall could say yes or no to this mission. He stood there for a moment in the smell of chalk dust and linseed oil thinking about it. He had been delegated.

THIRTEEN

Martin Levy was sitting in the chair opposite Sophie Green's desk. Stall stopped in the open doorway, considered leaving, then decided to knock. It looked to him as though professor and student were discussing literature, not politics—if that was what Jack Leaf's death had become. Several books were open on Sophie Green's desk, and one lay facedown across Levy's thigh. When Stall's knuckles rapped, the two looked up and Sophie Green smiled warmly. The look on Martin Levy's face was a little more complicated.

"I can come back later," Stall said.

Levy gave him a *please do* look.

Sophie Green said, "Martin, I believe we're about finished. Read those two pieces and we'll discuss them later." She said to Stall, "It looks as though Martin is going to be my very first advisee at this university."

"I make those assignments."

Sophie Green waited, puzzled.

Stall said, "You mean he's *requesting* you," and paused to let this sink in. Then he said, "It's fine with me. I'm sure you two will work together well. Professor Green, may I have a word?"

"Of course." She stood to let Martin Levy know he was dismissed.

Levy took his time gathering his books.

When he was gone, Stall put his hand on the chair. "May I?"

"Please."

Stall had read one of the books on her desk. He commented on it, said he had met Martin Levy in research methodologies and could tell he was a very bright young man, and mentioned that his brother Stephen had just been named editor of the *Alligator*.

Sophie Green's eyes narrowed at the mention of the newspaper. "Is *that* what you're here to talk about?"

"It's one thing, I guess."

"Just one or the big one?"

"Well, some people think it's pretty big."

"It is big in a way, but I wonder if we mean the same way. It's a big thing when a professor is harassed in his own classroom by thugs who represent some committee that has no authority, except what it grants itself because some moron gets to be governor when another moron drops dead . . ." she stopped in the middle of this complex syntax to catch her breath, "when these goons harass a professor to the point that he—"

"How much of that do you know to be true?"

"Well . . ."

"Do you know, does *anyone* know, that Jack was *harassed* by thugs or goons?"

Stall knew she couldn't prove half of what she had said. It was supposition, assumption. And he knew better than anyone else that most of it was true. Even *thug* was a pretty good word for Cyrus Tate, though the man had polished his manners and his haberdashery better than most who fit the type.

"Maybe we don't know all of it, but we'll find out."

We? "How much time do you plan to spend on this?" Stall smiled thinly, trying to keep things friendly. Trying to inch his way into the role of advisor rather than adversary.

"What do you mean by that?" Her fine little hand went to her throat where there had grown a small spot of red, the first flush of embarrassment or anger. The unruly lock of hair that had escaped her grandmother's mother-of-pearl comb the last time Stall had been in this office was obediently in place, and her face was a perfect Victorian cameo against the dark green of the oak trees outside the window.

Stall focused on his mission. "Well, I mean you've just started a new job. You've got, we've all got, a million things to do at the beginning of a school year." How could he get to the heart of it with a light hand? "You want to do *well* here, don't you?"

"Do well? Of course I do. I . . . Oh, I see what you're getting at."

When she stood up, just as she had to dismiss Martin Levy, Stall was surprised. He had thought his tack was subtle, as close to the wind as he could sail this boat. But she'd seen right through him. He didn't stand at her signal as Levy had done. He had to show her something, and right now. "Come on," he said, in the voice he used with Corey when she was headstrong. "Sit down and let's talk about this. I'm not your enemy."

"Are you my friend?" She was still standing.

"I'm trying to be. You're obviously interested in politics, so let's talk about that. We've got our version of politics here in the department. You just did something political, and I don't think you know that."

"I'm beginning to realize it." She settled back into her chair.

Stall held up his hand, lowered his voice. "Easy now. I'm not talking about what I think. Let's assume you and I agree on most of this. I'm here to tell you what some of the others will think and what, maybe, their opinions can do to you if you're not careful."

"You mean I could lose my job? Because I was interviewed by a student newspaper?"

Stall held up his hand again. "Sophie, I don't have to tell you who these older guys are here. You've read versions of them in a hundred novels. They're conservative. Insular. Some of them go back generations in this town. Their grandfathers sat in these offices, and they consider this department the family business. They think departmental business is ours and nobody else's, least of all a student newspaper. They think Jack Leaf is dirty laundry now, and no good can come of washing it out in public."

"This is dirty all right, but it's not laundry. A man is dead."

The few times Stall had been with Sophie Green, she had spoken in a voice he had once heard a theater professor describe as "stage English." She'd sounded vaguely like Bette Davis. No region in her voice, but definitely class. And the class was upper, or at least the Hollywood version of it. It was the sound of Davis and George Brent in *Dark Victory*. Now, she sounded different. Now that her anger was rising, her voice was falling toward the Lower East Side of Manhattan.

"Yes," Stall said, "a man is dead. By his own hand and for reasons we don't know yet. Reasons we may never know. And, Sophie, I'll say it again: I'm not here to give you an official message. I'm here to offer myself as an advisor, someone who knows the ways of this tribe, and who agrees with you that some of those ways are old-fashioned, ossified, and some of them are downright wrong. People like you and I can change those ways, but we have to do it carefully."

"So it's a choice between changing the English Department and getting justice for Jack Leaf? For whoever happens to be the next target of this nightmare committee you Floridians have invented for yourselves?"

"That's not what I said."

She took a deep breath and leaned back in her chair. "No, I guess it isn't. So what *do* you think about justice for Jack Leaf?"

Stall decided to be unusually honest with a woman he had known for only a few weeks, a woman whose actions had not justified much trust. "I think justice for Jack's wife and children comes first now. She's still here with us, and we don't know where Jack is."

Sophie Green looked at him for a long time, her eyes mixing a woman's natural skepticism with an intellectual's argumentative fire. Was he trying to move her to his side by appealing to her emotions, to female solidarity, or was he just using some Southern belle named Sarah Leaf as an excuse for moral cowardice? Her eyes softened. "Uh, how is Mrs. Leaf taking all this?"

"When I saw her she was devastated."

Stall remembered standing with Sarah in her kitchen, the two of them drinking rye. *See this ass? Doesn't it look a bit like a man's?*

What Sarah Leaf had been was more complicated than devastated, but there was enough truth in the statement to suffice for now. If Sophie Green cared about Sarah Leaf, she could easily find out for herself how the woman was doing.

Stall said, "Don't we care about the human side of things a little more than the political side? Isn't that why we chose this life for ourselves? Books are about people, individuals."

At this, Sophie Green shook her head a little sadly, as though Stall were a particularly slow student. "You can't separate humanity from politics. Politics is human beings in collective action. And books are about ideas too."

Ah, Stall thought, *the age-old debate*. "So, you'd choose to hurt the one and help the many?"

Since the war and the period of melancholy that had followed it, Stall had known that he must decide the question some faced and many avoided. Would he say yes or no to life? Live the everlasting yay or the nay? Whitman had loved and praised the many who crossed Brooklyn Ferry, and the poet's ecstatic yay to the life of his fellow man had become the anthem of Stall's days.

Sophie Green tightened her lips and looked hard at Stall. "I think so. Put it this way: I'd rather save the *million* than the one."

"But you don't know Sarah Leaf. You haven't looked into her eyes. It's different hurting someone when you've looked into her eyes, don't you think?" Every time Stall remembered his war, he thanked God he had not killed a man at close range.

"I don't know."

It was an odd thing for a woman to say, Stall thought. Weren't they supposed to be more sensitive than men, more attuned to the subtleties of human personality, of feelings? What would it be like when Sophie Green and Sarah Leaf met? The two couldn't be more different. The one an ambitious, groundbreaking scholar from New York City, the other a tennis-leaguer from the Ocala horse country who found more comfort in drunken gin rummy with Amos Harding's wife than in casseroles and platitudes about grief. Well, they were both competitive, that was clear. But much was murky. Stall was weary of this conversation. He stood.

"I hope you don't lose a friend to an idea."

"You mean you hope I *do*, so I'll learn my lesson?"

"I mean what I said. Thanks for talking with me about this, and remember, I came as a friend. Drop by my office if you need anything."

"I will." She said it with a nod that was ironic but peaceful.

Stall backed toward the door, then remembered something. "Tell me about our young Mr. Levy."

"What do you want to know? He seems like a fine prospect for English scholarship."

What should Stall say? "Well, he's been a bit . . . aggressive with me, if that's the right word."

"Is it?" She waited, small hands on slim hips.

Stall was about to say, *Sorry*, and make his exit, when she said,

"His father and mine know each other. Benjamin Levy and Solomon Green." She wobbled her head from side to side in a way that said, *A little of this, a little of that*. "It was Greenbaum in the old country. My father was a union man in the rag trade, an organizer. A tough guy. He was twenty when Triangle Shirtwaist went up in flames and he lived not far from there. You had to be tough in that business in those days. Those shop owners could sew a corset one day so you couldn't see the seam and the next day beat the hell out of a union man in the alley behind the building. You want to talk about two sides of the human personality? Those guys understood beauty and brass knuckles."

She had said, *You wanna twawk*, as she warmed to her story. Stall smiled at the power of family pride.

She said, "Martin's father was a journalist. Won a Pulitzer for a series of articles on working conditions in the Garment District. Sweatshops and all that. So they know each other, Benny and Solly, and now they're both retired to Miami Beach. They play shuffleboard and talk about the bad old days."

"So Martin's brother comes by journalism honestly?"

"Yeah, Martin's from good people, as we say. He's a little brash, but he means no disrespect."

"He has an odd way of showing it."

"Well, maybe what I mean to say is that you have to earn it with him. Respect."

"It's usually the other way down here. Students earn *our* respect."

"Maybe that's another thing that needs to change."

Stall bowed his head, shook it slowly, and retired from the field of battle.

FOURTEEN

People who had ignored the *Florida Alligator* for years now couldn't miss an issue. The *Gainesville Sun* tried, but couldn't keep up with the agile, up-to-the-minute *Alligator*. The student newspaper reported that professors all over the university system were falling into two camps, the militant and the timid. Most of the firebrands were the safest faculty, tenured in departments whose courses gave the least opportunity for controversy: how could a botanist corrupt American youth? The timid were the untenured, the unpublished, and those who could not afford to lose jobs that were, for myriad reasons, already none too secure. And though most did not say so, there were professors who agreed with the Committee if not with its methods. The *Alligator* reported all of this and more, and soon the whole university was in a state of watchful waiting, like an army in its trenches before stand-to at dawn.

Fraternities and sororities returned from summer break tanned and ready to begin their sybaritic courtship rituals. Professors returned from research travels to prepare for classes, but the usual noisy high spirits of fall were not heard in hallways and departmental offices. Expressions of impatience for the coming of football were shouted in bars and around Gainesville dinner tables, but even these sounded strained. An air of restraint, almost of paralysis, hung over the campus. A committee of men in Tallahassee had somehow managed to cast a pall over every part of life in the University City, as though a hissing gas had been released in the middle of the night to mix with the ground fog out in the pine forests where the kudzu crept toward the city, and this gas, colorless, odorless, but spiritually and intellectually toxic, had permeated every syllable and thought and even the smallest of gestures which only a few months before had been nothing but the dance of a beautiful world.

The *Alligator*'s most surprising story of the week before the fall semester began was its interview with Cyrus Tate. Tate, who could have chosen to hide behind the legal prerogatives of the Committee, walked into the offices of the newspaper in the student union building and offered himself, big, florid, and self-loving, for any and all conversations the student journalists might want to have. He began with a statement.

Yes, he and an associate had served Professor Jack Leaf with a subpoena requiring Leaf to sit before the Committee for an interview. The two men had waited politely until the professor's class ended, and then had entered the room. And yes, they had exited the building by the south door (as had been reported by a student at the scene), but they had seen nothing of the suicide itself (in fact had been surprised and dismayed to hear about it), and there had been no indication from Professor Leaf (in their estimation at least) that any such action would follow their brief, cordial encounter with him. Professor Leaf had simply said, "Thank you," when he received the legal document, and that was, as Cyrus Tate told the story, that.

Tate and his associate, a man he would not name (this refusal being one of the odd elements of an otherwise extraordinarily forthright statement), had left the building and walked to the College Inn for a cup of coffee and a brief conversation and had not heard about the death until a few hours later that afternoon when it was reported on a local radio news program.

All this the *Alligator* reported.

Questioning Cyrus Tate after his statement, student reporters asked for the reason Professor Leaf had been summoned by the Committee. Although it had already been reported elsewhere that Jack Leaf was suspected of being a homosexual, Cyrus Tate had surprised the student journalists by saying, "The Committee had reason to believe that Professor Leaf presented himself for employment by the State of Florida under false pretenses."

Stephen Levy, editor of the *Alligator*: "What pretenses?"

Cyrus Tate: "He was passing."

Stephen Levy: "Passing?"

Cyrus Tate: "Passing for white."

Stephen Levy: "Are you saying that the Committee suspected Professor Leaf of being a Negro?"

Cyrus Tate: "No. Professor Leaf presented himself for employment by the State of Florida as a white man when in fact he was a person of the Indian persuasion."

Stephen Levy: "Do you have proof of that?"

Cyrus Tate: "The Committee has certain documents in its possession, yes."

Stephen Levy: "What documents are these?"

Cyrus Tate: "Among other things, records of his schooling. He attended a high school for Indians in Oklahoma."

Stephen Levy: "Assuming that's true, do you believe that in 1958, four years after *Brown v. the Board of Education*, it is illegal for an Indian to be employed by the University of Florida?"

Cyrus Tate: "I know it is. The law on this is clear. No Indian or Negro can teach in any white school in the State of Florida."

Stephen Levy: "Do you think that's right?"

Cyrus Tate paused before answering. The student reporters in Stephen Levy's small Student Union office heard him chuckle under his breath.

Cyrus Tate: "Son, I *know* it's right. It's exactly as God Almighty Himself intended it to be. Jack Leaf lied his way into a job he never could have had if he'd told the truth about himself."

Stephen Levy: "And this alleged *passing* was the only reason the Committee wanted to interview Professor Leaf?"

Cyrus Tate: "There were other things."

Stephen Levy: "What other things?"

Cyrus Tate: "I try not to speak ill of the dead. My Bible tells me not to do that if I can avoid it."

Stephen Levy: "Where is the subpoena that was served to Professor Leaf?"

Cyrus Tate: "I don't know. The last time I saw it, it was in his hands."

Stephen Levy: "Do you have a copy of the subpoena?"

Cyrus Tate: "Not on me, if that's what you mean?"

Stephen Levy: "I mean, does the Committee have a copy?"

Cyrus Tate: "Of course."

Stephen Levy: "Is that document available to the public?"

Cyrus Tate: "That's not a question to ask me. I'm not a lawyer."

Stephen Levy: "Whom should we ask?"

Cyrus Tate produced a business card from his wallet and handed it to Stephen Levy. The card read: *Franklin Edward Vane, General Counsel, The Florida Legislative Investigation Committee.*

After reading the Tate interview in the *Alligator* a second time, Stall dropped the paper into his office wastebasket and breathed the sigh of Dante's damned. It was after five o'clock, but he did not want to go home. Lately he had taken to walking the corridors of Anderson Hall after the last afternoon bell had rung, when the building was dim and scented with chalk dust and linseed oil and the anxious sweat of generations bemused by Chaucer and Donne and Tennyson. Stall walked his rounds, checking for open windows, textbooks left behind, articles of clothing, and for anything else that might be amiss. He drifted along the dark, empty hallways trying not to think of this place as already belonging to him. Telling himself it was silly to feel such an ownership for this old pile of bricks and the people and the ideas that lived here.

A light slanted from the open doorway of an office down the hall, Jack Leaf's office. The sight alarmed Stall. Then he thought it was probably just the janitor, Jimmy Bright. He peered in. On her knees surrounded by boxes of books, Sarah Leaf was reaching far back into the bottom drawer of Jack's golden oak desk. Stall considered padding softly away but, thinking she might need help, he coughed and waited. He had never seen a woman spring to her feet with such violent readiness.

"Sorry," he said. "I didn't mean to startle you. I saw the light and—"

"Christ, Tom, you scared the shit out of me." She brushed some dust from the front of her blue cotton shorts. Her knees, Stall could see, were red from the rub of the oak floor.

He was damned if he'd ask what she was doing. She had as much right to be here as he did, but he wondered how she had opened the door and what she was looking for.

She rested a hand on a box of books. "I'm going to keep a few of these and give the rest away. Lord knows we've got enough books at home. Do you think Jack's students will want them?"

She was not a reader, Stall remembered. Smart as a whip, but not a reader. He let his eye fall to the bottom drawer.

Sarah shrugged. "I was looking for an insurance policy."

"Well," he said, "I saw the light, and I thought maybe . . ." But he did not know what he had thought—that a thief had broken in or someone had come looking for solutions to the mystery of Jack's death? Or even that somehow, miraculously, Jack Leaf had returned?

Sarah sat in one of the two chairs that faced Jack's desk and patted the other one. Stall sat beside her, thinking how strange they would look to someone passing by—the widow bereft and her husband's colleague who was not quite a friend.

Stall said, "An insurance policy?"

"Jack took it out a few months ago. He usually did the right things when it came to money. No gold mines in Alaska or shares of Bolivian copper." Her smile was thoughtful and wistful. "I'll get some dough from the insurance, I guess. Maybe I'll take the kids on a trip, after I pay Jack's"—she winced—"final expenses."

"Sarah . . ."

"When I told the boys about Jack, I think they took it pretty well, and Trent, he's our older son, you know what he said? Without any prompting from me, he said he was going to take care of his little brother. Well, you can imagine how much his little brother liked that. I could just see Brian thinking, *Take care of me? Like hell you will*. But I think the boys will be all right. I told them they would both make wonderful fathers, I just know it, and they should have no fear of having children of their own. I could see they thought I had completely lost my mind, but I think later on they'll appreciate my telling them that. Don't you think so, Tom?"

Stall nodded too emphatically. "I do, Sarah. Absolutely I do. Uh, did you find the policy?" *Insurance companies don't pay for suicides*.

"No, it's not here. I've looked everywhere, at home and now here. But the insurance company will have a copy, won't they, Tom?"

"Sure they will." He was trying to think of an exit line, something gentle but definite that would get him out the door.

She reached into the purse that lay on Jack's desk. "I did find this." She handed Stall a bank passbook, small, black, about the size of a pocket calendar, with *Dixie Fidelity Bank and Trust* printed on the cover. "Go ahead," she said, "open it."

The book held ten or so deposits totaling twenty thousand dollars. Stall blinked at the number. Almost three times his yearly salary, a salary he considered generous. The owners of the account were Jack Leaf and a Mr. R.T. Tyler.

Stall looked up from the book.

Sarah Leaf said, "I have no idea what this is about. I went to the bank and they told me it was none of my business. Did you know that? A dead husband's money is not his wife's business?"

Stall kept his expression neutral. He knew it. In the marriages he knew, men handled the money. "Who is this, uh, Tyler?"

Her shrug was the saddest thing Stall had seen in a while. "I have no idea."

He rested his hand on her forearm, and she returned the gesture. She dug in her nails.

"Tom, you've got to help me. You've got to stop them from putting Jack in that student newspaper. The boys are hearing things at school. Their friends, boys who used to be their friends, are saying things. Oh, I don't know how much boys that age understand about things like this, but there's always a boy, one boy who is precocious in the wrong ways, in horrible ways, and that boy can do awful damage. I tell you, Tom, if I could get that boy alone for a few minutes, I'd—"

Her tears were terrible in their suddenness and in what they did to Sarah Leaf's pretty face. In seconds, she was an old woman.

And holding her shuddering body in his arms, Stall thought, *The newspapers, they feed on the blood of suffering humanity.* Then he heard himself telling Sarah Leaf that he would do what he could to stop this, and heard in his own voice a certainty that was obscene in its hope, and then it occurred to him that he actually might be able to stop what was hurting Sarah Leaf and her two beautiful boys, boys who had their father's golden skin and lithe, athletic grace. After all, he knew Martin Levy, and that would get him to Stephen, the new editor of the *Alligator.*

FIFTEEN

Stall walked Sarah Leaf to her car carrying the box she had filled with things from Jack's desk. Back in his office, he called Maureen and told her he'd be a little late getting home.

"You're already a *little* late. What's up?"

"Just some extra grading I have to do for the research class—you know, the one I'm teaching for Jack."

"Oh, right." The voice of a woman whose baked chicken was waiting to be served softened at the mention of the dead. "Take your time then."

Stall went across the street to the Gold Coast and sat hunched over a sweating martini. He needed to think. Questions he could not answer were multiplying like maggots on a dead rat. Who was Jack Leaf? Jack Leaf, the underground man? Who else was down there in the underground waiting to be caught in the Committee's net?

Who was the man in the bus station with Jack Leaf? Was he just an accidental player, or did he somehow move the plot of this weird story? And who had taken the pictures? Obviously the photographer had known that the two men would meet that night.

Had Cyrus Tate told the truth about what had happened in Murphree Hall in the minutes before Jack Leaf had taken his walk in the air? Had Jack's walk been an impulsive act or had he planned it, or at least contemplated it before Cyrus Tate entered the classroom? Norman Mailer had said that Ernest Hemingway had lived as a suicide every day of his life. Stall had thought a good bit about this puzzling remark. Mailer must have meant that Hemingway's sense of personal honor was so heightened beyond all reason that on any day, any seemingly simple act could harbor the necessity of self-extinction. Maybe Jack Leaf had been that kind of man.

None of the students in Jack's class had seen Tate and his associate in or near the classroom. Since that day, subpoenas had been delivered to professors in front of students in classes. These outrages had received front-page news coverage. Why had Cyrus Tate used such discretion in his approach to Jack Leaf? Had there been prior contact between the two of them, or the three if you counted Frank Vane? Sipping the cold and soothing gin, Stall reflected that he would give a lot to know what had been said in that Murphree Hall classroom. Had Cyrus Tate told the truth about Jack's last words? If so, why would a man about to step out of a third-floor window say, "Thank you"? Was it a simple reflex of politeness, or was he thanking his tormentors for more than a piece of paper?

It occurred to Stall that Jack might have been involved with someone from the university, from the English Department. Maybe Jack's death had been a sacrifice, a thing done to protect someone else. But who? In his gin-soothed thoughts, Stall walked the gallery of the faces of his English colleagues. Were there secret signals by which such men recognized one another? Was it desperation or a thrill that caused men to meet in a bus station? Weren't there safer places? Stall finished the martini, set the inverted pyramid of empty glass in the exact center of his napkin, left a generous tip, and walked out into the fading sunlight to catch the bus home.

After eating more than his share of Maureen's wonderful chicken and seeing his daughter off to her room for whatever a preadolescent did up there, Stall poured his third martini and invited his wife out to the backyard to sit in a lawn chair and watch the sunset sky fade from salmon to black. They sipped gin, nibbled drunken olives, and Stall told Maureen about Sarah Leaf's visit to her husband's university office. He told her that Sarah had asked him to stop the savaging of her husband's reputation.

"You and Sarah," Maureen mused, "was that what kept you late?"

"Sarah came *after* what kept me late. Like I told you."

"Do I need to worry?"

"About Sarah's financial situation?"

"No."

He knew she meant *about you and Sarah*, and she knew he knew. "No."

"Okay, I won't then, but she's . . . attractive in her way. You be careful."

"She's attractive in a lot of ways, but not to me."

"Be careful."

"Careful it is."

"Can you do anything to help her?"

"Maybe. One of our new students, Martin Levy, his brother is the editor of the *Alligator*." Stall swallowed the last of his martini. The phone rang and he left the lawn chair reluctantly.

"Hello, Tom, this is Jim Connor."

"Pres . . . uh, Jim, how are you?" Stall's heart pounded adrenaline to his brain. *Calm down. Think straight.*

"Tom, is this a bad time?"

"Uh, no. Of course not."

"Well, I know it's the shinbone of the dinner hour, so I'll make this brief. I've got some good news for you."

Stall could hear ice clinking in the president's glass. He wondered how many bourbons were usual for Jim Connor in an evening.

"Tom, Amos Harding has decided to retire. I'd say he's taking *early* retirement, but we both know Amos has been in the traces too long for that to be an accurate statement. Between you and me and this whiskey in my hand, Amos has given this university a few too many years of loyal and visionary service, and while I'm grateful beyond measure to have had a man of his caliber among us, I think it's past time for a younger man to take over the leadership of the department. And I have a young man in mind."

Connor waited for Stall to understand the pregnancy of the pause. Stall's heart doubled its hydraulic effort.

"I've decided to make you chairman of the English Department. *Acting*, I should say. *Acting* chairman. We'll call you acting until you settle into the role, and we sort out some issues of, shall we say, legality—I'm talking about academic politics really, Tom. As you know, there are older and, some would say, more qualified men in the department who might have their caps set for the job, and we don't want to ruffle any feathers we don't have to." Connor paused to sip and sigh. "If I get any real pushback on this deal, I'll *pull* some feathers, but let's not get ahead of ourselves. Amos will call a meeting of the department to announce his retirement. He'll tell the assembled tribe that you'll take over—as naturally you should. You're his assistant, and you know the ropes. And Amos will say you're *his* choice. I'll have you officially appointed by the dean of Arts and Sciences, who tells me he reposes as much faith in you as I do." The president laughed quietly. "He reposes when he knows what's good for him."

Stall became obscurely aware that Maureen was standing a few feet to his right, with her beautiful backside pressed against the kitchen counter, and aware also of the fact that it was past time for him to say something. Into the growing pause, he stammered, "Well, Mr. President, Jim, I'm honored and flattered, and I want you to know that I'll do my best to justify the faith you're placing in me."

"I know you will, Tom. I know you will." Connor spoke with the voice of the father every man wished he'd had—even those who'd had the best ones. It was rough and loving, stern and understanding, and it carried just the smallest note of threat. *I know you won't disappoint me.* "I'm sure it's no secret that Amos Harding's wife has been a little under the weather for a while now. I know he'll welcome having more time to spend with her and to help her get better."

"Yes sir, I'm sure he will." *What a sad last act*, Stall thought, *nursing a gin-playing rummy.*

"And Tom, let's not forget that other business we have to take care of."

The shadow lurking offstage. You're my new chairman and my spy.

"We won't forget it, Jim."

"That's good. That's good, Tom. Well, I'll let you get back to whatever it is you're doing with that charming wife of yours. Please give my regards to the lovely Mrs. Stall."

"I will, Jim."

Stall cradled the phone and turned to the lovely Mrs. Stall. "You're looking at the new chairman of the English Department. Uh, *acting*."

She looked less surprised than Stall expected her to look. "How? Why?"

"Harding is taking early retirement to enjoy time with his family."

"Poor man . . . oh, forgive me for that."

The two of them stood paralyzed for a few seconds while the

new thing took hold of their imaginings. Then Maureen Stall smiled, stuck her finger into the dregs of her martini, and sucked it. "I saw the most fetching little cocktail dress in the window down at Wilson's Department Store."

Stall opened his arms, and she walked into them.

SIXTEEN

The student ghetto, locally known as Squalor Holler, looked quaint and bohemian to passersby, but life in it was harsh. Inhabited mostly by graduate students and the children they tried not to have but had anyway, the half square mile of run-down rooming houses and mildewed cracker shacks crawled with toddlers, wives who were quietly going insane while their husbands, living on teaching assistantships and the GI Bill, ground away at the MAs and PhDs they hoped would lift them to better lives. Some wives cared for the children of wives who worked to support husbands who could not get assistantships, some waitressed, and some typed the papers and lab reports of husbands whose wives were too busy with children to do it. During the day, the Holler was a world of wives who smelled of peanut butter and jelly, Wonder Bread, Spam, Kool-Aid, and Lysol. At night the odor was a more complicated perfume of cheap jug wine, cheaper beer, grilled cheese, hamburger that was more white with fat than red with meat, spaghetti sauce that started the week red and ended it watered to a pale pink, and the anxious sweat of men whose bodies were battered by alcohol, bad food, and the children they could not stop having. Their minds aimed at higher things—equations, and chromosomes, and epic poetry—their hope of salvation.

It was into this world that Tom Stall ventured in search of the home of Stephen Levy, recently named editor of the *Alligator*. After discovering that there was no listing in the phone book for Levy, Stall had asked Margaret Braithwaite to find the address for him. Using the mysterious powers of a president's secretary, in minutes she phoned it to him in his Anderson Hall office.

The warm night air carried hints of the coming fall, the faint, fickle season that finally gave way to Gainesville's often surprisingly cold winters. Stall walked slowly, remembering his own young married years after the war with Maureen and little Corey, those days of dreamy submersion in great books in his tiny wire carrel in the library and nights of Maureen's apprenticeship as a cook. They had argued sometimes as they'd learned love and marriage, but never bitterly, and there had never been any doubt of their devotion to each other and to making it work, and Stall, unlike some of his fellow students, had never doubted his role as a father. From the start, he had delighted in the time he'd spent with Corey. Now, as he neared the heart of the ghetto, straining to see street signs in the dim light, he could hear from far away and close by the voices of infants and children laughing and crying. It was bathtime in these hovels, and he remembered helping Maureen bathe their own slippery creature in the kitchen sink. Stall's job was to support her hot little head while Maureen poured cups of warm water over her fawn curls to wash away the shampoo that would make her cry if the parental hand was unsure. He remembered looking down into Corey's sweet, serious little face and marveling at the trust that gazed back at him.

Stall flicked sweat from his brow and stopped in the light from someone's front porch to read again the address he had written down. The house was just up ahead, an old bungalow that had probably been built in the 1930s when there was still hope that this neighborhood might improve rather than be consumed by the university's postwar need for cheap student housing. Stall stood on the weedy sidewalk and looked at the house. Voices came from it, not loud but contentious, the sound of steady, determined discussion. When he knocked, the talking stopped. After a pause and some whispering that Stall heard through the window screens, Martin Levy came to the door.

"Professor Stall?"

"Indeed." He was glad to surprise this young man for once. "Is your brother in?"

"Uh, yeah, he's—"

"Who is it, Marty?" The elder Levy brother, looking just like his picture on the masthead of the *Alligator*, stood behind young Martin peering at Stall through wire-framed glasses.

Perfect, thought Stall, *another Trotsky*. "May I come in for a minute?"

Stephen Levy didn't hide his reluctance to open the door. Stall smiled in his most disarming way and waited. Levy didn't move. Then Stall heard, "Let him *in*, for goodness sake," and Sophie Green stepped into view.

So, Stall thought, *I lose the contest of surprises*.

Sophie Green gently pushed the two Levys aside, and Stall stepped in. The first thing he noticed was the battered mimeograph machine on the dining room table surrounded by stacks of blurry blue leaflets proclaiming something about US policy somewhere, and the boxes of paper liberated from some university office, and the gallon cans of mimeograph fluid. All the makings of a revolution. It reminded Stall of a scene from a movie—two Reds and the machine that dyed their fingers blue.

He stifled the urge to chuckle, made his expression neutral, and said, "May I sit down for a minute?"

While contraband of some sort was not so artfully spirited out of sight, Stall reflected that Sophie Green was violating a tradition (if not a rule) of faculty conduct. After-hours socializing with students was restricted to sherry parties in honor of visiting scholars or to celebrate the publication of a faculty book, or holiday gatherings in the homes of the more generous and better-paid senior professors. It was understood that at these parties graduate students and their wives or dates would be especially mindful of their manners, especially when it came to drinking. The only exceptions to these practices were granted to students who were writing the most promising dissertations. When it was widely known that one of these was about to receive his degree, such a student might be seen at lunch with his dissertation advisor in a downtown restaurant or leaving that faculty member's house after a dinner with the man's wife and family. These fortunate students were about to cross over into the ranks of the professoriate. But even for them lunches and dinners with professors were trials and tests, and sometimes a gaffe was made that cost a young man his advisor's highest recommendation for a prized position. The department expected a young man to graduate not just with knowledge, but with social graces. The tradition was unforgiving, even cruel, but no one Stall knew had ever spoken against it.

Now, here was Sophie Green indulging in fevered off-campus discussions with a first-semester student and his brother. Hearing of this, some of Stall's colleagues would question her fitness for tenure.

All he could think of to say was, "Hello, Professor Green."

"Professor Stall." Sophie Green stood her ground unruffled. The upward curve of her lips said that she might even be enjoying his discomfort.

"Well," he said, "perhaps this isn't a good time."

"Oh, come on, Tom. We're just *talking*." She lifted her arms and let them fall to the sides of her faintly Victorian black dress. "I drove Martin home from a late conference, and he invited me in. These two wild men from the farthest reaches of Miami Beach will be living together." She glanced at each boy in turn. "If they don't kill each other."

"If I don't kill *him*," Stephen Levy muttered.

The three of them looked at Stall, and the question hung in the air: why are *you* here?

Stall took a chair that had not been offered. "I came to talk with Mr. Levy," he nodded at Stephen, "about what's been in the *Alligator* about Jack Leaf's death. Jack's wife came to my office today crying, very upset about things said to her sons at school about their father."

"I can't help that." Stephen Levy took a step toward Stall and looked down at him. The movement was aggressive.

Stall took a deep breath. "Sit down with me and let's talk." He knew you didn't tell a man to sit in his own house, but he didn't like this boy looming over him.

Sophie Green took a seat, as though to signal the boys to do the same. Reluctantly Stephen sat, and so did his younger brother.

We look like a discussion group, Stall thought. *Well, maybe that's what we are.* He stole a glance at Sophie, whose pleasant face said, *Your move.*

Stall said, "I understand you want to focus on the larger issues here, but human beings—the living, not the dead—are being hurt by what you're doing."

Stephen smiled grimly. "I have a certain sympathy for Mrs. Leaf and her children, but—"

"Two little boys," Stall said in his fatherly voice, "seven and nine. Just got back from a week at tennis camp to find out their father's dead, and now they're hearing a lot of . . . well, unfortunate talk from schoolmates about their dad. The sooner this blows over and you move on, the better for them. Surely there are other stories, better ones."

"As I was saying," Stephen's eyes bore into Stall's, "I do care about Mrs. Leaf and her children, but it's my job to expose injustice and hypocrisy where I see it—"

"Those are abstractions, these are *people*."

"That's twice you've interrupted me. I thought you Southern"—he pronounced it *Suth-run*—"gentlemen valued good manners."

"We do." Stall bit his upper lip. "I apologize."

"Thanks, but apologies don't matter much to me. To me, manners and the feelings of individuals are secondary to the needs of society. Right now the State of Florida needs to look hard at the bad laws made by a bunch of men in Tallahassee with good Southern manners and what they're doing to whole classes of people and their civil liberties. And I include homosexuals in that."

"So the more you drag Jack Leaf through the mud, the better off we'll all be?"

"Actually, the answer is yes. A man dies on a battlefield, and his death is ugly, but if his cause is beautiful, the uglier his death the better."

"And two little boys, their good feelings about their father, their sense of security in the world, their friendships—these aren't valuable things? Put yourself in their place."

"They're casualties of war. What happens to those little boys will break some hearts, and those hearts will become part of the momentum that leads to change. Feelings matter more in the aggregate than in the individual. Isn't that the way the world works, Professor Stall? Isn't that the way it's written in the books you teach? Slavery was called the South's 'peculiar institution' until abolitionists in the North examined their feelings about it, and their collective feelings, their disgust, started the movement that led to the Civil War. Dead children, flogged Negroes, start wars, sometimes good wars, but it's classes, armies that finish wars."

"Is that what you want? A civil war for homosexuals? Do you consider them an oppressed class?"

"What do you think they are? Sick? Diseased? Less than human? How well did you know Professor Leaf before you knew he was a homosexual? I'll bet you thought he was a great guy, and now, after all this, you think he was something less than that. Am I right?"

Stall folded his arms and took a deep breath. Somewhere in this exchange he'd become angry, very angry, and anger never improved his thinking. His adversary, young Stephen Levy, a PhD candidate in political science, gave Stall the uncomfortable feeling that he walked around angry every day, that he carried a burning furnace in him, that he had carried it a long time and had learned to damp its fires to fuel his words. Stall shook his head. "Haven't we gone a little far afield? My opinion of Jack Leaf or of homosexuals in general is not what matters here. I'm asking you to consider moving on to other news, maybe more important news, so that two little boys can mourn their father without being bullied at school."

"So you want me to write about some other homosexual professor? Or some Communist? A Negro from the NAACP? The Committee's after them too. There have been over two hundred subpoenas so far. But there's only been one suicide. Doesn't that make Professor Leaf's case the one I should concentrate on? You know, Professor Stall, there are a lot of unanswered questions, important questions, about Jack Leaf. We don't know yet if he fell, jumped, or was pushed. For all we know, this is a murder case."

"That's highly unlikely." Stall had stopped himself from saying, *That's crap*. And he had to admit, if only to himself, that his own list of questions about Jack Leaf's death was long and growing longer. He said, "The county medical examiner will make his decision about the cause of death any day now."

"What's taking him so long? Is he another Southern gentleman with good manners who wants to sweep this under the rug for the good old university?"

Coldly, Stall said, "I don't know the man personally. I tend to give professional men—people," he glanced at Sophie Green, "the benefit of the doubt when it comes to ethical behavior."

"Journalism is a profession, Professor Stall."

"And you're practicing it as an apprentice, Mr. Levy, as a young man learning." He did not say *his trade*, and was not sure if he did consider journalism a profession. In movies and novels it was often portrayed as a job held by ill-educated men who drank too much and ran around yelling, *Get me a rewrite!* Christ, this conversation was going haywire.

Calmly, Stephen Levy said, "I'll stand the *Alligator*'s coverage of the death of Professor Leaf up against that of any paper in this state. If you've read us and read the others with any objectivity, you'll have to say we've been fair, factual, and unintimidated."

"Have you thought about libel?"

Levy shook his head dismissively, stood, looked at Sophie Green in a way that said, *I did this for you*, and walked over to the table where the blue-stained mimeograph machine waited to crank out more broadsides against US policy somewhere. Right now, Stall did not care where. He stood wearily and took a step toward the door.

To Stephen Levy's back, he said, "Thank you for hearing me out."

Levy muttered, "Mmm."

Stall looked at Sophie Green, considered something like, *See you on campus*, or, *See you in the office*, but held his tongue. A loose word might reveal what he thought—that she should not be here in this house for any reason, and certainly not to witness his besting if not his humiliation by a boy half his age.

SEVENTEEN

In a rare tone of bonhomie, Amos Harding said, "Come up here, Tom."

Head bowed in the modesty that was proper and face warm with a blush that was real, Tom Stall walked to the front of the English faculty meeting and stood next to Harding, who let his hand rest for a moment on Stall's shoulder. Harding had called this special meeting, the second since Jack Leaf's death, but had told no one what was on the agenda. The old man was not known for dramatic flair, so it was generally, darkly assumed that Harding would "pull something" on the assembled faculty, possibly bad news about salaries, or some chicanery of the state legislature that might mean heavier teaching loads. The mood was expectancy and resignation.

Harding announced his retirement, gave his wife's health as his reason, and thanked his colleagues for their generous and loyal service to the university and their unfailing goodwill and gentlemanliness in their dealings with him. The reaction was relief rather than gratitude or concern for the old man. This was unfortunate and, worse, unintentionally funny. Observing the faces and the gestures, Stall read the collective mind. These professors were thinking that it was far better to lose a chairman who in his best years had been only fair at his job and who was, most felt, well beyond his prime, than to forgo their next salary increase. After the general sigh of relief had quieted, and the assembled tribe had noticed Harding's wounded surprise at their reaction, two senior professors rose to make rallying speeches. Struggling for words and compensating with dramatic hand gestures, they listed Harding's better qualities and thanked him from the bottoms of their tepid hearts.

Standing a respectful distance from Harding, Stall watched all of this unfold, thinking it would have been better for Harding to send a memo than to endure this display of humanity in the raw. But Harding had chosen to face the ranks and say his farewell, a graceful gesture, sadly received. This was not Stall's first sight of what it meant to lead. He had read and seen that it often meant disappointment. People often let you down, and sometimes they surprised you with glimmers of dignity and courage.

Harding put his hand on Stall's shoulder again and announced that Stall would succeed him as chairman in an *acting* capacity. The old man did a good job, Stall thought, of placing the final resolution of the matter in the middle distance where deans and vice presidents did their weighty deliberations. Stall scanned the audience as carefully as he dared for any outright dismay at the announcement, and especially for what the Bard had called the *lean and hungry looks* of men who might covet what Stall had just been given. He considered the position earned, not bestowed, but he knew that others might think differently.

"Tom, would you like to give us a few words?" Harding said.

"*Please*, only a few," came from one of Stall's senior colleagues, and there was muted laughter.

Stall was about to begin the brief speech he had memorized, confident that he could make it seem spontaneous, when a hand rose in the back. There was a faint clink as a bracelet shifted inches on the wrist of Sophie Green, whose slender arm was languidly waving. Stall was surprised and not sure if the new, acting chairman should recognize the hand or if Harding, who stood beside him, retained that right.

Amos Harding looked at Stall, smiled his resignation, and moved a step away.

Stall, who had completely forgotten the spontaneous words he had memorized, said, "Uh, yes, Professor Green. Is it a wild huzzah you want to give to my appointment?" *My God*, he thought, *where did that come from?* Predictably, no one laughed. Most looked confused. A few, he could see, were mouthing the word *huzzah* as though they'd just heard it for the first time.

Sophie Green looked embarrassed now, and not for herself. "Actually, no," she said, "that was not my intention. I was wondering if any thought was given to bringing in a chairman from the outside. You had a national search when you hired me. I competed for my position against people from Cornell and Yale." She left the question there, plain, unpolished, completely inappropriate.

Even as Stall tried to formulate an answer, and as his mind cursed her for ruining this moment for him, he wondered what his colleagues were thinking. Half of them were legacies in one way or another. Either a father or an uncle had held the job before them or they had been the favorite student of some long-gone professor. Stall expected at least a minor uproar to follow Sophie Green's question. He didn't know what to think now of the dead silence that was lengthening. Was this simply shock at her audacity, or were some of them thinking that perhaps a national search might have netted someone better than Tom Stall? He had to speak.

"Uh, actually, Professor Green, I don't know if any such thing was ever considered. If it was, the consideration was made at a level above my head." He said this in his best imitation of good-natured bemusement, as though he were speaking to a neighbor child who had brought some bad-smelling thing into the house and ought to have the good sense to take it back outside.

He said, "I will add that it has been the tradition of this department for the assistant chairman to take over the job in the event of . . ." What should he say here? He did not want to give the impression that Amos Harding's unforeseen departure was imprudent. "In the event of an unexpected, and I should say, lamented resignation." The only thing left for Stall to do, the only right thing, was to turn to Harding and offer his former boss the chance to speak. "Professor Harding, would you like to, uh . . ."

Harding looked at Sophie Green the way a man of his generation might look at the creature who bites the heads off chickens in a backwoods carnival sideshow. Such a creature is clinically interesting, but beyond the pale of humanity. "Professor Green," Harding began, "a national search had to be done to fill the position you now hold because the university was looking for a woman, and, as you know, there just aren't that many women to be had with records as distinguished as your own. As to the deliberations that led to the appointment of Professor Stall as acting chairman, those discussions have always taken place in private. Professor Stall has my complete confidence, and that of the dean, and, as far as I know, that of President Connor. If you'd like to suggest changes in hiring policy, I'm sure the president would be glad to hear you out on that subject. He's known as a man whose door is always open." And Harding was known for the kind of facial expression that said a subject was closed. His face slammed shut.

Sophie Green's face was hard to read. To Stall, she looked placid, cheerful even, like a smart student who had made an important contribution to the discussion. If she felt dismay at having had her knuckles rapped, she didn't show it. She said, "Thank you, Professor Harding, Professor Stall, and congratulations, Professor Stall, on your new job."

Stall did not make his speech. The meeting was adjourned.

EIGHTEEN

Two days after the departmental meeting, Amos Harding vacated his office. The Social Committee offered Harding a going-away party, but the former chairman politely declined, telling one of his trusted elder colleagues that he could not attend such a party without Mrs. Harding, and he was pretty sure she would not make it through the event standing up. It was a sad thing, all agreed, for a man of Harding's age and dignity to have to admit, but the faculty gave the old man credit for realism. At the end of Harding's last day, after his books and other possessions had been packed and shipped, he invited Stall to his office for what Stall assumed would be a ritual passing of the torch. Stall felt sad for the old man who had been good to him, but also found that he looked forward to their final meeting. He was sure that he could count on Harding for advice if he needed it later, and he planned to say so. As to the rest of it, he'd play it by ear.

On his way in, he passed Helen Markham on her way out. They exchanged complicated looks, Stall's hopeful, hers doubtful. He had known, of course, that he'd either have to work his way into her good graces or find an artful way to get rid of her. After all, she was at least as old as Harding.

He figured she was capable of loyalty to any man who sat at the chairman's desk, but he had no idea how she behaved when she actually liked someone.

Harding was standing at the tall window with the view of University Avenue that Stall planned to enjoy. The old man had grown more gaunt in the days since Jack Leaf's death and consequently looked taller and more funereal. His pale, pocked face managed a smile when Stall entered, a smile that was genuine if not generous.

Harding held out his hand and gave Stall a strong grip. "Hello,

Tom. I just wanted to have a final minute or two with you to wish you luck and give you something."

Stall glanced at the big Victorian desk he had so often coveted. The old leather blotter and calendar were gone, and gone were the ancient fountain pens and inkwell. Three things were left: the bronze figure of the man in knee breeches pushing a wheelbarrow piled high with books, the bust of Tennyson, and a half-empty jar of Sanka. *I want the toiling book lackey*, Stall thought. *He'll always remind me of my humble origins.*

He watched Harding's hand linger in the air above the desk and finally settle on Tennyson. Stall smiled as Harding handed him the bust. "Thank you, sir. I'll cherish this as a reminder of your kindness to me and of all the things you've taught me." He did not especially care for Tennyson's poetry, but he admired the poet's decency and his belief in the goodness of the world.

Harding picked up the bronze bookman and put it on Helen Markham's desk. He dropped the Sanka into the wastebasket. Then he pointed at the bust of the poet laureate that Stall cradled against his chest. "That thing isn't worth much, but it's been on every desk I've had since I started in this business. My wife's father gave it to me the day I got my doctoral degree and reminded me of two things: that I would take good care of his daughter or he'd horse-whip me, and I'd always be welcome in his coal-delivery business if I flopped as a teacher. We've seen the end of coal, at least delivered by mule and wagon, but I seem to be passing on to you a university in pretty good shape, though she's weathering some storms right now. I've been parsing symbols for forty years, and you've been at it ten or so. You'll understand that Tennyson is a symbol. He's the English Department. I'm giving him to you because I know he'll be in good hands. Goodbye, Tom."

Harding walked to the door. He stopped there and put on a hat, a rather jaunty one that Stall had never seen before, the kind of snap-brimmed hat that Englishmen wore when they drove open roadsters down Shropshire lanes. "I left something for you with Helen. She'll give it to you in the morning."

"Goodbye, Amos, and thanks again." Stall settled Tennyson back on the big desk

Harding adjusted the cap, waved, and was gone.

* * *

The next day, when Stall sat for the first time behind the big Victorian desk, colleagues dropped by to congratulate him either sincerely or politically. A few gave him words of warning or advice. Stall was neither instructed by the advice nor alarmed by the warnings. The former were mostly platitudes ("Steer the ship down the middle of the channel, young man, moderation in all things") and the latter mild paranoia ("It's a good thing you don't play golf with that martinet Connor"). Stall considered announcing that he had decided to take up the game, which seemed only right for a chairman, but restrained himself.

There were a few expressions of what Stall could see was a growing worry about the appropriateness of Professor Sophie Green. To these Stall said, "Oh, she's just doing what they do up North. Columbia University must be a real free-for-all. She'll tone it down when she sees how we operate here." But Stall, who had twice been the bull's-eye of Sophie Green's target, was not so sure this was true.

He'd spent some uneasy time the night before lying sleepless beside Maureen and thinking about the possibility that Sophie Green, not Tom Stall, was the future of this department. She came from a trade union family, and she seemed to think that a university should adopt the same ways and values. But a university, especially in the South, was not a democracy and certainly not a corporation. If it resembled anything, that thing was a fraternity, the kind of gentleman's club that Plato or Matthew Arnold or Scott Fitzgerald would have been comfortable joining. The sort of gathering of men that welcomed spirited discussion and some disagreement, but not vulgar disputation and certainly not revolution. Stall wanted more women to enter his profession (several were teaching now at the undergraduate level, staffing the required freshman English course), but he did not want to see standards lowered to accommodate women, nor to see the kinds of easy collegiality that he loved altered to accommodate the sensibilities of women.

By midmorning the drop-ins bearing congratulations and warnings had ceased, and Stall applied himself to the less-than-exalted business of emptying his old office and filling up his new one. By noon, he was covered with dust and sweat from hauling boxes of books and files.

Helen Markham had only said "Good morning" to him so far, but he could not fault her for that. The traffic past her desk to his office had been heavy, and then Stall had begun his labors with the books and files. She passed him in the hallway on her way out to lunch. Giving him a rather bleak look, she said, "You know I could have called a custodian to move those books."

Stall said, "Oh, uh, well, I . . ." He had not been certain that an acting chairman should accept such a service. Concealing this, he finished, "I wanted to do it myself." He tried to grin. "I have a rather eccentric system for shelving my books." This was not true. He shelved them alphabetically by the author's last name.

"Hmm," she said through pinched lips. She reached into an overlarge straw purse and withdrew a folder. "Professor Harding asked me to give you this."

Stall took the file, thanked her, went to the men's room to mop his grimy face with paper towels, then walked across University Avenue to the CI for lunch. He set the file on the table beside his BLT and a cup of coffee. The unassuming title was: *Faculty*.

The file contained notes written in Harding's old-fashioned school-boy hand, some of them long and some mere jottings on scraps of paper that seemed to have been dropped into the file according to no particular principle of organization. A few of the notes, the longer ones, had been typed, Stall assumed by Helen Markham. Some of the faculty whose actions were described in Harding's notes were gone, retired, or dead. Many were still active in the classrooms and meeting rooms of the English Department. Some of the notes were too cryptic for Stall to understand—such things as, *D reports that R and G duplicate.* Many were clear—*CB stopped for DD. EM called and we arranged release*. It took Stall no more than a few bites of his BLT to understand that *CB* was *Colin Broward*, a middle-aged scholar of the Romantic period, *DD* was *drunken driving*, and *EM* was *Ed McPhail*, the campus policeman. That particular note was dated March 1957. If there had been an arrest, the *Gainesville Sun* would have reported it, and the whole town would have known about it. It stood to reason that the campus and city police worked together on all sorts of cases.

One hand washed the other. Harding and McPhail had arranged the release, without charges, of Colin Broward. All for the good of the university, the English Department, and to the enormous relief of Colin Broward, who, come to think of it, continued to drink heavily at faculty parties and to drive away from them singing merrily through the open windows of his Buick Roadmaster.

With this first note as a sort of key, Stall deciphered more of the code. *WB* was *wife beating*. Stall got this one because the event had made the newspapers, and so had the divorce that followed. *PC* was *Peter Cameron*, the young eighteenth-century scholar who looked like a choir boy but had a penchant for punching his pretty young wife in places where the bruises would not show. After his story had been made public, Cameron had accepted a position in another state, leaving his wife in Gainesville to waitress in a local café. *LTC* was *late to class*, and Stall noted that both students and professors had reported this shortcoming to Harding. Harding's habit was to write, *Student*, followed by the kid's initials. *PH* was *poor hygiene*.

Stall sipped his coffee and looked around the CI at the students and faculty eating burgers and fries to the tune of the latest hit by the Silhouettes, "Get a Job." He couldn't stop the smirk that came to his face when he read on a scrap of paper, *PH reported by DB of TS—unshaven*. The date was September of 1957, the previous fall. Stall (TS) remembered that day. He'd overslept and, unshaven, had barely made it on time to his eight o'clock class. He remembered his surprise when he had reached up halfway through his lecture to stroke his chin and felt a day's growth. But who was *DB*, the student, staff member, or colleague who had reported Stall to Harding for poor hygiene? God, it was laughable, at least until Stall found the typewritten report about two faculty members who had been caught in *an unnatural embrace* in the men's room in the basement of Anderson Hall. For some reason, possibly because Harding had thought this document might find its way into official hands, he had abandoned abbreviations. The two men were not initials, they were named. They were Ted Baldwin and Jack Leaf. Baldwin was the senior medievalist, Sophie Green's mentor, or leader, or nominal boss. So . . . Harding had known about Jack Leaf.

Nothing in the report indicated that Harding had told anyone about Leaf and Baldwin, and nothing said he hadn't. Perhaps he had composed the report for later use or to protect himself. All of this was strange and unsettling to Stall, whose hands now felt soiled by Harding's file, but the strangest thing of all was the name of the man who had told Harding about the embrace in the men's room. It was Jimmy Bright, the custodian who had helped Stall carry Sophie Green's books from the parking lot to her office. Jimmy, the black man Stall had advised Professor Green not to insult with a tip.

Stall pushed his half-eaten sandwich away from him, and looked into the cooling dregs of his coffee. There was so much wrong with what he had just read that he did not know where to begin. The note about Leaf and Baldwin was dated March 1956. How on earth was it possible that the stiffly formal, deeply Southern Harding, a man who had brushed the dust of a North Carolina tobacco farm from his only blue serge suit to find his way to a teachers' college for his BS in agricultural sciences, could have the kind of relationship with a Negro janitor that would allow that black man to feel safe in reporting to Harding *an embrace* between two white professors? And there was Helen Markham. Surely she had typed the report and knew the contents of the file. What else did she know? Would she tell Stall any of it? Were there other files?

NINETEEN

Back in his office, Stall turned on his radio and heard the news. The medical examiner had called Jack Leaf's last act "death by misadventure." It was a careful and even a compassionate ruling, defining the event as neither suicide nor accident. Jack's body would now be released from refrigerated purgatory in the county morgue, and there would be a funeral. And now Jack's insurance policy would pay, and Sarah would have money to take her boys on that trip. Stall's good feeling about the medical examiner's report faded when he thought about the controversy it might cause. More grist for the mills of the newspapers, more grief for Sarah and her boys. The *Alligator* would probably question the ruling, say it was a mere convenience for the university.

Stall's phone rang.

"Uh, is this Mr. Tom Stall?"

It was a country voice, quiet, cautious, but musical.

Stall hesitated too, before saying. "This is Professor Stall. To whom am I speaking?"

The man waited, cleared his throat. "Uh, you ain't speaking to *whom*. This is, uh, Roney Tyler. I was a friend of Mr. Jack Leaf."

Stall's stomach tightened at the word *friend*. New meanings had been added to the word since Jack's death. Stall heard hammering where this man, Tyler, held a phone in his hand, and the low rumble of an engine. A garage?

He said, "Yes, go on, Mr. Tyler."

"Yeah, well, I seen it in the paper, about Jack's death. How they say it was a miss . . . adventure. I guess that means he didn't kill hisself?"

Stall said, "Yes, that's what it means." *Better this than*, It means they don't know.

The man at the other end covered the receiver with his hand, but not very well. Stall heard him yell, "I'll get that later. I'm gone out to lunch now!" The man uncovered the receiver. "Mr. Stall, could you maybe meet with me?"

Maybe meet? Mr. Stall? Irritated and intrigued by this friend of Jack Leaf, Stall said, "About what, Mr. Tyler?"

"Well, it's about a, uh, bank account."

Damn it, thought Stall. *That day in Jack's office. The bank book. Mr. R.T. Tyler.*

Before he could speak, Roney Tyler said, "They's a little café out to the Waldo Road, 'bout halfway to Newnans Lake. Could you meet me there?"

"When?"

"Uh, now. I only get a hour for lunch."

Stall heard in the background the whumping sound of the air compressor and the burring of a pneumatic wrench. It sounded like the rattle of the German Sturmgewehr assault rifle. He closed his eyes, wiped sweat from his forehead, and resolved to buy an electric fan for this office. (How had Harding sat in here all those summers in a blue serge suit never looking rumpled or damp?) It was mildly insulting that a stranger would think Stall could just get up and leave his office on short notice, but today he could do just that. The question was, should he?

There was only one café on the Waldo Road halfway to Newnans Lake. It was called Drawdy's Bait and Tackle. The store's business, Stall knew, was selling night crawlers, crickets, earthworms, top water plugs, cane poles, hooks, bobbers, and sinkers to fishermen on their way to the lake, but a hand-scrawled sign out by the road said, *Burgers, Beer, Sandwiches*. Stall pulled into the crushed-oystershell parking lot and stopped beside a battered International Harvester pickup truck. He looked at the truck through the window of Helen Markham's old Nash Rambler station wagon. As the dust settled around the car, he shook his head at the two marvels of the last half hour—that he had mustered the temerity to ask his secretary of one day if he could borrow her car, and that she had fished the keys from her giant straw bag and handed them to him without even looking up from the course list she was typing.

Stall examined the truck parked next to him for clues to the nature of Roney Tyler. Nothing spoke to him, except maybe the liberal use of a material known as Bondo, a quick and dirty way to patch holes and dents in an auto body. If Tyler was a mechanic, he was a sloppy one.

Stall pushed open the groaning screen door and saw that about a third of the small shadowed room was devoted to burgers, beer, and sandwiches. The rest of it was counters, racks, and coolers full of fishing tackle and creatures that would soon give up their lives to bass and shad. He could hear crickets cheeping from a rusting Coca-Cola cooler with a plywood lid. An old man sat behind a counter at the fishing end of the room, reading an *Argosy* magazine. He didn't welcome Stall. *Local color*, Stall thought, as he walked to the table where Roney Tyler waited for him behind a cup of coffee and a burger.

Tyler didn't stand or extend a hand. Stall took a chair. Tyler looked him up and down and Stall did the same. Tyler was darkly tanned, slim, and wiry, with bulging veins along his arms and a smile that revealed strong white teeth. He wore jeans and a shirt that had once been white, with *Bill's Body Shop* stitched in red over the left pocket. His sleeves were rolled up over hard biceps. The inevitable pack of Camels rode in one sleeve. "They ain't got table service," he said. "You gotta go to that hole in the wall."

Stall looked at the hole. Someone back there was playing a radio. Eddie Cochran singing "Summertime Blues." *True enough*, thought Stall. "I've had lunch, but thanks." Better to be polite and careful with this man who called himself a friend of Jack Leaf.

Tyler nodded as though anything was fine with him. He took a bite of his burger and chewed it thoughtfully. "Want to know how I got your name?"

"Sure," said Stall.

"Missus Leaf give it to me."

Stall nodded. Roney Tyler seemed to want him to ask a question. Stall waited.

Tyler said, "I called and told her Jack put me on that bank account, and I wanted to know how to get my money. She said to call you."

Roney Tyler didn't seem to think there was anything unusual

about Jack Leaf's widow telling him to call Tom Stall about a bank account. Stall wasn't sure how he felt about it. Why had Sarah Leaf decided to make him the agent of negotiations between her and a garage mechanic? "What did Mrs. Leaf say I would do for you?"

Tyler gave him the kind of look you'd direct at a slow child, wiped his hands on a paper napkin, and reached into his back pocket. He pulled out a passbook like the one Sarah Leaf had shown Stall and spread it out on the table. He said the words slowly: "She wants you to help me get my money."

Your money? My God, the endless complications of Jack Leaf. Stall did not touch the bank book. "You're saying Jack Leaf wanted *you* to have this money?"

"I tole you I'm on that account. Don't that say he wanted me to have it?" Tyler pushed the book across the greasy tabletop toward Stall. "Now there ain't no Jack, I'm the *only* one on it. Even a redneck like me knows the bank got to pay. So I called Missus Leaf, and she said to call you."

"But *why* did Jack want you to have this money?" *Rather than his wife and boys?*

A cunning pride filled Roney Tyler's cool blue eyes. "Well, professor, that's simple: he loved me."

Stall stared at Tyler, a man who did not seem the least bit lovable. But Stall knew from life, literature, and popular music that everybody loved somebody. Two weeks ago, he'd had no idea that Jack Leaf could love men, now he knew not only about the proclivity but about one of the men. Then the dizzying, damnable thought struck him: could this be the other man in the photograph? The man who had met Jack Leaf in a bus station men's room? And all of the other questions sprang into Stall's mind. How could this man possibly think that a wife, any wife, would happily help her husband's male lover filch twenty thousand dollars? Why hadn't Tyler simply gone to the bank? Why had he called Sarah Leaf? To threaten her? Was he just a common blackmailer, as common as the crickets whose cheeping cries came from the rusted Coca-Cola cooler?

Stall considered the possibility that Tyler had arranged for the photographer to be in that men's room, and that he had planned to threaten the Leafs with scandal if Jack didn't pay up. Was there guile enough in the creature who sat across from Stall chewing hamburger to do such a thing? Or had someone else put Roney Tyler up to the job?

Stall's mind was winding to some conclusions. "Do you want me to take the book with me and go to the bank?"

"Mr. Stall, you can see that I was *born* . . ." Tyler waited for this truth to penetrate Stall's brain, "but it wudn't *yesterday.*" He produced a stub of pencil and a Bill's Body Shop work order form from his pocket and handed them to Stall. "I want you to write down the account number and go talk to 'em. Say you represent me. You can do that, cain't you?"

I can indeed, thought Stall, *but why should I*? "Are you sure Mrs. Leaf won't, uh, contest this? She won't want the money herself? Try to keep you from getting it? There are ways she could do that."

"She didn't say nothing 'bout that. Sounded very nice on the phone. Told me to call the professor." Tyler said *professor* the way some of Stall's South Carolina country cousins had said *pissant* or *road whore*.

All through his youth, Stall had seen it. The contempt of men who'd studied in the school of hard knocks for those who had mere book learning. You could wear silk shirts and drive a Cadillac, and they still considered you stupid if you didn't know an oil-pan gasket from a fan belt.

Stall wrote down the account number. He knew the bank, of course, and the bank knew him. "How can I reach you, Mr. Tyler?"

"Oh, don't worry about that. I'll call you."

"No." Stall made as if to hand the order form back to Tyler. "You'll have to let me know how to get in touch with you."

Tyler clearly didn't like this, but decided to be reasonable. "Right now, I'm staying at the Oasis Motor Court on the Waldo Road. Number 6. Ain't no phone in the room, but they'll take a message at the office if it ain't too long."

"Give me a few days."

"Sure." Tyler pushed back in his chair and rubbed the flat little belly where hamburgers went to die. Thoughtfully, he said, "I gotta get out of this town."

"Where do you plan to go?"

Roney Tyler gave Stall a secret, satisfied look and shook his finger in the air between them. "That's for me to know."

"Give me a hint."

"Someplace cool. I'm sick of this damn heat."

It came to him that Tyler had said, *Gotta get out of this town*, not *want to* or *need to*. Stall went fishing: "Why do you have to leave Gainesville? Pressing business elsewhere? Problems at home? At work?"

The man's blue eyes darkened. "Let's just say ole Gainesville ain't friendly to me no more. Not after Jack."

"To hear you tell it, Jack's wife, his widow, is friendly enough to you."

"That ain't what I mean, and professor, you don't need to know no more about my life."

After Tyler left, Stall waited in Drawdy's Bait and Tackle for ten minutes. He justified his existence there by buying a paper container full of crickets who were pacified, it seemed, by a slice of raw potato dropped among them. He stopped a mile down the road and let the poor bastards crawl off into the grass. One for the Buddha.

He parked half a block from Bill's Body Shop, not far from the bowling emporium, Alley Gatorz, and watched Roney Tyler apply a belt sander to the rear fender of a 1956 Ford. The canny redneck worked earnestly in a cloud of rusty dust. *Maybe this dirty job*, Stall thought, *is why he's gotta get out of this town*. He suspected the reasons were darker.

He gave Helen Markham her keys and thanked her. "Had to do some emergency shopping for Maureen."

She took the keys with a mere "Mmm . . ." and said, "A delivery for you. It's on your desk."

It was a manila envelope from a courier service. A rare and expensive way to move information. The return address was, *F. Vane, Esq., Florida Legislative Investigation Committee*.

Fuck!

Stall hadn't settled into his chair when the phone rang.

"Tom, I'm so sorry. I didn't know what else to do."

Sarah Leaf.

She was crying, and her voice was thick and slow as though crying had led to drinking.

Stall said, "It's all right, Sarah, although it did take me by surprise." *Like so many things these days*.

"What did he say?"

"He wants what he calls *his* money." He told her about Tyler's bank book, a duplicate of the one she had found in Jack's office.

"Shit. His money. How could Jack do this to me?"

"I don't know, Sarah." *The mysterious ways of the human heart*.

She sobbed thickly, and he imagined her on the other end of this line—disheveled, aging fast, her hair going white at the temples. "Can you do anything, Tom?"

"I don't know. I've been thinking about it."

Her voice harder now: "He didn't say it in so many words, but I know he's a blackmailer. I'm afraid of what he'll do if I try to keep the money."

Stall considered saying, *That cat's already out of the bag*, but maybe there was another bag, more cats. More to know about Jack that would hurt Sarah and her boys.

"Will you do it, Tom? Handle this for me? I don't know what else he . . . knows about Jack."

"I'll do what I can, Sarah."

He told her that he had gone to Stephen Levy's revolutionary headquarters in the ghetto to appeal to the young journalist's better nature. "I asked him to find other news to write about. I'm afraid he didn't go for it."

Sarah Leaf's "Thanks, Tom" was almost inaudible.

TWENTY

The envelope delivered by courier lay on Stall's desk like a summons to an execution. He found a pair of scissors and opened it. It contained nothing but a photocopy of a check made out to *Brigitte Marie Raspeguy, Paris, France*. The check was drawn on the personal bank account of Frank Vane. Both sides of the check were shown, and there was Brigitte's neat endorsement. Stall traced the letters of her name with one finger.

He had never been an office tippler but, for contingencies, he had always kept a medicinal pint of bourbon behind some heavy volumes on his bookshelf. This was a contingency. He put on his serious new chairman's face and went to Helen Markham's desk. "Helen, we should have had an easy, restful summer, but these last few weeks have been, well, hard for all of us. Why don't you go home early today? Put your feet up. The fall hordes will be here in a week, and things will get crazy."

She had typed through his offer. Now she looked up, fingers still tapping keys, and gave him the doubtful gaze she'd used when she'd told him a janitor could have moved his books to this office. Through lips gathered as though by drawstrings, she said, "Are you telling me to go home, Professor Stall?"

Stall gave her the appearance of thinking about it. "Yes."

She gathered her things and left.

Stall locked the outer door, damned all possibility of interruption, and sat at the big Victorian desk with the bourbon in front of him. He took a long pull from the bottle and spoke to himself.

Stall, it's time for you to think seriously about some things, principally two: your integrity, such as it is, and the possibility that you are doomed no matter what you do about these entanglements you have found or that have found you.

The cloudy image of Tom Stall operating a belt sander in some shabby garage, a man without family or future, flickered across his mind. He banished it with a pull from the bottle. If only there had been no Brigitte. If there had been no Brigitte, then the possibilities for damnation and the death of a promising career would have been strong, but not certain. The only dilemma he would have faced would have been whether his ambition, his need to be chairman, could make him rat out a few homosexuals and Communists in his beloved English Department so as to satisfy Jim Connor or Frank Vane, or both of them, if that was possible. Literature told that such a thing, to become a rat, was enough to damn a man to the hell of everlasting ignominy, even if no one, neither stranger nor loved one, ever knew about it. And this was a terrible test for any man to face. Stall thought he could have passed the test.

He took another drink and swiveled his chair to look out at the oak trees that shaded the tall window and at University Avenue and the intermittent traffic of what was still the sleepy summer of a Southern university town. *If there were no Brigitte, no Françoise, you could have done it. You could have walked away from this job, your ambition, the department you love. You could have started over somewhere else. You could have told Connor and Vane to go fuck themselves. You could have delivered a pretty good speech to their smug faces, not that it would have mattered to either of them, about how a man could not, would not, rat out his friends because they loved the wrong people in the wrong ways or they harbored the wrong ideas. You could have said these things, resigned or been fired, and gathered up your books, your wife, your child, and your tattered ambition, and gone elsewhere.*

And he could have done it more or less happily, for he was young enough to start over somewhere—but there was a Brigitte, and Stall could not imagine his wife, the woman he loved more than anything or anyone else in the world, ever thinking the same way about him again or as well of him as he hoped she did now, after learning about a little girl in France who was his daughter.

Stall had known Brigitte before he married Maureen. Aside from an understandable haste in combining his flesh with hers and a forgivable misjudgment of her age (in a time and place where the mass delirium of freedom after years of war and occupation compelled everyone toward life), he did not think he was guilty of much. Surely he was not guilty of anything that stained the soul irrevocably.

And he had not known until a few days ago of the existence of a little girl who belonged to him as surely as did his beloved Corey. Had he known about Françoise at the time of her birth, or at any time before his marriage to Maureen, he would have done the right thing. He was as sure of this as he was of the sun rising tomorrow. The right thing was to take care of mother and child financially, whatever it cost him. And maybe he would have gone to France to marry Brigitte, to live there with her or to bring her home to live with him in America. He knew himself, his own moral pulse, well enough to be sure of these things. But he had not learned of the existence of Françoise until Frank Vane, who in Stall's place had done the right things for her and her mother, had told him about the child.

Stall pulled from the bottle and considered himself all right, not pure, but not eternally stained in his soul for not knowing about Françoise. Of course, there existed some man somewhere who would have taken seriously the possibility that a one-night stand in a Paris pension might lead to pregnancy, and who would have returned to France to investigate this possibility, but in Stall's moral universe, this was too much to ask of the common run of men. And Stall was no more than the common man.

If he didn't do what Connor or Vane asked (and the difference between the two of them and what they asked of him seemed to grow smaller as time passed), he would lose not just the job he had dreamed of, had worked for, but he stood a good chance of losing his wife and daughter. What was to prevent Maureen from leaving him and taking Corey with her? Perhaps he underestimated Maureen's compassion, her capacity for forgiveness, even her hard ability to recognize reality and adapt to it, but he was certain that after this he would be a different man to her, and almost certainly a lesser one. He could not bear the thought of passing the rest of his life as the man who slunk into and out of his wife's presence, the careless and corrupt father of a child in France.

With another pull from the bottle, and with the warm feeling of the bourbon slipping down his throat, he considered the possibility that Maureen might not take the existence of Françoise so hard. Why wouldn't she welcome into their life this other little girl, simply think of her as an addition to the family, a child of theirs that she, Maureen, didn't have to swell, and ache, and suffer pain to bring into the world? Stall's bleary eyes tried to read the small print on the label of the bourbon bottle. *What an ass you are!* it said. *Maureen is a lot of things, most of them wonderful, but she is not a woman who will forgive a child of yours by another woman.*

Stall walked home, hoping to sweat out some of the whiskey and to present himself at his own front door in a more or less plausible condition. Halfway there, the thought came to him: *What if I give them someone more corrupt than I am? Someone so black in his soul that I will be forgiven for ratting him out.*

TWENTY-ONE

"What's wrong with you, Tom?"

The question Stall had been dreading.

He and Maureen were driving the hot, dusty Newberry road back to Gainesville.

Jack Leaf's memorial service had been a dreary affair, thinly attended. Twenty or so of their colleagues had shown up, some with wives, all wearing faces that said they were not celebrating a life but doing an unpleasant duty. A half dozen of Jack's grad students came, two with wives. Stall figured they were mourning the dissertation advisor more than the man. Now they'd have to find someone else to sign off on their research. Jack's death could set them back years and cost tuition money they could ill afford. The two wives looked dazed from lack of sleep and bored with what was, even by the standards of contemporary liturgy, a lackluster affair.

The Leafs had not had what was locally known as "a church home," so Sarah Leaf had gone through the yellow pages until she'd found a minister willing to preside. The Mount Horeb Missionary Baptist Church stood in a grassy field, and the man was the Reverend Esau Conable. Stall sympathized with a preacher who had to bury a man he had never met (he'd seen his father do it several times), and knew that the job was almost impossible to do well even with help from the dead man's relatives. When relatives and friends were unavailable or did not care to contribute memories, the proceedings were doomed.

The Reverend Conable had relied on scripture and, unusual for a Baptist, one or two readings from the *Book of Common Prayer*. Stall appreciated the Anglican book for its poetry. And Conable left out the part about vile bodies. Stall expected Sarah Leaf to speak about Jack, but she didn't. Her face red and eyes swollen almost shut, she sat facing grimly forward with the two boys who were dressed identically in new blue blazers, black ties, and gray wool pants. Amos Harding gave a brief eulogy, citing Jack's professional accomplishments, his war record, and his popularity among students and colleagues. The words were vintage Harding, brief, careful, and just short of generous. He mentioned none of Jack's troubles.

If there was a surprise, it was that Sophie Green and the two Levy brothers attended the service. They sat in the back, Sophie Green with a black scarf covering her head, and the boys looking uncomfortable in white shirts and thin dark ties. Stall wondered if Stephen Levy was here in his professional capacity. Would there be an article in the *Alligator* about Jack Leaf's dreary memorial service? Sarah had chosen "He Leadeth Me" for the final hymn and the assembled company sang it earnestly to a wheezy organ played by an old country woman in a flowered dress. The Reverend Conable's fine baritone voice led them through the song. Stall was not surprised that President Connor had missed the service.

When it was over, as was the custom in South Carolina where Stall's father had toiled in a pulpit, Stall took the Reverend Conable aside and discreetly handed him forty dollars: "For the church," Stall said. The preacher would use the money as he liked, Stall knew, but decorum required Stall to say that the man of God had performed the service unpaid. Conable thanked him with a nod, and a "Bless you, brother." There was no trip to the graveyard. Sarah Leaf had asked her sons' tennis coach to take care of the boys while she alone accompanied Jack's body to the graveyard and saw it into the ground. "I don't want the boys to see that," she had told Maureen. "It will give them nightmares. They'll think of their father trapped in a coffin under all that dirt."

In the grassy churchyard with the crowd drifting away and sandspurs sticking to Stall's pant cuffs, Sophie Green separated from the Levy boys and approached, holding out her hand to Maureen. "This must be Mrs. Stall."

"None other," said Maureen with a neutral smile. Stall's wife looked austerely beautiful in a simple black dress and a black pillbox hat.

"I'm Sophie Green, *Dr.* Green. The new and still the only woman of the graduate faculty."

"Yes," said Maureen in the voice that Stall had come to know as speculating, "I know exactly how many women there are." She turned to Stall and gave him an approving pat on the arm as though he were responsible for keeping track of the women.

Sophie Green said, "Well, it's nice to meet you finally. I wish it had been in happier circumstances. Let's have lunch some time and some girl talk." She gave Stall a friendly smirk. "You see, Tom, I'm not all seriousness and work. I can talk frocks and handbags with the best of them. What do you say, Maureen?"

"I'm all for accessories," said Maureen. "And I think they're serious. Jewelry too, right, Tom?"

"That's right. You like jewelry as much as the next girl."

Sophie Green shook her head at the word *girl*. "I'll call you for a lunch, Maureen."

Watching Sophie Green walk away to her car, Maureen purred, "*So, you see, Tom, I'm not* all *seriousness and work*." She squeezed his arm. "What *else* is she, Tom?"

He looked back at the empty church doorway with the thought his father had given him: *Fear the Lord thy God*. "Not here, Maureen."

She took his arm, and they walked to the car.

Now he was pushing the Packard along the hot, dusty Newberry road back to Gainesville, and Maureen had said, "What's wrong with you, Tom?" in a tone that was deadly serious.

Despite his session the afternoon before with the bourbon bottle in what he still thought of as Harding's office, Stall could not bring himself to spill his secrets to her. *I'm being pressured to spy for both sides in a war of humiliation and bigotry, and I'm the father of another woman's child.*

"What do you mean?" His fingers drummed the steering wheel. "We've just seen the last of Jack Leaf, in this world anyway."

"I don't think that's what's bothering you. At least that's not all of it. And the last time I looked, this was the only world you believed in."

"I believe in *you*," Stall said resolutely. "And I believe in Corey. Isn't that enough for right now?"

"And you believe in changing the subject." She shifted on the seat, plucked the fabric of her dress away from her chest, and looked out at the scrub oak and palmetto. "While we're on the subject of Corey, why don't you take her out in the backyard and play catch with her once in a while? That's what she likes right now, and you should be glad about it, rather than muttering about her being better than the boys. She'll move on to the next phase soon enough, and you know what that'll be like. You had a sister."

In his dutiful voice, Stall said, "I will play catch with my daughter. I will meet her where she is—on the diamond of her dream to play shortstop for the Yankees."

"You know, Tom, we love it that you're smart, but nobody loves a smart-ass."

"Noted."

"On a related note, I can't remember the last time we went out as a family, to a movie or something."

Stall said, "Let's go buy that dress you mentioned. The one in the widow at Wilson's. We'll take Corey with us. Get her started on the main pursuit of her next phase: the acquisition of seductive apparel."

"I already bought it. It's hanging in the closet in the bedroom. I buy the dresses, you take me places where I can wear them, Mr. Chairman."

Stall nodded emphatically and drummed his fingers on the wheel wishing this was over.

Maureen's voice dropped into the octave of resignation. Through a sigh she said, "I know you're worried about more than Jack's death. I know it because I know *you*. I hope it's not me you're worried about."

"*You*? Why would I worry about you? You're okay, aren't you?"

"I'm fine, Tom. Healthy as a horse." She looked out into the last pasture they would pass before hitting the outskirts of Gainesville. She pointed. "As fit as that one right there."

And indeed, it was a fine horse, tall and black, holding its tail high like a fountain behind it. The animal lifted its head from grazing to watch their speeding Packard pass.

Stall drove on, thinking that his wife's discontent was misdirected now, though she was homing in. The beam of her instinct, of her knowledge of Stall, would soon cast its light into the darkness of his deception.

TWENTY-TWO

That night, Stall told Maureen he had to go to the library to do some research for the article he was writing on Graham Greene. She looked up from her *McCall*'s magazine, smiled, and said, "Mmm." His nocturnal runs to the library were well known to her. Early in their marriage, she'd said, "Can't it wait till tomorrow?" He'd explained to her the hot urge of the scholar to find the key fact while inspiration burned.

The library closed at ten. Stall figured he had two hours. He bought a fifth of Jim Beam at a liquor store on 13th Street, drove to the Oasis Motor Court not far from Alley Gatorz and Bill's Body Shop, and parked as far from Roney Tyler's door as he could. He was getting out of the Packard when Roney Tyler opened his door, surveyed the parking lot, and stared hard at Stall's car.

With the bottle in hand, Stall crossed the distance to Roney Tyler.

Tyler took a step back. "What *you* doin' here?"

There was blood in Tyler's eye, and his cheek was cut and swollen.

Stall put his hand on Tyler's shoulder. "Let's get you inside."

Tyler shrugged away from Stall's hand. "Get *away*, damn you!"

Stall was thinking that a trip to the emergency room might be in order, but he doubted that Roney Tyler would bother with such things, at least not until it was too late to save the eye.

Stall raised Mr. Beam into the range of the man's good eye. "Do I take this with me when I leave?"

Tyler made a sloppy grab for the bottle.

Stall swung it from harm's way. "Who was the other guy?"

"What guy?"

"The one whose ass you whipped."

"Awe, that's my goddamn wife's goddamn brother, and you better believe I give as good as I got."

"I believe it. How come you to be fighting with your brother-in-law?" Stall let a little of the old South Carolina slip into his speech. Kindred spirits. But the spirits he would mostly rely on were in the bottle. "Come on. Let's go inside, get you cleaned up, and share some of this panther piss."

"Ha! Professor, you don't know shit about bad whiskey. Hell, I done *made* bad whiskey in my time." Tyler made another feckless grab for the bottle.

"Let me put it this way," Stall said. "*If* we go inside, and *if* you let me take a look at that eye, then you and I will crack open this bottle of *pretty good* whiskey. Is that a deal?"

Roney Tyler let Stall turn him by his skinny, rock-hard upper arm and move him toward the door.

The motel room was what Stall had imagined it would be or a little worse. It smelled of mildew, stale beer, dirty socks, and fried onions. The linoleum was blistered and the carpet looked more like a layer of mold than anything from a textile mill. The kitchenette was piled with unwashed dishes and splashed with food. Roney Tyler was not a neat man, and apparently there was no one around who cared to straighten him up.

Stall washed two unmatched jelly glasses, poured healthy portions of bourbon into them, and searched the bathroom for some Mercurochrome or rubbing alcohol. Coming up dry, he poured whiskey on a wad of toilet paper. "Hold still," he said, and applied the wad to the cut under Tyler's eye. After an initial flinch and gasp, Roney Tyler held still. They both drank some Beam.

Tyler said, "How's it look?"

"Not as bad as it's gonna look in the morning. My guess is you won't be able to see out of it, Cyclops."

"Cy who? I've worked one-eyed before."

"I'm no doctor, but I'd advise you to take that eye to the hospital, let somebody smarter than us look at it."

"Aw, fuck it. I'm all right."

Stall put the wad of toilet paper in Tyler's hand and lifted it to the bloody cheek. "Hold it there." He checked the refrigerator for ice to slow the swelling. No luck. He moved some dirty laundry from one of the two dinette chairs, sat, and drank more of the sweet, hot Jim Beam. "So, why'd you fight your brother-in-law?"

"Called me a queer."

Stall remembered the bait shop, Roney Tyler saying it matter-of-factly. *He loved me.*

Jack Leaf had loved Roney Tyler and had made him twenty thousand dollars richer.

"Is that why you're living here? Your brother-in-law thinks you're unfit for his sister?"

"That's about right. How's it your bidnis?"

Everything about you is my business if you want that twenty thousand dollars. "Does *she* want you back? Your wife?"

"I doubt it. Doubt I want *her* back. Thank God we ain't got no kids."

Stall tried to imagine the offspring of Roney Tyler. "The other day you said you had to get out of this town. Is your brother-in-law coming after you again?"

Tyler threw the bloody wad of paper onto the floor and reached for the bourbon bottle. The gash under his eye had stopped weeping. A sane man would have wanted it stitched shut, but Roney Tyler didn't seem to care about that. Maybe he liked a good scar. He splashed some whiskey onto his cheek, cursed the pain, and poured some into his mouth. "Him and some of his friends, so he says. And you know what they do to queers."

Stall knew. He'd seen it in the army. Some of the boys in his barracks had talked about "rolling queers" to enhance their army pay. In an army town, the police considered homosexuals fair game for soldiers. The unwritten law was that if a soldier put himself in the way of a homosexual looking for rough trade, and if the soldier was propositioned, then he was justified in beating the man and taking his money. Stall had been delighted one night in the barracks when a tough young country boy from Georgia had come home covered with bloody welts and minus his wallet. He had rolled the wrong queer.

Before he'd reported for induction, his father had told him he'd meet all kinds in the army and he'd be the better for it. Some of the boys he'd met, louts, bullies, and creatures with the IQs of six-year-olds, had made his world worse. He had not been able to keep himself from looking at them and thinking, *Cannon fodder*. Later on, of course, he regretted this when he had seen them, the best and the worst of them, strewn in their macabre poses along the roadsides and across the snowy fields of France.

Stall drank bourbon. "Sure, Roney, I know what they do to queers. And I know they think it's right, but I don't agree with them."

"You queer too? That why you and Jack were friends?"

Stall considered telling Roney Tyler that he and Jack Leaf had not been friends, just colleagues. He considered saying that now, strangely, he wished he had known Jack better. He doubted that Roney in his present state would understand this. "No, I'm not queer, at least not that I know of." He could add that he was a married man, but Jack had been married and everyone had thought happily so. Then Stall remembered his drunken talk with Sarah Leaf after he had driven her home from the bowling alley. She had said nothing about any unhappiness with Jack. She had said, or at least implied, the opposite. *He liked me . . . sometimes. And I loved him.* For Sarah at least, theirs had been a strange but a happy accommodation.

Tyler finished his drink and poured another. For a thin man, Stall reflected, he had a large capacity. Tyler said, "If you ain't queer, what you doing here in the middle of the night?"

Stall looked at his watch. Half of his library time had passed. "I've got a proposition for you, Roney."

Tyler gave him an odd look with the crimson eye closed.

"Sorry," Stall said, "poor choice of words. I've got an idea. I know you want that money down at the Dixie Fidelity Bank, and now I know why you need it. If you don't get out of here, your loving brother-in-law will come back and beat you to death."

Roney Tyler bristled.

Stall raised a hand. "I know he couldn't do it by himself, but you said he'd bring his friends."

Tyler nodded grimly.

"Look, Roney, I believe you loved Jack and he loved you, but I think you had other reasons for being with Jack, especially on one particular night. Am I right about that?"

Roney Tyler hung his head again, and both of his eyes cried. One of them cried blood.

* * *

It was nine forty-five when Stall drove the Packard home. His alibi would hold. Right now the tired librarians would be shooing the last of the late-night scholars from the carrels and microfiche readers. He'd tell Maureen a story about rifling through the stacks looking for an obscure letter that Graham Greene had written to the Catholic priest he had met on the bus, the man who had been principally responsible for Greene's conversion to the One True Church. And Stall would reflect privately on the story he had pried from Roney Tyler with the help of some pretty good bourbon and some bloody tears.

Roney Tyler had lured Jack Leaf to the men's room in the bus station. He'd known the photographer would be there, and he'd done it to keep Cyrus Tate from telling Samantha Tyler, Roney's wife, about Roney's other life. None of this surprised Stall very much. What did surprise him was something Roney had said about Tate. "That Tate, he's a dangerous man. He don't care who he hurts, or how. I think he likes what he does a little too much. After that guy took them pictures of me and Jack, I ran like a scalded dog out of that men's room and Cy Tate was parked up the street where he told me to meet him. I got in his car, and he asked me how it went. I said it went, you know, like we planned it, but he wanted *details*. You know what I mean?"

"Yes," Stall said, "I think I do."

TWENTY-THREE

"Professor Green for you on line two."

Helen Markham didn't wait for Stall to speak. She put the call through.

Tell Helen to ask first. "Hello, Professor Green."

"I thought we decided to use first names."

That was before you told my department that a national search, which everyone knows would not be likely to land me in this chair, was a good idea. "Sorry. Hello, Sophie."

"Hi, Tom, do you have a lunch date yet?"

Stall looked at his watch as though it would tell him if he had lunch plans. It occurred to him that Sophie Green might tell him something he needed to know. "My dance card is empty. Shall we go over to the CI?"

She sighed into the phone. "No, I don't think so. I've hoisted too many greasy spoons in this town. You know, one of the things not so wonderful about leaving New York for the South is the . . . I guess I'll just say the food."

Stall had never been to New York, but he'd seen the movies. Delicatessens, famous restaurants, Chinese and Italian food, a gustatory cornucopia. He hoped to get there someday. Maybe on a chairman's raise he could afford a New York meeting of the Modern Language Association. "Where shall we go?"

"I don't know. I haven't tried that little place downtown. The Primrose Inn."

Stall and Maureen ate at the Primrose Inn when they could afford it. Fried chicken was the *spécialité de la maison.* "It's a long walk," he said.

"Sir, you're forgetting that I am the proud owner of an automobile. My father insisted I have one." She slid into her father's Lower East Side accent: "Kid, they don't have subways down there, and all the cab drivers are alcoholic Klansmen."

"Ah," Stall said, "Solomon Greenbaum, the union man. You do the voice well."

"I was on the stage, in an amateur sort of way."

Surely not playing an elderly New York trade unionist? "Where's your chariot parked?"

"Right across the street, gathering parking tickets as we speak."

In Sophie Green's DeSoto, the open wind wings only increased the late-August heat, and by the time they were seated at the Primrose Inn, Stall's collar was soggy. The restaurant tried for an English tea shop atmosphere, but as with many things people tried in Gainesville, there was more merit in the striving than in the results. At least there was a fresh red rose in a crystal vase on every tabletop. Sophie Green looked fresh if a little flushed in one of her vaguely old-fashioned frocks. She seemed to dress to emphasize her delicacy, or maybe to contrast it with the toughness that lived underneath. The effect seemed to Stall more like costuming than clothing.

When the waitress asked for their orders, Sophie Green looked at him with mischief in her dark eyes. "Would a glass of wine be completely out of order?"

Like your comments in our meetings? "I'll check my *Robert's Rules*." He let her think about that one for a few seconds, then said, "Not in my book."

"I'll have wine if you will."

"I'm not much for wine. I can barely tell a red from a white. I'll have a martini, but only in order to encourage you."

The drinks came, his Gordon's with a drop of vermouth and an olive, her Côtes du Rhône. Stall's respect for the Primrose Inn notched upward when she tasted the wine and smiled.

Lunch was her idea, so Stall figured he'd let her start the conversation. They covered her settling into her rented apartment, taking in a stray cat, not getting used to the heat, looking forward to teaching her first classes, and how strange it was to turn on the light at night and see what the locals quaintly called "palmetto bugs" scurrying for cover.

"I thought you had those up in New York too."

"Not like yours. You give them names down here, don't you?"

"Easy now," Stall said, "the lowest we go with names are yard dogs and third cousins. No buzzards, possums, or insects."

When his club sandwich and her chicken salad arrived, she picked up her fork and said, "Look, no grease."

"This is fun, Sophie, but I thought maybe there was something you wanted to talk about."

"You're right, Tom. I apologize for prattling on like some Southern belle. I wanted to offer you this lunch as a way to make up for what I said at the meeting. That was . . . well, sometimes I spout off before I've completely thought things through. I hope you'll believe me when I say I had no intention of questioning your qualifications for the position. I just want faculty to have a say in things."

"You wouldn't be here if they did."

His bluntness caused her eyes to blaze for a second, then they cooled.

"The people who hired you knew most of the men here wouldn't want you. For the good of the university, they didn't ask for any opinions. I'm not the only man who's glad you're here, but there aren't many of us. I want to see women in my classes too, and I think you can help make that happen." He paused and rolled some cold gin on his tongue.

"So, my opinions about progress put me on the side of the big decision-makers? The boys behind the scenes?"

"In this case they do." He gave her his *such are the ironies* smile. "Welcome to the smoke-filled room."

"Well," she said, "I'll have to think about that." Just a hint of concession in her tone. She touched the corners of her bow-shaped mouth with the point of her folded napkin. "I wanted to talk about Stephen and Martin too, if that's all right with you."

Stall smiled, nodded. The two Trotskys from Miami.

She said, "They're not bad boys."

"Good boys do bad things. Stephen's in political science. Nothing I can do about him and the newspaper he runs, apparently without any advice or counsel from grown-ups, but I will say this: Martin's a grad student in the English Department. I admit that he and I got off to a bad start. I've acknowledged my part in that, at least to myself, and I plan to call him in and try to start over with him, but if he continues here with the attitude he's shown so far, he'll have trouble with many of his professors. He can't take all his classes from you, and I'm by no means the most conservative or the most irascible of the men he'll encounter." When he saw how seriously Sophie Green was taking this, and sadly too, he said in a softer tone, "I take it you approve of my calling him in?"

"I don't know," she said. "I don't know how *he'll* take it."

Stall took a long breath and another sip of gin. "Go on."

"Well, you probably won't like this, but I don't think Martin and others of his generation, especially those with roots in the Northeast, are going to like being 'called in.'" She set down her wineglass and peered carefully into his eyes. Stall was surprised to realize that she was cautioning him. She said, "Boys like Martin think of men like you as 'The Man.' Have you heard that phrase?"

Stall had heard it, but he couldn't remember where. He stopped himself before saying, *It's a Negro thing, isn't it?* He settled on, "I believe so." He was thinking: *Martin will do things our way here, or he won't thrive. Discipline and a dose of humility will make him a better man and a better scholar.*

Sophie Green said, "I'll talk to Martin."

"Haven't you already done that? Wouldn't it be better if he came and talked to *me*? You said once that we have to earn our students' respect, and I said it was the other way around. Respect is both internal and external. Externally, it's good manners. Down here we show good manners to people, even if maybe we don't feel any respect for them. I believe the one grows out of the other. When two people treat each other with good manners, what's inside can change."

"Have you told that to the Negroes who say *yes sir* and *no sir* and don't have the right to vote?"

"I believe what I said is true for us and them too. We live together as well as we do down here partly because of our manners."

"Not because of nightsticks and police dogs?"

"I haven't seen any of those around here."

"When the time comes, you'll see them."

Stall shook his head and looked into the bottom of his empty martini glass, and then at the scraps of his club sandwich.

Sophie Green reached out and put her hand on top of his. "When Martin interrupts or speaks out of turn, it's just a difference of style. He doesn't think he's showing disrespect when he disagrees with you. Taking you on as an intellectual equal is his way of showing respect."

"Did his brother think he was showing respect when he turned his back on me?" Stall knew what she was thinking: *Stephen turned his back on a weak argument.*

They had reached an impasse, and they both knew it. Any more of this, and real damage might be done.

Stall said, "Despite our differences, I respect you for asking me to lunch, and for a great many other reasons."

"Thank you for that, Tom. I respect you too, but I have to say that history is not on your side."

God help us, Stall thought. *Historical inevitability, the Marxist line, the argument that trumps all others.*

On the way back to the university, they talked about their research.

TWENTY-FOUR

For Immediate Release

James Connor, president of the University of Florida, gave a brief statement today from his office in Gainesville about what he called "unrest" at Florida's flagship university: "Of course nobody wants radicals and deviants teaching our children, but we have to obey the laws of the land and demonstrate a proper respect for civil liberties."

Professor Stanley Margolis of the Political Science Department, representing the Faculty Senate, praised President Connor for his "moderation in the face of the extremism of a right-wing state government." Margolis added that he hoped the president could bring himself to move closer to positions taken by representatives of the faculty who strongly disapproved of the recent activities of the Johns Committee on their campus in Gainesville. President Connor responded that he always intended to be fair to all sides in his decision-making about the university's responsibilities to the Board of Governors and the state government who "after all, have only the highest regard for our universities and their faculty and students, and only their best interests at heart. Let's not be too quick to take sides and draw the battle lines." The president added, "Moderation in all things."

The *Alligator* ran a cartoon of President Connor dressed in a chicken suit and dangling the scales of justice from his thumb. One side read: *Johns Committee*. The other, the empty cup, read: *The people*.

Helen Markham covered her typewriter, locked her box of Earl Grey tea and her Spode cup and saucer in her desk drawer, and left for the day. So far, she had treated Stall as though he might be temporary. A few times, he had caught her looking tensely at the outer doorway like a dog whose owner has not come home at the usual time. *Maybe*, he thought, *I should remind her that Harding won't be back*.

Stall was about to call it a day himself when there was a strong knock, and Ted Baldwin thrust his head into the office, bobbling his eyebrows like Groucho Marx. Baldwin was the faculty comedian, the sort of man who stopped colleagues in hallways and told jokes from a supply that he refreshed periodically so that no one ever heard him repeat himself. He told the jokes impeccably, with voices that suited the characters, pauses for emphasis, and, usually, a drolly understated punch line that got him the laughter he wanted. Stall had always liked Baldwin in the way he liked men who played necessary roles and demanded little more than an occasional audience. But now that he had seen Harding's file, he could no longer think of Baldwin as merely the faculty funny man. Sitting in the CI and reading about the embrace in the men's room downstairs, Stall had known instantly, sadly, that he would never again see Baldwin as simple and safe.

Baldwin stood in the doorway examining Stall's new office, a survey punctuated by exaggerated "Ahhs" and "Ooos," and finger-pointings. He nodded sagely when he saw the bust of Tennyson resting in its usual place. "Ah, so," he said in a mock-Chinese accent, "I see that the world will continue to turn on its axis. Alfred Lord Tennyson stands at his post."

"And so will he always," said Stall, playing the game. "Come in, Ted. Take a load off."

Baldwin unbuttoned his moss-green Harris Tweed jacket and sank with a satisfied sigh into the chair in front of the big Victorian desk. He dressed the part of the English professor. He wore the clothing of an Oxford don, or the closest approximation of it he could find in Gainesville's haberdasheries. When he summered in England and Scotland, he brought home expensive shoes and ties. The brogues he wore now had probably cost him a week's pay. *But*, Stall reflected, *if he has them soled and heeled they'll last the rest of his life, and there are rumors that he has a private income*. Teaching was a good life for a single man with tenure in a none-too-demanding discipline. How much more, how much that was new, could Baldwin learn about Geoffrey Chaucer, and how many students would ever want to specialize in the medieval period? Baldwin was genuinely enthusiastic about a field that bored most grad students nowadays. Their boredom lightened Ted Baldwin's workload. He was handsome, and at forty, probably weighed not a pound more than he had at twenty. He played a wicked game of tennis, and Stall had seen him at parties with several very presentable middle-aged women, all of whom seemed to adore him. He was said to be an excellent ballroom dancer. Stall shook his head to dismiss from his mind images of Jack Leaf and Ted Baldwin embracing—whatever that meant.

Baldwin winked. "So, Tom, how are you settling in?" He looked around the office again with theatrical gravity. "Is it true what we hear? *Uneasy lies the head . . .* ?"

The rest of it was, *that wears a crown*. Famous words from *Henry IV*. Several replies occurred to Stall: *I've been doing the old man's job for years now anyway. Nothing new for me but this boat of a desk and old Tennyson over there.* Or the more earnest, *I'm feeling my way into the job, Ted. Pretty sure I can do it with a lot of help from senior fellows like you.*

The truth was, he didn't know how he was doing. He thought again of Helen Markham gazing doglike at the open door.

Baldwin lit a filter-tipped Parliament and glanced around for an ashtray. Stall took one from his desk drawer and set it in front of him.

"The usual travels this summer, Ted? Anything new over there in old Blighty?"

"Actually, some interesting documents coming to light in Kent. Old Geoffrey did some work for the king there."

"So if they dig up a pewter mug or something that old Geoffrey or one of his cronies might have drunk mead from, this tells you something you can pass on to adoring mobs of students here in Ye Olde Gainesville?"

"No, the mugs are all in museums. I did pass a lovely afternoon picnicking near a Roman dig site and watching some keen lads and lasses from the local university toiling on their hands and knees with toothbrushes."

Stall pictured Ted Baldwin sprawled on a plaid ground cloth with a wicker basket full of cheese, fruit, and finger sandwiches, sipping chilled champagne and watching the lads . . . and lasses. "Nice work if you can get it."

"Indeed." Baldwin took a long pull of his Parliament and blew a thoughtful plume of smoke into the air above Stall's head. "This life we've chosen for ourselves. Almost too good, I think sometimes."

"Yeah, I think that more and more these days."

"You are thinking," Baldwin said archly, "of the troglodytes who want to take this life away from us."

"In an oblique way." Stall put a finger to his lips as though someone might be listening.

Baldwin nodded sadly. "I'm going to miss Jack Leaf."

"Me too." Their eyes met. *What is this dance we are doing?*

"I hope nobody else jumps."

"Goes without saying."

"Of course, sorry."

"And it was misadventure."

"Yes, of course."

Ted Baldwin finished his Parliament and lit another. Stall waited. The silence was not uncomfortable.

Finally Baldwin said, "So, Tom, there are, uh, rumors."

"Aren't there always."

"Not always like these."

They had hit a bump Stall hadn't seen coming. Baldwin was not talking colleague to colleague now but professor to chairman. Stall sat up and leaned forward. "Any particular rumor, Ted?"

"Well . . ." Baldwin looked through the cloud of smoke at the canopy of great oaks beyond the tall window. "Some are saying that we . . . the English Department, are under investigation."

"Investigation? For what reason?"

"Oh, you know, Tom. All this Johns Committee bother. Commies, subversives, agitators, the NAACP."

But not men who embrace. Firmly, chairmanly, Stall said, "It'll pass."

Baldwin's voice was suddenly full of a strain that Stall had never heard in it before. "So will I. So will you. We'll all pass, Tom. But when will *this* pass? How long do we have to endure this damned destructive stupidity before someone calls bullshit on it?"

And who will that someone be? Stall recalled the newsreel footage of Joseph Welch, the lawyer who had said to Senator Joe McCarthy, *Have you no sense of decency, sir?* Where was Florida's Joseph Welch? He said, "I don't know how long it'll be, but universities, in America anyway, tend to outlast Bible-thumping demagogues."

"This isn't America. This is Florida."

Stall laughed and shook his head. "Yeah, well, we're a bit behind the times here, but we'll be all right." He didn't say, *We'll catch up*, because he was not sure he wanted to be in time with everything that was happening in the North and West. *I'm an old-fashioned guy*, Stall often said to himself, *and there's nothing wrong with that*. He could hear Maureen saying, *Somebody has to do it*. Until recently he had found this to be reassuring.

"Any other rumors, Ted?" Stall hoped this question would send Baldwin on his way.

"Actually, Tom, there is one. Some say you've been appointed to head this . . . investigation of *us* . . . the department."

The top of Stall's head went hot and light. His hands made involuntary fists on the desk. He closed his eyes and repeated in the sanctum of his self-control: *Patience, Stall. Patience infinite*. He managed a strained smile. "Who are the . . . *some* who say this, Ted?"

Baldwin waved an impatient hand at the smoke in the air. "You know I can't tell you that."

So, Baldwin had not come here to inform on the rumor-mongers. Protecting them could mean that he agreed with them, or simply that he would not violate confidences.

Stall managed, "Well, when change comes, when a . . . new man comes into a job like this one, some people are bound to be anxious. But . . . you all know me. Surely you don't think I'd take this position knowing I'd be asked to . . . investigate my colleagues."

"Well, *I* don't think it." Baldwin waved his hand at the smoke again.

Stall wondered if he had come here on his own or had been sent as the representative of "some who were saying." Wondered if this conversation was really a warning: *We're on to you, Stall. Better watch your step*.

And he wondered if he, as the new chairman, should return fire.

"Next time you hear a rumor, Ted, tell the folks you hear it from to drop by and see me. I'm happy to talk about this with anyone who has . . . concerns. But . . ." Stall stretched his arms elaborately above his head and yawned so that the message was clear. He was ready for this talk to end. "The semester's about to start, and we all have work to do. Let's not let this Committee business panic us into any rash action."

Baldwin stood and imitated Stall's stretch and yawn. *They say it's catching.* He bobbled his Groucho eyebrows again. The faculty funny man. "How's it going with Helen?" He shot a look at the outer office where Earl Grey was safely locked in Helen Markham's desk.

"We're getting along fine. She's the soul of efficiency."

"Did you know she's a friend of mine? Quite a dancer, Helen. In another life, we partner down at the armory. She can still shake a leg." Baldwin waited.

Stall smiled. "I envy you that, Ted." *You and Helen?* "I could never do much more than a dignified shuffle."

Baldwin stepped gracefully backward toward the door. "Yes, Helen and I are dance partners. That's a secret you can share with anyone."

Several minutes later it hit Stall. What Ted Baldwin was telling him. *She warned me*, Ted Baldwin was saying. *Helen Markham typed that file.*

Before going home, Stall walked his inspection of Anderson Hall looking for anything abandoned or amiss. In a classroom on the third floor he found a copy of Lattimore's translation of *The Iliad*. A magnificent work, mostly detested by students. He was on his way back to his office to drop the book in the unofficial lost-and-found, a cardboard box behind Helen Markham's desk, when he saw Jimmy Bright backing out of the faculty mail room, mopping as he went. Bright's big wheeled bucket with attached brushes, bottles, and rags stood in the empty hallway behind him. The smell of pine cleaner was strong as Stall approached. Bright looked up, his eyes sending fear, then blinking to his standard meet-the-white-man gaze. The expression was a bland friendliness with a dash of obsequious cringe. Stall had seen the look in many black faces, and he hated it, not because it was wrong or unnecessary but because men like him were its cause. In the world he loved, this should not be the way men of different colors met in an empty hallway.

Bright stood almost at attention, his mop dripping at his side.

"Hello, Jimmy."

Bright flashed a smile. "Hello, Dr. Stall. How are you, suh?"

"Fine, Jimmy, and you?" On a whim, Stall reached out, took the mop from Bright's hand, put it into the bucket of water, and said, "Jimmy, let's talk a minute." He turned and walked back to his office, knowing Bright would follow.

In the office, Stall behind the big desk, Jimmy Bright standing, Stall said, "Have a seat, Jimmy. Please."

"Ah . . . yes suh." Bright's green university work shirt and trousers were sweated through in spots, and he seemed reluctant to rest a workingman's body in Stall's chair.

"It's all right, Jimmy. Go ahead and sit." Stall added, "It's been a long day," because it was the close of the day for him, and he was tired. He had no idea when Jimmy Bright's work day began or when it ended. The custodian gave Stall's chair a last dubious look and sat down.

"What can I do for you, Dr. Stall?"

There was no good way to go ahead with this. No way it would not be awkward for both of them. "Jimmy, I want to ask you about something. You clean the basement men's room?"

"Yes suh, clean them all. This my building. Take me my whole shift to give her a good cleaning. Do it one day, then again the next. How I make my week."

Stall tried to read Bright's face. Was this longer-than-expected description of the man's job a hedge against an accusation of laziness or incompetence? Stall smiled. "We all appreciate the work you do here, Jimmy, the way you keep the place clean for us. I want you to know that."

Bright's face gave nothing back, neither pride nor appreciation.

"But, Jimmy, it's the basement men's room I'm interested in."

There it was, the narrowing of the eyes, a tightness around the mouth. "The men's room, suh? Anybody complaining, I sure can fix it. You just let me know what's wrong. Course, that old plumbing down there got some leaks, and ain't nothing I can do about that."

"The room's clean enough, Jimmy. It's fine as far as I know. That's not what I want to talk to you about."

It was hard for him to guess Jimmy Bright's age. He could have been thirty or forty-five. Stall knew from his youth in South Carolina that blacks talked among themselves about this agelessness. *Black don't crack* meant that their skin didn't wrinkle as white skin did. Bright was maybe an inch shorter than Stall, about six feet even, and had no fat on him. When he rolled up his shirtsleeves on the hottest days, his arms looked rock hard. Stall had never seen him do anything but work at a steady pace. If he took smoke breaks, ever sat down to rest, ate lunch from a paper sack, Stall had never seen it.

"Jimmy, Dr. Harding, when he retired, gave me a file, a report on something you told him happened in the basement men's room."

With Stall's words, Bright's head moved back an inch. "Dr. Harding told you about that?"

"He gave me the report, Jimmy."

"Well, yes suh, it happened."

"Why did you tell Dr. Harding about what you saw?"

"He asked me to. Said it be better for me and him if I told him about anything like that."

For me and him. "Yes, I imagine he would say that."

"You know what he mean, suh?"

"Yes, I do."

Amos Harding, a man of the generation before Stall's, had understood the many ways an encounter between a Negro custodian and two white professors in a men's room could go terribly wrong. And things hadn't changed much since Harding had learned this hard truth. Stall knew it too.

"You trusted Dr. Harding with that . . . information?"

"Yes suh, I did." *And I'm trusting you now.*

"All right, Jimmy. Thank you."

"That all then, Dr. Stall?"

"That's all, Jimmy. Thank you."

Stall sat still in his office until he heard Jimmy Bright push the wheeled bucket to the end of the hallway and out the door that led to the iron staircase.

Riding the bus home, he asked himself, *Why did you question Jimmy Bright? Isn't seeking information about other people for no good reason exactly what the Committee does?* He searched his thoughts for a reason, and something came ringing back to him. *Maybe you wanted to know something good about Amos Harding. Know that he put names in a file not just to protect himself and his department but to protect the least of them, a mere custodian.*

TWENTY-FIVE

The next day, Stall heard a dull roar through his office window. It came from the south side of the campus. He asked Helen Markham if she knew what was going on. She shook her head.

He went up a flight to Sophie Green's office. She knew.

"Some students demonstrating at the *Alligator.*"

She was writing, possibly one of her brilliant papers for the *Publications of the Modern Language Association.* Stall glanced at the rows of neatly penned sentences, hardly a scratch-out or a smudgy hesitation. The words seemed to flow on as though from some location beyond them both. Writing was a hard thing for Stall, thoughts stumbling from his mind like stunned soldiers from smoky thickets. He pulled his eyes from her words to her untroubled face.

"At the *Alligator*?"

"Yes." She stood and went to her window. He stood beside her looking out. They could see nothing but the green mysteries of the old oak boughs and the sidewalk below. Students drifted along carrying books, smoking, talking. The sounds of cheering, then of someone speaking into a microphone, were faint and theatrical through the trees.

"Demonstrating against what?" *Or for it?*

"The *Alligator* has decided to tell the stories of students who have been approached by the Committee."

"Approached? You mean students the Committee asked to inform on professors?"

"No, I mean homosexual students who've been harassed, in some cases by university officials. Or by the Committee. According to Stephen, the Committee has asked the dean of students to dismiss students who are homosexual. Or to force them to submit to treatment for mental illness as a condition of staying in school." She gave him a baleful look. "The Committee's position is that contact with homosexuals is dangerous for normal people."

Stall moved away from the widow, to the other side of her desk. "And Stephen thinks it's right to put these students' stories in the newspaper."

"He won't use their real names."

"A lot of protection that'll give them. Don't you think he's taking the freedom of the press a little too far?" Stall remembered Stephen Levy's tired arguments about classes and individuals and how change comes about.

"A freedom is absolute. By definition it can't be taken too far."

"Oh, Sophie, you know that's absurd." *And it's the kind of bullshit that makes universities vulnerable to people like Charley Johns who believe the Bible is the literal truth.*

She said archly, "We've established that we disagree about these things."

"How did the, uh, demonstrators find out about this?"

"Someone on the *Alligator* staff must have talked."

"God help those kids when their *stories* are told."

That night, by order of President James Connor, the campus police entered the office of the *Alligator* and stood guard while the locks were changed. The student newspaper was closed until further notice. Connor called it a press holiday, a hiatus to coincide with the opening of the fall semester and the arrival of the new freshman class. He assured the campus community that the *Alligator* would reopen soon and that he would be in conversations with the newspaper's leadership about some of the editorial positions they had taken—and about moving forward in a responsible way. The next day on the quadrangle in front of the library, Stephen Levy, his staff, and about fifty representatives of various clubs, groups, and organizations, including a few members of the local klavern of the Ku Klux Klan, held rallies that soon degenerated into a shouting match that became a brawl. It took both the campus police and some officers of the Gainesville Police Department to restore order. After separating the various factions and assessing the damage (black eyes, bruised knuckles, and one or two bloody noses), the police huddled and decided to declare the quadrangle off limits and send everyone home without any arrests.

Hearing the ruckus, Stall walked over from his office and watched the last of it from the sidelines along with a handful of professors and librarians, and some students who had spilled from the library and classroom buildings. From Stall's vantage point, the melee looked like a scene from a Mack Sennett flick, and he wasn't the only one to chuckle at the awkward struggle. Stephen Levy left the fight with some honorable bruises, and Stall watched the boy walk away with his *Alligator* comrades. They swaggered, proud of their battle scars. *Battle? What am I laughing at?* On the way back to the English building, he fell into step with Ed McPhail, the balletic campus cop. McPhail was breathing hard, but bore no signs of damage from the fracas.

"Admirable restraint, Ed," Stall said.

"Thanks, professor. Next time maybe not." McPhail touched the billy club at his hip.

"Yes," said Stall. *How easily these things can get out of hand.* He and McPhail knew that passions could outpace reason at the drop of a hat. Or of a leaflet, or a banner, or a woman's glove. Civilization was fragile. A cop's business was to keep passionate people from breaking what was fragile. Stall wanted to reach over and rest his hand on McPhail's shoulder. Show the man his gratitude. Instead, he turned toward the steps that led to his office with a friendly, "Take care, Ed. See you at the opening game."

Stall sat looking out his office window at University Avenue through the gap in the oak boughs. Soon the street would teem with students and their parents unloading the sustaining goods of the new academic year. He would see the tearful goodbyes of parents, fathers giving their final advice, and in some cases a "Good riddance." Stall had ignored the mission Jim Connor had designed for him as long as he safely could. As the days passed, he had come to dread the ringing of the phone. He had all but considered telling Helen Markham, *If the president calls, I'm out.* With Connor, Stall figured he had two options: he could throw Ted Baldwin into the threshing machine of the Committee, or he could find a way to get Frank Vane and Cyrus Tate to look elsewhere. If he gave up Baldwin, he could tell Connor, *He's the only one. There are no other homosexuals in my department, and there are no Communists.* If Connor pressed him, he could produce Harding's file as his proof. *See, just one embrace in my building, and one of the two lovers is dead.*

Stall had argued with Stephen Levy and Sophie Green that individuals mattered more than classes or "the masses," and since the war, that had been his creed. He had seen the individuals lying in their twisted, obscene poses in the snow, their bloated, frozen hands reaching up from the white drifts as though to implore the skies for mercy. If he gave up Ted Baldwin, he'd prove Sophie Green and Stephen Levy right. *To make an omelet, you have to break eggs.* And if he broke Baldwin to save English, the Committee might concentrate on other prey, probably the Political Science Department where faculty with left-wing sympathies were rife.

After Baldwin, maybe he could convince Jim Connor to stand up to Frank Vane. *Isn't one lamb to the slaughter enough?*

The other option lay somehow with Roney Tyler in the murky underground where the man had met Jack Leaf. Roney had done the bidding of Cyrus Tate. He had lured Jack Leaf to a bus station. Stall had to assume that Roney had known Jack before that night, and that Cyrus Tate had recruited Roney somewhere in the underground where men like Jack found men like Roney. But where was that underground, and who else lived there?

Stall picked the Red Lion, a shabby bar on 441, for a meeting with Roney Tyler. The place was a dreary imitation of a British pub. It sported a dartboard, a display of pewter mugs, and a framed Union Jack, convincing enough for the college boys who lived in the apartments that lined 441. Stall figured an English professor and an auto mechanic with an eye patch would fit right in.

He bought a pitcher of beer and set two mugs on the table. Roney poured the beer.

"Did you take that eye to the hospital?" The makeshift blood-crusted patch looked fetid.

"Naw, a girl at the motor court. She put this bandage on me. I been putting ice on it at night like you said."

"Look, Roney, you need to see a doctor. If I pay for it, will you go?"

Sulky, Roney looked around at the empty pub. "Maybe."

Stall pulled a twenty from his wallet. "This'll cover a trip to the emergency room."

Roney put the money in his Bill's Body Shop shirt pocket.

They drank in silence for a few minutes, then Stall said quietly, "Are there . . . bars where you meet other men?"

Roney winced. "In this city? You kidding me?"

"You must meet them somewhere."

"Look professor, there are bars everywhere, and there are men in them, all kinds of men, and you have to be careful."

"Where'd you meet Jack?"

"At a guy's house."

"Who?"

"I ain't telling you that." Roney's clear eye filled with suspicion. "You said you wasn't interested in meeting men."

"I'm not. Not in the way you mean."

Roney shook his head like a redneck who was born, but not yesterday.

"Look, Roney, you said you need that money fast, and I said I'd help you get it. I can do that, or Mrs. Leaf can get a lawyer and contest the bank account. She might not win, but she can sure as hell cost you time and money. If you want my help, I need yours."

TWENTY-SIX

The house was perched on a bluff at the edge of Paynes Prairie, with an expansive view of what William Bartram, in his *Travels*, had called "the Great North Florida Savanna." Stall had seen the house many times while driving north from Micanopy. It stood alone on its promontory with cantilevered beams supporting a terrace that jutted forty feet or so out over the saw grass and palmetto. When Roney parked his dented International Harvester pickup in the sandy circular drive and they got out, Stall heard the faint tinkle of a jazz piano, a recording of "You're the Top." Stall counted the cars in the drive—a Lincoln, a Cadillac, two foreign jobs, a Jaguar and a sporty MG, two beleaguered Chevys, and a Ford Fairlane with a missing hood ornament. He looked over at Roney, who pointed at the Jaguar. "The guy owns this house don't take his car to Bill's."

"Am I welcome here?"

"I'm welcome, and you with me, ain't you?"

"I'm with you." *In for a penny*.

Roney knocked and a man in what Stall thought might be called lounging pajamas answered the door. He was about forty with black hair combed straight back and a golden tan. The kind you had to work at. You had to have time to work at it.

The man smiled at Roney and gave Stall a friendly nod. "Ah, Roney! And who's this?"

"This here's Tom. He's shy, don't want me to tell his last name."

The man shifted his drink from right to left and gave Stall a strong grip. He spoke to Roney: "You know that's all right here, Roney." A look at Tom. "But only the first time. We find that it's better for everyone if, let's say, the levels of knowledge are equal."

The man stepped aside and, as they passed, said, "Welcome,

Tom. The bar's open, help yourself. We don't stand on ceremony."

Stall thanked him, thinking of how he might describe this to Maureen someday. How this story might elicit a very rare "Holy *shit!*" from her.

He went to the bar where he made some acquaintances, careful to give his first name only. This raised eyebrows. He was answered in kind by a Gerry, a Leonard, and a Keith. It had occurred to him on the drive out here that he might see someone he knew. Or even that Cyrus Tate might be here. This was the place, Roney had told him, where he had met Tate.

Stall stood at the bar drinking a martini and watching Roney circulate. From the way the mechanic was received, it was clear to Stall that Roney was a regular, well-liked and more or less comfortable in this company. Another surprise was that the jazz piano was not a recording. A handsome man dressed in a loosely constructed black silk jacket and a green paisley cravat was playing it. He had moved on to "Begin the Beguine," rendering it flawlessly to Stall's admittedly uneducated ear. The man looked familiar. Stall had seen him somewhere.

He was feeling conspicuously alone when Roney finally returned to the bar. Roney poured himself a bourbon and water and they turned to face the room. Roney leaned toward Stall and whispered, "That's Eugen Brugge. He pronounces his first name *Oy-gen*. Funny, if you ask me. I just call him Eugene, and he's okay with it. With me, anyway. He don't like it if other people get it wrong."

Ah, thought Stall, *Eugen Brugge. The genius enfant terrible of the University College.*

The University College was the university's quaint name for the general education courses of the first two undergraduate years—logic, math, the sciences that did not lead to medicine or engineering, American institutions, and freshman English. The University College faculty were, for the most part, capable and dedicated, and some of them, like Eugen Brugge, the Belgian polyglot, were brilliant. They all had in common the inability or the disinclination to publish. A few, perhaps even many, resented the graduate faculty, calling them snobs and prima donnas whose comparatively light teaching loads and higher pay made them lords of the campus. But as everyone knew, it was publish or perish on the rarified heights where Stall and his colleagues lived and worked, and it was easy enough to fall from those heights.

It was rumored that Eugen Brugge did not even have an undergraduate degree, much less a PhD. People Stall knew said the guy was just so damned brilliant, and could do so many things that nobody else in Gainesville could even attempt, that every possible exception had been made to keep him here and happy. It was said that he spoke Russian, French, German, Italian, Spanish, and, of course, Belgian fluently, and could read Latin, Greek, Sanskrit, Farsi, and Arabic passably well. He knew opera and could sing and play it. He had been a concert pianist before an injury to one of his hands had ended what had promised to be a brilliant career. His skill at the jazz piano was on display right now. He knew more about Continental literature, especially the emerging theater of the absurd, than anyone south of Charlottesville. He spoke of having met Beckett and Pirandello, and was said to be on close personal terms with Ionesco and Giraudoux. Stall guessed that some of the paintings that hung on the wall, reminiscent of Magritte, were his, and he had heard that Brugge had acted in plays in the university's Theater Department and in the local community theater. When the University College needed someone to lecture on anything, Brugge was called into service. His air of authority was absolute, and even if he was fraudulent on some exotic subject, who in Gainesville could prove it? When the opera singer Richard Tucker had come to town for a concert, the *Gainesville Sun* had reported that he stayed at Brugge's house. The house where Stall and Roney Tyler now stood sipping their drinks.

Men came and went, mixed and mingled. This seemed to be an after-work gathering, an airlock for the relaxation of men who would soon go home to lives that might be a lot like Stall's.

Roney said, "Come on. I got something to show you."

The cantilevered terrace Stall had seen from highway 441 was a pool deck. Several men swam or lounged in the late-afternoon sunlight, two of them nude. *Christ*, Stall thought, *the underground is the high ground*.

Roney pointed at a man who sat by himself in a bathing suit, smoking and gazing out over the prairie. "That's the guy who knows Cyrus Tate."

Stall gave Roney a discrete double take. "Knows?"

"Yeah," Roney said.

"You mean . . . ?"

"I think so. I seen them together a few times here." Roney headed back toward the house.

Stall walked over to the man in the bathing suit. "Hell of a view."

"Your first time seeing it, I take it."

Stall nodded. "My name's Tom."

"Ah, a Tom. I'm a Ron." The man lifted his cigarette pack to Stall.

Stall said, "Somehow I never picked up the habit. Although the army tried hard to get me hooked."

"The army. The bad old days, right?"

"Right you are."

"Sit down, Tom. Looking up at you makes my neck hurt."

"Sorry." Stall sat on a deck chair where a wet bathing suit had recently been.

"What do you do, Tom?"

"I profess."

"You what?"

"I teach at the university. And you?"

"I doctor. Pediatric surgery." The man held up two manicured hands. "Hands of a surgeon." He laughed quietly.

"That's impressive."

"It's a job."

"It's a bit more than that. You save the lives of children."

"When I can. Sometimes they die."

Stall immediately liked the man, partly because he seemed completely comfortable in this place talking about who he was and what he did, and because *sometimes they die* was a truth that seemed neither to trouble nor to please him. It simply was.

The surgeon said, "So, how did you find your way to this oasis above the prairie of Payne?"

Stall decided to risk it. It was what he had come for. "A man I know told me about it. Cyrus Tate. He said I might be welcome here."

The doctor seemed surprised. "Oh, so you know Cy Tate? Somehow you don't seem like his type."

Stall gave his best imitation of an easy chuckle. "Yeah, Cy can be . . . rough around the edges." He remembered Tate sitting in his office, Stall wondering if the man's fashionable suit concealed a gun.

"Surprisingly cultured in his way too. If you don't let him preach the gospel to you. Actually, he's pretty good at the preaching, but I'm afraid my churchgoing days are over."

Stall wasn't sure about this, but he said it anyway: "Mine too."

"The war?" The doctor gave Stall a soldier's brotherly expression.

"Mostly, and some studying I did."

The doctor looked out at the prairie again. "I did my first surgery on a hospital ship off Okinawa. You learn a lot very quickly, and you don't have much time to think about the bodies that pass under your knife. You fix what you can and move on. When I got home, I never wanted to cut on a grown man again. That's why I specialize in children. Do you think that's strange?"

All Stall could think to say was, "An army doctor saved my life in Germany."

The man lifted his glass. "Well, here's to the medical profession. May we know them only when we need them."

Stall touched his glass to the doctor's. "My name's Tom Stall."

"Ron Davidson. What do you profess, Tom Stall?"

"English. Modern British and American."

"Ah, the modern stuff. How do you know what's good, what will last?"

"That's part of the fun. You trust your instincts." But Stall knew it was more complicated than that. Reputations came and went. Greatness could be buried for centuries, and mediocrity could reign for just as long. He said as much.

Davidson considered it. "We don't have a lot of greatness in my business, but incompetence becomes apparent very quickly."

Stall said, "I assume you know what Cy Tate does for a living?"

"Yeah, I know. We all do, but he doesn't do it here."

"I guess that makes him some sort of hypocrite."

"Oh, he's worse than that. Much worse, but even a moral crusader needs a doctor from time to time."

"Have you seen Tate . . . professionally?"

"That would be a professional confidence, wouldn't it, Professor

Stall?" Davidson stubbed out his cigarette and looked around the deck and into the gloom of the house where the piano tinkled out "Just a Summer Love Affair." Then the doctor said, "I suppose we're all hypocrites here."

"Sorry," and Stall really was. Not for trying to learn about Tate, but for putting a good man in a hard spot.

Dr. Ron Davidson glanced at his watch. "Well, I've got rounds tonight. Better go get into my doctor disguise." He walked to a nearby table and retrieved his wallet from a jacket slung over a chair. "Here's my card. Call me if you like. We'll have a drink." The doctor waited for Stall to respond in kind, but Stall could not give him a phone number. He stammered, "Thank you, I will."

"Maybe you will. And, uh, don't worry, Tom, I won't tell anyone I saw you here."

Roney drove Stall to his bus stop.

"You get what you wanted, professor?"

"Some of it."

"When do I get my money?"

"As soon as possible. I might need your help with a few more things before you do."

"Don't get me in no more trouble, professor."

Stall was suddenly angry. "Tell you what, Roney. You stop calling me professor and I won't *start* calling you an asshole. Who names a kid Roney, anyway?"

Roney looked hurt. "Assholes, I guess. It was my grandfather's name."

Stall took a deep breath, sighed it out. "Sorry, Roney. I shouldn't have said that."

"What do you want me to call you?"

"Tom will do."

Roney took Stall's twenty dollars from his shirt pocket and handed it back. "That place was crawling with doctors. One of 'em took me in the bathroom and looked at my eye. He thinks it'll be all right, looks worse than it is. I'm going to see him again tomorrow."

Stall got out and leaned into the window. "I'll talk to Mrs. Leaf about the money."

* * *

Stall called Sarah Leaf and told her he considered it to be in her best interest not to contest the bank account. He said that Roney Tyler was a volatile and possibly even a dangerous individual, and that, even though twenty thousand dollars was a lot of money to lose, it would not be wise or even safe for her to get into an argument with Tyler. "And," Stall softened his voice, almost whispering into the phone, "after all, it was Jack's intention to do this, however strange it seems to us."

"But why didn't he do something like this for *me*, for his children?" There was an infinite sadness in the voice at the other end.

She had not said much to Stall about the Leaf family's finances. She had mentioned an insurance policy that would cover Jack's final expenses. He had no idea what savings or additional assets Sarah had. She lived in a lovely house in a fashionable neighborhood. If she sold the house, she would do well. Stall thought he recalled that she had majored in math in college. Surely with such a background she could get work. But even with a job, Sarah Leaf was almost certainly looking at what was politely called reduced circumstances.

Quietly, sadly, she said, "All right, Tom. I'll just forget about the money."

Stall called an officer he knew at the Dixie Fidelity Bank and Trust and in confidence told him the story of Jack, Sarah, and Roney Tyler. The banker said, "Bring Mr. Tyler in, and I'll guide him through the process, if that's what you and Mrs. Leaf want me to do."

TWENTY-SEVEN

"Since when do you stop off at the Gold Coast for a drink before coming home for your *first* martini with me?"

They were finishing a dinner of beef spare ribs, steamed asparagus, and mashed potatoes. Stall was hoping for a bowl of vanilla ice cream after he made short work of his last rib. Corey had been excused to watch TV, the sound of gunshots and stampeding cattle murmuring from the next room. Stall gave his wife an offended look, but his heart was not in it.

She shook her head at his bad acting. "You're wondering how I know? Well, two things. The smell of your breath and the look in your eye when you come home later than usual acting sober as a judge. Remember, my grandfather *was* a judge, and I know what a sober one *really* looks like. And number two: Eileen Mears saw you in the Gold Coast, twice. She thought it would be a good idea to let me know."

Maureen's expression looked to Stall more like disgust at being *told something* about her husband than triumph at having the goods on him. Eileen Mears, who lived down the block and sometimes visited Maureen for coffee in the afternoons, was the wife of a sociologist whose area of research was "the family."

Stall was all for families, but held sociology in an esteem about the equal of phrenology. "Well, I'll have to be more careful when Eileen Mears is lurking about."

Maureen's gaze was steely.

He shrugged and raised his hands in the I-give-up way. Gunshots crescendoed from the other room. He tried humor: "You got me, podner. I'm guilty of drinkage. I guess it's straight to the dipso wing at the old hoosegow."

Maureen took a significantly slow sip of her ice water. Her only beverage tonight.

"So, Carrie Nation," Stall said, "when did you start counting my drinks?"

"When you started . . . acting strange."

"Strangely," Stall said.

"Pedantically," Maureen said.

"Okay, at least I'm guilty of that. But you knew that when you married me." He gave her a half smile, inviting her to relent a little, and looked down at his plate where the last rib was getting cold. "All right, I guess there's nothing to do but tell the truth. I've been under a lot of strain at work, so yeah, I stop off for a . . . a little buck-me-up before getting on the bus. It's probably a bad thing to . . . start, so I promise you I'll stop." When the words were out of his mouth, he thought, *What if I told her everything?*

"What strain?"

"Well, obviously Jack's death, and this new job . . . and people *dropping by* to talk about that damned Committee and what I'm going to do to protect the department. And some of them, apparently, think I've been made *acting* chairman so that I can sneak around peering through the transoms to see who's . . . Christ, I don't know what to tell them. And . . ." Here Stall knew he might go wrong, even in his evasion and his avoidance, but he had to give Maureen something she didn't already know. "And Sarah, Sarah Leaf, called to tell me that Jack gave some money, actually quite a lot of it, to . . . a man."

"A man? What man?"

"One of his . . . you know, friends."

"You mean one of his lovers?"

"I guess so."

"That bastard. Did he give *any* money to Sarah and the kids?"

"I don't know. Of course, there's the house and other assets. It's not as though they'll be destitute or anything."

There were tears in Maureen's eyes. Stall got up, poured his martini into the sink, and went to her. He leaned over and pressed his cheek to hers, hot and wet.

"Don't worry about Sarah. She'll be all right."

Stall's wife withdrew her warm face from his and stood. "I'm not worried about *her*. I'm worried about *us*."

Stall knew the answer could be terrible, but he had to ask: "Why, honey? Why are you worried about us?"

"Because *I'm* supposed to be your buck-me-up after work, not some damned drink at the Gold Coast. I thought you knew that."

She ran for the stairs. When her heels tattooed the oak floor at the top, Stall heard the first wracking sob. The bedroom door slammed.

TWENTY-EIGHT

It became known in Gainesville that the Committee was holding interrogations in the Thomas Hotel. Persons to be interviewed received polite phone calls inviting them to conversations with the Committee. Those who demurred received assurances as to the Committee's good intentions: the investigators only wished to gather information about important matters regarding the university, its faculty, students, and administrators. When subjects were seated before the Committee, and the tape recorder blinked red, and the yellow legal pads lay flat on the table, and pens were poised, it was a different matter entirely. Politeness fled. Little by little, questions became more insistent and more intimate. Interviews often lasted three hours and, at the end, wrung-out subjects had been skillfully pressed to reveal their most shocking secrets. Charley Johns asked one witness, "Now, when you suck another man's penis, do you get the same sensation out of it as when you have yours sucked?" Some witnesses came away feeling that they had provided a strange pornographic entertainment for the members of the Committee.

In the early days of the Committee's work, few subjects considered themselves to be at serious risk and few took advantage of legal counsel. It was only after some declined invitations to these conversations that the Committee began to issue subpoenas.

These men and women, a few of them students, left their sessions with the Committee and returned to their jobs and friends and families and told no one—but still Gainesville knew. Some people who passed the Thomas Hotel did not look, as some turn away from a bloody accident on the highway, but others did look and sometimes the hotel drew small crowds of the curious, people hoping to see the Committee come and go, to see the brightest star of the chamber, Charley Johns, walk to his car carrying his briefcase full of names, careers, lives. Some people who gathered hoped to see the subjects of the Committee's inquiry emerge into the light.

At the west end of the second-floor hallway, the faculty mail room stood opposite a large, glassed-in bulletin board that listed English courses in the fall and winter, and exam results for the winter and spring. Four times a year, the bulletin board drew crowds of students. The mail room, with its mimeograph machine and coffee pot, was a faculty gathering place. Faculty boxes yielded both the dreary campus mail and the more exciting mail from the Great Out There where acceptances and rejections of scholarly articles and books, and sometimes even job offers, percolated like the passable coffee in the Sunbeam pot grudgingly serviced by Helen Markham.

As Stall entered the mail room and walked to his box, a quiet conversation among four of his colleagues ceased. One man walked out before Stall could look up from the trivia he had pulled from his box; the other three stood looking at Stall as though they expected him to explain something. *What the hell?* Hands full of mail, Stall faced them. *I'm your chairman. If there's something I need to know, tell me.* He waited. No one spoke. What was it they shared—a secret? A fear?

Stall slapped the mail against his palm like a man punishing a dog. "What's up, you guys? The coffee *that* bad?" A second man walked out without a word and with only a glance back from the door.

"Fred, what's going on here?" Stall hated his own exasperated tone.

Fred Parsons, who taught American lit with a specialization in Washington Irving, was middle-aged, a middle-grade teacher, and middling in scholarship. His face was round and red, and his pale blue eyes were set too close together. He had tenure, was fully promoted, and probably couldn't be moved to publish another word. Parsons said, "*You* haven't heard?"

"Oh, for Christ's sake, Fred, what's going on? Heard *what*?"

"Well," Parsons said breezily, "not for *me* to put *you* in the know."

The other man who had stayed, Bob Reynard, an eighteenth-century scholar who specialized in Dryden, said, "You should ask Gilson."

"Yes," Parsons added definitively, "he's the one to ask." He moved to leave.

Stall realized that he was blocking the door and stepped aside.

When their footsteps had receded on the old boards of the hallway, Stall shook his head and wiped his brow with the white handkerchief that Maureen had tucked into his pocket as he'd left the house that morning. He looked at the greasy sweat on the cloth in his hand and wished he could wipe away this sudden strangeness that had fouled the faculty mail room. He ground his jaws and set off for the basement and the office of Roland Gilson, the newly hired assistant professor of the medieval period.

The basement was dank, Florida's water table being what it was, and despite the best efforts of Jimmy Bright, the faint smell of urine from the men's room midway down the hall mingled with the odor of pine-scented cleaner. Roland Gilson's door was closed and locked. A hand-lettered sign was tacked to it: *Classes are canceled for the rest of the week*. A signature slanted across the bottom of the page: *Dr. Roland Gilson*.

Gilson had left no explanation (though explanations to students must be kept to a minimum, the usual falsehood being *due to illness*), and not a word about a date of return or whom to contact for assignments or other information. Departmental policy called for notification of the chairman of any canceled classes. Most faculty, especially the senior men, simply telephoned Helen Markham, who did not bother the chairman with the details, but still . . . this was sloppy work by an untenured man in only his second year. Stall searched his memory for Roland Gilson and found only a few cordial words at faculty parties, an encounter or two in hallways ("How's that article on Gower coming along?" "Soon, sir, soon." The usual young-man-in-a-hurry smile). And there was a vague recollection of a nervous but conventionally pretty young wife.

And why am I here seeking Roland Gilson?

In a fast walk, Stall made the end of the hallway and took the stairs three at a time. Surely Helen Markham would know what was going on.

She was sitting at her desk, glasses perched at the end of her nose, pink sweater hanging from her bony shoulders, and the phone in her hand. "Just in time!" By two fingers, she held the phone out to him. Her eyes were unusually large.

Stall's lips formed a silent *Who?*

Helen Markham's lips formed *Him!* She rolled her eyes in the direction of Tigert Hall.

Stall took the phone. *Him who?*

The president. His fear confirmed.

"Hello, Jim."

"Tom, can you come over here for a minute?" The president's voice was excited but not unpleasantly so.

"Sure. Be right there."

Stall stepped out of the powerful sunlight into the cool dim of Tigert Hall and heard scraping footsteps in the stairwell to his right. Roland Gilson emerged from the well, and in a way that was almost comical rocked back on his heels at the sight of Stall. Stall fitted a smile to his face and prepared himself to greet young Gilson, to ask in his most affable way what the hell Bob Reynard had meant. *You should ask Gilson*.

What Stall saw stopped his tongue. Roland Gilson looked like hell. His light-green summer suit coat was sweated through at the armpits, and his darker-green tie was askew and looked like it had been knotted for a month. His swollen face was gray and his eyes seemed to swim in a viscous red liquid above his cheeks. The smell of whiskey found its way across the three feet between them.

Gilson rocked forward but not comically, and a look of sly speculation came into his eyes. "Aha," he said, "our new chairman, entering the storied halls of Tigert. See how boldly he walks, and with what assurance. No doubt not his first visit to this capital of the empire, no doubt one of many visits, and what *messages* he brings with him . . ."

How long could this . . . epic recitation of Gilson's go on? Stall raised his hand in the *stop now* gesture. "Roland, is there something I can *do* for you? You don't look . . . very well. I'll be happy to . . ." Stall glanced at his watch. The president was waiting for him. He wasn't sure what is was he'd be happy to do.

"Aha!" Again Gilson rocked on feet set wide apart as though the floor moved beneath him. "Aha! Our chairman, *my* chairman, wants to do something for me. How nice! How very, very nice! In fact, *très gentil!* But . . . *actually*, Dr. Stall, you clever dog, it's what you've done *to* me that we should talk about."

Gilson balled his fists and looked at them as though they belonged to someone else. He went into a wobbly boxer's stance and threw a few loose punches into the air. His eyes took on a wild hilarity. "Stall, you miserable son of a bitch, I ought to knock your pearly teeth out. Every goddamned one of them."

Three students entered from the halo of summer light at the door and stood behind Stall. He stepped aside for them, two boys and a girl, older and well dressed, the boys in ties and shirtsleeves, "student leaders" probably, on their way to some business here in the administration building. Stall and Gilson watched them take in the situation, its strangeness furrowing their brows as they hurried on past the two men.

Stall tried, "Roland, I just don't—"

"Aw, go to hell," and Gilson shuffled toward the door on wide-set feet. As he made the hot light and raised a shaking hand to shield his eyes, Stall noticed that one of his shoes was unlaced. A green sock had fallen down over the shoe like shed skin. Stall took the handkerchief from his coat pocket and blotted his face, pressing fingers into his eyes where a headache had begun to pound.

Margaret Braithwaite glanced up from the rattling Olivetti and said, "Right on through." She looked, as always, perfectly coiffed and dressed, and as cool as a spring day, but her eyes roamed Stall with questions. Had young Gilson passed this way? Had she seen, smelled him?

Two men stood before President Connor's desk: Connor himself, in shirtsleeves, apparently too full of nervous energy to sit, and Amos Harding, a man Stall had thought he'd seen the last of. Harding wore the usual black suit and narrow black tie and held a file folder in his right hand. Connor's coat hung on the rack by the door with the Panama hat on its shoulders. The rack looked to Stall like a very thin man with a large head.

Connor gave Stall a stern, approving look, the look of a man who has sent a boy on a difficult errand and seen him return with the goods. "I want to thank you, Tom."

Stall had only seconds to decide. Accept this man's thanks or question it.

Connor held out his small, tough hand and said, again, "Thank you."

Stall shook the hand, his own feeling too large and too soft. "You're welcome, sir"—better not to say *Jim* with Harding here—"but . . ."

But Connor had turned and was pacing the space in front of his desk, his eyes on the ceiling miles away. Stall stole a glance at Harding, whose face gave nothing away. Connor stopped at the window that looked down on the main entrance to the campus. The avenue was extravagantly wide, as though the planners had imagined the chariots of victorious armies passing in review.

With his back to the room, Connor said, "Of course, this will be hard on young Gilson, but he'll find his footing . . . eventually. A good man always does, although it's difficult for me to see any good in a man who does what Gilson does."

Stall looked directly at Harding. Harding stiffened and turned slightly away.

Stall's mind staggered. *What the . . . ?* Connor turned from the window, looked at him, expecting . . . something.

Stall's mind gave him: "Uh, yes, uh. Gilson. Well, he—"

"Is he much of a loss, Tom? A promising young scholar, or . . . ?"

This Stall could answer. "By no means a star, sir, but, uh, the best our search committee could find . . . at the time."

"Good," said Connor. "Good."

Stall was not sure what was good. He nodded. Waited.

Connor went to his desk, picked up a sheaf of papers. "I've had him in. Dismissed him for cause. It's all here. These are your copies." He handed the papers to Stall.

At last. Stall scanned the pages, his eyes stopping at *dismissal* and then *moral turpitude.* He looked up at Connor, hoping to seem knowing—even agreeing. *Gilson. What had the man done?*

"Again, Tom, I appreciate your letting me know about this. This will help your department and the entire university a great deal, I think."

Stall allowed himself the brief, resolute half smile of a good soldier, a man who had done his duty. He hoped that his face said the right thing. He searched the papers in his hand again, looking for what it was exactly that he had done to please Connor so completely, and there it was, a letter from the chairman of the English Department addressed to the president of the university. The letter claimed that Assistant Professor Roland Gilson had been caught by custodian Jimmy Bright in an unnatural embrace in the basement men's room of Anderson Hall. The style of the letter was blandly official, and there at the bottom was a reasonable facsimile of Stall's own signature.

Connor pressed the small, tough fist to his mouth, coughed into it, and cleared his throat. "Professor Harding has let me know that he had no knowledge of Professor Gilson's activities. That's right, isn't it, Amos?"

"Yes sir, it is."

Harding offered Stall the file he had held since Stall entered this office. Stall could do nothing but take it. The contents were carbon copies of the file Helen Markham had given Stall, the file he had spent an unhappy hour reading in the College Inn. The file that damned Jack Leaf and Ted Baldwin, but said nothing at all about Roland Gilson. It was Harding's proof, Stall supposed, that the Gilson outrage had not happened on his watch.

President Connor waited to be sure that Stall recognized the contents of the file, then said, "Professor Gilson will vacate his office by five o'clock tomorrow. I'm sorry this is such short notice, but I know you'll find a suitable man to take his place. You've done it before. You and Amos, that is." An appreciative glance at Harding.

Stall handed the file back to Harding.

Connor cleared his throat again. "All right then, Tom." A statement not a question. Stall's cue to exit.

He backed to the door, opened it with a small bow, and departed.

In the outer office, the magic Olivetti, which had paused to let its smoking organs cool, began again its machine-gun rattle. Mrs. Braithwaite did not look up from her work.

TWENTY-NINE

All right then, Tom.
All's right, Tom.
All's well that ends well.

The words rang in Stall's aching head as he walked toward Anderson Hall.

God, poor Gilson. A guy with a new job, good prospects, and a young wife. All of it over. The end.

And who in God's name or in the Devil's had stolen stationery from Stall's office and written that letter? And was it even true, *the cause* for which Gilson had been summarily dismissed? There were any number of ways to get the stationery, starting at the printshop where it was made. One very ugly possibility was Helen Markham, who handled the stuff on an hourly basis. *But wait a minute.* The wording of the letter—*an unnatural embrace*—was from Harding's file. Had the letter been written by someone who'd seen the file? (Again, Helen Markham?) And who was the other man, the man with Gilson in the basement men's room? Why wasn't he named? Someone from the town? A man who could not be fired summarily by a university president? Roney Tyler's bloody eye came painfully into Stall's thoughts.

Had Connor read Harding's file, and if so, when? Had he known about Baldwin, even before calling Stall the day after Jack Leaf's walk in the air? And if so, why had he done nothing about Baldwin? The most merciful interpretation of this intelligence was that Connor really did want only one sacrifice from the English Department. A new man, a younger man, fit the butcher's bill.

Stall crossed University Avenue to the College Inn and bought two cups of coffee and a cardboard tray to support them. Carrying the coffee and his best intentions, he took the alley between Anderson and Matherly, the business administration building, and then the stairs to the basement. The light was on in Roland Gilson's office.

Stall knocked and waited.

"Come in!" Gilson's voice was too high and too loud.

Stall had to summon courage to cross the threshold. Holding the coffee out in front of him, he said, "I come in peace."

Gilson's head lay on his arms atop the gray metal desk. A small semiautomatic pistol rested on the desk beside his head. Stall, who'd had the standard hour of training with the army's Colt 1911, a .45 caliber semiautomatic sidearm, knew the type if not the make of the pistol and could see that the safety was off. His blood jumped, and the hands that held the cardboard tray sprang sweat.

Gilson looked up, his hostility seeming only a little abated since Tigert Hall. "Well," he said, "the chairman has more guts than I thought he did. Shall we go out to the curbstone and see how this turns out? As you see, I have my gun. I'll give you a decent interval to go get yours."

For a second Stall imagined it, two English professors in sport coats with leather elbow patches shooting it out for all to see. He shook his head and took a long, calming breath. "May I sit down? I'm unarmed except for coffee, and I think maybe you could use a cup." His voice sounded fatherly though he hadn't meant it to. He hoped the tone was right.

"To hell with your coffee." But Gilson held out a hand for the cup.

Stall gave it to him, considered snatching the pistol from the desktop while Gilson was distracted, but thought better of it and sat. He held his own cup in both hands and breathed in the heat and aroma. "I want you to know I had nothing to do with this."

"You expect me to believe that?" Gilson sipped the coffee greedily, gave Stall a defiant look, and opened his desk drawer. Again Stall considered lunging for the pistol.

Gilson pulled the cork from a pint of bourbon and poured liberally into his cup.

Stall held out his own cup toward Gilson, who raised his eyebrows theatrically and poured more.

Stall said, "When this runs out, I've got a bottle up in my office.

And yes, I expect you to believe it, though I can't go into the details right now."

"And you can't change them either." Gilson put the cup down and drank from the bottle, chasing the bourbon with coffee.

"No, I don't think I can, or anyone else can, but it matters to me that you know I didn't report you to the president."

"Then who did?"

"I don't know. I'm going to find out." When the words were out of Stall's mouth, he knew that he believed them.

Gilson shook his head, picked up the coffee cup, then put it back down. "Do you know what this does to me? Do you have any idea?"

"I think so." Stall looked at the pistol. "You're finished in this town, maybe in this profession." No sense, Stall thought, in pretending it was otherwise. If Gilson were more experienced, with solid publications, he might go north looking for work, but things as they were . . . Softly he said, "What will you do?" *Assuming you live through this day.*

"Oh, there are . . . possibilities." Gilson drank from the bottle again, offered it to Stall.

Stall took it, poured a portion into his coffee, and set the bottle on the floor beside his chair.

A sudden hilarity came into Gilson's eyes. "*Possibilities!* I may be a cocksucker, but I'm not an idiot." He reached up and screwed his forefinger into the side of his head to show that he had brains. Stall winced. *Just the place where a man might press the barrel of a pistol.* "There are things I can do. There's the family business, and let me tell you, boy, back home they can't understand why a promising young man would choose this genteel poverty we call the profession of English."

Let him bluster, Stall thought, *he's entitled to the courage of his whiskey.* "What's the family business?"

"Why it's business machines, or so they're called now. You know, cash registers, adding machines, we've even started a line of electric punch-card calculators, soon to be all the rage."

We've started, Stall thought. He's calculating the new life. I wonder how his wife is taking this. Does she even know about it yet? "I'll help you in any way I can. Will you let me do that?"

"How can you help me?"

Stall thought, *Go north, young man, maybe there's a chance up there where they don't care who you love as long as you know your Gower*. "I'll write you a reference letter if you want one. I'll make it good, and it won't mention any . . . of this."

Stall stood and Gilson looked up at him, eyes clouded with hope. "Thanks . . . I'll let you know what I decide."

Stall leaned over the desk and covered the pistol with his hand, thinking, *So small you are, little instrument, and capable of such big things*. He slid the gun across the desk and into his pocket. "I'll keep this for a few days. Just until you feel better."

Some of that sly hilarity came back to Gilson's eyes, and he gave Stall a look almost of contempt. "There are other ways."

"Hundreds," said Stall, "but you're thinking about the future now, and I'm going to help you."

"All right," said Gilson. "For now."

"Go on home to your wife. Think about her, not yourself. Do something for her." *Imagine her seeing you here with a hole in your head*.

Stall backed to the door, remembered the whiskey bottle on the floor, and bent to pick it up.

"You confiscating that too?"

Stall smiled. "Naw." He handed it to Gilson.

"Thank you, sir."

Stall knew that Gilson's thank you was for more than the bottle.

And Stall was *sir* again, no longer *you miserable son of a bitch*.

When he reached the stairs that ascended from the dank basement, he put his moist hand into his pocket and felt the cold little pistol. *Christ, maybe he planned to use it on me*.

THIRTY

Stall could barely stand the sight of Helen Markham, harboring as he now did the suspicion that she had either written the letter or given the stationery to Ted Baldwin. Baldwin had danced not only with Helen Markham in a ballroom somewhere, but with Jack Leaf in a men's room, and after Jack was gone the dance had put him at risk. Stall knew of no animosity between Baldwin and Gilson, but neither had he noticed any warmth. Baldwin's reasoning might have gone this way: Gilson is young, he can come back from disgrace, get a job elsewhere, or do something entirely else. (Perhaps Baldwin knew about the Gilson family and the new world of business machines.) *But* I, Baldwin had thought, *I must finish out my better-than-average (or better-than-nothing) career here in this place. I cannot afford disgrace, exile, and penury.* And who but Ted Baldwin would know that Roland Gilson was homosexual? Who else could read the signals, whatever they were?

At five o'clock, Stall walked past Helen Markham's desk with a "See you tomorrow, Helen," and a resolve to have a private talk with her. It would have to be a careful, thoughtful talk. He wasn't sure what to say. He was sure that she had never been loyal to him. Now she was his enemy.

Stall's headache throbbed as he rode home on the city bus. Schoolchildren, housekeepers, and law students got on and off, carrying with them the cares and joys of the day. Stall's heart went out to them. They were crossing Brooklyn Ferry. He was one of them, always had been, always would be. *You furnish your parts toward eternity; great or small you furnish your parts toward the soul.* Stall believed, had to believe, that he had done nothing, yet, that was bad enough to separate his soul from theirs.

Getting off the bus, starting his walk up the gentle rise, a Floridian excuse for a hill, carrying his battered briefcase full of the dog-eared pages of the article he had been rewriting far too long, his new sport coat folded over his forearm and his dirty collar open to a stingy excuse for a breeze, he wanted to hold this mood, this feeling of oneness, of merging with the great, muddy, glorious river of humanity. With the world he had resolved to love.

Stall and Maureen had handled each other with careful reserve since the night she had slammed the bedroom door, the night of her tearful complaint that her husband took solace in liquor rather than in his wife. His prouder self had said, *Well, damn it, be my solace then, and let me handle things my own way.* His humility had answered, *Christ, man, you've got to tell her some time, and some time soon, by the look of things.*

The house was quiet. No sound came from the kitchen, no soothing smells of food. Stall carried his battered leather satchel to the kitchen table and dropped it there with an assertive thud he hoped would raise some answering sound. Nothing. He arranged his coat on the shoulders of a kitchen chair and called out, "I'm home!" Then after a space, "Anybody here?"

This was more than strange, and he stood in the soundless house feeling his heart begin to hammer. *If I stay right here*, he thought, *everything will be all right.* A car pulled into the driveway. Stall went to the living room window and looked out. Dressed in a smart black skirt, black pumps, and a conservative but formfitting silk blouse, Maureen got out of the Packard. Stall considered walking to the front porch and greeting his wife with open arms, or at least in a way that might quiet the pounding of his heart. He thought better of it. The most he could do was turn on the lights in the living room so that he would not be discovered by Maureen standing here in half darkness. She came through the door carrying her black patent-leather handbag and a pair of white gloves. When she saw Stall, her eyes hardened but not to the steely point of hostility. She put her bag and gloves on the hall table beside the coat rack. "When were you going to tell me?"

"Where's Corey?" If everything had fallen from beneath him, at least Stall could get the elements of his world in some kind of order before . . .

"She asked me this morning if she could spend the day with Jeannie."

Jeannie was the Mears's daughter. Her mother Eileen was the helpful neighbor who had reported Stall for drinking at the Gold Coast. Jeannie was about Corey's age and a decent enough kid if you didn't hold her parents against her.

"So," Stall said, "is Eileen protecting our daughter from her drunken father today?"

On her way to the kitchen table, Maureen kicked off her black pumps, leaving them behind on the carpet. "You changed the subject. Again. So I'll ask *again* . . . when were you going to tell me?"

It was all at the back of Stall's throat now, a great vomitous purging of his secrets. For a second he wondered if his past would actually emerge in some reeking physical form.

With a long, tired breath, Maureen settled herself into a kitchen chair. "I had lunch with *Dr.* Sophie Green today."

Stall's hands made fists that wanted to pound the table. Wanted to beat his own eyes.

Maureen's voice was full of an unnatural froth. "You remember . . . at Jack's funeral. She said we should have lunch. Girl talk, shoes and handbags. Professor Green's chance to let the new chairman's wife know that a New York intellectual could be just one of us gals here down South."

Christ, there might be hope. "What did she say that's got you so . . . upset?"

"Oh, we did talk about shoes and bags, but only for a few minutes. It took her," Maureen glanced at the Lady Timex on her wrist, "exactly seventeen minutes at a table in the Primrose Inn to tell me that you ratted on Roland Gilson."

There was no name for the feeling that flooded Stall's body—and his soul, if he still had one. It was far beyond relief. It was more than a stay of execution but less than salvation. He sat down across from Maureen—suddenly, desperately craving the martini that usually waited for him at this table. He tried to keep surprise and relief from his voice. "Well, I'm *sorry* to disappoint Dr. Green . . ." *That bitch*. "But I'm *happy* to assure you that your husband is not a . . . goddamned fink. I did *not* report Gilson to the president. Someone did, but not me."

Maureen looked up from a hopeless examination of the tabletop. The look in her eyes was both resistance and curiosity.

Stall said, "Someone sent a letter to Connor naming Gilson as a homosexual. The letter was written on Harding's, I mean *my* stationery, and *my* signature is at the bottom. But I did *not* write the letter. The signature's an obvious fake."

Maureen's wide blue eyes flooded with relief, and tears followed. "That sounds . . . I don't know, too crazy to be true."

"Well, it is true, and you're right, it's so crazy that sane people will think I'm lying."

"Why would Connor believe . . . you'd send a letter rather than just call him, or walk over there and tell him to his face?"

"Because a chairman would know the president needs a letter. Connor wouldn't act without something official. And he wanted to think . . ."

"Think what?"

"I'm the kind of man who'd handle a matter like this by mail rather than in person."

The look in Maureen's eyes was complicated. Was he, was her husband, that kind of man now? Did ascending to a chairmanship make you the kind of man who coldly, by campus mail, denounced a colleague for the greater good of the department and the university?

Stall wanted to know more about his wife's luncheon at the Primrose Inn. "Why did Dr. Green think it was her business to tell you this story?"

Maureen glanced at the cupboard above the refrigerator where the gin bottle waited, bereft, unopened since their talk about Stall's afternoon stops at the Gold Coast. Stall got up and, reversing their roles, made a pitcher of martinis. He poured the drinks cold and clear, the gin adulterated only by the briny sweat of two olives.

Maureen sipped, then remembered and touched the rim of her glass to Stall's. He felt the touch even in the risen hackles at the back of his neck. Maureen said, "You know how women are. Don't you?"

It seemed to be an honest question. Stall knew better than to answer it.

Maureen speared her olive with the nail of her little finger. "I think Dr. Green wanted to hurt us, both of us, because she thinks I'm the wife of a phony, an *organization man* or some such thing."

Murder in my eyes, but don't let her see it.

"I asked her, I mean after I got over the shock, how the department was taking the news about Gilson, and she just shook her head and looked into her wineglass." She gave him a grim smile. "Oh, hey, guess what? I'm one martini ahead of you today. I had one at lunch with Sophie Green. And I ordered it even before I heard her shitty news about you. How's that for sophisticated?"

Stall shook his head, sipped, allowed himself to imagine various ways of torturing Sophie Green. The ways were vivid and ugly. "What did she say? About how the department is taking the news?"

"She said not well, not well at all."

"Did she say who'd be leading the assault on my office?"

"Say? No. She hinted. Ted Baldwin seems to be in what she called *the highest dudgeon* about the situation. What, by the way, is *dudgeon*?"

God, Stall thought, *I love you.* "It's, uh, I don't know. I'll have to look it up. Probably somewhere uphill from *chagrin*."

"Well, according to Professor Green, Ted Baldwin is highly in it. And others are not far behind him in the, uh, muck and mire of this dudgeon. But she, Dr. Green, is sympathetic to you and me."

"Christ." Stall sipped, the cool gin calling words to his tongue. "All these years of working with and for those bastards and all it takes is one . . . misunderstanding to make them turn against me like some mob of Transylvanian peasants."

"I'm so glad it's not true. It's a hell of a crazy thing somebody did to Gilson and to you, but you're innocent. That's what matters."

Other things matter, but oh, to be innocent in your eyes.

As though she'd read his thoughts, Maureen said, "I don't know about you, but I need Sophie Green's sympathy like I need a hole in my head, and if those bastards over there in Anderson never get the truth into their thick skulls, it's all right with me as long as I know it. Know you."

The gin turned to acid in his throat. He told her the whole story of his trip to Tigert Hall, the meeting with President Connor and Amos Harding, and his two encounters with Roland Gilson.

"He actually has a gun?"

"He *had* it." Stall pulled the little pistol from his pocket and put it on the table between them.

Maureen's eyes double-took the black message on the table. "Tom, *don't!*"

Stall palmed the gun, got up, and put it in the cupboard above the refrigerator.

"No," Maureen said, "that's not good enough. I don't want it anywhere Corey might find it."

Stall extended a calming hand toward her. "I'll put it in the garage. I'll lock it up out there . . . in, uh, one of the steamer trunks."

She looked less than half convinced and only inches mollified. "You took it away so he wouldn't use it on himself?"

"That's right." *Or on me.*

"Well, that's a good thing." She finished her martini. "But I want it out of here."

He stood. "You pour us another one while I take this to the garage?"

"Sure, and then there's something I need to tell you."

THIRTY-ONE

"I've got a job."

Stall had the key to the steamer trunk in his hand, was trying to think of where to store it so that he would not lose it forever. He couldn't quite take in what Maureen had said. "You what?"

"I've got a job."

She held up her beautiful left hand in the calming gesture Stall had used on her only minutes ago. He couldn't help but notice the two rings, the wedding band and the engagement ring with its two carats, far more than he could afford at the time of purchase. His father's sister, his only aunt of any gemstone sophistication, had stood by him for the purchase. *Tom, it's a ring she can wear for the rest of her life, and she'll never have to worry about that diamond.*

At the time, Stall had not even been dimly aware of what it meant for a woman to worry about her diamond. Later, of course, he had learned that two carats were the dividing line between cheap and showy. Now, the way Maureen inclined her left thumb to the inside of her third finger to move the wedding band as she raised her calming hand to him, this told Stall a long and complicated story of marriage.

"After Sophie Green told me about you and poor Roland Gilson, with that phony concern for you, for us, in her voice, and something else in her eyes that I couldn't make out, I wanted so badly to get up and just leave her there with that glass of Burgundy she pronounced passable for *this* town, but I couldn't do that. I just couldn't be that rude, even though every ounce of me wanted to spill my water glass in her lap and just, as you sometimes say, haul ass, so I just sat there listening to her talk and she started in ever so sweetly on the subject of my boring life. No, that's not what she said, that's not the word she used. She was more subtle than that. She asked me, *What do you do all day, Maureen?* That's what she did. And you know, Tom, I couldn't really think of an answer. I couldn't sit there in the Primrose Inn sipping my martini, all dressed up to look right for lunch with this New York intellectual, and start telling her about doing the laundry and shopping for our meals and getting Corey's new school supplies and her clothes ready for the school year. I couldn't do that, so I just sat there saying nothing until it got weird and I finally had to speak, and then I said, *Oh, you know, Sophie, I do lots of things. I read a lot. I just can't keep up with all the books I want to read. You know what I mean?* She knew, Tom. She knew exactly what I meant."

Stunned, sorry, guilty for reasons he didn't understand, Stall said nothing.

Maureen peered into his eyes. "Right. You do understand. So, you know what I did?"

Stall shook his head, but he knew.

"I said a polite goodbye to her, and I left the Primrose Inn, went to the Rexall Drugstore, bought a toothbrush and some toothpaste, brushed the hell out of my teeth in the ladies' room, until I was pretty damned sure there was no martini smell on this girl's breath, and then I drove to the office of the superintendent of schools. I was dressed just right for it, you know. It was almost as though I knew I was going there when I got up this morning and got ready for my girl-talk lunch with Dr. Sophie Green.

"So anyway, I wasn't in the superintendent's office five minutes before his secretary told me they'd just had a very unfortunate last-minute resignation by a woman whose husband had received the job offer of a lifetime in Jacksonville, and they just didn't know how they would fill a position for a fourth-grade teacher at Kirby Smith Elementary School on such short notice. Well, Tom, Kirby Smith's practically right up the street and three blocks from Corey's school, and I could drop her off there in the morning, and we'd get out at about the same time so I could bring her home with me at three o'clock or three thirty, and if there's just the teensiest time difference, well, she can sit in the library and read. That'll do her good.

"So I talked with the superintendent's secretary for a while, and I could tell she was impressed with me. Then she asked if I was certified in the State of Florida, and I had to say no, but she said if the superintendent liked me and thought I was suitable for the position, then I could teach on a probationary basis until my certification came through, and you know, Tom, I'm sure it will. There's nothing in the world I can think of that would stop it."

She was not exactly out of breath, but pretty close to it. Stall would have laughed at the length of this monologue if he had not wanted to cry. He didn't know what bothered him more, that his wife wanted to work rather than to stay home and take care of her house, husband, and daughter, or that Sophie Green, fresh from telling Maureen the tale of Stall's ratting on a colleague, had planted this poisonous seed in his wife's mind.

"And you know what, Tom? He hired me. His name is Frank Lundy, and after we talked in his office for a few minutes and he asked me about my educational philosophy, he said he liked the way I presented myself, the way I had dressed for my visit to his office, and how well-spoken I was. He asked me for references, and I gave him the names of some of my college teachers. He even knew one of them. God, Tom, I hope those guys are still working. Some of them were pretty old when I graduated. And anyway, Mr. Lundy called the principal at Kirby Smith, Mr. Dalton, and talked to him on the phone right in front of me. And when they finished, Lundy said if my references checked out, and I'd do whatever the state required after they looked at my application, Mr. Dalton would hire me on a probationary basis, and I could start next week in that fourth-grade classroom at Kirby Smith."

Maureen reached into her handbag and pulled out the application for certification. She held it up for Stall to inspect.

"And how do you think Corey will feel about having the only mother in the neighborhood who works?"

Stall had thrown his daughter into the breach without having any idea of how she would take to the idea of her mother working. The transportation plan, as Maureen had described it, did sound plausible. Images floated through Stall's mind: He and Maureen grading papers together at the dining room table. Stall ironing his own shirts. Stall in an apron making breakfasts for everyone, or worse, dinners—the only things he did with any confidence were scrambled eggs and hamburgers cooked as hard and black as hockey pucks. And he thought finally, *When she leaves me, later on when she leaves me because I have an illegitimate daughter in France, this job of hers will come in handy. In fact, it will seem like a thing that fell from heaven.*

That night, recalling the day from his place beside Maureen in their bed where she had rewarded his forbearance with the endlessly inspiring plenty of her body, Stall reflected on the charm of her excitement at getting a job so easily and at telling him about it. His heart was touched because she had enjoyed telling him about it so much. The telling had stripped years from her voice if not from her face. She had told the story as the girl he remembered from that first year after the war would have told it. She had turned an awful day with Sophie Green into a good day, a good job. It mattered little to her now that the job had been Sophie Green's idea and that the idea itself had sprung from Sophie Green's immutable certainty about the Proper Life of Woman. Stall would have to live with his wife's job, and he was pretty sure that he would have to live with her eventual disillusionment in it—the lot of an elementary school teacher, however dedicated and talented she was, could be hard. He was damned sure of one thing: he no longer had to live with Sophie Green's certainties about life as it should be lived in his English department.

The next morning in his office, Stall received another message by courier from Frank Vane: *You've done good work for us, Tom. We hope you won't stop now. Les Deux Copains must talk soon. Frank Vane.*

The *Alligator* was still enjoying its press holiday, which meant that Stephen Levy and his staff were still in negotiations with President Connor for the rules by which it would henceforth have to live, but the *Gainesville Sun* carried the story of Dr. Roland Gilson's dismissal with no comment from Gilson himself, who had, apparently, left town before the paper could send a reporter to his house. The *Sun* cited simply *for cause* as the reason for Gilson's termination.

In the hallways of Anderson and within its general districts where faculty and students knew that Stall was a new chairman and a rat, he was snubbed or shunned. Men and boys, and even a few women and girls, dropped their eyes when they passed him, or did not respond to his cordial good mornings or good afternoons. Some even crossed hallways to avoid the stain of his presence. A few men, members of the old guard, congratulated him for what they called *the Gilson business*. Sometimes they spoke in loud, outright ways, and other times with the raised eyebrows and sober nods that said, *We are the wise old heads*.

For a while, Stall looked forward to his next encounter with Sophie Green, and he rehearsed in his thoughts the volcanic eruptions that would spew forth when he met her, but eventually a coldness, if not a wisdom, invaded his thinking. He would wait and plan. During her first few weeks in Gainesville, he had seen himself as her advisor, even her defender, but she, apparently, had seen him only as a hopelessly backward bumpkin and an impediment to the plans she had brought with her from Columbia University to the bootless South. She was adept at politics, both personal and public, Stall now realized. Her fey gestures, the back of a hand to a flushed forehead, the blush rising up that delicate Victorian neck, these were arrows in her quiver—hell, they were bullets and bombs. She knew, at all times in all places, exactly what she was doing. She calculated to the last word, to the last man and woman, the gains and the damages of her actions.

Stall met her by accident several days later on the old iron stairway between Anderson and Matherly. He was going down for a quick lunch at the CI, and she was ascending. They stopped and she said, "How *are* you, Tom?" The words were any day's greeting, and her expression was concern, but her intention was, Stall knew, to probe him. *How are you—after the Gilson business*? And what would she do with what he revealed?

"Fine," he said breezily, "and you?" He showed her the bland face of business-as-usual.

It was the first time since she'd tried to tip the custodian Jimmy Bright for carrying her books that Stall had seen her off balance. Her face colored and she moved her slight body into the path of his much larger one. She wanted more from him. Stall put his hand as lightly as he could on her shoulder, moved her out of the way, and kept going down the stairs. Behind him, he heard what sounded almost like a whine: "But Tom, we . . ."

In the CI, with a hamburger in front of him, he planned what he would say at the faculty meeting he had called. He'd be goddamned if he would give them what they wanted—an explanation of what they all but one believed were his actions. He'd be equally goddamned if he would name the person who had done what they were convinced Stall had done: that would be the work of a rat. Staring at the congealing burger and a clot of french fries, Stall allowed himself a cruel grin and a quiet chuckle. He knew what to do.

THIRTY-TWO

Stall did not stand, as Harding had always done, for the opening of his first meeting as the new chairman of the English graduate faculty. He had arrived early, pulled a desk from the first row of classroom seats, and settled into it, crossed his legs comfortably, and, not quite lounging, watched the men and one woman of the faculty drift in.

As they entered, Stall looked each one in the eye. In return, he received punishing or shunning glances and even the kind of disgusted slide of eye that said Stall resembled something a man might step in on a hot summer sidewalk. Stall knew that the men who shunned him were the innocent ones. They had only bought the consignment of crap that some other man had sold them by sending a letter to the president of the university. The man who gave Stall a sad but sympathetic eye—that would be the man who had forged Stall's name.

By the time a quorum was assembled, Stall's failure to look defiant or ashamed had thoroughly unsettled the room. The smile on his face, selected to resemble the expression of a hangman who enjoys his work, had caused the voices in the room to fall from the hum of the righteous to an uneasy silence. Stall waited until he could hear the footfall of an ant on a window casement. Sophie Green and Ted Baldwin were the last two to enter. Neither met his gaze.

"All right," he said, beginning without a welcome, "as you know, the first meeting of the fall semester is usually scheduled for next Monday. I've called this ad hoc get-together because we have a problem to discuss. Or rather because some of you have let me know that you have concerns." Still sitting, just short of sprawled like the student he had been long ago in better days, he gave them the executioner's smile. "Well?"

He waited. Nothing.

"Well," he said again, "let's hear your *concerns*."

He counted eight before Fred Parsons, the tenured slacker who had confronted him in the mail room, said, "What about Roland Gilson?"

"What about him?"

This brought a general disturbance. Could Stall cravenly deny what everyone knew to be true? The expression on Stall's face said, well, yes, he could. He looked over at Helen Markham, who sat in the corner scribbling the meeting's minutes. He let his eyes rest on her until he was certain everyone in the room knew there was a reason for it, and until his pause caused her to look up at him. Then he said, "I asked you, Fred, what about Roland Gilson?"

Parsons sputtered, "Well!" It sounded like *Whelp*.

Apt, thought Stall. He let his grim gaze rest on Parsons until the man looked down at his desktop, then Stall's eyes searched the room. "Anyone here know anything about what happened to Dr. Gilson?"

No one spoke.

Stall's gaze fixed on Sophie Green. "Professor Green? Anything from you? You seem to have sources of information unavailable to the rest of us. The *Alligator*? Anything from that beacon of truth and light you'd care to share with us about Roland Gilson?" He leaned toward his faculty in the desk not quite big enough for him. "Well," he said, "Dr. Gilson and I talked in his office on Tuesday *after* he was dismissed for cause by President Connor. Dr. Gilson, *Roland*, and I shared a glass of bourbon. I'm sure that at least some of you will consider a late-afternoon drink on a working day forgivable in a situation like the one in which Roland and I found ourselves. We had our drink and he told me that someone had denounced him as a homosexual. I assured him that I would find out who had done such a thing. And I will."

Stall waited. No one spoke. A few faces told him that his performance was not just false but crazy. Most just looked stunned. One or two glanced around for whom it might be that Stall intended to accuse.

"Is Professor Baldwin here?" Stall had seen Ted Baldwin enter. "Ted, you're Dr. Gilson's senior colleague. Do you have anything to tell us about what happened? I assume he confided in you."

Stall watched them, all of them, their shocked faces, watched as they all looked around, located Baldwin sitting beside Sophie Green. Stall untangled his long form from the student desk and walked to the door, thinking, *So this is what it feels like to be unemployed. Well, I've got a wife to support me.*

He stopped at the door and let his eyes search the room again, let them rest on the face of Ted Baldwin. "I should tell you," he said, "that I think I know who denounced Roland Gilson. It goes without saying, I'm sure you'll agree, that the man who did it is a dirty yellow dog. It may be true, as some say, that there is guilt in being homosexual." He looked up. Was his South Carolina father's God looking down? He looked back down at this group of grounded men. "But that's not for me to say. What I can say with some assurance is that there is guilt in betraying a friend."

In the hallway, as he made his measured pace, Stall heard at first silence from the room behind him, and then a hum, growing, and then a confused and anxious uproar.

THIRTY-THREE

At five o'clock that afternoon, Helen Markham placed, without comment, a sealed envelope on Stall's desk. She stood waiting, hands folded in front of her, as though for a response. Stall broke the seal and read, "*Tom, I heard about your comments to the English faculty today. Either they were the truth, your truth at least, and you are not the choice I thought you'd be for the chairmanship, or they were a very questionable way for you to conceal the fact that we are working together. I choose to believe the latter. Let's talk. Yours, Jim Connor.*"

Each afternoon at five o'clock exactly, it was Helen Markham's practice to stand before the big Victorian desk that Stall had inherited from Amos Harding and wait for him to tell her she could go home. Before coming to the desk, she always covered her typewriter with its crackling green oilcloth canopy and locked away her Spode cup and Earl Grey tea. Since occupying this office, Stall had always acted his part in this ritual, saying, "Thank you, Helen. See you tomorrow."

Now he said, "Where are the minutes for today's meeting?"

"I haven't typed them yet. They're in shorthand on my desk. I thought tomorrow—"

"Type them now. I want to read them before you leave today." The minutes were an official document, and Stall wanted them to be accurate.

"Yes sir."

She returned to the outer room, and Stall heard the oilcloth canopy crackle from her typewriter. He reviewed some lecture notes to the sound of her methodical typing. Ten minutes later, she stood in front of his desk again, offering him the record of his ad hoc meeting. He read. She stood. He marked a few errors, looking up at her after each one. She looked down unmoved.

"Sit down, Helen."

She did, to the side of Stall's desk where students sat. She smoothed the linen of her dress across her lap and adjusted the horn-rimmed glasses that hung from a string of pink coral beads around her neck.

"Helen, do you know that you serve at the pleasure of the chairman? My pleasure?" Stall reached into his desk drawer and retrieved the university's *Personnel Policies and Procedures Manual*. He set it on his blotter, turned it so that she could see the cover. "*At the pleasure* means that I can let you go at any time, for any reason."

"You wouldn't do that." She didn't look at him, only stared at the windows behind him with their view of University Avenue, though her voice had lost its usual flatness. There was something in it that reminded Stall of a bleat.

"I would, Helen. I would."

The tiniest of smiles, tidy and ungenerous, came to her lips. "I've been here thirty years. The others wouldn't let you fire me."

The others should know by now that they can kiss my ass.

Stall rested his hand on the manual, patted it. "All I have to do is call the personnel office and let them know I'm dismissing you, and I'll be interviewing candidates for your position tomorrow. And you will be gone, Helen. And you might be surprised to learn how many of *the others* will not be sorry to see you go."

She shook her head, stared at the window. But in her lap, her hands had begun to tremble.

Easy, Stall.

He lowered his voice, made it a measure more soft, a little soothing: "Helen, did you write that letter to the president?"

She shook her head, the slightest of movements. Her eyes, never bright, never animated, had fear in them now. Stall reached into his desk for the box of Kleenex he kept there for students. He offered it to her, but she gave a stiff, angry wave.

"The letter, Helen?"

"No, I did not."

"Lying is cause for dismissal, Helen. You know about *cause*. It's mentioned in the minutes you just typed."

She broke. The tears gathered, then fell, spotting the linen at her chest. Stall offered the box of tissues again, and she clutched it with both hands, took a wad of them, and blotted her eyes with ugly stabs.

"I didn't write it. I couldn't do that. I have a carbon of Dr. Harding's file. He asked to see it, and I showed it to him. I know I shouldn't have done it, but . . ."

But you love him. You love him and he knows it, and though he can't return your love the way you want him to, he does appreciate you in his way, and the two of you are the missing pieces of each other's lives.

Stall only said, "I understand, Helen. You gave Ted Baldwin the file, and he wrote the letter." He had tried to keep the sad fatigue from his voice, but it was there. This was the end of a long run. One of them anyway. It was clear now. Baldwin had read Harding's note about the basement men's room and panicked. He had to save himself before Stall, the new chairman, the rat, did something with the information.

She sat stiff upright, her eyes stricken as though by the sight of a sudden injustice. "No! Not him. Not Professor Baldwin."

Stall rocked back in his chair, examining her eyes for any deception, guile, cunning. He saw nothing but her shock. "Who then?"

"I thought you knew. The way you talked at that meeting, I thought you knew it was Professor Parsons."

Christ, Stall thought, *Parsons*. The guy whose outrage at my cowardice made me the worm of the faculty mail room.

Stall shut his eyes, shook his head. He didn't try to conceal his surprise. In the darkness of his eyes, he considered Parsons, who was a lot of things and none of them extraordinary, but who was not, at least to Stall's understanding, a homosexual.

"So you gave Ted Baldwin the faculty file, and he . . ."

She nodded, looking at her lap. "He told Professor Parsons."

"Did you give Fred Parsons my stationery?"

"No, but one day when you were in class, he came by and asked me to leave the office, and I did, and when I got back, he was gone."

"Did you know what Parsons planned to do?"

She shook her head, then hung it and would not look up again.

Had she guessed it would be Gilson? Had she danced with Parsons too? Did she love him too? Or was she simply too weak to say no, or too full of contempt for Stall, Harding's successor, to care who forged his signature? He could ask her, fill out the bill of her indictment. But no, Stall thought, she's nothing but the instrument of other people's actions, a dance partner, infinitely stepping backward. And Parsons's reasons for writing the letter, for sacrificing young Gilson, were clear enough. Ted Baldwin was his friend, and Gilson, new to the department, was nothing.

Stall stood behind the big desk. "Helen, give me the key."

"The key? I'm sorry, what key?"

Stall held out his hand. "The key to the desk out there." He pointed at the door.

"To *my* desk?"

"The key, Helen." His hand was open between them.

She got up, and he followed her to the outer office, where she unclasped her big bag and found the key. She handed it to him.

He opened her desk drawers, all of them, and removed her Spode teacup and tin of Earl Grey. He set them on the desk. "Take these and anything else that's personal, that belongs to you, and leave. And Helen, I will not see you tomorrow."

He watched her until she had shifted her few belongings—a bottle of aspirin, some breath mints, a small box of tissues, a lipstick and compact—to the big purse and walked to the door.

THIRTY-FOUR

At six o'clock, Stall's phone rang and Margaret Braithwaite, her own typewriter no doubt neatly covered, the magic Olivetti beginning its well-earned nightly rest, said in a not quite clipped tone, "Dr. Stall, President Connor would like to see you at the residence. He'd like you there as soon as possible."

There was, of course, no question, at least none spoken, of Stall's having plans of his own. "Of course. Tell him I'll be there."

"Thank you, Dr. Stall."

He dialed Maureen, then hung up the phone to think. To imagine. He saw Maureen sitting at the kitchen table filling out the application for teacher certification. She'd have Stall's old Royal portable out of its scuffed little suitcase, and she'd be pecking away at her answers to the state's questions (she was an excellent typist). Or maybe she had already filled out the application and with her usual efficiency was moving around their bedroom in quick but graceful teacher steps, assessing her wardrobe and jotting a list of items she would need to purchase for the new job. (One thing Stall knew about women was that every change in life was an opportunity to shop.) Or maybe she was sitting in the garage at what was comically called Stall's workbench (he did little work with his hands unless you counted rifling through drawers in the library card catalog), and her hands were lovingly caressing the spines of the teacher education textbooks she had taken from the dusty cartons that lined the walls.

With the phone in his hand, his index finger holding down the cradle that could bring the line to life, Stall found that he did not exactly detest these images of Maureen's new life. He dialed and told his wife he'd be late for dinner. He was not sure how late. "I've been summoned to the residence."

"The president's residence?"

"The very one."

"What for?"

"Your guess is as good as mine."

"Come on. You know what for."

"I'm sure it has something to do with Roland Gilson."

"Me too. Want me to pick you up when you're finished with *El Presidente*, or he with you?"

"No. It's a short walk. I'll burn some calories before I sit down to whatever lovely dinner you'll have ready for me."

"Sorry, just tuna sandwiches tonight, but I know you like them."

"I do like them." Stall thinking, *So it begins, the life of the Sandwich Eaters.*

The residence was the university president's house, a colonial mansion situated at the spot where University Avenue divided to become state roads 24 and 26. The V-shaped lot was narrow at the front but widened until it was plenty large for the big white columns and verandas of the grand old house. Stall got off the bus at his usual stop across from the hole in the ground that would be the new law school and started the short walk to the residence.

When he knocked and was admitted to the foyer with its view of the grand staircase and the elegant spaces on either side, he saw that big doings were afoot. Negro men and women in tuxedos and starched black dresses with white aprons and ruffled white caps hurried here and there preparing for some sort of party. Food had already been set out, and Stall's stomach growled as he waited for the man or woman in charge to notice him and escort him to the president. A tall Negro, all energy and confidence, emerged from one of the doorways behind the big staircase and approached Stall with the gravity of a battleship. His tuxedo trouser creases were razor sharp and his patent-leather shoes were blinding. A head taller than Stall, he inclined a torso as big as a boiler and smiled large and bright. "Dr. Stall?"

Stall nodded.

"Follow me, please, sir."

Stall did.

* * *

Stall had not known what to expect, and certainly not the president's private dressing room, and not its walk-in closet. The closet was as large as Stall's living room. Half-dressed and attended by a tuxedoed Negro, Jim Connor gestured distractedly for Stall to sit on a leather-covered stool, the kind you saw in shoe stores. It featured the sort of ramp where a customer could rest a foot while a salesman fitted a shoe. Rows of suits and sport coats lined both sides of the closet, and at the back, a stack of drawers held, Stall supposed, cuff links, studs, braces, belts, and other accessories. Beneath the suits and coats, rows of shoes freshly shined waited for the presidential foot. The mingled smells were intoxicating. If there was a perfume for men, Stall thought, this was it.

Connor noticed Stall. His boxer's legs, short but still powerful, with quadriceps that split above the knee with a dangerous vitality, moved here and there under his old-fashioned long shirttails. *Any other man*, Stall thought, *would look ridiculous here.*

Connor said to the Negro, "Cornelius, will you give me a minute or two with Dr. Stall?"

The man bowed almost imperceptibly and backed toward the entrance to the closet. Soundlessly he was gone.

Connor held up two bow ties. "Which one do you think, Tom?"

Stall shook his head. "They look alike to me, Jim."

"They're different." The president shook the one in his right hand like it was a black snake he had just killed. "This one's got a little weave in it, almost like bombazine, barely noticeable, but in a certain light it'll shine. In a certain light, it'll make me look like a man dealing cards on a paddle wheel riverboat."

"Is that a good look for you, sir?"

"Believe it or not, it might be good for tonight. My wife and I, we're having a little reception for some donors, some folks we want to help us expand the medical school. Might be a good thing for me to look just a little bit like a man who'd slip his hand into a drunk's pocket. You know the whiskey's gonna *flow* tonight."

"I imagine so."

"Well, we aren't here to talk about bow ties, are we?"

"No sir."

Connor opened a drawer, produced an old-fashioned silver flask, and handed it to Stall. "Try this."

Stall did as told. It was a very fine, very old bourbon.

"Comes from a private distillery not far from here but very far from the prying eyes of the revenue services."

Stall handed back the flask. "You mean it's bootleg whiskey, sir?"

Connor drank. "It's far too good to go by that name. Let's just say it isn't bonded. You'll find, Tom, that many of the best things in life are not, shall we say, officially sanctioned."

"Will I, sir?"

"You will, and I told you a long time ago to stop all that *sirring* with me. Just call me Jim, and you're Tom to me."

"Sorry, Jim."

Connor looked at his watch, furrowed his brow, glanced at the closet door. "Cornelius will be back here in a minute to help me get my trousers on right, so let's get down to it. Why didn't you tell me in my office the day I fired professor Gilson that you did not write that letter?"

Stall hesitated. Did it matter what he said? Of course the truth mattered, especially here in these close quarters, but it had seemed to Stall for a while now that he was destined to be sent back to the ranks of the common professoriate. No more Chairman Tom Stall. He had tenure, but in strange times like these he could be fired. He did not believe that his actions that day in President Connor's office amounted to a firing offence, moral or any other kind of turpitude, but then, Gibbon had written that Emperor Nero had declared his horse a god and made the Roman Senate bow to the beast. Connor could do anything with Stall he wanted to do.

"Jim, when you called me to your office, I had no idea why. In the circumstances, I thought it might be best to play it by ear."

"Yes, but what tune were you playing?"

The small black man, Cornelius, appeared, assessed, and like a puff of smoke in a magic act, disappeared.

Stall took a long, deep breath. "I've thought about this a lot since that day, Jim. Right now it seems to me that it might serve your purposes best if the world believes I did write that letter. If I did, then as the world sees things, especially the world that's about to arrive here to drink your whiskey and eat that wonderful food down there and let you put your gambler's hands in its pockets for the good of the medical school—that world needs to believe that crazy things like somebody writing a letter and signing somebody else's name to it don't happen in a well-run university."

Connor's laugh was loud, and better, genuine.

Well, Stall thought, *perhaps my next career will be in comedy*.

"I see your point, Tom, I certainly do, but didn't you just convince that bunch over in Anderson Hall that you didn't write the letter? I heard you were eloquent . . . and angry. And aren't they earnestly searching for the man who did write it?"

"About the convincing, I don't know. About the search, I'd say maybe now the English faculty just want to let sleeping dogs lie."

"Are the dogs sleeping over there?"

"Not yet, but they will be. Come the first football game."

"So what's our deal now, Tom? I'm sure you have one in mind."

"The best one I can think of right now is you move on. You let the Committee know that two dead dogs from the English Department are enough. There are other dogs for them to chase."

"You got any other dogs in mind, Tom?"

The words formed in Stall's mind. There are some likely dogs in political science, dogs who truly believe that all means of production and distribution of goods and services should belong to the government. But he had already come dangerously close to losing his soul to that kind of accommodation. He said, "Jim, I think it's perfectly obvious where the dogs are. You and the Committee can find them."

Connor looked at him sharply. "You think I'm with *them*, Tom? Is that what you think?"

"With them? No. I just think some of them will be ringing your doorbell pretty soon with money for the medical school. Or better yet, maybe you can convince the Committee that they've done enough here in Gainesville."

"All right, Tom. All right. The hour is late, and I have to pull on my trousers."

Small, neat, discreet Cornelius appeared as if from nowhere.

Stall found his way to the bottom of the stairs where party preparations had reached a pitch of controlled fury. He cut across the lawn taking the shortest way home, aiming his footsteps for a spot just east of where the first limousines had begun to disgorge gentlemen and their ladies all tuxedoed and bejeweled and smiling. As Stall reached the street, trying to look inconspicuous in his sweaty, loosened collar and scuffed shoes, a big Lincoln pulled up. Out of it stepped Frank Vane, followed by Dr. Ron Davidson. Stall lowered his head and kept walking. He had just stepped off the curb when Vane called out, "Hey, Tom! You coming to the party?"

Stall stopped, walked over to them. They both wore tuxedos, Vane's empty sleeve as usual pinned up neatly under his arm. Stall said, "Uh, no, not invited, but, uh, mightily impressed by all the pomp." He shook hands with the two men. Dr. Davidson smiled warmly. "Good to see you again, Tom. Sorry you won't be with us tonight."

Stall aimed a deferential glance back at the wealthy residence, then turned his gaze to Vane. He could not suppress the question in his eyes.

Vane nodded, smiled with a practiced charm. "Surprised to see me here, Tom? I don't know why. I'm rich, and I might give some of my filthy lucre to Jim Connor for his medical school, just to make Dr. Davidson here happy."

At a loss, Stall said, "All in a good cause." They shook hands again, and Stall watched the two men walk across the lawn.

Even in Stall's neighborhood up the hill, the music and laughter of the president's party could be heard well into the early-morning hours. The following afternoon, University City learned that Professor Stan Margolis, a nationally recognized political science scholar, and, Stall knew, Stephen Levy's dissertation director, had been dismissed for devoting an entire semester to the works of Karl Marx.

THIRTY-FIVE

"You fired her?"

Maureen put down her tuna sandwich, touched the corners of her mouth with a paper napkin, and picked up her glass of milk.

Paper napkins. Stall had started a mental list of the changes that Maureen's new job, or at least her preparations for it, had already caused in the Stall household. What would be next, TV dinners? He had guessed right about Maureen's old textbooks. They were everywhere in the house where she could sit for a moment and study, their pages marked with gas company envelopes and torn pieces of newsprint. *Classroom Management* was open on the kitchen counter next to an empty tuna can.

Stall ate a potato chip. "I did. She had no loyalty, at least not to me."

Corey looked up from her bowl of tomato soup, the remains of her sandwich in the same hand that held a spoon. "Dad, you fired somebody? Who?"

Stall gave her his Serious Father look. "You know, don't you, Corey, that you can't talk to anyone outside the family about things we say at the dinner table."

"Nothing?"

"Your father means important things." Maureen reached over and touched Corey's shoulder.

"How do I *know*?" Corey looked at her mother, then at Stall.

He ate another chip and loosened Serious Father into Best Pal Dad. "Don't worry about it, honey. Your mom and I will let you know when things come up that you can't share with anyone. And we'll trust your discretion."

Corey smiled wisely. "I know what that is."

"Was it a vocabulary word?" Maureen was already teaching.

Corey nodded. Back at the beginning of the summer, a time that seemed now a long time ago, Maureen had given Corey a calendar that featured a daily vocabulary word, its definition, and the word used in a sentence. This so their daughter's brain would not rot during the long vacation.

"And she left without a fight?" Maureen scraped her plate into the sink, and turned to wait for an answer.

"I don't even know if I have the authority to fire someone. I bluffed her with the *Policies and Procedures Manual*. Dropped it on the desk in front of her with an ominous thud, but I haven't read it."

"You will now."

Stall gave her a grim nod. "Carefully."

There was a knock at the front door, Corey answered it, and the sociologist's daughter was heard asking if Corey could come out to play. Stall wondered abstractly what *to play* meant to two rising seventh graders in training bras—when they weren't fielding ground balls. Did they regress to dolls, a last longing for childhood before the prospect of real babies loomed?

Maureen gave their child her permission.

Stall had told his wife everything he could recall about the strange meeting with Jim Connor in the walk-in closet as large as their living room. Telling Maureen the story, it had seemed important to recall as many details as he could of the opulence of President Connor's entertainment.

"They really had shrimp as big as lobster tails?"

"They did, I swear it, and lobster tails as big as Jim Connor's feet."

"Ugh! That takes the lobster right out of a girl's mouth."

"Yeah," Stall had said, "that simile fails, but they were the biggest lobster tails I've ever seen."

"And you saw his legs, and you think they're good legs?"

"Better than good. The strong legs of a boxer."

"Damn interesting. I wonder what he meant by it. Having you meet him in his dressing room."

"What he meant by it, I can only guess. Maybe that we needed to be in his most secret place. Or maybe that we were not, at least right then, president and chairman, just two guys, one of them without pants."

"Down to the basics," Maureen said, "elemental."

"That's a guess. Another is that he was just in a hurry as any president might be, and he wanted to do two things at the same time—get dressed and give me my marching orders."

"I thought you gave him his."

"We agreed on a new deal."

"Sounds Rooseveltian."

"I think Connor is more Caesarian."

"What does that make you? I hope not Ciceronian. We know what happened to him."

"You *have* been studying."

Now, with the sounds of Corey and Jeannie, the sociologist's perfectly adjusted offspring, fading away on the sidewalk outside, Stall wondered if he could suggest a martini to follow a tuna sandwich. Or was there brandy somewhere in the house?

University classes would commence on the coming Tuesday, and Stall hoped for a hiatus from the Committee's depredations, at least in his own department. He was thinking that even the politicians, petty bureaucrats, lawyers, and enforcers of the Committee would respect the beginning of the fall semester as a time to honor students, their parents, and matters higher than who slept with whom and with what parts. Stall's duties would include making last-minute adjustments to classroom assignments and course schedules, the annoying business of hiring someone from the shallow local talent pool to cover Roland Gilson's classes in medieval lit, and deciding which of the arriving graduate students would get the last two or three of the teaching assistantships the department always held in reserve for promising late admissions. These late admissions were often excellent students who had brokered to the very end their prospects for financial aid at better schools. Having failed to close their deals at Vanderbilt and the University of Virginia, they would gladly accept last-minute offers from Florida. And, there was the business of naming a new assistant chairman, the man who would assume Stall's former position. The talent pool for this position was, in Stall estimation, the shallowest of all. Perhaps he should suggest, as Sophie Green had done a few days ago, a national search for an assistant chairman.

Then a bolt of inspiration blazed in Stall's brain. There was only one man in Gainesville certain to have the expertise to fill in for Gilson while a search committee did its work.

THIRTY-SIX

Before the trouble of the forged letter had come to Stall's office door, he had allowed himself to imagine standing before the assembled graduate faculty for the first time as their chairman, gaveling them (metaphorically) to order, and leading them with gentlemanly good humor and wit in the light business of a new academic year. It was mostly a matter of a few introductions, approving the minutes of last spring's final meeting, and some pomp and ceremony for the benefit of the newest initiates, the graduate students. Stall remembered from his own first faculty meeting at Virginia wanting desperately to believe that a professor's job offered the kind of gowned-and-mortarboarded magic he had seen in *A Yank at Oxford*. The reality, he had soon learned, was often drab, but some gestures and courtesies survived that would have been familiar to the men of Heidelberg when Karl Jaspers strode its cobbled streets.

Yet Stall had already chaired his first meeting. The hands of that clock could not be turned back. This was Stall's second meeting as chairman, and he walked to it with a burdened heart and an intention do business with dispatch.

He waited in the stingy breeze on the iron staircase between Anderson and Matherly until they were all assembled, then he walked into the classroom and stood before them as had been Harding's style. Of course there was no gavel, not even a podium, only a wobbly music stand, useless for a man of Stall's height. With nods and smiles he acknowledged some of the students from Jack Leaf's research methodologies class, and some of the new graduate students who, unlike the summer grinds, had chosen to vacation after finishing college. The ambitious ones had dropped by his office to introduce themselves. He knew only the college grades and tests score of other boys, but would soon put faces to names, and he noted the one girl, Martha Kenny, who was bespectacled, drab of dress, intensely serious of demeanor, and looking a little daunted to find herself surrounded by so many men with only Dr. Sophie Green as her ally in womanhood.

Martha Kenny was a type, Stall thought, as he waited for the group to quiet. Versions of Martha Kenny taught now in the University College freshman English program, and that was where with some luck this one might find employment after completing her PhD. She had high test scores and straight As from Smith College.

Stall gave his welcome with little ceremony, got last spring's minutes approved by voice vote, and asked each new student to stand and say his (and now her) name and where he or she came from, and what his or her intended area of study was to be. "And remember, brevity is the soul of wit."

The students did well. One or two of them attempted eloquence or bragged a bit, but Stall's mordant gaze sat them down before too much damage was done. When Martin Levy's turn came, he had to be called twice, and then with a great show of reluctance shoved himself out of his chair and said, "Martin Levy. The University of Miami. Medieval lit under Professor Green." He sat. Eyebrows rose, some faculty who had been out of town for the summer gave Levy double takes. *Charming*, Stall thought, but said only, "Thank you, Martin. Next."

Stall was beginning to worry. His guest was late. He could announce the man, but preferred the full effect of an introduction. When the new students finished, he called for a round of applause, and when the clapping ended, said, "This might be the last time you'll hear such easy appreciation from your professors." The students smiled, grimaced, laughed.

Stall introduced Sophie Green. "Most of you have already met our first faculty member of the fairer sex, Dr. Sophie Green, who completed her doctoral degree at Columbia University last spring. Dr. Green has already begun to make her mark here at Florida. I'm sure that those of you who are just returning from summer travels will want to welcome her to our ranks."

Stall gestured to Sophie Green so that she could stand and speak. She stood.

The door opened and a tall, thin man in a black suit with a floppy bow tie that would have suited Oscar Wilde, swept into the room. He carried a black satchel in one hand and a white handkerchief in the other. He stood just inside the doorway blotting his brow and surveying the crowd with an expression somewhere between boredom and unmet expectation.

He noticed Stall, and walked with stately pace to Stall's extended hand. The tall man brushed the hand aside and kissed Stall on both cheeks. Stall received this greeting with calm good humor as he had promised himself he would. "Eugen Brugge," he said loudly enough for all to hear.

From a corner of his eye, he saw Sophie Green slowly sink back into her chair.

Before Stall could go on, Brugge gave the room an Elizabethan bow. "Most of you know me from one or another of my lectures or performances here in the . . . *lower* college. Professor Stall, my dear friend Tom, has asked me to substitute for Dr. Gilson, and I have reluctantly agreed. Mind you, I say reluctantly only because I have such a busy schedule. Now, I don't want any of you *doctors* of philosophy to worry about this old Belgian hack getting his toe in the door." He glanced at the door, smiled sphinxlike, and said, "Well, I'm already in the room with you, but please believe me, I have no desire to remain. I'm just *filling in* as a favor to my dear friend Tom. I promise you all that I shall do my very best to illuminate Gower and Boethius competently for your very fine students and possibly even with some flare." He glanced at one or two of the young people in the room. "And I always learn as much as I teach, so I have high expectations of you young scamps."

And with that, before Stall could say another word, Eugen Brugge checked his Girard-Perregaux wristwatch, shook his head at the impossible busyness of his schedule, blotted his brow, and strode out the door.

When it had closed, Stall said to the shocked or comically surprised or offended faces of his colleagues, and especially to the death masks that were Ted Baldwin and Fred Parsons, "As per my prerogative as chairman, I approached Eugen about helping us out, and he graciously agreed. Any questions about that?" Stall looked at his own watch, the homely Timex.

No one spoke.

"Good, then. Again, welcome to you all. Let's have a wonderful academic year."

He wished his own exit could be like Brugge's, but it was his duty to stay and field questions if there were any.

Sophie Green walked past him looking puzzled and hurt. He gave her only a glance before listening to young Martha Kenny say how much she looked forward to Stall's class in the modern American novel.

THIRTY-SEVEN

On the Sunday afternoon before Eugen Brugge's surprise visit to the English faculty, while Maureen Stall had studied classroom management, and Corey Stall had laid out her clothes and readied her notebooks and pencil box for the first day of school, Roney Tyler had turned his brand-new midnight-blue Cadillac Sedan de Ville into the Stall's driveway. The big gleaming machine rocked on its leaf springs as Roney braked it hard.

Maureen looked up from the pad she was covering with notes. "Who's your new friend?"

Stall said, "I'll tell you all about it."

"Hmm. When?"

"When you have time." He gave her book and notepad his most innocent attention.

When the point was wordlessly made, he walked outside and got into the Cadillac.

The Dixie Fidelity Bank and Trust had come through, Roney had told Stall, and he was considering not leaving town. His wife and her brother had decided, apparently, that a rich man who was queer could be tolerated, possibly even loved, better than a poor man who drove a battered truck and lived at the Oasis Motor Court.

Stall had considered it his duty to warn Roney, but in exchange for his warning he had received for the third time Roney's line about being born, but not yesterday. Stall's final word on the subject of family love was, "Roney, if they'll kill you for being queer, they'll kill you for the money."

"Naw, they'll wait until we spend it all, then they'll kill me."

Roney's injured eye had cleared of all but a tinge of pink in the outside corner, and the cut beneath it had healed to a handsome scar. The eye patch was gone, but Stall worried that worse things might be in store for this bank-account pirate.

Roney parked the new Cadillac in front of Eugen Brugge's cantilevered house. Before they could knock, Brugge threw open the door and called, "Come in! *Entre! Willkommen!*"

Stall smiled gratefully for the welcome and looked over at Roney, marveling not for the first time at his redneck friend's ingenuity. "He noticed you," Roney had told Stall. "That time we went to his house. He plays that piano, but he don't miss much."

Roney had told Stall that Brugge would welcome a second visit. Stall thought of it as a private audience.

Inside the house with the late-summer light pouring in through the floor-to-ceiling glass doors and the pool sparkling blue under the sun, Stall marveled again at what was not so much a house as a private museum and a testament to a learned man's tastes. Eugen Brugge wore black light-wool trousers, an open-throated white silk shirt, and black shoes of soft leather. He served them coffee in demitasse cups with cubed molasses, sugar, and cream, and, after a few sips, told Roney in a soft but commanding tone to "wander about while I talk to Dr. Stall."

Roney didn't appear to mind this a bit and seemed also to know where to go. The mechanic turned and walked into a wing of the house that Stall thought must hold bedrooms.

Brugge tilted his handsome face up to the sun. "I noticed you the other day. And after you left, my friends told me you gave only your first name."

"That's right."

"Are you gay, Dr. Stall?"

Stall considered the same answer he had given Roney—*Not that I know of*—but it didn't seem appropriate here and now. He said a simple no.

"Then why did you come to my house?"

"Roney said I'd be welcome."

"Well, yes, Roney was right about that. He's one of our, shall I say, rough-trade mascots, and very dear to all of us, but Roney's approval of you does not answer my question. Were you just slumming?"

Stall looked around. "This is hardly a slum."

Brugge put down his demitasse and sighed. "Somehow I thought you'd be more direct with me, Dr. Stall. Ron Davidson said he liked you, that you and he had some things in common."

"We talked about the war. A lot of men our age have that in common."

"Well then, if you won't tell me why you came here last time, tell me why you're here today. Roney said you have a proposition for me."

"A proposal, yes."

"I suppose there is a difference. Go on."

"I want you to teach two courses to English graduate students. Courses in medieval literature."

"But I'm not even a graduate myself."

"But you could do it?"

"If I wanted to. Why should I?"

Stall shrugged. Of course he had anticipated this question and had known he could not answer it satisfactorily. He tried: "For the good of the university."

"Well, the university does employ me, but as you know, I work at a level far below your own. I'm just a University College drudge, and I do harbor some resentment at the condescension I have to endure."

"Hardly a drudge." Stall looked around the house again.

"Do you know what I heard, Dr. Stall?"

"How could I know?"

"I heard that you did *not* tattle on Roland Gilson. I heard that someone else did."

Stall wanted to ask who had told Brugge the truth, but not very badly. He figured the news had come from Gilson himself; he had probably found his way to this house not long after arriving in Gainesville.

"Do you know who put poor Gilson in the way of the Committee?" Brugge asked.

"I think so."

"Will you tell me?"

"No."

"Good. There's really not much difference between denouncing in one place and telling in another. In this house, in my house, we pride ourselves on . . . enjoying life and not talking about it."

"I understand." Stall finished his coffee.

"I hope so, Tom. I hope you did not come here that first time looking for intelligence about one of my guests."

Tate. "One of your guests has hurt some people, and he wants to hurt more of them."

"Yes, and that's regrettable, but he won't hurt me, or any of my friends, because he is one of us. Do you understand that, Tom?"

"I think so." Actually, in several ways it was unfathomable, but it was not a thing to explore here and now.

"Then I will help you if you will help me. You'll be welcome here for whatever reasons bring you to us, but not for that one."

Stall nodded.

Eugen Brugge set his demitasse in the exact center of its tiny saucer and touched his mouth with a linen napkin ringed with Belgian lace. "It will be tedious teaching your young dullards about a time in human history they can never hope to understand, a time that even I struggle to comprehend, but I will do it for you, my new friend Tom. And I will enjoy, oh so much, being the new queer in the English Department that has just purged itself of my kind. I'll be your very newest and most obvious queer, and I'll be unassailable."

Stall rose and received, to his surprise, kisses on both cheeks. The hand he had held out for shaking hung limp in the air.

And Stall thought, *No one is unassailable.*

THIRTY-EIGHT

Secretary-less, Stall was answering his own phone. He had moved Helen Markham's empty chair to the front of the outer office and taped a hand-lettered sign to its back: *Walk through*.

Sophie Green called him.

"Word's out you sacked Helen Markham."

"As it happens, this time the word is right."

He waited while she breathed into the phone, apparently cooling her temper.

"What did she do that caused you to take such a drastic step?"

"Drastic? I don't call it that. People come and go. Gilson's gone. Jack is gone. Don't worry about Helen. She'll be fine."

"I'm not worried, not about Helen anyway. It just seems that things are getting . . ."

"Getting what, Dr. Green?"

"I don't know, a little strange."

"Very strange, I'd say. Now, did you call to talk to me about my former secretary or something else?"

"I want to see you. I want an appointment with the chairman."

Stall checked the calendar that Helen Markham had been keeping for him in her neat hand. He struggled to read his own scribble. "I can see you this afternoon at three o'clock."

"Good then. Thank you."

It had been a busy morning, the first of the new semester. Stall was always moved by the invasion of quiet little Gainesville by the thousands of automobiles that disgorged students, their parents, their siblings, grandparents, and friends, all dedicated to the solemn mission of delivering one or two brilliant young minds to the university where it was devoutly hoped that these minds would be improved. And some were improved, to be sure. Stall had seen the proof. Most, he was pretty sure, would just enjoy watching football, muddle through their first paroxysms of sex, earn Cs, refine their manners (at least those who joined fraternities and sororities), and make the connections that would later get them the jobs that would earn the modest livings that would make it possible some years hence for them to invade Gainesville on some cool fall day and park on the grass outside Stall's office window while they unloaded suitcases, trunks, food, record players, hot plates, a few books, and their own offspring.

Stall had come to regard the twice yearly invasion of the thousands of automobiles that delivered and then retrieved the young scholars as reassuring and even beautiful, like the waxing and waning of the tides.

His morning and his early afternoon would be routine—a few disgruntled students whose stipends did not seem to them generous enough, a few whose course schedules did not suit them, a few who wanted to have their first man-to-man chats with Stall about literature and life (he'd make short work of these), and a few professors who'd bring him problems they could have solved themselves with a little more ingenuity and a little less self-regard. And then there was Sophie Green.

At noon, he locked his office and walked to the College Inn for a sandwich and coffee. The crowd was thick and boisterous. New students and their parents milled, the youngsters agog, the oldsters reliving college days, and veteran students preening and sizing up the newcomers. Stall kept his head down over his BLT and the copy of Abrams's *The Mirror and the Lamp* he had brought with him. When he raised it, he saw Martha Kenny at a nearby table addressing herself to a glass of water. His curiosity piqued, he continued to watch as she opened her purse and removed some crackers wrapped in cellophane and a small jar of peanut butter.

She had not applied for an assistantship which would have given her the meager income that kept so many graduate students alive if not well. When Stall had asked her about it, implying that she could have had the stipend if she'd asked for it, she'd said, "I didn't want my time to be divided between teaching freshman English and my studies." *God*, he had thought, *the earnestness*. It was touching, and now this, a lunch of water and crackers.

He finished eating and walked to her table. "How are you, Martha?"

"Oh!" Startled, flustered, rallying. "I'm fine. How are you, Dr. Stall?"

"I'm well, Martha. Is that, uh, your usual luncheon fare?"

Her face reddened. "Oh, this . . ." She seemed so completely at sea that Stall almost regretted this approach. Then the idea came to him.

"Look, Martha, how would you like to do some typing and light office work for me to earn extra spending money?"

Her face was like sunrise after a stormy night. "Oh, Professor Stall! That would be wonderful! And you know, I worked in an office back at Smith. I know my way around a typewriter and a filing cabinet."

They both looked down at the crackers and the water. She swallowed and smiled.

"Good, Martha. Come by my office and we'll work out a schedule for you. Nothing too heavy, of course."

Stall walked back across University Avenue into the melee of moving in and tearful goodbyes. His hiring the girl would further outrage the rank and file. Of course he would restrict her duties to matters not confidential. *If pressed, I'll tell them Harding's faculty file is locked away from prying eyes.*

At three o'clock on the dot Sophie Green settled herself into the chair beside his desk with a rustle of skirt and a brisk crossing of legs. "Tom, have you been avoiding me?"

The air in Stall's office was instantly charged as it always was in ways that he could not entirely understand when he was with Sophie Green.

"No, I haven't," he said. "I've been busy, and I'm sure you have too."

"I thought you wanted to be my friend." Her tone was adamant.

He calmed his thoughts, tried to sort them. Had he wanted to be Sophie Green's friend? Did he now? He remembered their first days, reading her wonderful scholarship, helping Jimmy Bright carry her books up from the old DeSoto with New York plates. So brief a time and so much had happened. Could he afford to have friends in this department now? Did he want them?

To Sophie Green he said, "I wanted to be a good colleague, maybe even an advisor. When you got here, I wasn't your chairman. Now I want to be a good chairman. That's about it."

"That's it? Nothing more?"

What was she digging for? "Look, Dr. Green, Sophie, I've tried to help you, and it seems to me, if you'll forgive this, that you've needed a lot of help in the very short time you've been here. I've advised you to the best of my abilities about how to get along, how to succeed, but at every turn you've debated, or misinterpreted, or ignored my advice. So, let's say I've gotten the message. You'll do things your own way."

"Really, Tom, what have I done that's so wrong?"

"*Wrong* is not the word I'd use. It's too metaphysical. I'm talking about tone and, yes, manners, about what's appropriate for a new person to say and do and what's not. We've been over this more than once. I see no reason to go through it again." *Well*, Stall thought, *at least she didn't correct me on the meaning of* metaphysical.

She smiled for the first time in this meeting, and it was a cruel smile. "There's something you don't understand about me, Tom. Mr. Chairman. I didn't come down here to fit in, to get along, to be appropriate. I came here to change things."

Despite what he knew about her, or thought he knew, Stall was surprised. On top of being arrogant and foolhardy, this was the statement of a woman who did not care if she kept her job. And it came to Stall that she, unlike him and most others here, could easily get work elsewhere. He remembered times before when her stage English accent had slipped and the Lower East Side of Manhattan had rung in. Now, he had the strong impression that she was acting, playing a part.

"Well," he said, his voice low and a little sad, "if you see yourself as a crusader, then get on with the crusade and accept the consequences."

"Is that a threat?"

"Of course not."

"Are you man enough to tell me right now that you think I can't *succeed* here?"

"Man enough?" Stall gave her a bitter chuckle. "I don't think it requires any manhood to tell you that your success or failure is up to you. If you define getting tenure as success—and most of us do—that decision won't be made until your fifth year of probation."

"Probation? Christ, am I already a convicted felon?"

"You signed the contract, Dr. Green. The terms are clearly stated in it. A five-year probationary period is one of those terms."

"There are other ways to define success."

"Of course."

"Maybe you'll be surprised to see who changes."

"Maybe. But it's a busy day, and I have more pressing things to think about."

Sophie Green stood and put her hands, steady as two little alabaster rocks, on the back of the chair. "There's nothing more pressing than change."

"Maybe so, but I have to decide who gets the last of these assistantships, and you may not know it, but this piddling money means the difference between a wife who works and one who can stay at home with the baby."

"You hired Brugge without consulting the medievalists."

Nor did I speak with the Americanists. "Ah," said Stall, leaning back in his chair and lacing his fingers behind his head. "Honestly, I thought Brugge would please you. You above all others."

"Why?"

"Think about it, Dr. Green. You'll come up with an answer."

"Do you know that there's a chapter of the American Association of University Professors on this campus?"

"Yes, and I know they're the only club in town that has fewer members than the United Daughters of the Confederacy."

She turned, walked to his doorway, her back to him, then turned again. "By the way, this ludicrous so-called press holiday that your friend Connor has declared, it won't matter. The *Alligator* staff, at least the ones who count, have voted to take the paper off campus. It'll be independent from now on, published out of Stephen Levy's house. They'll take donations from people of conscience, but no advertising money. You can tell Connor this: when he shows up to negotiate his terms with the *Alligator*, the office he locked up will be empty. He can fill it with his stooges. I'm sure that's what he planned to do anyway."

Stall said, "My days will be full and satisfying without reading the *Alligator*, on or off campus."

With a flounce of fabric, a flash of patent leather, a glance of penetrating disdain, and a spin of well-turned ankle, Sophie Green was gone.

THIRTY-NINE

Before returning to the papers on his desk, Stall gave himself some time to think. Was Sophie Green a danger now or just an annoyance? An asp who could kill or a gadfly who merely stung? He was certain of one thing: from now on he'd be careful with her. She would watch and wait, and he might bitterly regret any slip of hand or tongue.

When five o'clock came, Stall turned his mind to the vital question: what waited for him at home? *Paper plates, plastic cutlery, boiled hot dogs?* Frank Vane walked in.

Vane held an envelope in his hand. "I found this on the floor outside. Someone must have left it for you."

Christ, Stall thought, *more Restoration Comedy*. Vane leaned over Stall's desk to hand him the envelope, and Stall noticed that Vane's stump, the half arm that war had given him, moved in tandem with his good one. The sight almost brought tears to Stall's eyes.

"God, Stall," Vane sat in the chair recently warmed by Sophie Green, "envelopes under the door? I didn't think an English teacher lived a life of such intrigue. Go ahead, open it."

Stall did. The envelope contained an unsigned letter from *a concerned group of faculty* who averred that it might be time for Stall to resign his chairmanship. This concerned group averred additionally that if Stall did not do as they suggested, they might call for a vote of no confidence at the next faculty meeting. "The group," Stall supposed, was Parsons and Baldwin, and a few others. He doubted that they were a majority.

In a pig's ass I'll resign.

Stall knew that, however uncomfortable this office might become for him, his job was secure as long as Jim Connor wanted him in it.

He remembered telling Connor that the dogs of English would go back to sleep with the first football game. It was still possible.

"In a *what?*" Vane was laughing. "There you go. That's the Tom Stall I knew and loved all those years ago."

Loved? "Did I say that aloud?"

"You sure did. You said, *In a pig's ass*, and then something I didn't get. Hard day?"

"It was fine until the last half hour or so."

"I hope you don't include me in the last half hour's hardship. I'm here to congratulate you for showing leadership and good judgment. That Gilson was a bad piece of work."

There was a lot Stall might have said. *Gilson is a decent young man, and he was a promising teacher, and now he's God knows where facing an uncertain future because of you and your committee.* None of it would be worth the expense of breath. Stall said, "What can I do for you, Frank?"

"Tell me what's in that envelope, or does it stay in the pig's ass."

"It stays there."

"Ah!" Vane laughed again, as though Stall were a fine afternoon's entertainment. He held his hand up into a shaft of bright light from the window behind Stall and examined his manicured nails. Satisfied with them, he rested the hand in his lap. "I went to see your friend Roney Tyler yesterday."

"How was he?"

"I don't know. I couldn't find him. His boss at the body shop says he just quit coming to work, and the charming proprietor of the Oasis Motor Court told me he cleared out of there in the middle of the night. Left the money he owed her on the kitchen counter. I find it strange."

So did Stall, but he could think of several good reasons for Roney Tyler to lam it out of Gainesville. The lack of any necessity to continue to apply Bondo to bent fenders was one, and his wife's brother was another. "Cy Tate told me about Roney's windfall. Maybe he decided to spend some of his newfound wealth in a more exciting place." Stall shrugged. "Maybe he'll be back."

"Did he say anything to you about leaving?"

"Many times. I'm surprised he waited as long as he did." It bothered Stall that Roney had not said goodbye.

"Well," Frank Vane said, "it's a mystery." He examined his buffed nails again as though to say he was finished with the subject.

Stall waited.

"What did you think of Connor getting rid of that Communist Stan Margolis?"

"Think of it? I think it stinks, but it's a practical strategy for a president with his eye on a bigger medical school. Rich men don't endow political science."

Vane shook his head, and the glow of good humor returned to his eyes. "No, we don't. Science can save your liver if you drink too much of Jim Connor's whiskey, but political science is just horse shit wrapped in jargon." He looked around Stall's office, his eyes lighting on the bust of Tennyson. He reached out and patted the poet's head. "Stall, you've gone from idealist to cynic in record time."

"I've had a lot of help."

"Strange. I'm the same idealist I always was. We just have different ideals."

"As I said, Frank, what can I do for you? My dinner's waiting." *On a paper plate.*

"Funny, I haven't ever met the lovely young woman who's cooking it for you. Maureen's her name, isn't it?"

"It is. How many operatives of the Florida Legislative Investigation Committee did it take to find that out?"

"Oh, that's casual information. Mrs. Tom Stall is known around here as a more than ordinarily good-looking young woman."

Stall stood and pressed balled fists to his desktop. Strangely, he wondered if Amos Harding had ever had to endure such unction in this office. "Yes, Frank, my wife is a beautiful woman." *And you just said you loved me*. "Again, what's your point?"

Frank Vane stood too, looked at his watch. "My point? Oh, just that you're a lucky man. How many men ever have the love of *two* beautiful women? I wonder if the two of them will ever meet. That would make quite a picture."

Something broke in Stall, or maybe it was born, or it died. "You're a sad man, Frank. And this, the thing you're doing, it's very sad. I feel sorry for you. Not as sorry as I feel for the people you're hurting, but really, genuinely sorry. And Frank, I'm afraid that's all I have for you.

All I will ever have. I don't know where you're going when you leave here, what you'll do or who you'll do it with, but I know I'm going home to a wife and daughter who love me. Good afternoon, Frank."

"Does Connor know you didn't write that letter?'

"I don't know. Ask him."

"I did, just after I handed him a check for the medical school. He said you didn't. Said one of the queers in your department sacrificed the kid, Gilson, to save his own sorry ass." Vane gave a philosophical sigh. "But the sum of it all is that another dangerous influence on our youth is gone. Eliminated. The public knows your department was dirty, and they'll know soon that others are too."

"So, you're happy with your work?"

"Happy? No, I'm sad. Sad that we live in this kind of world. But I'm content to be making progress. I've already thanked you for your part in that progress."

Stall let himself hope. "So, you're finished with me, are you?"

"Oh, no. No, I don't think so. Enjoy your dinner, Tom, and give my regards to the lovely Mrs. Stall."

As Frank Vane left the office and walked off down the silent, empty hallway, it came to Stall that there was a special malice in the man's heart for him, for Tom Stall. So far, its source was a mystery, a thing hidden from Stall and perhaps also from Vane himself. It wasn't only that Vane had undertaken responsibilities that should have been Stall's, or even that in his way Vane had loved Brigitte. There was something more, something in the love Vane had said he felt for Tom Stall.

FORTY

The first thing Tom Stall saw when he walked into the office of Discreet Investigations, Inc. was a camera. It was about the size of the radio that stood on the bedside table in the bedroom he shared with Maureen. He had seen cameras like this one only in the movies and on television. He remembered the storms of flashbulbs in the news coverage of the House Un-American Activities Committee hearings, so many bulbs exploding in the faces of bewildered witnesses that the hearing room in Washington seemed to be full of summer lightning.

A half-dozen bulbs with *Sylvania* written on them lay on the table next to the camera.

A man called from a back room, "Help you?"

From the small foyer, Stall called back, "Maybe."

The investigator was well dressed, well built, and casually on his guard. He stood in the doorway of a back room looking Stall up and down. He was about Stall's own height, six one, with brown eyes, sandy, close-cropped hair, and he moved with a careful grace. He wore dark-blue suit trousers, black cap-toe shoes, a white shirt, and a silk tie that was modestly tropical. Except for the tie and an empty black leather holster clipped to his belt, he could have passed for one of the lawyers or bankers who walked Gainesville's downtown streets. The holster looked about right for a snub-nosed .38.

This small office was on a side street south of a town landmark, the aptly named Commercial Hotel. Some of the hotel's commerce was hourly. Stall composed himself in pleasantness and waited. The man stepped forward and said it again: "Can I help you?"

May I, thought Stall. *Can* is a capability, *may* is an offer. "I hope so. I couldn't help noticing the camera. What kind is it?"

"It's a Graflex. They're common as dirt. You notice something about it I should know?"

The man's voice was businesslike, but there was a hint of impatience. Stall took out his wallet. "I know your time is valuable. Let's call this a consultation. I'm happy to pay you for an hour at the going rate." He smiled like he was buying sliced ham at the local butcher shop.

"All right," the investigator said, "ten dollars will buy you a half hour, but only because I'm stuck here waiting for a phone call. I see clients by appointment."

A man who was this brusque had many clients, Stall thought, or very few. He handed over the money, followed the man into the back room, and took the chair in front of an old golden oak desk. "My name's Tom Stall."

"And you're a professor and a friend of Jack Leaf. And you just got promoted. Congratulations."

"And you took Jack Leaf's picture. In a men's room."

"That stupid hillbilly ought to keep his mouth shut."

"I can't argue with that. Roney told me he had to get out of town before somebody shut it for him."

"And you're helping him?"

Stall nodded. "I'd like to. For my own reasons, and Roney's too. Mine are good ones, I think."

"I don't deal much in reasons." The investigator held up his thumb and first two fingers and rubbed them together in the age-old way that said legal tender, moolah, scratch, jack, money.

Stall nodded again. "I figured. So I'm thinking maybe you don't care where the compensation comes from as long as it's the going rate, and not too much complication comes with it."

The investigator nodded, took a pack of Lucky Strikes from the desk drawer in front of him, and lit one with a kitchen match he took from a sawed-off brass shell casing. Although Stall had never caught the habit of smoking, he'd always liked the smell of burning tobacco. He enjoyed the smoke the investigator blew across the desk at him. The shell casing, he knew, came from a twenty-millimeter cannon round. Stall had seen the empty brass before and not in happy circumstances. The German Messerschmitt Bf 109 had fired the twenty-millimeter round from a cannon in its propeller hub. After the American infantry had been strafed, soldiers could, if they cared to, pick up these casings along the frozen roadsides.

The investigator said, "So we've established that we know some of the same people, and my services are for sale. What do you want?"

From another man, the words might have been unpleasant, but they didn't seem so to Stall. Just clear and efficient. The effect was bracing.

"May I consider this conversation confidential."

The PI nodded.

"Can you find out something about Roney's brother-in-law?"

"Do you know the man's name?"

"No."

"Shouldn't be hard to get you something. The courthouse over there . . ." the PI gestured with the half-finished cigarette, "will give me the wife's maiden name. That'll get me her brother. Why you want to know about this guy?"

"He promised to kill Roney for being queer. Nobody's seen Roney in a while."

"You just said Roney planned to leave town."

"I don't think he would have left without saying something to me first."

"That's touching. You don't *think*?"

Stall shook his head. "Let's say I've got a bad feeling about this. I saw what the brother-in-law did to Roney."

"What was that?"

"Beat the shit out of him."

"Anything else for your money?"

"I don't know your name."

The PI took a business card from a tray on the desk and put it on the table. Stall read it—*Rudolph D. Silber*—and looked up.

"People call me Rudy."

"Am I people?"

"Sure, why not?"

Rudy Silber stood up behind the desk and stubbed out his Lucky Strike. He looked at Stall with raised eyebrows until Stall understood and took out this wallet a second time. The moulah, scratch, jack, money Stall handed over for the retainer was painful, but he figured he'd recoup what he spent in one way or another, maybe by keeping his job. Roney was connected to Rudy Silber through Cyrus Tate and thus to Frank Vane, who had just given a large sum of money to President James Connor for a medical school wing. Stall's thinking ran this way: a safe-and-sound Roney was a friendly link in this chain that held a midnight men's room and a president's office together. Stall and the discreet investigator shook hands on their deal, and Stall was about to go when it came to him.

"You're the other man, aren't you? The day Jack Leaf jumped, I saw you with Cyrus Tate. I was crossing the street. You two came out of the College Inn. That's right, isn't it?"

The PI nodded.

"Did Jack know? Did he know it was you who took the pictures?"

"Yeah, I think so. It all happened pretty fast."

"Why were you there? In Jack's classroom with Tate?"

"Purely by accident. Tate and me, we were on our way to lunch, and he said he had to see Leaf, serve him. You know what serving means?"

"I know."

"So that's what we did. Tate gave Leaf the subpoena, and we left. By the south entrance to the building, just like those kids said. The last time I saw Leaf, he was alive and well. Upset, sure, but nothing desperate that I could see. If I'd thought he was going to kill himself, I'd have stayed there."

"What did he say? I mean when Tate served him."

There had been questions, speculation. Many times Stall had wondered: *What were Jack Leaf's last words?* That August afternoon, Stall had heard the dying fall, the strange sound that was not words.

The PI lit another Lucky. "He said, *Thank you.* Polite, like it was nothing at all. He put the subpoena in his coat pocket. We left him standing by the desk in that classroom. That's it, professor."

Stall wanted more. He wanted the look on Jack's face, an interpretation of the scene. There had to be more. It couldn't be as simple and as bad as "Thank you" and then seconds later a walk in the air. Since the war, Stall the Spectator had spent his life interpreting stories, investigating moments of literary time that stretched on infinitely because great books were forever, their scenes available to generations of teachers and students for their endless speculation. And now it seemed there was nothing to learn, nothing to think, about Jack Leaf's last seconds alive.

The practical, methodical man with the empty holster and the big camera put Stall's money in his desk drawer. "So, you bought ten dollars' worth of nothing. I'll get you something for the fifty."

"I'll hear from you?"

"You will."

FORTY-ONE

By most reports, Eugen Brugge was a great success with the students of medieval literature. He brought in a recorder and played what he claimed was music from the time of Chaucer. (Who knew if it was true? There were only surviving scraps.) He assigned students parts and had them act out scenes from *The Canterbury Tales* (stopping short of full costuming), and he regaled them at great length about life as it was lived in Chaucer's day—the appalling sanitation, the frequent wars, the rampant disease, the starvation, the grueling agricultural work, the absolute *droit du seigneur* of the nobility, and the brief, miserable lives of everybody else. He read them Auden's "Musée des Beaux Arts," and showed them Bruegel's painting of the peasant plowing his field, oblivious to Icarus plummeting from the sky. "That about sums it up," he told them one afternoon. "Most people kept their heads down, and a few, like Chaucer and his pals, looked up."

His students did little writing or even talking in his seminars. (He told them that their work would be tedious for him to read, and in any case he was far too busy to do it.) He promised them a party at the end of the semester at his house and said they'd never see a house like it again in their lives. Brugge developed special feelings for two of the boys in his class and took them out for lavish lunches at the Primrose Inn where he ordered wine and talked late into the afternoon while neighboring diners and staff muttered darkly. Stall, of course, was delighted by this, almost as much as the rest of his faculty were appalled. He told the one or two who complained to his face, "The proof's in the pudding. We'll see how the students do on their master's exams." And he added to their incredulity, "It's been my experience that sometimes the reading of the difficult primary works comes after the enrichment experiences have lit the fires of enthusiasm." In plain terms, *They'll read the hard books if the music and the pageantry excite them.* Stall knew as well as anyone that in an American university just about anything could be justified by an impressive string of Latinate abstract nouns.

And Stall saw from the beginning that most of Brugge's students simply liked the man because his enthusiasm for what he claimed he knew was so infectious. How many of Stall's colleagues could say the same thing about their own classes? Stall believed that he could claim to radiate a certain excitement when he talked about the writers he loved, and that he could see this excitement reflected back to him from the eyes of his students, at least the best of them, though lately his worries burdened him so much that he found himself walking to his classes more annoyed than excited.

Stall appointed Jed Burwell, a Shakespearian and the oldest man in the department, as his assistant chairman. There had been so much uproar lately that the ruckus which attended this absurd act seemed muted to Stall.

He had walked to Burwell's office on the third floor, found the seventy-five-year-old sleeping with his head on his desk amid piles of lecture notes, soiled coffee cups, and stacks of old manuscript pages, the books Burwell had been promising to finish for years. As Stall waited for Burwell to rouse, he resolved that he would send Jimmy Bright up here to tidy things as much as was possible, but caution Bright not to alarm Dr. Burwell. Stall cleared his throat twice. Burwell snorted and woke with a wild swiveling of his snowy old head, as though an alarm had gone off somewhere.

"Jed," Stall said officially, "will you do me a favor?"

"Of course, Smith. Anything."

"I'm Stall, Jed, Tom Stall."

"Ah, Stall." Burwell smacked his lips and unstuck a mucky tongue from the roof of his mouth.

"Jed, I want you to serve a term as assistant chairman. Will you do that for me?"

"Well, uh, sure I will, but who's the chairman?"

"Oh, I thought you knew. I am."

"Ah." Burwell still not fully awake. "So what shall I do?"

"Oh, I'll let you know, Jed."

"All right, Stall. You can count on me."

"Thanks, Jed. Go Gators!"

Burwell was an avid fan when he remembered to attend the games.

Stall announced the appointment by memo.

The graduate faculty met to consider a vote of no confidence.

Stall's bill of indictment, he later heard from Jed Burwell, was his high-handed and unprofessional behavior as chairman—to wit, that he had appointed Eugen Brugge to replace Roland Gilson without consulting the specialists in medieval literature, and that he had appointed Jed Burwell assistant chairman in the same imperial way. Apparently, the question of Stall's having written or not written the letter denouncing Roland Gilson had been so muddied by rumor and speculation that the faculty had no stomach for including it in their list of his sins. What Burwell could remember from attending the meeting and from the sketchy notes he had taken indicated that the discussion had ranged all the way from Stall being a stooge of President Connor to Stall being simply incompetent and not up to the complexities of the job. Although Burwell's account was muddled, Stall got the impression that the older, more conservative members of the faculty who remembered the Red Scare of the 1930s, and the more recent Army–McCarthy hearings, rather liked President Connor and could not accept the trade unionist slant of the stooge accusation. According to Burwell, the meeting was soon fractured, no agreement could be reached for an actual vote, and so a straw poll was taken instead. Stall won it, according to Jed Burwell, by a slim majority. "I tell you, Tom, it was touch and go there for a while."

Stall could see that Burwell was ready to tell the whole story, name names, who had said what, but Stall didn't want to know. His only curiosity lay in wondering what President Connor would have done had the English faculty dropped a vote of no confidence on his desk. Stall was not even certain that such a thing was allowed under university rules. He could imagine anything from Connor thanking them politely and just ignoring it, to the president thundering at the English teachers, *No confidence! No confidence in a man I hand-picked for the job! I've got about as much confidence in you bunch of participle parsers as I do in a three-legged quail dog with a head cold!*

* * *

The department always held its Fall Social at the home of Fred Parsons. People said that Parsons had a gift for the stock market, and this was how he owned the grandest of all faculty houses. It was a rambling, split-level Prairie-style structure made of sandstone and redwood that sprawled on a little rise above Hogtown Creek, the trickle that could become a torrent in a hard rain. The Parsonses' backyard sloped down to a swimming pool that drained into the creek, its chlorine bleaching the banks downstream for a hundred yards or so and killing all but the hardiest fish. Nobody cared about a few ditch perch as long as life was good in the yards along the stream.

Parsons's Fall Socials were the stuff of lively English Department memories. The food was always good, the liquor flowed liberally, the house was a fine place for a gathering, and spirits were always high when a new semester began.

Stall wore his only suit, dark blue, and one of his two festive ties, the one with palm trees. Maureen pulled out all the stops. Her black cocktail dress plunged to an ample cleavage where more than a few men's eyes had gone blind, and her long white neck sported a single strand of pearls. Her black heels were high enough to lift her above most of the wives and many of the men. As the Stalls drove to the party, he could tell that she was more than ordinarily excited.

"So, party girl, you looking forward to this?"

"Yup."

"I thought so." He stopped himself before saying, *You'll have more to talk about tonight than you usually do. It won't just be childhood diseases, cleaning products, soap operas, and stretch marks. You have a job.*

Again, she read his mind. "I wonder what people will say when I tell them I'll be teaching next week."

"Will it be fun to find out?"

"I think so. A few of the women will be happy for me, some will be jealous, and some will worry about you and Corey"—she looked over at him, Poor Tom, the Tuna Sandwich Eater—"and one or two won't be surprised at all because everybody knows everything about everybody in this town."

And there's Sophie Green.

Stall would wait for his wife to mention Dr. Green if she wanted to, or he'd wait to hear what Dr. Green had to say about Maureen's job when they met tonight.

Maureen reached over and turned the rearview mirror toward herself to give her lipstick a last review. She frowned at it as she always did, and picked with a fingernail at the corners of her mouth, removing an infinitesimal amount of the red goo. She rested her hand on Stall's shoulder. "How do I look?"

"You've taken away my mirror, and now you want me to take my eyes off the road? Dangerous woman."

"No really. How do I look?"

"Like a million bucks, of course. Like a dangerous woman. Like we're on a journey to the end of the night." Stall's head swiveled from the road to the beauty beside him and back again.

"That sounds like the title of a bad movie."

"It probably is." *And a French novel too.*

Maureen cupped her breasts with both hands, a thing he'd never before seen her do, and lifted them thoughtfully, then let them settle gently. His groin tightened. Her frown deepened. "This dress is tighter than I remember it."

Stall knew exactly what to say. "The, uh, tightness is just right."

"Would you tell me if it wasn't?"

"Of course. Would I want the chairman's wife to outrage the Fall Social?"

She laughed and squeezed his shoulder. They parked in front of Fred and Mary Beth Parsons's house.

FORTY-TWO

They had planned to be a little late and enter a party that was in full swing. Stall, who was not exactly persona grata with this crowd, wanted to plant himself in a corner and let whoever would, approach him. If any did, he'd be cordial. If none did, he'd enjoy his whiskey, collect his wife when the time was right, and take her home for a nightcap and anything else that came up.

Maureen would begin the evening as she usually did, standing beside him and listening to the book talk that his colleagues inevitably brought with them. Funny, he had thought more than once, that there was no prohibition against talk of work at faculty parties. According to their usual custom, after standing beside her husband for a while, Maureen would drift off to practice her wiles wherever she found victims. Stall watched her walk away admiring the curves of her buttocks in the black dress that, despite what he had said earlier, he now saw might actually be a little too tight. Maureen had just inclined her head to a group of wives who seemed to be in deep colloquy about something that needed whispering when the front door opened and Sophie Green entered on the arm of Stephen Levy. In a Jane Austen novel, a collective gasp would have greeted the sight of social unequals, a professor and a student, arriving as a couple. In Fred Parsons's house, the hum of cordial conversation subsided to nothing.

And then, "Dr. Green, welcome! And this must be . . . ?"

It was Mary Beth Parsons saving the night. Their hostess had almost run, at the risk of broken ankles on her tipping heels, across the room, bracelets rattling on her wrists as she extended both hands to Sophie Green. This act of good manners, genuine or not, gave cover to the rest of the faculty and their wives, so that conversation began again at first archly, and then more naturally. From his redoubt in the corner where he drank alone, waiting for any who cared to stop for a word with him, Stall could not hear what Sophie Green said to Mary Beth Parsons as the two stood gripping each other's hands, but he saw Sophie Green introduce her date to Mrs. Parsons. Stephen Levy shook the woman's hand, gave her a look that told her she was not worth his attention beyond hello, and looked over her shoulder for men whose conversation offered meat. This was English, not political science, but there still might be men here whose meager intellects Levy could conquer.

The strain in Sophie Green's face, and the defiance in young Levy's manner, told the graduate faculty that this was not a miscalculation, but an intentional affront. Watching the two, professor and student, her arm in his, walk to the bar, Stall recalled Sophie Green saying, *I came here to change things.* And then he thought, *Well, at least my sins won't be the most memorable from tonight's party.*

Fred Parsons approached Stall, a very brown whiskey in his hand. Stall looked at the bar again. Maureen was standing next to Stephen Levy. Parsons said to Stall in a voice that was not quite invitational, "Let's go outside and get some air."

The backyard sloped to the pool and the creek, and walking beside Parsons, Stall remembered one of the two fistfights he'd had growing up. In the bad one, a boy shorter than him, a boy he later learned had studied boxing in another city, in the Police Athletic League, had fallen behind Stall on sloping ground and said, *Is this all right?*

And stupidly, Stall had taken another step downhill, turned, and said, *It's fine.*

And then the boy was on him, and it wasn't boxing, it was more medieval than that, and the advantage of the slope, of the boy's weight hitting Stall's chest from uphill, was decisive. Stall never got the boy off his chest, and after a while, all he could do was protect his face with folded arms. The boy had beaten him until he grew tired of it and walked away. Stall had earned a broken nose and a good lesson: terrain was all.

He stopped and let Fred Parsons take the fatal step downhill. If this was to be the well-known let's-step-outside, then Stall would not make the same mistake twice.

"All right," Parsons said, "so you know I wrote that letter."

Stall waited, sipped his drink. Not much occurred to him to say. The situation seemed to be at rest. Jack Leaf was dead, Gilson had been sacrificed but had not blown his brains out in the basement of Anderson Hall, Helen Markham and her tin of tea were gone, the graduate English Department was wounded but not fatally, not yet, and Connor had moved on to political science.

Parsons said, "I ought to take you down to that creek and soak your head."

Christ, Stall thought, *what a pathetic threat. At least Gilson wanted to knock my teeth out.*

Parsons was ten years older than Stall, flabby at the middle, and audibly wheezy when he climbed the Anderson Hall stairs. But he had been tenured and fully promoted years before Stall had been, so maybe Parsons thought seniority was enough to make the threat of a head-soaking in toxic Hogtown Creek matter to Stall.

"You're welcome to try." Stall measured the distance for the toss of a tumbler of bourbon into Fred Parsons's face.

Parsons groaned like an old dog waking up and looked up at the starry night, then at the lights from his back porch where the party carried on with its tinkling of ice in glasses, phonograph music, and the hum of talk. When he looked back at Stall, his eyes were anguished. "Goddamnit, Stall, do you think I wanted to do it?"

"Yes, I do." He didn't see how a man could do such a thing without *wanting* to.

"I had to protect Ted. Oh, you may not think much of Ted, or of me for that matter, but Ted is my friend and I had to protect him."

I thought you were both my *friends before this mess got started.* "From what?"

Parsons gave Stall the *are you insane* look. "Well, isn't that obvious?"

At this, Stall shook his head. "I don't know, Fred. Maybe we could have saved Ted another way. We'd already lost Jack. Maybe that would have been enough for Connor. Maybe I could have convinced him to let us alone after Jack died—but now we'll never know, will we?"

"*You*? Convince Connor?"

"Sure. Why not? I was trying. Didn't you know that? Didn't my friends, my colleagues, believe I'd do my best to protect the department?"

No, you believed I was a rat.

"Oh, damn it, Stall, you don't understand." Another anguished glance at the starry night where God, if you believed in Him, looked down on a sorry scene.

"What don't I understand?"

"There's more. Things you don't know."

"What things?" Stall let himself relax, gave up his uphill advantage. His curiosity was awake now. He faced Parsons on even ground.

"Sure, Ted's queer, gay as a bird, if you like, but he's not bad enough to destroy Roland Gilson to save himself from what most of us knew already."

But you did. You destroyed Roland Gilson.

"Ted would just leave quietly. He wouldn't throw himself out any window. There's something else."

"But you won't tell me what it is? Is it Helen?"

"Helen?" Parsons waved his hand. "Of course not, Helen will be all right."

"Okay, Fred, I'm going to stop guessing. But there's something I want you to do. Something I think you owe me and the department." Stall glanced up the hill at the happy frivolity of Parsons's party. "I want you to tell the faculty, our colleagues, the people up there I thought were friends who trusted me, I want you to tell them *you* wrote that letter."

"But they'll want to know *why*!" Parsons's voice was a whiny hiss in the starlight.

"Of course they will, Fred. And you'll have to tell them that too. I'll call a special meeting for you, and you'll say you wrote the letter, and I can't see you getting out of that meeting alive without giving up your reasons. If, as you say, everyone knows Ted is gay as a bird, then you can leave that out. But you'll have to tell us the rest of it."

Parsons hung his head. Bourbon spilled from the tilted glass in his hand. Stall waited, sipping, enjoying the cool night.

Finally: "Let's go back to the party, Fred."

Parsons walked downhill toward the pool and the creek.

Stall ascended, tossing the ice from his empty glass onto the dewy grass.

I know enough for one night.

FORTY-THREE

Stall found Maureen, Sophie Green, and Stephen Levy near the grand piano that begged for a good playing by Eugen Brugge. Stall wondered if Brugge had been invited. A little Cole Porter would be just the thing for this gathering. Stall said hellos all around and touched his wife at the small of her back where no other man could put his hand.

Maureen said, "We were just talking about you." She gave him one of their several secret smiles. This one said, *Just wait till I tell you.*

Stall smiled back his, *Can't wait to hear it.* He said, "I'm a little disappointed that you can't find something more interesting to talk about."

Sophie Green said, "Don't sell yourself short, Tom. There are lots of interesting things about you. Not many men would react so well to a wife who came home one day and out of the blue said she had a job."

You mean not many men down here? In the sunny South?

Stephen Levy's expression said that the topic of Maureen Stall's new job only just crossed the border of the permissible.

Stall said, "Well, I'm progressive that way. A real forward-looker, actually." *What was I supposed to do? Instruct my wife to go down to the office of the superintendent of schools and unhire herself?* He started counting, betting that he wouldn't make it to ten before Sophie Green took credit for Maureen's job.

Six, seven, eight . . .

"We should have another lunch, Maureen. Put our heads together and think of some other things you can do that will make Tom look . . . forward."

Maureen gave Stall a loving glance. "Oh, he's indulged me quite enough for now. What about you two? Isn't this . . ." Maureen's hand gestured at the couple in front of her and then at the party, the Fall Social of the graduate English faculty, "new?"

Only you, Maureen, could do this.

Sophie Green handled the question with a girlish toss of curls that was almost Southern. "I've only been in town since July. Everything here is new to me."

Stephen Levy ignored Maureen. To Stall he said, "The invitation said *faculty member and guest*. Nothing there about race or class."

Stall had decided to let Sophie Green go her own way without further counsel from her chairman. Her guest could go with her. "Fine with me. The more the merrier."

Sophie Green leaned toward him, pulling young Levy by his arm. "It's kind of you and Maureen to talk with us like this. I get the impression that we've made some of our colleagues uncomfortable."

"Why?" *Let her explain it.*

Sophie Green looked to Maureen for a woman's understanding. "Oh, you know. Tradition. The way *we* do things down here." With her last few words, Sophie Green had tried out a Southern accent. Her acting fell short of the mark.

"Don't forget good manners." Stephen Levy dug into the breast pocket of his shabby black suit coat. "I brought the invitation in case we were braced at the door." He offered the paper to Stall.

Stall had to say it: "So, you two are changing things here tonight?"

Sophie Green gave Maureen a sweet girl wink, let go of her escort's arm, and dramatically laced her fingers in Levy's. "Let's go mingle with the English."

"They're in love," Maureen said.

She was rolling a silk stocking down her left thigh, making the careful roll that meant she would give the sheer little darlings one more good wearing before she washed them. She'd wrap them in white tissue paper and put them in her underwear drawer to wait for another night out. She sat with her legs slightly splayed, the other stocking with its old-fashioned black seam running down the back still attached to her garter. During the war, when most of the silk in the world had gone to parachute canopies, American women had used mascara to draw those black lines down the backs of their bare legs. It took a steady hand or a roommate's help. Not all of America's ingenuity had gone to tanks and warplanes, Stall mused.

"How do you know they're in love?" He sat in a chair in the corner of the bedroom, sipping a bourbon nightcap. "How could you tell it from a political alliance?"

"Oh, a woman knows."

He waited.

"By her voice mostly. There's a little tremble in there when she talks about him."

"About Stephen Levy?"

"Yes, and the way she never took her arm from his. Didn't you see she was the only woman in the room who held onto her man the whole night?" She gave Stall one of her *how could you miss that* looks. He hoped there'd be many more.

"Now that you mention it, I didn't. Anything else?"

"Her makeup. It was party makeup, and we all did a little better than usual, but she put some real time into hers. She wanted to look younger."

"I didn't notice any makeup."

"That's what I mean. The harder you work at it, the less it's noticeable."

"She's only, what, twenty-nine or thirty?"

"Yeah, but he's only twenty-five or so, and at their age, at the very beginning, that matters a lot."

"Ah." Stall sipped and tried to imagine if an age difference, if Maureen had been older than he, would have mattered to him.

Maureen went into the bathroom to slip into her nightie. Her voice drifted, a little dreamy, out to Stall: "If she'd showed up alone, she wouldn't have worn makeup so as not to threaten the wives. Coming with a man and all made up says love."

Stall considered it promising that she had chosen the black nightgown. He had already been rewarded for receiving with good grace the news of her job. So far, she'd mentioned nothing about the party that hinted at a reward tonight.

He tried this: "Did you tell anyone about your new job?"

"No." She crawled into their bed and pulled the covers up to her chin.

"Why not?"

"I don't know. It all just seemed so sad."

"Sad? Jesus, Maureen, it was a party. I'm the one with the troubles. I thought you were happy tonight."

"I was. Then I saw you go outside with Fred. When were you going to tell me about that?"

"It was going to be the very next thing."

"Well?"

"Well, there isn't much to tell, really. He admitted writing the letter, but he wouldn't share his reasons for doing it."

"Did you tell him you might want to prosecute him for forgery?"

"What good would that do?"

"Well, he deserves some kind of punishment. A good kick in the ass at the very least."

Stall sighed. "I guess we don't kick asses in the English Department. But I want you to know I was ready for anything out there in the backyard."

Maureen rolled away from him. After a while her breathing became long and slow. When he thought she was asleep, he took the last of his bourbon in a sloppy gulp and set the glass on the table by the chair.

From the bed: "Did you put a coaster under that?"

"No, but I will. Tell you what. I'll take it downstairs and wash it."

"In the morning."

Stall realized that he was very tired. There would be no reward tonight.

And from the bed: "Your troubles are mine too. Don't you forget that. Ever."

But Stall was thinking about *it all just seemed so sad.* From what chasm of his wife's unexplored self had such a thing come?

FORTY-FOUR

Having bagged two homosexuals and a Communist in Gainesville, the Johns Committee went on the road. The legislators, lawyers, investigators, secretaries, stenographers, and associated coat-holders of the Committee decamped for Miami to find communism in the NAACP. They planned to interrogate the Miami chapter of the NAACP and to call in prominent members of the organization from across the state. Things went differently for the Committee in Miami. The national headquarters of the NAACP in New York, under the direction of a Negro attorney named Thurgood Marshall, funded lawyers for many of the subpoenaed witnesses. On the advice of attorneys who challenged the subpoena powers of the Committee and thus its power to cite witnesses for contempt and to mete out punishment other than public embarrassment, many witnesses refused to appear. The mostly Negro leadership of Florida's NAACP chapters considered themselves to be soldiers in the crusade for civil rights, and they were proud to defy publicly the authority of the Committee in the Miami hearings. The *Miami Herald*, the *Tallahassee Democrat*, the *Jacksonville Florida Times-Union*, and the *Gainesville Sun* gave plenty of space to their outcry against the Committee. The Committee, and especially its chairman Charley Johns, emerged wounded from the confrontation in Miami. No one could yet tell how serious were these wounds. Would they soon heal or would they fester and their odor become intolerable to citizens of the state and the nation?

Tom Stall and his colleagues, indeed all of Gainesville, paid close attention to the reports of the Miami hearings. The *Independent Alligator*, now a smeared blue mimeographed broadside that emanated, it was rumored, from somewhere in Squalor Holler, gave lavish coverage to what Stephen Levy described as the humiliation of Charley Johns. Stall, whose offenses, imagined and otherwise, to the English Department had not been forgiven, remained estranged from his colleagues. He taught his classes, performed his administrative duties, attended or chaired the meetings on his docket, and otherwise kept to himself.

Although he had access to the opinions of his colleagues only through the often comically unreliable Jed Burwell, Stall could sense, and thought they did too, that the noxious fog of fear and paranoia that had drifted across the university after Jack Leaf's death had thinned, if not lifted. Fred Parsons remained silent.

Maureen Stall was in her glory as a probationary fourth grade teacher at Kirby Smith Elementary School.

After three weeks of teaching from eight until three o'clock and then spending long evenings refreshing her knowledge of her college textbooks, she had hit her stride. She told Stall that her students were adorable, although a few needed special attention for behavior or academic deficits (and one or two were what was compassionately called "slow"). The other teachers had welcomed her, and some were becoming her friends. The principal could be severe at times and was never much of a personality, but he ran a well-organized school and had dropped by Maureen's classroom to praise her decorations of the walls and bulletin boards and had even stayed on for one of her lessons with math flash cards. The Stalls had banked Maureen's first paycheck and, while the amount was modest, it would help. They had talked of setting aside her salary to purchase air conditioners, or perhaps for a real vacation next summer, something less frugal than the usual drive to South Carolina and Ohio for stays with their parents.

On Monday morning of the fourth week of Stall's semester and the third of Maureen's, Stall awoke earlier than usual to find the bed empty bedside him. He lay in the half darkness, expecting to see Maureen emerge from the bathroom in her nightgown to glide across the floor and back to her place with him. No light seeped from under the bathroom door. This was odd. He heard something downstairs. He couldn't identify the sound. Human, animal, mechanical? It came again. Whatever it was, it put him instantly on the alert.

He padded to the top of the stairs. Corey's room was dark. She was still sleeping. At the bottom of the stairs, he saw light from the kitchen, heard the sound again.

Maureen kneeled on the kitchen floor with her face in the garbage can they kept under the sink. She gave another wracking, shuddering retch, and Stall heard her mutter, "God, oh God."

Even before he reached her and put his hands on her shoulders to steady her, to reassure her, the image formed in his mind of his wife in the front seat of their Packard, of beautiful Maureen in her black party dress, lifting both hands to cup her breasts and then raising these treasures with an evaluating expression on her face. *This dress is tighter than I remember it.*

Upstairs, Stall held Maureen's head on his shoulder and remembered her face lifted to him from the garbage can, pale and full of despair in the harsh light of the kitchen. He didn't think he'd ever seen her face so drained of color, of hope. Trying, he whispered, "It'll be Christmas before you . . . show. They'll let you finish out the year."

"No. The policy is absolute. I looked it up." Her voice was as drained as her face.

"What did it say exactly?"

"A woman who, as you say, *shows*, has to quit. The little darlings can't be allowed to see *that*, although most of them have figured out they came from *somewhere*, don't you think?"

Stall had been thinking hard ever since he had mopped his wife's face with a warm cloth and offered her tea, a piece of toast, a glass of warm milk. The contortions in her face at the mention of milk had moved him a step back from her. His thoughts had traveled well beyond the question of whether or not she might keep the job she obviously loved, the job that had put a lightness in her step and a glow in her eyes he had not seen for a long time. Even if she could make it through a year of teaching undetected or at least disguised and tolerated, what would she do after a summer off with their new baby? Yes, *theirs*. When they were young, Stall had done his meager share of caring for Corey while also navigating the shoals and deeps of graduate school. It had been no easy thing for Maureen or for him. Could they afford to hire a woman to care for the baby while Maureen taught? Stall could imagine the arrangement as plausible, but he doubted that his neighbors in this slightly higher than middle-class neighborhood would see it that way. The Stalls would be considered odd at best, neglectful at worst. And wouldn't Maureen suffer the guilts of hell itself if she left her new baby to the care of another woman for seven hours a day? No, the likeliest thing was that Maureen would give up the job that was probationary. She would return to the life of laundry, pot roasts, short ribs, pancakes, and scrambled eggs, the life that Stall and Corey had known and loved (more than they knew) before Maureen's lunch with Sophie Green and her chance encounter with the superintendent of schools.

"I thought we were careful," Maureen whispered into Stall shoulder.

"So did I." This was dangerous. It would do no good now to find the bottom of it.

"Are you going to school?"

"I have to."

She bit the flesh of his shoulder, not too hard. Stall wondered what the message was. Her teeth telling him, *You hurt me*, or just expressing the anguish of a girl who might bite her pillow in the night to stop her tears.

Stall wracked his brain for something to say. Finally, "Is there anything you can take for the nausea?"

"Dramamine, I suppose." Her voice so sad.

"Will that, uh, hurt the baby?"

"I don't know."

When they heard Corey start her morning in the bathroom, Maureen turned away from Stall's wounded shoulder.

FORTY-FIVE

Late one afternoon, just before Stall began his tour of the building to make sure nothing was amiss, Fred Parsons appeared at his office door. Stall's battered briefcase was packed with the article he had promised himself he would soon finish, and his mind was uncluttering itself of the day's cares in preparation for an evening's work at home. Parsons walked past Stall and stood at Helen Markham's empty desk, where Martha Kenny had left the work she was doing for Stall beside the uncovered typewriter. Stall had considered telling her to cover the machine, but the daily crackle of Helen Markham's typewriter cover had irritated him more than he had realized until the woman was blessedly gone. Not hearing it when Martha Kenny came and went was a pleasure.

Parsons's chubby hands picked up the pile of manuscript pages that Martha had left behind. "Aha," he said, reading from Stall's title page, "'The Unlikely Conversion of Graham Greene and the Changes It Wrought in His Fiction.' It'll be interesting to see what you found that's original in this well-worn topic. Seems to me that Greene's Catholicism is a vein that's been pretty well mined."

Thank you, Fred, for pronouncing my article dead. "I think I've found something of my own to say."

"Yes, sorry. Goes without saying, I suppose." Parsons walked on to the inner office and settled his spreading hips into the chair opposite the big Victorian desk. There was nothing for Stall to do but follow him.

Stall sat. "What can I do for you, Fred?"

Parsons crossed his legs and looked around the office. His thinning hair, combed from just above his right ear across the top of his head, revealed liver spots, and his close-set brown eyes seemed to

Stall smaller than usual. "I haven't spent much time in this chair, but I have a few good memories of conversations with Amos Harding. Times change, don't they?"

"They do." Stall looked at his watch. "Fred, what is it you want?"

"We're subtle people, we academic types, but today I'll be blunt. I assume you've heard that Dr. Green's behavior is raising eyebrows. As you know, I chair the tenure committee, and I can tell you, informally of course, that members of the committee have grave doubts about Dr. Green's fitness for our department."

Stall considered saying, *What makes you think* I *want to keep her?*

Parsons waited, then shrugged. "Well, I just naturally assumed you'd want to help the girl . . . in your official capacity as chairman, of course."

"As always, Fred, I want to do what's best for the department and the university."

"Of course, of course. So, assuming that you want her to stay . . ."

"Assume as you like, Fred. I want her to get a fair shake like everybody else."

"I remember you and your lovely wife taking care to talk with Dr. Green and her escort at my party."

"Just being polite."

"Of course."

"My dinner's waiting, Fred."

"All right, then, continuing in bluntness, I want to offer you a deal. I'll use my influence with the committee to see to it that Professor Green gets, shall we say, the most careful consideration of her application for tenure, if you'll forget this entire business of a letter that was sent to President Connor."

"That *you* sent."

"If you say so."

"*You* said so, Fred. That night in your backyard after you threatened to soak my head in the creek."

"No one but you heard me say it, and now I've offered you a deal. Dr. Green gets tenure if you forget about that letter."

Christ, you bastard, you want to put my soul on the block again. Stall stood. "Fred, I'm confident that you and the committee will do the right thing when it comes to Dr. Green's tenure application. As to the other matter, it's up to you and your conscience. What I want you to do remains unchanged. Stand before the department and admit you wrote that goddamned letter." He picked up his briefcase. "Shut the door on your way out, Fred."

"Wait!" Parsons stood at Helen Markham's desk again. He fingered the pages that lay beside the typewriter. "You and Martha. How's that going, Stall?"

"She's a crackerjack typist, Fred. If she has some time I'm not using, I'll send her your way. She can type up the volumes of work I'm sure you're producing."

In the hallway, Stall considered his habitual walk to see what might be amiss in the old building. Behind him, plenty was amiss. He made for the nearest exit and the promise of fresh air.

The next morning, Martha Kenny arrived early for her day's work with Stall. He heard her come in and sit at the outer desk, but the typewriter was silent. He had found that he looked forward to seeing her. After some awkwardness, they had developed an easy relationship. She was respectful and efficient here in his office and entirely appropriate in his class. She did the typing and filing Stall required and accepted the money he paid her for it gratefully. Stall had put off interviewing applicants for the job of full-time secretary.

Now Martha was sitting quietly in the outer office in the lingering effluvium of Helen Markham's rosewater cologne and Earl Grey tea. Stall got up from his desk and walked to the door. "Hello, Martha." He looked at his watch. "You're a bit early."

"I'd like to talk with you about something."

"Come in, then."

Shyly but resolutely, she did, and took the chair he offered.

"What can I do for you?"

She smoothed her tartan skirt, a garment better suited to winters at Smith than to early fall in steamy Gainesville, and crossed her legs. She was nobody's beauty queen, but Stall had seen already that she gave back to the world only its goodness. She was one of ten students in Stall's modern American novels course. So far, she had shown herself to be hardworking, well prepared, enthusiastic about the books, and congenial with her fellow students, all men. The high quality of her intelligence was obvious: she had deserved her As at Smith College. She seemed to enjoy life and literature, to emphasize their affirmations while fully aware of their darkness. Stall liked her.

"Oh, I know I probably shouldn't ask, but I'm wondering how I'm doing—in your class, I mean."

No, you probably shouldn't. Stall had always disliked this question. It usually came from wheedlers who fished for compliments or wanted to negotiate grades. With Martha Kenny he would make an exception. "It's early yet, Martha, but so far indications are good." He gave her a fatherly smile.

She sighed. She seemed genuinely relieved. Stall found this touching. He thought she would rise and leave now, but she said, "I was afraid I might be talking too much in class or annoying people, you especially, but if . . ."

"No," Stall said, "you're talking about right, I'd say. Keep it up. We're all enjoying what you have to say." Of course, he couldn't speak for the enjoyments of all nine men in the class. Probably some of them resented her, but these would have resented any woman who took a chair around their table. He also knew that Martha had perfected the skill of disarming the male ego. She was deferential to good ideas and never scornful of bad ones. Her attitude toward the latter was that of a kitten playing with the mouse it has not yet practiced the courage to kill. She gave the smarter men in the class admiring looks when they spoke well and looked into her lap when they didn't.

Despite reservations about the question, Stall asked, "How are things going for you generally? Are you enjoying your other classes?" The best students understood that enjoying a graduate education meant submitting to a certain amount of destruction. Flabby opinions and beloved old appreciations had to be purged.

Martha Kenny's brows furrowed up to her hairline. "Yes sir, they're all good. All except one."

"Which one?" Before becoming chairman Stall would not have plucked this thread, but his new position required that he know the running of things.

"Dr. Green's class."

Stall cleared his throat. "Which of her classes?"

"American lit."

The class Sophie Green had offered to teach after Jack Leaf's walk in the air. Stall remembered opening the note from Sophie Green while he waited in President Connor's office:

I wrote my master's thesis on The Leatherstocking Tales, and, though I later moved on to specialize in Chaucer (a lot of distance between those two!), I remember a good bit about American Romanticism, and I will certainly bone up on it if you repose faith in me to take over the course.

"What bothers you about the class, Martha?"

"Well, she overpraises some writers and denigrates others, and she favors some students—well, really just one."

"Which writers does she overpraise?"

"The women."

"Hmm." Stall examined Martha Kenny's face for any sign of currying his favor, any sign that she was telling him what she thought he'd want to hear. "Well," he said, "I doubt that anyone would argue with the notion that few women in those days had the requisite education or opportunity to become known in literary circles."

Martha Kenny watched him while she thought her way through his careful answer. What he'd said didn't seem to help.

Oh hell, Stall thought. "Martha, what women does Professor Green overpraise?"

"Fanny Fern, and she just wrote potboilers. Sentimental stories for women."

Stall shifted in his chair. "I have to agree with you there. Now tell me about the student she favors."

"Martin Levy. They sit together at the end of the table and talk like two friends rather than professor and student."

"And this offends you?"

"Not offends. It just sets the wrong tone. It's like the rest of us are there to watch and listen. Like we're inferior beings or something."

"I assure you, Martha, you are not an inferior being."

"Thank you. I know that. It's why I'm here, to make the most of my talent and brains. And that's why I'm talking to you. I don't think

I can learn much in a class that's really just a conversation between two people."

"Martha, do you want to be a teacher someday? A professor?"

"Yes sir." Her fervent tone told Stall how much she wanted it.

"Can you imagine yourself someday sitting where I'm sitting now?"

She thought about this for a while, probably strategically. Should she tell her professor, her chairman, that she might someday become what he was? "Yes, I think so."

"What do you think I should do?"

"I don't know, Dr. Stall. Maybe there's nothing you should do. But I thought you'd want to know." She considered her words carefully. "And I felt that I had to tell you."

Stall leaned back in his chair and laced his fingers behind his head. He closed his eyes and found that he could imagine very well the scene Martha Kenny described, the kind of conversation that Sophie Green and Martin Levy would have while the other students looked on in admiration. He opened his eyes to the expectations of Martha Kenny.

"I'll talk with Dr. Green. And Martha, let's keep this conversation to ourselves. All right?"

"I promise."

"Good. I do too."

FORTY-SIX

Stall called Sophie Green and asked her to come down.

A few minutes later she was at his office door. She gave him a cold look. "I've been summoned?"

Stall permitted himself a little chuckle. "I suppose you have."

She stepped past him into his office, sat, smoothed her skirt, and looked pointedly at her watch.

Stall put the desk between them. "How's American lit going? I remember you saying you'd done your MA thesis on Cooper. Are you including him? Is it all coming back to you?"

"What isn't *coming back* will come with preparation. I'm a good little swot."

"Ah, a swot. Aren't we all?" *Swotting* was British slang for cramming, grinding the books.

"So, yes, things are going fine in American lit. Why do you ask?" Her eyes narrowed.

"Oh, no reason really, uh, just that I've heard—"

"Heard what?" Sophie Green pushed forward in her chair, squared her feet on the floor, and elevated her chin.

Stall cleared his throat. "Well, that you and Mr. Levy have a lot to say to each other in class."

"Look, Stall!"

"Dr. Green?"

"All right, I'll play the game with you. Heard from whom?"

"Well, from several people actually." A little lie to protect Martha Kenny.

"Several? Right. You mean Martha Kenny?"

"Why do you mention her?"

"She's a clever little thing, little Martha. I'll bet she's been in here to see you with her . . ."

"Her what?"

"Oh, that Smith College nose-in-the-air attitude of hers."

Damned if Stall would admit that Martha Kenny had come to him with a concern. "Hmm. Strange. In my class she's been nothing but productive. Gets along well with everyone."

"You mean with the boys."

"Well, strictly that's true, but it's not what I meant. Martha seems like a reasonable person to me."

The look she gave him disputed his knowledge of reason.

Stall said flatly, "Is it possible that you're giving so much attention to Martin Levy that you may be neglecting the needs of other students?"

"In a word, no, it's not. And Martha Kenny would do well to listen to what Martin and I have to say on any and all topics related to American Romanticism."

"Dr. Green, I'd be remiss in my role as your chairman if I didn't suggest that you divide your attentions a little more evenly among your students. I'm sure you want all of them to have the same exciting learning experience."

"Alas, they're not all capable of the same experience. But for the record, your advice on pedagogy is duly noted."

Stall looked at the door, signaling his thought that this meeting was over. Sophie Green reached down for the bag at her feet, a stylish and expensive combination of purse and portfolio. She took from it a blurry blue mimeographed sheet. "Are you reading the *Independent Alligator* these days?"

Stall shook his head.

"Well, I thought I'd bring this with me to save you the trouble of hearing about it from some of our colleagues." She leaned forward and put the blue sheet on Stall's blotter.

He glanced at a headline: "UF AAUP Chapter Gets Makeover. New Officers Installed." He looked up at Sophie Green. "And you're . . ."

"Recording secretary, duly elected. They wanted me for vice president, but I said no."

Stall shook his head in good-natured bemusement. "I suppose congratulations are in order."

The UF chapter of the American Association of University Professors was a local joke. It rarely met, could never agree on an agenda when it did, and had never in living memory caused anything to happen. It was little more than a social club.

"If your congratulations are sincere, I'm happy to have them." She paused to let Stall smile his sincerity. "And I didn't come here just because you summoned me. I was planning to come anyway. I had, shall we say, an impromptu meeting with Fred Parsons and some of his friends on the tenure committee."

"A meeting?" This got Stall's attention. The tenure committee met in private on a regularly scheduled basis, and never had, as far as Stall knew, interviewed a probationary faculty member. "On the face of it," he said carefully, "this seems unusual." *Unprecedented.*

"It's good to hear you say that. I thought maybe it was a regular thing—one of this department's many medieval rites."

"Tell me about it."

"Fred caught me coming out of class and took me to an empty classroom. Ted Ruggles and Bob Reynard were waiting. So, there I sat in a circle with three senior men. They got right down to business. Fred asked me if I planned to stay here. I said yes, I thought I would like to do that, although no one could read the future, and you know, career opportunities do come one's way from time to time."

"You said that?"

"Yeah, well, I figured why not enhance my value? No good ever comes from underselling yourself, right?"

Stall didn't know the answer to that one. He suspected that he had always been a little too slow to put himself forward. "Go on."

"Fred told me that things had been noticed, and things were being said about me. It had come to the attention of the tenure committee that I had been elected to a leadership position in the AAUP. He said, *And I hardly need tell you that your performance at the Fall Social caused some consternation*."

"Your performance?"

"Of course he meant showing up there with Stephen Levy on my arm—or me on his. When Fred mentioned that, the other two gave me their gravest looks."

Christ, Stall thought, *Parsons works fast. First the deal he offered, and now a threat*. "Surely you knew the party would cause problems."

"Not this kind of problem."

"But I told you a month ago exactly what could happen to you."

She pointed at the blue sheet on Stall's blotter. "This is precisely the kind of problem the AAUP exists to solve."

"If you joined that club to get yourself tenure, I'm afraid you miscalculated."

"Of course I didn't. I joined it to fight Charley Johns, as you very well know."

"And I assume you know that the AAUP has a lousy track record when it comes to fighting for faculty rights."

"We're going to change all that."

"What do you want me to do?"

She drew herself back into her chair, her chin elevated. The red daubs of a blush appeared under her cheekbones. "Well, I . . ." She shook her head. At what? Stall's failure to understand, his lack of interest, of nerve?

He said, "Look, my stock is about as low as it can get around here, and partly because of you and others who came here to change things. A month ago I could have talked to Fred Parsons and the others, maybe spent some political capital on this. But that's all over now. That account is empty."

"Aren't there rules against what they did?"

"Yeah, there are rules, and they're intentionally vague. Anyone can be denied tenure for any reason. It's a blackball situation, just like what happens down on fraternity row. From the day you set foot on this campus, you've made it clear that you want to change things. Well, some people don't want things to change. And the men who run the tenure committee don't want them to. They'd rather just get rid of you."

"Can I appeal?"

"You can go to the dean, the president even." Stall shrugged in a way that said, *Good luck with that.*

She pulled the portfolio purse into her lap and wrapped her arms around it as though to shield herself from Stall. "So, you won't do *anything* about this?"

Stall sighed. He could remember no time when Harding, in his capacity as chairman, had attempted to sway the tenure committee. And the decisions the committee had made since Stall had been hired had all been widely approved, although only the committee actually made them.

With a sad smile that opened to Stall her first vulnerability, Sophie Green stood and turned to leave.

To her back he said, "I'll talk to Fred."

She turned.

"I can't guarantee anything, of course, but I'll talk to him. If he shows some willingness to relent on this, can I tell him you'll play things with a little less brass?"

Anger flashed in her eyes, and then just as quickly died. "Yes, Tom, Mr. Chairman, you can tell him that." She reached out and lifted the blue sheet from his blotter and dropped it in his wastebasket. "I'll start by resigning from the AAUP."

"Oh, and Dr. Green, remember this for the record: I did not mention Martha Kenny in connection with problems in your class, and I'm confident that you will treat Miss Kenny with perfect fairness from now on."

Sophie Green couldn't make words come out, but she nodded twice, the second time with more resolution, and then she was drifting past Helen Markham's empty desk like a Victorian wraith.

Stall glanced at the blue sheet at the bottom of his wastebasket, the brief career of a recording secretary.

He rolled a piece of paper into his typewriter and began his own faculty file:

This date, student MK reported to me that Prof. Sophie Green favors student ML in American Romanticism class. According to MK, Dr. Green spends much of the class hour in conversation with one student, ML, while other students look on. MK indicates that Prof. Green's behavior diminishes the quality of her experience here at the University of Florida.

FORTY-SEVEN

In a dark mind, Stall walked to Tigert Hall and another meeting with President Connor. Students came and went, near and far. Did they stop talking as he approached? Were they alarmed by his shambling gait, his chin scraping the knot of his tie, the grim set of his mouth? He remembered an aphorism: *Be kind, for everyone you meet is fighting a hard battle.* A strong breeze ruffled the long tassels of the loblolly pines that lined the walk, and the air smelled of fall. Florida cheated in so many ways, and one of them was her seasons. Some years, ninety-degree temperatures lasted into October, and some, like this one, gave Gainesville a week or two when the perfume in the air was a gentle warning of cold to come and a sad reminder of summer. Such things moved the heart.

President Connor's call had come at eight thirty, only seconds after Stall had settled into his office chair and spread some lecture notes on the blotter in front of him. Connor's voice on the phone had given nothing away. "Come over, Tom. Something I want to talk with you about."

Margaret Braithwaite, immaculate in a stylish wool suit of harvest yellow, stood behind her desk uncovering the Olivetti. She looked up as if caught.

Stall said, "Hello, Margaret," and nodded at the inner office. "He asked for me."

Mrs. Braithwaite, keeper of the president's time, raised her chin an inch and narrowed her eyes at Stall. "He said nothing to me about it, but . . . go on in. Here, take this with you." She handed Stall a cup of black coffee, then remembered hospitality. "Would you like one?"

"No thanks. I've had breakfast."

She nodded approval of breakfast if not of Stall.

James Connor stood in shirtsleeves at the window, looking down on the grand entrance to the university with its beds of azaleas and rows of boxwood hedges.

Stall settled the coffee in its saucer on the president's blotter. The rattle of the cup announced him, and Connor turned from the window.

There was something in the president's face Stall had not seen before. Connor's expression said, *This will be brief.*

"Tom, what do you know about the Committee's hearings in Miami?"

"Just what everybody knows. They didn't go all that well. At the very least it was an anticlimax for Charley Johns."

"It was a disaster." Connor sat, pulled the coffee toward him, looked into its hot black surface as though he could see some grim future there. "Did Margaret offer you a cup?"

"Yes sir, she did." Stall waited. He had not been invited to sit.

"Tom, I want you to go back to Jack Leaf."

"Go back to him . . . Jim?"

"Leaf's death was an opportunity we missed. It should have been the beginning of an investigation, a systematic inquiry into the possibility that Leaf was the leader of a homosexual ring here in Gainesville. I say in Gainesville because simple logic tells me that it's not limited to the English Department or even to the university."

A systematic inquiry? "Do you mean a police investigation?"

"No, I mean I want you to look into it for me . . . in a more *energetic* way."

So, my efforts have lacked energy. Stall remembered their talk in Connor's dressing room. They had agreed that English had sacrificed enough. With brutal dispatch, Connor had moved on to the Political Science Department and the dismissal of Stan Margolis.

"The woman," Connor said, "Leaf's wife. What's her name?"

"Her name is Sarah."

"Ah, Sarah. Not a bad-looking girl if I remember right. I want you to go see her and find out what you can about their friends, Leaf's friends, his activities. Anything she knows about his associates."

"I talked to her after Jack died. I doubt she knows anything about his associates." Of course Sarah had known Jack's friends, but she'd had no idea that her husband met men in public restrooms. Stall shook his head. "Whatever the truth is about Sarah and Jack, I'm not going to *inquire* into it for you. If you think something illegal took place, then maybe you should refer the matter to the police, or to the Committee's investigators. They've granted themselves police powers. A 'homosexual ring' is beyond my meager investigative abilities and certainly beyond my interest." *My interest in both senses of the word. You've put me in the place where I can destroy myself or you can destroy me. Either way, the end is destruction. Better my destruction on your conscience than on my own.*

"Look, Tom, I know you liked Jack Leaf and cared about him, and I think you care about his wife. Go to her, and tell her there'll be more about her husband in the newspapers if she doesn't help you with your investigation. She'll find that persuasive."

Stall remembered a poem he loved by E. E. Cummings in which a beleaguered character says, *there is some shit I will not eat*. "I won't do it."

Connor sipped his coffee and let his fighter's eyes relent. "You think I'm going back on a deal, don't you, Tom?"

"I won't say that, Jim. But I did think we . . . reached an understanding the last time we talked." *You were pulling on your pants with the help of a smiling retainer.*

"Well, things have changed." Connor took a folded newspaper from the desktop and held it out to Stall.

Stall read the banner headline: "Homosexual Ring Alleged at University."

"I can't ignore this, Tom."

The newspaper was the *Marianna Eagle and Intelligencer*. Stall turned the paper toward Connor. "This is hardly the *New York Times*." They both knew that Marianna, a northwest Florida tobacco town, was the seat of pork chop power. Charley Johns was from Starke, not far away. "Who cares what Marianna says?"

"A majority of the state legislature, that's who. And if you don't know this, you should: in this state, the legislature has the Board of Regents by the short and curly hair." Connor snapped his fingers in the air between them. "They can fire a university president quick as that. Hell, somebody in the legislature probably wrote that headline."

Stall took a step backward. "I'm sorry, Jim. I can't do what you ask. I did think we had a deal, and now you say *circumstances are different*." Stall shrugged. "To me, a deal's a deal."

"Damn it, Tom, you'd better think about this before you walk out of here. I can hurt you in more places than your wallet, and Frank Vane can too." The look on the president's face was sad now. "I knew from the start they had something on you, Tom."

There was no mistaking what he meant. Frank Vane had told him about Brigitte.

Connor turned to look out the window. His voice was low and almost soothing. "Tom, you know I had to find out why Frank Vane thought he could work you. It was only right that I should know that, don't you think?"

"I think private lives should be kept private. I've told you that before."

"You're naive." With a flick of his hand, Connor waved Stall's innocence away like a fly that circled between them.

Stall said, "I know what you and Frank Vane can do to me." And he was about to say something bold—*And I'm not worried about it.* But he was worried. He certainly was. Instead, he said, "How much did Frank Vane give you for the medical school?"

"It was a substantial gift for a good cause. You object to that?"

Stall stepped back toward Connor's desk and leaned over it, looked into the man's eyes, saw the fear in them. "You're afraid, Jim, just like me. I can see it. I understand fear. We both learned all about fear in a French forest. But I have to tell you, Jim, this thing you're doing with Frank Vane is beneath you. It's lower than you ever thought you'd go."

Connor looked away at the big windows that opened onto the fragrant fall day, the season of dying, of the red leaves poets described. There was no poetry in his eyes when he turned back to Stall. They were dead. "Stall, you made this trouble for yourself. You should have left that girl alone, and you should have told your wife about the child the day you learned of it. I can't have a man carrying your kind of baggage stay on as one of my chairmen. Not if people know about it."

"You're probably right about what I should have told my wife, and there was once a time when you could have instructed me about it, but that day is gone. You and Frank Vane ought to confine yourselves to building medical schools. We both know this shit with homosexuals and Commies will pass. Universities last."

"And marriages?"

"Some do."

"They'll name the new wing of the medical school after me, Stall. I'll bet you that one dollars to doughnuts."

"Maybe it's not too late to earn the honor."

As Stall walked through the outer office past Margaret Braithwaite, who had not yet fired up the typewriter that reminded Stall of the war he had survived not by wit or guts but by luck, it occurred to him that Frank Vane and James Connor had wanted the same thing from the beginning. In his uneasy alliance with Connor, Stall had never been on the right side. Only on the side of a brutal practicality. He had been the tool of two men's ambitions. He had given the investigation of English the shabby imprimatur of the minor position he held, and now they wanted more of his bureaucratic zeal. Not some gumshoe or state cop, but a bright young chairman to root out a ring of queers. He had understood this at least dimly since the night of the president's big party. Connor and Vane had been allies from the start. Fate and Charley Johns had presented Connor with a surprise ending to an honorable career. Now all the president cared about was winning the final round and sliding easy into retirement, his old gray head covered with laurel.

Let him find someone else to expose his ring of homosexuals . . . or invent it.

Walking the beautiful fall sidewalks back to the office that probably wouldn't be his much longer, Stall breathed in the strange, unnameable perfume of the changing seasons. Halfway to Anderson Hall, a thought stopped him in his tracks: *There is a ring.*

There is a ring of homosexuals, although Jack Leaf was not its center, only a man at the margin. The center is Eugen Brugge.

FORTY-EIGHT

Wearing one of Maureen's aprons, Stall stood at the kitchen stove stirring a pot of tomato soup. He'd made it the good way, with milk rather than water, and had put together a simple salad of lettuce, tomato slices, and grated carrot.

Maureen was upstairs alternately vomiting and lying in the dark with a wet cloth across her eyes. Corey sat at the kitchen table doing her homework. They'd exchanged glances, Stall's too cheerful, Corey's worried. When he lifted his eyebrows and the corners of his mouth to show his daughter his Daddy in Charge face, it was a labor of Hercules. Stall had sent the girl up to invite her mother down for dinner, but Maureen hadn't even let her into the bedroom. Corey had returned with, "Mom says to start without her."

Stall whisked some vinegar and vegetable oil with salt and pepper and dried mustard for a salad dressing and spread egg salad onto toasted bread for the main course. He poured a glass of milk for Corey, made himself a second martini, and laid their dinner out on the table.

The doorbell rang. Corey looked up from dipping her sandwich into her soup. Stall said, "I'll get it." Then, "You expecting Jeannie Mears?"

"Nope. She's got homework too."

Well, Stall thought, *some things still work. The Great American Compulsory Public School System is grinding away at the minds of our young.*

He headed for the front door, but stopped midway through the living room and looked down at the stained apron that covered the white shirt and gray suit trousers he had worn to work. He considered stripping off the apron before answering the door, but thought what the hell. He'd just have to put it on again to do the dishes. *Stall, you look the fool that life has made of you. Comic relief. But what tragedy awaits beyond yonder door?*

When he opened the door, Frank Vane said, "Something smells good. Is there enough for one more?" He was past Stall and into the living room before words came to Stall's fuddled tongue.

"Uh, Frank, this isn't . . ."

But Vane strode on into the kitchen, and Stall, a few steps behind him, heard him greet Corey like her long-lost uncle. "You must be Corey. I've been looking forward to meeting you. No, don't get up. I don't want to interrupt your . . . Say, that looks like some good grub. Good simple American food. Did your daddy make that for you?"

Stall, in the kitchen doorway now, heard Corey's polite "Yes sir," saw her nod, saucer-eyed and expecting . . . what? *God,* Stall thought, *you're a good kid. You'd yes-sir the devil until you saw his cloven hoof.*

Ignoring Stall, Vane said, "I see your daddy has a . . . little drink. Where does he, uh, keep that?"

Corey was approaching her limit. She looked at Stall with an expression of complete bafflement, then at the cupboard above the refrigerator, signal enough for Vane.

Frank Vane opened the cupboard, rummaged, and came down with a bottle of bourbon. "Well," he said ebulliently, "good for you, Tom. I see you've got the brown stuff too. Up where I come from, I mean the, uh, *family* I come from, they consider that stuff in your glass, well, that's for *women*. It's a lady drink. But this good old dark-brown John Barleycorn, it's a buck's liquor." His back to Stall, Vane dumped the dregs from the martini shaker into the sink, poured the ice into an orange juice glass, and gave himself a generous portion of whiskey.

Stall put his hand on his daughter's shoulder, applied a gentle squeeze. "It's all right, Corey. Eat your dinner. Mr. Vane and I will sit with you for a while, then you can go upstairs and finish your homework."

"No, no!" Vane took a long draw of bourbon, rolled it on his tongue, and swallowed appreciatively. "Stay with us, Corey. When will I ever have another chance to share a table with the child of my good friend Tom Stall?" He winked at the girl. "Sort of thought I'd be invited here before now."

Stall thought, *Now, now is the time, before this goes any further, before it gets out of hand, now is the time to take this man by the lapels of his expensive suit coat, jerk him up out of this chair, and toss him into the front yard*. But then he saw his daughter staring at the sleeve of Frank Vane's coat, turned up and neatly pinned under what remained of his arm. She looked at her father for an explanation of something she had never seen before. An awful thing. A thing that should not exist in a child's good world.

Quietly, Stall said, "Corey, honey, Mr. Vane was hurt in the war. It happened a long time ago and now he . . ." But he couldn't finish it. *Now he has made his peace with it. Now he has come to grips. Now he hates with a violent, vicious, unstoppable force every whole thing he sees. You, my whole thing, my beautiful daughter, should not have to see this. Not yet.*

"Oh this!" Vane took another sip of bourbon, set his glass down, and used his only hand to pinch, speculatively, the cloth at his stump. "This? Don't let it worry you, honey. It doesn't worry me anymore. It's just something that . . . happened. I get along just fine without it. Look."

Vane let go of the expensive cloth and showed Corey how well he could use his only hand. He pulled his wallet and a cigarette case, then a notepad and pen, from the inside pockets of his suit coat.

He was undoing his belt when Maureen, looking half dead, said from the doorway, "Don't. That's enough." She wore a housecoat over her nightgown. Her face without makeup was drawn, a gray mask. She took two steps into the kitchen. "Tom, who is this man?"

Standing behind Corey, one hand on her shoulder, the other holding his martini, Stall said, "This is Frank Vane, honey. We, uh, knew each other in the army."

Maureen looked at the kitchen table, the food, and Frank Vane's wallet, case, pad, and pen. "Mr. Vane, please put those things back in your pockets." She waited until Vane complied, then said, "You're welcome to eat with us if you like," and to Stall, "Tom, I don't think I'll want anything. Mr. Vane is welcome to whatever you prepared for me."

Frank Vane looked at—no, examined—Stall's wife, the lovely Mrs. Stall who was not quite the beauty Vane had said she was that day in Stall's office, and seemed to lose some of the courage of his mission. He sat and settled his drink on the plastic place mat in front of him. "Thank you, Mrs. Stall. I'm pleased to meet you. I've heard a lot about you . . . from Tom, of course, and from others too. By all accounts, you're one of Gainesville's belles."

"Not today I'm not." It broke Stall's heart to see his wife touch a hand hopelessly to the hair that her pillow had crushed to the side of her head. "Not for a while, I'm afraid."

Stall supplied the obvious: "Maureen hasn't been feeling well these last few days."

"Well . . ." Vane sipped his bourbon and looked at the stove where the tomato soup was congealing in its pot, "I hope it's nothing serious."

"Oh, it's serious." Maureen's eyes shared with Stall what they had told no one else. "But it's nothing for you to worry about, Mr. Vane."

Frank Vane's face came alight with realization. "Oh my goodness, Mrs. Stall, is this what I think it is? Are you . . . how to put it most delicately? Are you in the family way?"

"Look, Frank. That's none—"

Maureen leaned on the sink, looked into the soup pot, and put her hand over her mouth. She turned to Vane. "It's neither delicate nor appropriate right now, Mr. Vane." She slid her gaze to Corey.

"Oh, well then, I'm sorry. The news is . . . *new*. The, uh, thing has come as a surprise to you. Well, not for the first time, of course. I'd venture to say that half the human race since the days of Methuselah came along as a surprise. But, of course, *always*, as they say, a bundle of joy."

"Corey," Stall said, "go on up to your room and finish your homework."

Corey stood and backed toward the kitchen door.

Maureen took a bowl from the cupboard, ladled tomato soup into it, and set it on the table in front of Frank Vane. "There you go, Mr. Vane." She looked at the egg salad on Stall's plate, covered her mouth again, closed her eyes, and said, "Would you like a sandwich?"

"Well, if you're offering . . ."

Maureen made the sandwich and placed it in front of Frank Vane, who watched her with an open, avid curiosity. She walked around the table, took Corey's place, and sat with the careful balance of the sick. As she let herself down, her housecoat came open, and she reached up to close it.

Stall sat too. He was beginning to feel a dizzy uneasiness, worse than before because it was clear to him that something was to happen now between Frank Vane and Maureen and he could only watch.

Maureen's face was gray and slack when she said, "You knew Tom in the army? Tell me about that. Is that what brought you here?"

But Vane turned to Corey, who still hung in the doorway staring at him. "That's it in a roundabout way. I wanted to see Tom's family. When we were soldiers together, and"—he took a long drink of bourbon, the taste seeming to fuel his memory—"shot to pieces together, although your Tom kept more of himself than I did, we developed what you might call a bond. Yes, a bond. It was more than the comradeship of two guys in the same unit. They put us side by side completely by accident in a field hospital, and a lot of guys who were carried in were also carried out, if you know what I mean, but Tom and I, we got better, and when we could, we talked about where we came from, who we were, what we wanted to do with the lives that had been, you know, sort of taken and then given back to us, and we went to Paris together on a weekend pass, and we had some fun there, different kinds of fun, and then old Tom here got sent home to meet you, I guess, and . . ." He glanced over at Corey, whose eyes had reached their widest, "to have you. And I never saw him again until about two months ago back in August. But the point," he drank again, "the point is that I knew Tom would go home and meet someone—if not you, the lovely Mrs. Stall, then someone else—and he and the wife would have a couple, maybe three, of the very best of our wholesome, disciplined, polite American children, and . . ." Frank Vane took a long breath and finished the brown whiskey in his glass, "and here I am, and here you are, and everything I thought would happen to my friend, my pal, *mon copain* Tom Stall, has happened. Except one thing."

Vane got up from the table and helped himself to another pour of bourbon, swirling the whiskey in his glass.

"And what is that?" Maureen had put both hands on the table in front of her as though to keep from falling forward.

"That?"

"The thing you didn't expect, Mr. Vane?"

"Well, it's that I would have to father one of your husband's three children."

Maureen bowed her head, and then looked up at Stall from under gray, furrowed brows.

All he could say was, "Maureen, I'm sorry."

"You're sorry?" She turned her gaze to Frank Vane. "Mr. Vane, what is my husband sorry about?"

Frank Vane looked at her for a long time, whether it was for dramatic effect or he was making up his mind, Stall could not tell. Finally, he said not to Maureen but to Corey, "Honey, did you ever want to have a sister? I know most kids, uh, you know, only children like you, they want to have a brother or a sister, and I imagine most of them, when they think about it, want to have a *little* sister, or a *little* brother. Did you ever think about that?"

Maureen said, "Corey, go to your room."

For the first time in her life, Stall's daughter disobeyed.

Frank Vane drank again, swirled the whiskey, watched the vortex it made in his glass. He looked up at Corey. "Well, honey, your very dearest wish has come true. But it's an *older* sister you have, not a younger one."

When Stall lunged, seized Vane by the lapels of the coat, intending to drag him out of the house, and then to return and do whatever he could to keep three bodies and souls together, Frank Vane shrugged out of the coat and it hung torn in Stall's hands. With a look of pure hatred on his face, Vane tore off his tie and stripped the buttons down the front of his shirt until Stall heard them rain with rattling sounds on the tile floor. And there it was, Vane's wound, his half arm, the testament to his service, the source of his everlasting hatred of all that was whole. Stall and his family could do nothing but stare at it. Frank Vane's half arm ended above the elbow joint in a puckered nozzle-like gathering that was shocking in its crudeness. The surgeon must have been in a great hurry. It was bright red as though it had never healed. The symbolism hit Stall with thunderous effect. But perhaps the most disturbing thing was the asymmetricality of Vane's torso. Years of doing everything with one arm had given him one pectoral muscle and one biceps that would have been the envy of a bodybuilder. From the middle to the left his chest was emaciated, the chest of a sickly boy.

Maureen stood on unsteady legs. "All right, Mr. Vane, you've delivered your message. It's time for you to go."

"Go? Like this? For all the world to see?" Vane laughed, rolled his eyes with comic exaggeration. He reached down to the table for his glass, took a pull of whiskey, and held out his hand to Stall for his coat. His eyes never left Maureen's. Like a porter or a footman, Stall handed him the coat.

When Vane had dressed himself with practiced quickness that should not have been a surprise, he took a last sip of the bourbon and said, "Well, Mrs. Stall, I just wanted you to know what kind of man your husband is." At the door, he turned back and said, "Oh, and Tom will show you the pictures of his . . . wartime souvenirs."

When the door closed behind Frank Vane, Maureen looked over at Stall. She lowered a hand to her belly and cradled it. "I want you to know, Tom, I welcome this baby."

FORTY-NINE

For three days, Stall had climbed the hill from the bus stop to his house with the sadness and dread of a man walking to the scaffold. The afternoons of late October had been cool. Stall's collar still held some starch and his face was dry. The coat he carried folded over his arm reminded him as always of the August afternoon when he had covered Jack Leaf's face. It seemed to him now an ill-omened thing that he and Maureen had decided to keep the coat President Connor had sent and had returned the one that was Maureen's gift. Connor's coat had come from calculation and, Stall knew now, like so many other things from Connor, to create an obligation. Maureen's coat had come from love. A block from their house, Stall stopped and shifted his battered briefcase with its increasingly heavy burden of unpublished work from one hand to the other. He sighed and looked around the neighborhood, at the quiet, peaceful houses, in the way he had lately looked at many things—as though they would soon be gone. He took a deep breath and started again up the little hill, bracing himself for the look in Maureen's eyes.

The Packard was not in the driveway, which told Stall Maureen was out. She did not risk driving it into the garage where the clearances were narrow. She'd scraped a fender once and from that day on it had been Stall's job to garage the car before they turned in for the night. In the dark living room, habit made him call out as usual, "I'm home!" This announcement of himself had held a frightening uncertainty since the afternoon of Frank Vane's visit.

He found the note on the kitchen table, a salt shaker centered on it. He knew Maureen. She had put the shaker there so that in the event of earthquake or revolution, the note would not fall off the table and become lost like one of Thomas Hardy's fated missives.

Tom,

I'm going to Ohio to spend some time with my parents and think things over. Mr. Lundy was very kind about letting me leave my job. He said he thought he could get one of their retired teachers to come back for the remainder of the year, or maybe just half of it if he could find the right person to replace me full time. He said some very nice things about my teaching that I really needed to hear. He was sorry I'm having such a hard time with the new baby.

I thought about leaving Corey here with you. God knows she doesn't need to be taken out of school and relocated at this point in her life, but I didn't think you could take care of her here as well as I can with my mother's help in Oberlin. Corey was sad to leave. She cried when I told her and wants you to come and join us. I don't know what I want right now. I told her things would work out. Isn't that what parents tell their children? You've got some decisions to make. We both know that. I suppose I do too.

As you know, it's been hell with this baby. I don't know why it's so hard. Maybe an Ohio doctor can explain it to me. We didn't have this kind of trouble with Corey her first few months. I'm hoping for the best. Corey and I will spend the night somewhere halfway, and I'll call you when I get home to let you know we made it all right.

Maureen

Well, Stall thought, *the note is a piece of work and so is she*. There was no *Dear Tom* to start and no *Love* at the end. There were subtle and not so subtle knives for Stall's heart. The world, Stall had learned, was about some simply opposing notions. Two of them were thought and emotion, and discovering the relationship between the two was the work of a lifetime.

Stall drank gin warm from the bottle before finding the martini pitcher and a glass and cracking an ice tray. He walked with the bottle in his hand to the dining room where he found the tablet of paper Maureen had used for her note. He could see on it the impressions of her writing, layers of versions of her message to him. Artistry, Stall had learned from his literary studies, lay not in the display but in the concealing of hard, meticulous work. The note she'd left had the simple, straightforward quality that was Maureen herself. She had worked hard at her message to him.

The hell of it, Stall's third long drink of gin told him, was that he was not even surprised. Maureen had refused to talk to him about Frank Vane's visit and had shown no interest in the photographs Vane had said Stall would show to her. For three days, the Stalls had lived life in silence, punctuated by a few necessary monosyllables. His walks up the hill of late, foreboding in every step, had told him that something was coming, and there were only so many possibilities for the fractured future of a suburban couple of modest income with one child and another on the way. So, home to mother it was. But in Ohio there was also Maureen's father. And from the beginning of their marriage, he, Mr. Wiggins, lawyer by profession, had never quite bought what Stall was selling. There had always been the look at Stall from under his brows that said Maureen might have done better in the marriage market. Another sip of gin, cold now and sparkling in a crystalline glass, told Stall that no father, probably, could ever quite entirely buy what a son-in-law was selling, and briefly Stall allowed himself speculations about a future in which Corey brought home young men who would not be entirely adequate.

With a wobble in his step that surprised him, Stall went to the refrigerator to see what might be there for his dinner. Aha! Maureen had left two casseroles covered in wax paper. Cooking instructions in her neat handwriting were taped to them. *Well*, Stall thought largely, *fuck casseroles, especially you, Mr. Chicken and Mushroom*. The buses were still running. What in the world would be wrong with a trip straight up University Avenue to the College Inn or even farther to that other Inn, the Primrose, for the *spécialité de la maison*. Delicious, hot fried chicken.

Stall grabbed his coat from the back of a kitchen chair, crumpled Maureen's note into insignificance, tossed it into the garbage can under the sink, and spun on his heel to head for the front door . . . but spinning once became spinning twice and then half of a third time, almost a pirouette, and he was on his ass looking up at the kitchen ceiling with blood spouting from his right wrist which featured, in a way that seemed almost comical to him now, a long, knifelike piece of broken martini glass protruding from an artery.

Stall watched the blood resolutely pumping, little jets of it mixing with spilled gin to make an orange that reminded him of the university's colors. *Well then, Go Gators!* A heat came to his face, and he recognized it for the first flush of fear, and with an effort that seemed greater even than the one he had used earlier to climb the hill to this house, he flung his left arm across his chest and squeezed his right wrist hard. Hard enough to stop the jetting blood. *Christ*, he thought, *what now?*

It seemed to take all of the strength he had to get to his knees and open the drawer next to the refrigerator that held the household's odds and ends—pliers, screwdrivers, balls of twine, a small jar of assorted nuts and bolts, and bingo! A roll of electrician's tape. Stall wrapped his right wrist as best he could with the sticky tape, and resolved to crawl to the phone. On that long journey, he occupied himself with questions of reputation and propriety. He did not want an ambulance to arrive, siren blaring, at this address, his neighbors to see him carried out by two men in white smocks, blood dripping from his hand, his head lolling from gin and misery. *Who has a car? Who do I know, do I trust, that has a car?*

His hand turning blue, Stall dragged the phone book off its little table in the living room and pawed it, smearing blood, until he found the number. With what seemed like his last strength, he dialed. He smiled at his luck when Sarah Leaf answered.

The young intern who stitched Stall's wrist waved his hand in front of his face. "Whew! Your breath is making my eyes water. How much . . . ?"

"Gin," Stall said, "elixir of the gods. Not enough, really."

"I'm sure, but how much? Do I have to admit you for observation while you dry out?"

"Naw," Stall said, "the, uh, lady who brought me in will see to it I get home. She'll sit with me for a while if I need her."

The doctor said, "This'll pinch a little. Ready?"

"Ready, doc."

The intern had shot Stall's wrist with Xylocaine, but Stall doubted he'd have felt much pain without it. Now he felt the first gripping of the talons of the Mad Bird Hangover in his head. She was a big, vicious bird.

The intern seemed to enjoy his work. "If you'd been in your right mind, you could have handled this yourself at home with a compression bandage, but you're not in your right mind, so I get to practice my suturing."

When he finished and snapped off his gloves, he gave Stall the look you'd give a boy who needs a spanking. "All right. I'll sign you out into the lady's care, but lay off the ethanol for a few days, okay?"

"Okay."

Stall lay alone on the gurney in the white-curtained cubicle for a few minutes before Sarah Leaf entered and looked down at him. "I'd believe you just had some bad luck and fell, but . . . you reek."

Eureka! "My wife left me." The words were out of his mouth before he knew he'd even thought them.

"Jesus! Maureen?"

"The only wife I have." The irony of this arrived too late to shut Stall's mouth. "Two mothers of my children, but I married only one of them."

Sarah Leaf gave him an almost motherly smile. "You *are* drunk. Two mothers? What the hell are you talking about, Stall?"

"I'll tell you when I feel better . . . maybe." It occurred to him that somewhere in the murky depths of what some called the unconscious mind there lurked hidden motivation. Maybe his drunken, bloody hands had pawed the phone book not for a trustworthy friend who had a car, but for the only other person he knew in Gainesville whose life had fallen into utter disorder. In a way it was rotten to choose Sarah Leaf for this favor, but in another way, well, who could be held accountable for what the unconscious mind did in gin and fear?

Sarah Leaf looked down at Stall, and it was a mother's smile that broke across her face, soft and generous. "Let's go back," she said, "to what you said a minute ago. Maureen left you?"

"Yeah," Stall sighed so big it was almost a word, "this morning, I guess. While I was at work, she took Corey and went to her parents' house in Ohio."

Sarah Leaf put her hand on Stall's forearm, gave it a little squeeze. "Why, Tom? Why did she leave?"

He closed his eyes, liking the warm consolation that gripped his arm. "So many things happened so fast. She's pregnant and the morning sickness has been terrible, and she had to quit her job, and she loved that job, and . . ."

"Jeez, Tom, I didn't know Maureen had a job."

"Well, we haven't been in touch since . . ."

"No, we haven't. Not since you called me about the bank account and that slimy redneck Jack gave it to."

Stall wasn't going to tell her right now that Roney Tyler actually had his points, even a certain working-class nobility. He probably never would. He said, "I'm sorry we haven't called, invited you over. A lot's been going on." It hit him: there was no *we* anymore, at least not here in Gainesville. There might be a *we* again, here or somewhere else, but it was by no means certain.

Sarah Leaf squeezed his forearm again, the gentle warmth better than any drug. "I've got a job too. Maureen and I could have compared notes. Of course, I'm a bookkeeper, dull as dirt, not much to talk about."

"Where do you keep . . . books?"

"Two places actually: a hardware store in the morning and an auto parts warehouse in the afternoon. It's not bad. Keeps body and soul together."

Ah, thought Stall, *body and soul together—the work of a lifetime*.

He swung his legs off the gurney, sat up, and reached out both hands for Sarah Leaf's shoulders because the white walls of the little cubicle had begun to tilt and turn around him. He found that he could not grip her shoulder without an uncomfortable pulling in the new stitches.

The intern stuck his head in. "You still here? I'm afraid we need this space. Busy day."

"All right," Sarah Leaf said, "we'll get this guy up and moving." To Stall, "You ready?"

"As I'll ever be."

When they left the hospital parking lot, she said, "You can come to my place if you want to. The boys are home from school, but they'll be quiet. You can lie down until you feel well enough to go home."

Stall, whose shirt and trousers were smeared with blood, asked her to take him to a used car lot on north 441. "I have to buy a car."

"This'll be interesting."

"I hope not. I might need a bookkeeper's help."

Stall picked a 1948 Plymouth coupe in an obnoxious light-blue color. A two-seater with a small compartment behind the seats, it was not a car for a family man. The salesman looked at Stall's bloody clothes, and Stall swore he could hear the man thinking, *I've sold cars to stranger guys than you, bud.* He assured Stall that the Plymouth was good transportation. Stall took this to mean that it was mechanically sound and not much more. Right now, soundness was all he wanted. The asking price was two hundred dollars. Stall agreed to it.

Sarah Leaf frowned and took him aside. "Bargain with him, Tom. He'll take one fifty or I'm no skinflint."

She was right.

Leaving the lot, she said, "You took me home from the bowling alley that day when I was too tight to drive. Want me to follow you home, make sure you get there? Drag you out of a ditch if you don't?"

"Naw," Stall said, "I'll make it. And thanks, Sarah. It was awfully kind of you to do this."

"*De nada, hombre.* Anything for a friend." She got into the new Buick Jack had bought for them, started the engine, then turned it off and got out again. She walked to Stall and held him by the shoulders. "You're a good man, Tom. Whatever this is with Maureen, it'll pass. You'll be all right."

At home, Stall confronted the bloody mess of the kitchen and living room. He decided to worry about it later. Upstairs in bed, with the Mad Bird Hangover flexing its talons into his brainpan, he thought about Sarah. She looked better. Not as thin, not as gray, not as haggard as she had looked the last time he had seen her. And she was dressing differently. Not so mannish, none of the Katharine Hepburn look. She'd walked into the hospital cubicle in a blue cotton dress that she filled out very well. Maybe there was a chance for her, another life.

Stall had just fallen into a restless sleep when the phone rang downstairs. He rushed down to it, thinking it was Maureen calling to tell him where she had stopped halfway. Maybe give him a number where he could reach her at least for the night. His mother-in-law's voice crossed the distance to Stall, and distant it was. "Hello, Tom, this is Grace Wiggins."

Not *your mother-in-law*, or as she had been in better times, *Mom*.

"Hello, um, Grace."

"I'm calling to tell you that Maureen got here. She drove straight through, the poor thing. In her condition. Anyway, she's here now, safe and sound, and she and Corey are sleeping up in her bedroom." That would be Maureen's childhood bedroom which her parents had kept exactly as she had left it as a college girl.

There was a long pause during which Stall could think of nothing to say. Finally he blurted, "Well, I'm glad. Uh, please tell her I'm glad she made it all right. And—"

"Oh, Tom! I just don't know what to say about this . . ."

And then tears, a torrent of them far away in Ohio, and then a man's voice. The father-in-law who had never quite bought what Stall was selling. "Hello, Tom."

"Hello, Ed." Again, *Hello, Dad* out of the question.

"I'm afraid you won't be able to talk with her tonight. We'll see what we can do for you tomorrow."

We'll see. A project for the entire Wiggins tribe?

"Well, uh . . . thanks, Ed. I hope you all have a good night."

"I doubt that. But, uh, thank you, Tom. Maybe tomorrow."

And the line was dead.

And Stall thought, *Maybe tomorrow and maybe not*. He thought about killing the Mad Bird Hangover with the only poison that would bring the creature down: more gin. He decided against it. Better for him to endure the Bird and hope to sleep.

In his dream just before dawn, Stall met a man on a park bench. The man seemed to know all about him and his various predicaments and they fell into an earnest and forthright conversation. "After all," the man said, "what are you really guilty of?"

There were ducks in the park and they came crowding around. Stall said, "I don't know, really. And that's the hell of it. I just don't know."

"What *do* you know?" the man asked gently, almost in the way of a confessor.

"I know that I should not have concealed from my wife the knowledge of a second daughter."

"But you only learned of the daughter . . . how long ago?"

"A few weeks."

"So, for a few weeks you did not tell what you should have told?"

"I dreaded what she might think, what she might do."

"Did it not occur to you that she might have responded well to your honesty if not so well to the news?"

In the dream, on the bench with the man, with the ducks coming closer, wanting what Stall could not give them, it came to him that he had not in fact considered the possibility that Maureen might respond generously to his honesty. And why had this not seemed to him a possibility? Why couldn't he have granted her the possibility of a generous reaction?

The man beside him seemed to have the ability to know Stall's thoughts. "Do you see that there are really two parts to this thing? The first is that you did not tell her, the second is what to do about the child now that she knows. Assuming that your wife can forgive you for the first part, how do you think she will react to the second?"

"I don't know. I fear it."

"Perhaps when you did not tell her, you were afraid of something else."

"Of what?"

"Only you can know that."

So the man would not be Stall's oracle. He would only define for Stall his dilemma.

Stall did not often remember his dreams, but when he awoke and made his way to the bathroom in the dawn light on a desperate hunt for aspirin, he knew he would remember this one.

Perhaps you were afraid of something else.

FIFTY

Stall parked the '48 Plymouth with the obnoxious blue paint job down the block from Discreet Investigations, Inc. So far, the car had lived up to its reputation. It was good transportation. It leaked oil and had soiled the floor of his garage before he had thought to slide a stack of newsprint under the oil pan, and the windshield wipers worked when they wanted to, but otherwise, it got him around. He found that he rather enjoyed the stares of his neighbors when they saw him driving the old coupe. They'd be talking soon about the missing Packard, and then about the missing Maureen. Stall had wondered what he would say to the wife of the sociologist who studied "the family" when she came knocking with questions about Maureen, her coffee friend. Perhaps he'd answer the door with a spade in his hand and say that Maureen had . . . gone away.

The holster clipped to Rudy Silber's belt was not empty. The neat blue-steel .38 was snug in its black leather bed. Silber eyed the bandage on Stall's wrist, but didn't ask. He opened the desk drawer, retrieved a file, and handed it over. "I got what you asked for on Roney Tyler's brother-in-law."

Stall flipped through it. Roney's brother-in-law was named Buddy Carwin. Buddy was not a nickname, it was on his birth certificate. "Give me the highlights."

"Not a pretty picture." The PI picked tobacco from the corner of his mouth and examined the find. "Violent tendencies. Extreme. Two jolts at Raiford, one for assault with a deadly weapon, in this case a knife, and another for attempted vehicular homicide. He tried to drive his car over a guy in the parking lot of a bar, and that was *after* he beat the guy senseless with a pool cue."

Stall's admiration for Roney Tyler grew. He had fought the bad brother-in-law. *And gave as good as he got.* "Tried to? What stopped him?"

"According to witnesses, the car stalled."

"Roney knows this?"

"Who knows what Roney knows? *You* know it. You paid for it. I didn't talk to any of Carwin's known associates. They'd just tell him somebody's asking about him."

"I want you to do another job for me. I want you to use that big camera again."

"Sorry, professor. It's too dangerous."

"It was dangerous when you took pictures of Jack Leaf and Roney Tyler. What's changed?"

"When I took those pictures, I was on the right side of Cyrus Tate."

Rudy Silber lit a Lucky Strike, blew smoke at the ceiling above Stall's head, and adjusted the lie of his tropical tie along the seam of his button-down white shirt. "Charley Johns got mud on his skirts down in Miami. Reputations are at stake now. Going after a bunch of queers who'll do anything to stay in the dark is one thing. Those Negroes in Miami are different. They've got money for lawyers, and they don't care about exposure. Hell, they like it, at least until it brings the Klan down on their heads. What you're asking could get me . . . hurt."

Rudy Silber stubbed out his Lucky, unlocked a gray metal filing cabinet, and reached inside. "Here's what I can do for you. *All* I can do." He laid a tiny camera on his desktop, and beside it a roll of film no bigger than a thimble. He looked up at Stall's puzzled face. "Spies use these. Us and the Russians. Mostly to photograph documents, but they're good for other work too. They're quiet, they're obviously concealable, and you don't need a flash, at least in normal daylight."

Without thinking, Stall said, "I can't . . ."

"Of course you can, professor. I won't do it, so you'll have to. If you've got . . ." he looked Stall up and down, "what it takes."

The balls, Stall thought, *the stones, the* cojones, *the guts, the sand. The rot in your soul.*

The PI wrote a name and phone number on a slip of paper. "You'll have to pay him, but he's reliable. I've worked with him before. He knows the place and the people, the ones *he* can trust."

Stall read the name, said it aloud. "Allard Bryce."

"Al for short," the PI said, "and remember this, professor: the kind of trouble you can get into is nothing like what can happen to him."

"How much will I owe him?"

"He'll tell you. He's not shy about money."

Stall was walking back to the old Plymouth when the PI caught up with him on the sidewalk. "Wait a minute, professor. There's something else."

Stall had noticed long ago that when practical men called him *professor* they often meant something else, something like *little girl* or *sissy*. He had come to think of it as part of the price he paid for the safety of observation. He followed the PI into the lobby of the Commercial Hotel and through to the bar, empty at this time of day but smelling strongly of the previous night's enjoyments.

The PI took a table by a window and Stall joined him. He lit another Lucky and blew some thoughtful smoke at the grimy ceiling. "Something Tate told Jack Leaf before he served the subpoena. He said Jack could get somebody killed if he wasn't careful."

"Somebody?"

"I think his exact words were *that cracker*."

"Was he talking about Roney?"

"I don't know, professor. It's possible. One thing's for sure: Jack Leaf knew who he meant."

For three days Stall was allowed to talk only to Mr. and Mrs. Wiggins. He asked them to call Maureen to the phone, then he begged them, then he said things he should not have said about people who interfered in other people's marriages. Then he apologized.

FIFTY-ONE

Stall waited by the loading dock behind the Thomas Hotel. Allard Bryce came not from the kitchen where he worked in various capacities, but from behind Stall, suddenly there and tapping Stall's shoulder. Startled, Stall turned in a half crouch, hands raised.

"Easy, professor, easy." Allard Bryce was a tall, solidly built Negro of middle years with a Clark Gable mustache and a wide, confident smile. His starched white smock was yellowed by sweat at the neck and under the arms, and variously stained by food. His eyes, the way they stared unblinking into Stall's, made Stall think, *He's a hard man when he wants to be.*

Stall extended his hand. Bryce looked down at it for a count of three before giving Stall a brief strong grip. He pulled a pack of Camels and a Ronson lighter from the front pocket of his white cotton trousers, offered Stall one, then lit up, smoking with the greed of a man on a short break from hard work. He didn't stand on ceremony.

"They come sometimes in the afternoon, round three o'clock usually, Mr. Tate and Mr. Vane. Mr. Tate, he use the room with several men. Mr. Vane, he confine himself to Mr. Tate."

There it was, Stall's proof, at least the testimony of a voice. He'd need more, and he intended to get it.

"So, Mr. Silber said you know how to do this?"

"How *you* can do it."

"You're going to help, aren't you, like you help Mr. Silber?"

Bryce answered with a wise smile that made Stall wonder. Did the handsome black man enjoy his work? The hotel was for whites only.

That Tate and Vane should meet in the same hotel where the Committee held its interrogations puzzled Stall, but stranger things had happened. Perhaps the risk was part of the thrill. Or perhaps the two believed they were, like Caesar's wife, above reproach.

Stall looked at his watch. It was two thirty. He left Allard Bryce stubbing out his cigarette on the rubber bumper of the loading dock and walked to his car a block away. He'd brought his copy of Greene's *Stamboul Train* to read and he'd brought something else. Before leaving the house that morning, he'd passed through the garage, and it had been a small matter to open the steamer trunk and retrieve Roland Gilson's pistol. Its weight was both small and large in the hip pocket of his gray suit trousers.

Allard Bryce appeared on the loading dock again at ten of three and waved to Stall in a way that could have been the swatting of a mosquito. He led Stall through the kitchen without a word to the two busboys playing a desultory game of gin, and the elderly cook sleeping away the hiatus between lunch and dinner with his head on a freshly cleaned chopping block. None of them seemed to think it was strange, Bryce in his white smock leading a white man in a shirt and tie through their kitchen. *They don't mess with his business.* And business it was. Stall had paid Bryce fifty dollars for the help he was about to get, whatever it was.

Bryce took a flight of fire stairs up to a third-floor hallway where he opened the stairwell door an inch and looked out. "Wait here," he whispered. Through the aperture Stall watched him walk almost too nonchalantly down the hallway to a closet and emerge with a broom and a long-handled dustpan. He headed to the end of the hallway, made a few swipes with the broom at nothing Stall could see, then turned and came back again, stopping at the door of room 309. *Do Not Disturb* hung from the knob.

Bryce looked meaningfully at the door, then up at the transom which was open to let air escape from the room, then he looked rather theatrically at Stall. Stall opened the stairwell door another two inches and mouthed, *I understand*. Bryce nodded and walked toward him in the same nonchalant way, stopping again at the broom closet, from which he emerged without the broom and pan but with a stepladder.

The sordid story that would star Tom Stall played out in Stall's imagination. The Tom Stall who watched Tom Stall saw him padding down the hall, opening the ladder, removing the little camera from his pocket, climbing the ladder, and . . .

Charley Johns walked out of a room two doors down from 309, stood stretching and yawning in the dim hallway, and began walking along behind Allard Bryce, who was halfway from the closet to the stairwell where Stall hid. *He looks like a dyspeptic office clerk, like a small-town bank teller.* Of course, Stall had seen grainy newspaper photos of Johns. The pictures did not endow the man with any particular majesty, but this creature walking toward him now, unnoticed by Allard Bryce so soft was the Committee chairman's footfall, looked small, tired, and seedy, like some commercial traveler who had not sold his quota of brushes or corsets and now had to leave the hotel in his disheveled suit to find a cheap diner before catching the Atlantic Coast Line Pullman out of town.

Stall thought, *I should warn Bryce somehow*, then thought, *But why, he's just doing what hotel workers do . . . Up here in a third-floor hallway wearing a greasy kitchen smock?*

Before Stall could speak or gesture, Charley Johns said, "Say, uh, boy!"

Allard Bryce stopped and Stall saw his eyes burn like the embers of hell, then the fires went out and he shaped to his face the meet-the-white-man gaze. The look of bland friendliness with a hint of obsequious cringe. He pivoted neatly, almost militarily. "Suh," he said evenly.

"Boy, I need some cigarettes. Run down and get me a pack of Chesterfields." Johns dug into the pocket of his trousers and tossed Allard Bryce a fifty-cent piece, enough for cigarettes and a tip.

"Yes suh, Mr. Johns. I bring 'em . . . ?"

"I'll be in my room, 312. Quick now, boy!"

"Like a bunny, suh!"

Charley Johns turned and walked back up the hallway.

In the stairwell, Allard Bryce showed no sign of his encounter with Johns, only said, "Best you wait till I get him his cigarettes before you go down there."

Stall nodded. *Christ, he's two men. The grafter I'm paying fifty dollars and the cringer who smiles for a twenty-cent tip.*

Five minutes later, the hallway quiet, Stall climbed the ladder, aimed the camera through the transom at an angle he thought would capture the bed. He took ten shots. He could not see what the camera saw, could only reach both hands up high enough to position it at the open transom. Finished, he crept to the closet and returned the ladder. On the loading dock, he gave Bryce the camera. Bryce had explained how the film would be developed.

"You ever seen them ads in the men's magazines? *Argosy*, *Police Gazette*, and the like?"

Stall had seen the ads. They usually started with something like: *Does your marriage need spice?* The gist of it was that couples could take pictures, send the film to a developer who promised secrecy, and get the photos back in a brown paper parcel with an innocuous return address. Something like, *Artfilms, Inc*. Reading the ads, Stall had always chuckled, not at the need for such a service, but at the naivete that believed in the secrecy.

Allard Bryce said, "Mr. Silber and me, we send our film to a guy in Ocala runs a lab out on a rural route. He do good work."

"And I'll pay him . . . ?"

"Included in my price." Bryce climbed the steps to the loading dock and disappeared into the kitchen.

The following night, Stall called the number Bryce had given him. "How'd they turn out?"

"You did all right, professor."

Maybe you'll have work for me when they purge me from this academic trade. "You surprised?"

"Ain't much surprises me no more."

FIFTY-TWO

The same night, Sophie Green called Stall at nine p.m. "I'm sorry to intrude on your home life."

He considered telling her he no longer had one. "That's all right. What can I do for you, Dr. Green?"

"You can call me Sophie again. We need to get back onto a better footing with each other." It was hard to read her voice on the phone. Sad? Worried? Resigned?

"All right, Sophie. What *else* can I do for you?"

"Meet me somewhere? A bar if you know a good one."

Meet you? At night? Did she know that Stall was now a bachelor? It did not seem likely. There must be some urgency in this, whatever it was. "I don't know what qualifies as a good bar in the eyes of a New Yorker, but there are one or two I like." Then it occurred to him. "Sophie, are we, uh, looking for a bar where we won't be seen by people who know us?"

"Yes, I think we are."

They met at Alley Gatorz. Stall got there first.

"Quaint," Sophie Green said. With a tired sigh, she took the chair across from him.

He had chosen a table as far as possible from the nearest game. The rumble of falling pins echoed to them from the lanes.

She set a folder on the table. "I owe you an apology."

Yes, you do. Several, actually. "What for?"

She slid the folder across to him.

Stall looked down at it, back up at her. "Somehow, I think this calls for hard liquor."

"Whatever is right . . ." she looked around at the place, "here at the Gator Bowl."

Stall laughed.

"What?"

"Never mind. It would take too long to explain. What'll you have?"

"Like I said, whatever's right."

Stall went to the bar and returned with rye shots, draft beers, and soggy coasters to set them on. Eyes wide, Sophie Green lifted her rye and sniffed it.

"Better not to do that." Stall tossed back half of his shot, and chased it with the yeasty beer. "Like that, and not too long between the two. You don't want to actually taste this whiskey."

She did as he had shown her, finishing with eyes watered and cheeks flushed.

"So?" Stall put his hand on the folder.

She nodded.

In it was a photocopy of an article published in an obscure literary journal. The author was Roland Gilson. It had been published, Stall calculated, two years before Gilson had come to Gainesville. The article had helped Gilson get the job he had recently lost. Evidence of scholarly industry was always a good thing in a young faculty member. Stall looked up at Sophie Green. She finished her shot and chased it.

"I'll read this later if you like, but at first glance I don't see why you owe me an apology."

"That comes later. For now, let's concentrate on Fred Parsons."

I'd rather not. "What about him?"

"Plagiarism. Not his, Ted Baldwin's."

Stall looked down again at the article in his hand. "Baldwin stole from Gilson? From *this*?"

Sophie Green nodded solemnly, then stood. "Another round?"

"I guess we'll have to."

She returned from the bar with a tall, gaunt man in tow. The man wore a white apron and carried a tray. She looked down at Stall, then up at the tall man. "He wouldn't let the little lady carry the drinks."

Stall thanked the bartender, who answered, "Of course."

Sophie Green told him the story. It was, apparently, Ted Baldwin's appallingly bad luck that he had lifted large portions of Roland Gilson's article for one of his own, later published in a much more prestigious place, and that through the inexorable workings of fate or justice Gilson later became Baldwin's colleague. Baldwin had forgotten the name of the insignificant young scholar whose work he had stolen, and had participated enthusiastically in the hiring of Gilson. Gilson had not, so far at least, learned of the theft. It was Fred Parsons, Baldwin's colleague, who had discovered it, again by simple bad luck, while doing some research of his own.

Under the starry sky in Fred Parsons's backyard with Hogtown Creek singing its trickle down below, an anguished Parsons had said, *There's more. Things you don't know*. This, Stall reasoned, was the more. Parsons had decided to kill two birds for his friend Ted Baldwin with one stone. He had written the letter denouncing Gilson to save Baldwin from the Committee and to save the English Department from double opprobrium—perversion and plagiarism.

"How'd you find out about all of this?"

"Before I came here, as a professional courtesy, I read my senior colleagues' research. Last week a friend of mine from grad school recommended Gilson's article. He thought it might help me with something I'm writing. He'd heard that Roland and I were colleagues here."

"How'd you know Parsons wrote the letter?"

"The way you looked at him in that meeting you called. You as much as asked him what he knew about it. I just put two and two together."

"Christ." Stall shot his whiskey and chased it, looked at the bowling world through the prism of his murky beer glass. "They ought to clean the taps."

Sophie Green finished her second round. "I'm getting to like this. You'll make me Southern yet."

Doubtful. "So . . ."

"So, you're not the fink I thought you were. You didn't rat out Gilson, and I owe you an apology."

Stall searched her eyes, saw no deception, nothing withheld. "Well then, thank you. Apology accepted."

She tapped her empty shot glass on the tabletop. "Don't get me wrong. We still disagree on miles and miles of things, but on this one we're in accord. You are not a fink."

Stall waved to the tall man in the apron behind the bar and, like his daughter at shortstop signaling to the outfield, held up two fingers. The man nodded, poured, and brought the third round. They drank in silence for a while, the cheap rye getting better by the minute. Finally, Stall said, "So, what are you going to do about this?"

"You're the chairman."

"A chairman who's a fink in the eyes of all but one . . . junior faculty member. If I go before the department and say, *It has come to my attention*, I'll be a petty bureaucrat acting on intelligence from an informer. I've had enough of that. *We've* had enough." He watched her as she listened to him. She nodded solemnly, weighing, it seemed, every word. Stall continued, "I see two options. One is you tell what you know . . ."

"Me?"

"You. Or did you plan to keep your part in this hidden?"

She frowned into her half-empty shot glass.

"And the other is you go to Baldwin and Parsons and give them the opportunity to resign . . . for the good of the department they ruined Gilson to protect."

"I'll have to think this through."

"Yes, you should do that, and very carefully. And consider this: that night at Stephen Levy's house, you took the side that's for sacrificing the individual for the benefit of the masses. If you bring this information to light, you'll hurt Baldwin and Parsons. And you'll look them in the eyes. Are you willing to do that?"

"Let them resign, fall on their swords? Isn't that covering it up?"

"Maybe, but it's also not giving the Committee another brush to tar us with. And don't forget Connor. Do we want to force him to deal publicly with the forged letter he used to fire a faculty member?"

Stall was fully aware of the fact that he had just plied Sophie Green with the same reasoning Parsons had given him in that starry backyard.

"Maybe it's a case of the greater good," she said.

"It always is, isn't it?"

"Or the least offense."

They drank and she considered it. Stall didn't think her courage was rising to an encounter with Baldwin and Parsons.

She said for the second time, "I'll have to think it through."

In the parking lot, it was clear that Sophie Green was too far into her cheap rye to drive home. Stall got her into his car and headed in the direction of the small house she had rented. After a while she roused, looked around, and said, "I'm not there anymore."

"Where are you?"

Her voice was small, almost little-girl small. "Turn there, please."

He did. When he stopped the Plymouth in front of Stephen Levy's house in Squalor Holler, Levy was waiting on the screened porch. He came down the walk and met them halfway. Stall passed Sophie Green's elbow into young Levy's care. To Sophie Green he said, "You're uh . . . here?"

"I am."

So, Stall thought, *she's made her bed.* He lingered in the blue coupe watching Stephen Levy help Sophie Green into the shabby old cracker shack. And then he stayed longer thinking about what life was like for the two of them in this love nest that smelled of mimeograph fluid. Was Sophie Green reliving her youth while Stephen Levy learned to be a man?

Levy appeared on the porch and stood looking at Stall in his unlikely automobile. Stall put the car in gear. Levy raised a hand, came down the steps, and leaned into Stall's open window. "I'm leaving. I'm following Dr. Margolis to the University of California. He got me admitted as a condition of his appointment, and he'll be my thesis advisor."

Who'll lead the crusaders of the Independent Alligator? Stall decided not to ask. Gainesville would know the answer soon enough. Then another question came to mind: what about the woman whose pretty head rests inebriated in yonder hovel? Would Sophie Green follow her new love to the golden West? Stall's eyes moved from Levy's always serious face to the cracker house where every line was off plumb and every angle oblique.

Reading Stall, Levy said, "I don't know what she'll do. We haven't decided yet. In my opinion, she'd be well rid of this place."

Stall had no ready answer to this. He couldn't say, *And it of her*; he wasn't sure he believed it. A future of Sophie Green's kind of change might be—if not what Gainesville needed, then a least what she would inevitably get. He said, "Well, good luck to you both, whatever you decide," and slid the coupe away from the curb.

FIFTY-THREE

Every night at seven o'clock Stall called Maureen. Every night Mrs. Wiggins answered, and then one night she handed the phone to Maureen. This was progress, and it lifted Stall's heart to hear his wife's voice, though she sounded deadly tired.

"How are you?"

"A little better, not as sick as I was down there with you."

To an English teacher, all was metaphor. *Sick with you* was fraught. Stall dismissed it from his mind. "Have you seen a doctor?"

"Yeah, he doesn't know what to think. He's small-town conservative and says I just have to get through this. He's not prescribing anything. But I'm worried about the baby. If I can't keep anything down, how will the poor thing thrive?"

Stall had no idea what to say. He tried, "I'm sorry this has been so awful for you." Most of what he meant was in the tone of his voice. *I'm sorry* I *was so awful.*

"It'll get better." But she didn't sound convinced. "Tom, I should get off. I'm feeling . . . you know . . . erpy."

He looked at his watch. Two minutes they'd talked. He had hoped they'd get to their questions, *the* question: when was she coming home? He had only recently let himself think about the possibility that she might not come back to Gainesville at all. Might stay in Ohio where Corey could have a better school and the care and support of two loving grandparents. And where she, Maureen, might pick up again the threads of the life she'd left there years ago—old friends, the things she had loved to do in the winter, tobogganing, skating, and . . . Stall dreaded the thought: old boyfriends. There were several, and last year's batch of Christmas cards had told the Stalls that one of them was now a widower.

"I love you, Maureen," hearing the tremble in his voice, "and I'm sorry."

"I know. I appreciate that, Tom. Good night."

"Night, baby."

Stall sent the photos of Vane and Tate to the president's office by campus mail in a sealed envelope marked, *President Connor, Private and Confidential*. If Margaret Braithwaite took time from the magic Olivetti to open the envelope despite its warning, well then, she would be shocked. Stall had been only mildly surprised by the photos. He had been prepared for them by the photos he had seen of ancient Greek pottery, which could be viewed by qualified scholars in the rare book room of the university library under the watchful eye of a male librarian. He included no cover letter. The president could think what he wanted to think and do what he thought was right, or if not that, then what he thought would serve his interests.

Stall had thought it through this way: Connor feared being fired by a legislature under the thrall of a renegade committee headed by Governor Charley Johns. Frank Vane and Cyrus Tate, two men highly placed in Charley Johns's star chamber, had compromised themselves, and now Connor had the proof. Connor had worked with Vane behind the scenes. If he chose to, Connor could save his job and the careers and even the lives of others in his university by using the evidence Stall had provided—that Vane and Tate *were* what they hated and persecuted—to convince Charley Johns to back down or at least back away. If Johns would not see reason (or self-interest), then liberals in the legislature, the so-called lambchoppers, would see it. They would use the photos to attack the Committee and possibly even force a vote to disband it by ending its funding. Failing this, few newspapers in the state, even those who favored the Committee's work, and there were some, would pass on the chance to publish such a salacious story. Of course, they couldn't publish the photos, and many had never even published the word *homosexual*, but they would, Stall was certain, get the necessary news to their readers. The Miami hearings had taken first blood from the Committee, and this second wound, Stall believed, might be fatal. He had given Connor salvation, though without honor, if only the man would take it.

Connor called Stall in his Anderson Hall office. "Come over, Tom. I want to talk to you."

"No thank you, Jim." Jack Leaf had said thank you to his fate. This, in its way, was Stall's homage to a man's dignity.

After a long pause during which Stall tried to imagine the look on Connor's face, the president said, "So, Stall, I see you're as dirty as anyone, or should I say as ever?"

"You and I are about equal. I sometimes think the main purpose of this world is to get us all dirty."

"The Bible says we arrive that way."

"So it does. What will you do with those pictures?"

"I'll do what I do. A word to the wise: be careful, Tom." And the president hung up.

You be careful, thought Stall. *Think it through.*

He went to his bank downtown, rented a safe-deposit box, and put copies of the photos and the negatives in it. Connor would assume that he had kept the negatives.

Sarah Leaf dropped by to check on him. Stall had done a bad job of cleaning up the blood he had spilled on the kitchen floor. When Sarah saw it, she insisted on eliminating the traces of his fall. Stall protested, said he'd do it later, but there was no stopping her. In no time, she had mixed Lysol with water in a big saucepan and was on her knees in front of Stall scrubbing. Nothing for him to do but join her on his hands and knees, both using rags, the saucepan of soapy water between them. They dipped their rags in the water, pink now with blood, and their hands touched. Stall felt something he did not want to feel. He told her about the safe-deposit box. Someone had to hold the duplicate key. Who else could he trust?

She leaned back, letting the rag drop to the floor beside her. "You're scaring me, Tom."

He wanted to reach out and touch her shoulder as she had done for him in the hospital, reassure her. He kept his eyes on the floor, working at a stubborn spot of blood in the tile grout. "Don't worry about it. I shouldn't have said anything. You're not in any danger."

"Why won't you tell me what's in the box?"

"I can't." *That would put you in harm's way.*

But he hadn't thought it through. If he gave her the key, weren't there ways the Committee, Tate or Vane, might find out she had it? Wasn't it, given the logic of irony and revenge, the right, the obvious thing for him to do? This had all started with Jack Leaf. If the photos Stall had taken—and yes, *taken* was the right word, he had stolen the images of two men in an intimate embrace—could end the work of the Committee, wouldn't the men who wanted to keep the Committee alive know he'd give Sarah Leaf the key? Stall took a deep breath and sighed it out. The tendency of literature was to endow evil with omnipotent powers, but this was the world, dirty, confused, and groping. These operatives of the Committee were not supermen. They were thugs and bumblers who preyed on the fears of the weak.

Lying drunk as a lord on a gurney in the hospital, he had told Sarah that Maureen had left him. With those words, he had made her his confidante. But the key was something else; it was dangerous. He stopped scrubbing. "Sarah, I'm sorry about this. I didn't think it through. If anything happens, go to the police and tell them about the box at the bank. If anyone else approaches you after I'm . . . after something happens, you don't know anything about the box. Okay?"

Sarah stood and dropped her rag in the sink. "I think we've done about as much as we can do with this." She meant Stall's bloody mess. "I'll do whatever you want. I want to help, but I don't want to complicate things."

Stall stood too, and poured the water from the pan into the sink. It left a residue of tiny glass fragments. Such a mess from one martini. He'd had the sutures removed. In a few days, the wound wouldn't need its dressing. Strange that no one at work had asked him about it, but so much was strange now. The quiet of the house without Maureen and Corey, things they had touched gathering dust. He'd cut his drinking to two before dinner. The truth was that he didn't much enjoy his six o'clock martinis without Maureen to touch her glass to his. And dinner was hardly worthy of the name. Canned soups and sandwiches, frozen TV dinners, burgers he brought home from the CI—driving the preposterous blue roadster home with a greasy paper bag on the seat beside him. Marriage, he had decided, existed not for the lofty reasons legends and theology proclaimed, but simply to keep men of a certain age from coming apart.

Sarah Leaf took a chair at the kitchen table. "So, what about Maureen and you?"

"I call every night at the same time. It was several days before she'd even speak to me."

"Are you going to tell me what this is all about, or are you going to be like that box down at the bank with a deep, dark secret inside?" She gave him a smile that encouraged sharing. Stall had not been a man who shared his life with others. She encouraged him with a hand on his on the tabletop. "When you were on that gurney in the hospital full of gin and remorse, you said you had two wives. I thought you were just martini-silly, but Tom, is it true?"

He rubbed his eyes with his palms, struggled to remember it. "I think I said *women*, not *wives*."

"Oh, I see."

Her eyes narrowed and her mouth drew tight. Was she pairing him now in her thoughts with her gone husband? Was Stall just another adulterous male? He had to tell her more. The story he should have told Maureen, the story that several times had been at the back of his throat like a blazing eruption, came pouring out. He told Sarah Leaf about Paris, Brigitte, Françoise, and how the past had come back into his life through the evil offices of a blackmailer. He did not say Frank Vane's name.

When he finished, she seemed neither surprised nor relieved that he was not a garden-variety adulterer. After a long look into his eyes, she said, "I'm trying to decide what I would do. I mean, if I were Maureen, and I just don't know. You said some other man has been taking care of this woman in France, giving her money all these years."

"We were in the army together. He has family money, a fortune."

"So it's no skin off his—"

"I don't mean that."

"Of course you don't." If skeptical had a face, it was Sarah Leaf's. "Are they . . . ?"

"No. He's not . . . interested in women."

"I see."

And Stall knew she did.

"Sarah, I knew nothing about any of this until the end of August."

"That night in Paris, you had no idea you had . . . ?" She raised her eyebrows.

"Fathered a child? No. None. Of course, it's always possible."

"No, it's likely."

"All right, but the main point is, if you were Maureen, what would you do?"

"Well, I'm not Maureen, and I won't, *we* won't, go into the differences between her and me. What I'd do, what I'd *have*, is a good honest talk with myself about what I want from this life. But I don't think I could have that talk with myself until after I got over some things, or as far over them as you can ever get." She gave him her most honest eyes. "I mean, if the situation were reversed, wouldn't you have some things to get over, get through? If Maureen had a child by another man and that news just fell into your life out of nowhere? I mean, when I figured out who Jack really was and what he was up to, at least some of it, I had that talk with myself."

"What did you decide?"

"I already told you that, in the bowling alley after Jack killed himself. I decided what was good between us was better than what wasn't, or in my case, our case, what was just not mine. What belonged to other people."

"Were you happy?"

"In some ways I was happier. The mystery was solved, you know what I mean? I knew what the rules were. We had the kids, a life, we were good together in a lot of ways most people would never understand. I told you about that too. We were in my kitchen drinking rye whiskey."

Stall remembered what she had said. *See this ass? Doesn't it look a bit like a man's?*

Remembering it now, she did not seem embarrassed. "I thought Jack and I had found . . . stability. Of course, I didn't see this damned Committee thing coming, nobody did, and I didn't know my husband was taking the risks he was taking."

"So I should . . ."

"Give her time. If I know Maureen, she'll have that talk with herself. Of course, there's no telling what she'll do after she has it."

Was there any telling, even guessing? How well did any husband know his wife? And what would life be like after, if Maureen decided that stability was good enough for them?

Softly, Sarah Leaf said, "Tom, isn't it good to know you have this other child? I don't mean would you *prefer* it, I mean she exists, and isn't it better to know than not know?"

Stall said he'd have to think it through.

"Well, I think a person *should* want to know if there's another human being somewhere in the world because of him, because of what he did. Isn't there some good in this, a lot of it, really?"

At the front door, Stall and Sarah Leaf stood looking back at the clean kitchen and listening to the empty house. She pulled Stall close and hugged him. "She'll have that talk with herself, Tom, but first you need to say the right things to her."

FIFTY-FOUR

Frank Vane called and asked for a meeting.

It felt good to tell Vane they'd meet in the bowling alley bar. It was neutral ground, anonymous, and Stall's choice. No more surprise visits, invasions of his office and home by General Counsel Frank Vane, who had granted himself the power to appear where he chose to appear and do what he liked there. No more worry about who saw them together and what those observers supposed about their business. Stall felt the happy lightness of his liberation from Vane the puppet master. He knew that like a puppet learning to walk free, he should be careful not to stumble, but he could not help the exaltation he felt in his freedom.

Vane sat across from Stall at the same table Stall and Sophie Green had used. This time of day, early afternoon, the place smelled more dank than usual, chief among the odors stale beer and rented shoes.

"You look like hell, Frank." It wasn't entirely true, but Stall enjoyed saying it. Vane's eyes were gray and sunken, and his cheeks were sallow. His charcoal-gray suit, usually fresh and crisp at the lapels and trouser creases, looked like he had slept in it.

"What are you drinking, Stall? I hear that's a problem with you."

"Just Coke." It was true. He was keeping to the regimen of two martinis before dinner.

Vane shook his head slowly. "I didn't think you had it in you."

"A lot of people didn't."

"How did it feel, taking those pictures like a common sneak, a Peeping Tom?"

"You ought to know all about that, Frank. Or does your legal work keep you above all the everyday stuff?"

"I thought we were friends, Tom. *Les Deux Copains*. Army buddies. I thought there was a bond that couldn't be broken."

Stall shook his head. "How could you do those things to a friend?" It was a simple question. He really wanted to know the answer. If not for the truth in it, then for the perversity.

"I believed you'd finally see the light, Tom." Vane put his cigarette case on the table and in his practiced way extracted one and lit it. "Sure, I put some pressure on you, but I thought in the end you'd come round to seeing things my way. About the menace these degenerates pose to us, our children, our country. And I thought you'd want to know about Brigitte and the child, and want your wife to know. Tom, I was truly surprised when you didn't tell her the same day I told you."

"But you gave me the information as blackmail, Frank. You didn't want me to tell her. That would have robbed you of your power over me. Some of it anyway. You still had Connor to play against me and you did."

"And you wanted to be chairman, Tom. You wanted to rise in your paltry career."

"Yes, I did, and so did you. The difference is, your career resembles that of Joseph Goebbels."

"You've disappointed me, Tom. Truly you have."

"Likewise. No, let me amend that. I had no idea who you were, so how could I have been disappointed? We knew each other for a few weeks in a hospital in France thirteen years ago when we were both not much more than boys. I had no idea who you were then, and you didn't cross my mind more than a few times in all the years since. There was no bond, just some closeness caused by the relief we felt because we didn't do what we should have done. We didn't die. So I'm not disappointed in you, Frank, that would mean I know you. That would be like being disappointed in an insect for biting me. All I know is that you're a creature of the Committee. You did exactly what I or anyone else would expect you to do—blackmail, coerce, intimidate, and probably violate the law. You should be disbarred."

A look of misery came into Frank Vane's face. "He called my father, Tom. Connor told my father about those pictures. I won't tell you all of it, but my father said he'd disinherit me if any of this came out."

"So you care more about the money than you do about your mission?"

"Don't you see, Tom? The money, when it's *all* mine, can allow me to do more, much more, than the Committee can ever accomplish. It can lift me to things you can't even imagine."

Stall imagined what he could. The Committee going to Washington as one of a hundred organizations with offices near Capitol Hill, all the houses of power, something called the Vane Foundation, trying its best to inflame a new era of McCarthyism. Even sitting here in a bowling alley in benighted Gainesville where the Committee had waged its war of weakness and fear, Stall considered it unlikely.

He asked the question that had hovered, like the silence of intimidated minds, the fog of suspicion and paranoia, over the university, over all of the schools, the entire state, since the Committee had begun its work: "How could you defame and persecute the people whose only crime is that they do exactly what you and Tate did in that hotel room? How could you do that, Frank?"

"I had to. Don't you see that? If I could purge that evil from the world, then I could purge it from myself."

Stall wanted to laugh, but even now, after all that had happened, he could not allow himself that cruelty. He only sighed and shook his head. "Frank, you're not making sense. You never have. None of this has. Why not just be what you are and let others do the same?"

"This isn't about sense, Tom. Don't you see that? Don't you feel it? Didn't you know it then, in that army hospital? We loved each other."

Stall's voice was tired. "Maybe you did, Frank. Maybe *you* loved *me*."

"You knew it."

"No, I didn't. But I heard you say it. In my office at the university. *The Tom Stall I knew and loved*, you said. And that's what got me to the Thomas Hotel, a guy standing on a ladder with a camera in his hand. It wasn't my finest hour, Frank, but it got things done." Stall thought of Stephen Levy, and added more for himself than for Vane: "I broke some eggs."

"Eggs?"

"Never mind, Frank. We've said all we need to say."

"I know you loved me."

"No, Frank. I liked you, sure. I appreciated your young innocence and your sacrifice, your bravery, your intellect. We had some good talks, and like boys do, we shared some confidences. But that's as far as it went for me. And Frank, you went after me with a special ferocity, with personal malice. You didn't just do the Committee's dirty work, you had to punish a man who didn't love you."

Frank Vane shook his head. "No. I loved you, and you loved me. I went with you to that pension in Paris expecting love and you gave me betrayal. You betrayed me with that girl."

What more could Stall say? It was all fantasy, and to the mind that saw fantasy in all its brilliance, fantasy was real. In a quiet, sad voice, Stall said, "Frank, I love my wife, and you've done your best to ruin that for me."

"I only told her the truth you should have told."

"Look, Frank, Charley Johns is finished. There's an election in November, and Johns is going to lose. LeRoy Collins will bring a new majority to Tallahassee, and they'll pull the funding from your kangaroo committee his first day in office. You've got another month, Frank, and you can do some good in the time that's left. And maybe if you do, the lambchoppers will never see those photos of you and Tate. Use your influence, Frank, right now, to stop this. Maybe you can get your boss, Johns, out of this mess he's made for himself gracefully, before Collins puts a boot in his ass."

Vane just shook his head, at first with resolution and then with what seemed to be misery.

"One last thing, Frank. Thank you for taking care of Brigitte and the child."

"She has a name, Tom. It's Françoise."

Stall left Vane sitting in the dim, malodorous Alley Gatorz bar. There was action on only one lane. As he walked to the door, two teenage girls shrieked their laughter at a gutter ball.

FIFTY-FIVE

Stall called Eugen Brugge to ask the Belgian if he had seen Roney Tyler.

"No, *mon bon* chairman, our mascot of the mangled English and the midnight-blue Cadillac has not been my guest in some time. When, may I ask, will we see *you* again?"

"Soon," Stall said, "soon," not planning a visit to the house overlooking the prairie.

Roney's number was in the phone book.

Roney's wife answered. "No, I ain't seen him in a long time. I don't know where he's gone to." Her tone was not what Stall had expected. He had expected anger, resistance to the stranger. She sounded aggrieved by her husband's absence, or possibly by the absence of Roney's newfound wealth. In either case, she'd put a tremor into her voice. After Stall hung up, it occurred to him that he had heard two false notes. The woman hadn't even asked him who he was.

Stall called Rudy Silber.

"Do I have any credit left in my account with you?"

"Yeah. Your fifty buys a couple more hours of work. Why?"

"I want to know what became of Roney Tyler." *That stupid cracker.* "I've called everyone I can think of to ask about him. Nobody's seen him for at least two weeks."

"I'll look into it for you."

Every night at seven, Stall called Maureen. Night after night, it was the same thing. When was she coming home? She didn't know. How did she feel about him? She wasn't sure. Yet. Things might change. She had to wait and see. She couldn't think about him, about them, as much as she wanted to, as he wanted her to, when she was so sick.

Sometimes she seemed to offer hope . . . on a thin thread of what? His changing? His saying something to her, the right thing, about the past? The phone bills mounted. Their calls became weirdly routine. What was it she wanted him to say? How much more sorrow did she expect from him before he gave up?

Rudy Silber called back. "I went over to Tyler's house, talked to the wife. She says she has no idea where he is. I talked to some of the neighbors. A nice lady told me Roney's brother-in-law is a really great guy. Just built his sister a new driveway. The lady said he spent all day and all night on it. Moving dirt, mixing and pouring concrete. A real Boy Scout. That's all I got for you, professor."

"Well," Stall said, "I guess every man has his virtues."

Silber called again. "They found Roney Tyler."

"They . . . who?"

"The police. Remember the driveway I told you about? The one the good brother-in-law built for his sweet sister?"

"Sure," Stall said. "The man has his virtues."

"Not really." Stall heard Rudy Silber breathe some cigarette smoke, imagined him at the desk in his bare-necessities office adjusting his loud tropical tie. *Those Luckys are going to kill you.* "The new driveway bothered me. I don't know, after a while you develop a nose for what's not right. I went back over there at night to look at it, the driveway, and there were dogs."

"Dogs?"

"Yeah, two of them, just standing there. Staring at the new concrete."

"Staring?"

"Well, yeah, staring and sniffing. They were sniffing it, around the edges. So I got out of the car and went over there, and let me tell you, professor, you don't need the nose of a dog to smell it."

"It?"

"Roney."

"Oh Christ."

"I guess so. Anyway, the cops dug up the driveway, and there was your friend Roney, shot once through the forehead."

"Poor guy, he said they'd kill him for the money."

"The brother-in-law, Buddy Carwin, is over there with the cops right now explaining that a good Christian man, a guy who confines his carnal desires strictly to women, does not, as the Bible says, tolerate men who lie with men. That a good Christian man has a perfect right to end the life of a man who does that. Funny thing is, the guy was too good with his concrete. He put those expansion joints in the sections of the driveway so it wouldn't crack. They're made of felt. That's why the dogs could smell Roney."

"So he admits it?"

"As we speak. Thinks he did the right thing. They're holding the sister for luring Roney to a meeting with Carwin somewhere in the woods near Alachua. You'll read about it in the *Gainesville Sun* tomorrow."

"They killed him for the money."

"That's most of it, but the guy, our Buddy, he really believes he had the right to rid the world of his sister's queer husband."

"Thanks, Rudy."

"You bet, Tom."

There was a knock at Stall's door. When he opened it, a young blond man in a cheap black suit handed him a sealed envelope. As soon as the paper touched Stall's hand, the man said, "You're served," turned on his heel, and walked to the motorcycle parked in the driveway.

Stall stood in the open doorway in his undershirt looking down at the envelope. It carried the official seal of the Florida Legislative Investigation Committee. FLIC. The Johns Committee. Across the street, a neighbor boy mowing the lawn stopped to mop his brow with a red bandanna. The fragrant smoke from the lawn mower's engine mixed with the smell of mown grass drifted to Stall. The kid saw him in his doorway and waved. Stall moved the envelope to his other hand and waved back. The place where the sliver of broken glass had pierced his wrist hurt him. All this—the kid, the good smells of grass and a Briggs & Stratton engine—was normal life. Hell, it was Florida, where lawns were mowed in November. The envelope in Stall's hand was malignant insanity.

At the kitchen table, Stall opened it. On pain of contempt of the Florida state legislature, Stall was summoned to appear at nine o'clock the following morning at the Thomas Hotel to meet with investigators of the Committee. The summons spelled out in detail the penalties Stall might suffer if, for any reason except poor health or an act of God, he failed to appear at the appointed time. It said nothing about any offenses Stall might have committed, or any other reasons for the summons.

He tossed the official paper aside and considered his options. Should he hire an attorney? If he did, would the Committee allow the man to sit with him during the proceedings? Should he go it alone or not go at all? For a moment he imagined himself in the little blue Plymouth coupe crossing the Florida–Georgia line in a dash for Ohio where he would woo Maureen back to their marriage and somehow make a new life for himself, for them, in the small town of Oberlin. Hell, maybe there was a job for Tom Stall in the Oberlin College English Department. Stall would chafe, he was sure, at the smallness of it all compared to Gainesville, University City, but Oberlin College had her charms. A very fine school by most reports, and surely Tom Stall's credentials would impress the department chairman there, whoever the man was.

If he made his run for Ohio, surely the subpoena powers of the Florida legislature and their punishments would end at the state line. Surely the "full faith and credit" clause of the Constitution did not extend to the police powers of a spurious committee in a backward Southern state. But the things Stall's imagination saw—the wind from the Plymouth's vents bracing in his face as the little car pushed on reliably toward Ohio, the tearful then passionate reunion with Maureen—faded. He couldn't just leave his job, though he found little pleasure in it now. And what about the house? His other obligations? No, the dash for the state line and freedom was out of the question.

His choices, he decided, were two: he could obey the summons or he could defy it and take the consequences, whatever they were. Taking them did not mean lying down in their way. If he defied the subpoena, he'd fight the Committee in whatever way he could, and that included using the photos. In the end, part of what swayed Stall was simple curiosity. A part of him wanted to know what would happen in a room at the Thomas Hotel when the door was closed and the tape recorders were turned on and the questions came. What questions would they ask? Stall's child in France was a known thing now, and if the little girl in Paris lost him his chairmanship and even his job, well, he had always served in the first post at the pleasure of the president. In the second? He was tenured, but in these times he was no more secure than poor Gilson had been. He doubted that the Committee would use the child against him. What was it they wanted to ask him?

Stall called an attorney he and Maureen knew casually and told the man he was going before the Committee and might want to engage his services after he met with them. The attorney, Billy Davis, had represented some colorful clients, including a lurid murderer and a politician who had dipped his hands into the city till, and had a reputation for courtroom dramatics.

"Not before?" the lawyer asked.

"No, I don't think so."

"Just as well," the lawyer said. "I've heard that they sometimes deny lawyers admittance to their hearings. On what legal grounds, I have no idea. I think they make that decision on the basis of a determination of how much they can intimidate the subject of the inquiry."

"So, if they think they can leak damaging information about a person, they deny him legal counsel?"

"Basically, yes. But they don't formally deny it, and they certainly don't put anything about that in writing. They just advise against it. *You'll fare better with us if you don't show up with a lawyer*. That kind of thing."

Stall considered bravado. *Well, they can't intimidate me.* He thought better of it. Under the right circumstances, literature had taught him, anyone could be intimidated. "Thanks, Billy. I'll let you know how this turns out."

"You do that. And good luck."

FIFTY-SIX

Stall entered the Thomas Hotel for the second time, this time through the front door. A desk clerk told him that the Committee was conducting its business in a conference room on the second floor, front. Stall thanked the man and walked to the stairs, stopping for a moment to examine himself in the mirror of a machine that vended peanuts, gum, and cigarettes. His dark-blue suit and gray tie seemed appropriate, his eyes were clear, and his jaw was firmly set. *You look resolute but not belligerent.* He patted the hip pocket of his trousers. He had left the house that morning with Gilson's little pistol in his pocket, but then had thought better of it and returned the gun to the trunk in the garage. It might be against the law to take a gun to a meeting of the Committee. If they patted him down and found the weapon, he might buy himself trouble for no reason but a dubious feeling of security.

On the second floor, two conference rooms, A and B, faced the street. Stall knocked on both doors but got no answer. He was a few minutes early. He paced the hallway, checking his watch with each turn. A pale woman in a skirt and jacket the same sober blue as Stall's suit approached from the opposite stairwell. She wore black pumps and carried a black zipper portfolio. She stopped in front of Stall without greeting him, and reached into her coat pocket for a ring of keys. She opened the door of conference room B and held it for him.

Inside, Stall turned to thank her and ask her name, but she had already started down the hallway, her shoes softly brushing the carpet. What was this? Some Committee trick to chafe his nerves? Or was she just used to the appearances of nervous people and trying to be as unobtrusive as possible? Either way, she was ominous, her manor saying, *I am nothing. What follows me is your trouble.*

Stall glanced around the room. The polished mahogany conference table could seat ten or twelve, but only four chairs were arranged around it. There was nothing on the walls. The only other furnishings were ashtrays, an empty wastebasket, and, at the far end of the room under the window overlooking the street, a smaller mahogany table. The floor was carpeted in the same blue checked pattern as the hallway. Here and there Stall saw cigarette burns in the carpet and along the edges of the table. The room smelled of smoke. There were no signs of the room's purpose, certainly nothing that identified it as the star chamber of Charley Johns.

Cyrus Tate entered carrying a scuffed brown briefcase in one hand and a large black suitcase in the other. The suitcase was obviously heavy. Tate's massive shoulders tilted with its weight. Casually, he set the briefcase on the table before one of the chairs, then with a soft grunt he hefted the suitcase onto the small table by the window. He said nothing to Stall, only opened the suitcase and began to assemble what Stall knew from movies he had seen was a lie detector machine. Was it called a polygraph? Seeing it brought back scenes from films—men sweating as electrodes were attached to their skin; technicians in cones of bright light hunched over scrolling paper watching the swinging stylus that recorded truth or falsehood; detectives, usually the good guys but not always, sitting in adjacent rooms waiting for the results of tests, results that sometimes determined life or death.

It took Tate awhile to assemble and tune the machine, if that's what it was he did with the dials and switches, and Stall watched him at his work, thinking, *Surely that thing is not for me. What should I do if he wants to put me in that harness? Resist? Go along with it?* And of course, as Tate worked, Stall took in the spectacle of the man himself. A former linebacker for the Miami Hurricanes who looked like he could still play the position, a man whose trim waist, broad shoulders, and bulging arms and thighs proved either that he lived a clean life or was some sort of monster of inheritance. After the age of twenty-five, few men were granted what Tate had. The thick blond hair, the ruddy face, the big square jaw were billboard All-American, and Stall figured that was exactly how Tate saw himself. He remembered Tate sitting in his Anderson Hall office like he owned it, dismissively plucking a volume of poetry from the shelf, then returning it with a shrug while Stall sat behind his desk wondering if Tate carried a gun. He wondered it now and, with the man's back to him, looked for the telltale swelling under the arm or at the waist. Nothing was obvious.

Finished with the machine, Tate stepped back, looked at his work, then at the window whose curtain was half open. He leaned across the machine and drew the curtain closed. He turned to Stall and flashed a brilliant smile. "So, Professor Stall, we meet again."

"We do," was all Stall could think to say.

"Have a seat, please."

Stall made for a chair, but Cyrus Tate said, "No, over here, this one." He motioned to a chair with its back to the lie detector machine. Stall sat and Tate took the chair across from him.

Stall looked at the bare tabletop and wished he'd brought paper for his own notes. He always carried a pen. Briefly, he considered asking to borrow paper, but discarded the idea. Nothing, not the smallest thing, should put him in the Committee's debt.

"So, you take pictures, do you, Professor Stall?"

Stall said nothing, noting that there was no tape recorder, no way for Tate to make a transcript of what was said. Maybe the pale woman in the blue suit would return to write what they said. Stall felt his hands growing warm and moist. His coat seemed suddenly too tight, and the room too warm. He considered asking if the window might be opened.

"Who developed those pictures?" Tate's face held a pleasant expression, but his voice had gone low and cold.

"I don't know." Strictly, this was true. Allard Bryce had been the intermediary. He had not given Stall the name or location of the developer.

"You don't know? Who does know?"

"I won't reveal that."

"Didn't it occur to you that some lab technician might keep copies of the pictures for himself?"

Stall had thought about it, and hadn't much cared one way or the other. For one thing, Allard Bryce would not tell the lab who the two men in the photos were, and for another, in the photographic underground where pictures "for marriages that need spicing" were handled and, Stall supposed, occasionally traded on some sort of pornographic black market, it was caveat emptor. Let the buyer beware, or the lover, as the case may be. Treating Tate and Vane to a measure of their own method of intimidation seemed only right to Stall. But he hadn't anticipated sitting here talking to Cyrus Tate about it.

Tate said, "I need to know where that lab is and what you did with the negatives. Do you have them?"

"They're in a safe place."

"Sweet suffering Jesus, Stall, do you *know* what I'm willing to do to get those negatives?"

"No, but I can imagine."

"You should do that. Use your imagination." Tate seemed almost happy with Stall's answer.

"Look, Tate, how is this . . . interview supposed to go? Does the Committee have questions for me?" Stall looked at the closed door behind the man. "Charley Johns, does he have anything to ask me? I'm pretty sure he doesn't know about those photographs. Yet."

Tate leaned forward and rested his blond head in both hands. When he looked up there was a malice in his eyes that put Frank Vane's hatred to shame. Only once before had Stall seen a human face so full of violence—in the frozen fields of the Bulge. Those had been dead faces, twisted in their last agony, the last seconds of their killing and dying plain in their contorted features.

Words seethed through Tate's clenched teeth: "One more chance, Stall. Where are those negatives?"

Stall shook his head.

Cyrus Tate took a long, slow breath, rubbed his eyes with the backs of his hands. "All right. I'll have to put you on the machine." He rose and took the scuffed leather briefcase from the table in front of him.

Stall turned in his chair to watch Tate and the machine.

Tate said sharply, as though speaking to an animal, "No! Sit facing as you were. You are not permitted to watch this."

Thinking this absurd, Stall nevertheless obeyed. He closed his eyes and listened hard to what was happening behind him. But it was his nose that warned him too late.

There was a sudden bitter chemical odor, and then strong hands pressed a cloth to his mouth and nose. Stall fought, punching and clawing behind him at the arms that locked his head in their vise and held the reeking, smothering cloth to his face. He tried not to breathe and then he tried desperately to breathe. And then the table, the chairs, the wall in front of him began to fade into a universal gray. The last thing he saw through a shimmery gray haze was the door opening and a man entering the room. Stall could not make out the face, but saw the man's hands swinging from white cotton sleeves. They were black.

Stall came to consciousness with sensations of heat and motion, and the hum of wheels and road. He tried his limbs and knew that he was bound, his cheeks split painfully by a gag. His legs were pressed to his chest so that he could not test the dimensions of his prison by feeling with them. A loud thump flung his body upward and then dropped him again. *Christ, I'm in the trunk of a car.*

In the darkness, he could not tell if it was day or night, but he knew when the car turned off the pavement onto a rough dirt road. Before this turn, once or twice, he had heard the swish of cars passing or being overtaken. This vehicle was alone now on a bumpy dirt road. After a space, it stopped, and Stall heard faint sounds, birds chirping, wind in the trees. When he heard a key in the trunk latch, he closed his eyes. *Let them think I'm still drugged.*

"Get his legs."

Two men lifted him. He let his body loll as it would if he were still unconscious. The men carried him across a length of ground, up some steps, and one of them pressed his hip against Stall's shoulder while he groped in his pocket. A key rattled in a lock, a door swung open, and Stall was dropped onto the floor. It took all his concentration not to open his eyes in shock at the pain and surprise of being released two feet above the ground.

"In the chair." Stall recognized Cyrus Tate's voice.

The other man said, "Yes suh."

One of them cut the cord that bound Stall's legs and they lifted him into a chair. With new cords, they bound his chest to the back of the chair.

"I think he's awake. Or almost. Let's see." The slap was so violent that it rocked Stall's eyeballs in their sockets. He thought his cheekbone might be broken. The cry that erupted behind the gag in his mouth caused him to retch.

"Take that out of his mouth before he pukes into his lungs."

"Yes suh."

From behind Stall came two hands to release the gag from his mouth. With it out, Stall kept retching until he finally conquered the spasms, his eyes running with tears of nausea and pain.

"You can go on back now," Tate said. "Take the truck." He tossed keys to the Negro standing behind Stall.

"Yes suh."

The Negro walked past Stall to the door. His starched white kitchen smock was stained with food and blood. At the door, he stopped and looked back at Stall. The look that Stall and Allard Bryce exchanged was complicated. Bryce's eyes apologized for what he had done to Stall, but in them also was that unmistakable steel that Stall had seen the day they'd met. *He's a hard man when he wants to be*. Stall was obscurely proud when his eyes said only that he understood. The last lynching in Alachua County had been only thirteen years ago.

Stall sat watching Cyrus Tate roll up his sleeves while outside an old engine coughed and started up and the truck bounced away down the dirt road on sprung suspension.

For a long time, Tate beat Stall methodically and without heat, careful not to render Stall unconscious or to do too much damage. After a while, Stall took some comfort from the brutal delicacy of the beating, thinking that Tate probably did not plan to kill him. Only to rearrange his features permanently. Tate slapped and punched Stall's face, and then stopped to ask him, "Where are those negatives?"

When Stall only shook his head, Tate stood behind him and punched his kidneys through the ladder-back of the chair until Stall pissed himself. When the odor of urine and blood rose to the rafters of the old hunting cabin, Tate retreated to the small kitchen behind Stall and lit a cigarette. Stall heard him blow a plume of smoke and say, "If I let you out of here, will you take me to those negatives?"

Through blood and mucous, Stall said, "If they see me where I hid those negatives, they'll call the cops. You can't get them without me, and you can't take me with you like this."

"Well then, I'll have to get me somebody you don't want me to hurt and hold her while you take your ugly face in and get the negatives. How about Sarah Leaf, that queer Indian's wife? You like her, don't you?"

"I can take her or leave her alone."

Tate laughed quietly, smoked. "Sure you can. I'm going to let you think about this a while. Sit there in your piss and think. Maybe I don't really need you to get the negatives. Maybe that cute twist knows where they are. She was at your house for quite a while the other day. Maybe you told her."

"Why would I tell her? Why would I tell anybody, Tate? Think about it."

Carrying a pump shotgun, Tate walked from the kitchen to the front door. "It stinks in here. I'm going for a walk in the woods. Like I said, think about it."

They both knew Stall was past trying to get himself untied. He might even be past walking. Tate would not have to worry about finding him here when he returned.

Stall let his chin fall to his chest and tried to rest, to think. There was no use wasting time on regret for involving Sarah Leaf in these troubles. Tate had been watching Stall's house. It was only natural for him to assume that Stall and Sarah were confederates in the theft of those images—pictures of two men in bed at the Thomas Hotel. He sent out his heart to Sarah, wherever she was. He knew now that Tate would not hesitate to take her if he thought she would get him what he wanted. It occurred to him that the simplest thing, and maybe now the right thing, was to give up the negatives. Connor had the copies Stall had sent him. Vane had said that Connor had spoken to his father, so either Connor had shown the old Croesus the pictures, or had described them to him. This had been enough to change Frank Vane's course, if not his mind. Stall didn't think Tate would kidnap the president of the university and take him to a hunting cabin in the woods for a discussion like the one Stall had endured. How much more could he take? Was it the best strategy to keep taking this beating? When it ended, Tate might kill him and then go after Sarah.

The door opened and Tate stepped in, still carrying the shotgun.

He walked past Stall and stowed the gun, washed his hands, and came back to stand in front of the chair. *Here it comes again.*

The door opened. Rudy Silber stood in the rectangle of light with the blue-steel .38 in his right hand.

Tate spun, saw Silber, slowly raised his hands, then lowered them. "You know what, Silber? I don't think you're gonna use that gun."

The confederacy of these two flashed through Stall's mind—the night they had worked together to capture the image of Jack Leaf and Roney Tyler in a men's room. And how many other nights of entrapment and intimidation had they spent together? Stall remembered Rudy Silber's thumb and forefinger rubbing together. *Moulah, scratch, jack, money.* Why would Silber want to help Tom Stall now? It couldn't be money. Stall figured Tate was right: Silber would not use the gun.

Hands at his sides now, Tate walked past Stall's chair toward the kitchen. Did Silber see the pump gun?

Silber raised the .38 and aimed it across Stall's left shoulder. "Don't touch that, Tate. I mean it. You pick that up and I'll—"

Silber's pistol snapped twice, a sound Stall had hoped never to hear again. With all his strength, Stall rocked the chair backward and landed on his back, staring at the ceiling. The blast from the pump gun would have taken off Stall's head if he had not fallen. Some of it caught Rudy Silber's left arm as the PI aimed again and two more shots cracked. The shotgun . . . again, and this time its lethal pattern tore holes in the rafters above Stall. Dust and bits of pine sifted down into his eyes.

Allard Bryce walked into the cabin, took in the scene, and went to Silber, examining the buckshot holes in the left sleeve of his shirt. The holes oozed blood.

Silber looked down at his own arm, shook his head, "Shit!" and walked past Stall toward Tate. He held the gun now at his thigh. A tendril of smoke rose from its barrel. Stall could not see Tate, but figured by the way Silber held the pistol that there was no more threat from the shotgun. When Silber was out of Stall's sight, Bryce was in it, unfolding a barlow knife to cut Stall's bonds.

FIFTY-SEVEN

Allard Bryce helped Stall to Cyrus Tate's car and drove him to the hospital in Gainesville. Rudy Silber drove his own car to a gas station in the town of Alachua and called for an ambulance for Tate, who was still breathing. The PI told the dispatcher he'd wait for the ambulance at the station and guide the men in white smocks to the cabin in the woods. Leaning on Bryce and limping to Tate's car, Stall nodded to Rudy Silber, whose arm Stall could see was bloody but functioning. Silber lit a Lucky Strike and nodded back. The look on his face was frustration and anger. *He's wondering how things got so indiscreet so quickly.*

The young intern who had stitched Stall's wrist saw him limp in through the emergency entrance. "You again?"

Stall muttered, "Sober as a judge."

The good doctors X-rayed Stall's skull and kidneys and discovered a cracked cheekbone and two badly swollen but otherwise uncritical internal organs. They prescribed remarkably little—IV fluids, ice, and rest.

When Stall was established in a private room and punctured for intravenous saline, Rudy Silber visited him. Silber's arm was bandaged and in a sling. His bloody shirt was split from cuff to armpit.

The PI looked down at his slung arm. "Two pellets, through and through. Lucky they missed bone. If that shotgun didn't have a choked barrel, I'd probably be dead."

"You checked the barrel?"

"Sure."

"Tate?"

"He's a miracle of physical fitness, or I don't shoot as straight as I used to. Hit him four times, but nothing vital. Spoiled his looks, though."

"How so?"

"One slug took off half his left ear."

Tired and hurting, Stall could only shudder at this revelation.

"Well," Silber tapped the pack of Luckys in his shirt pocket, "they won't let me smoke in here, so I better get going. Hope you feel better soon."

"Wait a minute, Rudy. You can't just walk out of here and leave me pissing blood in a bedpan. Tell me what happened."

Silber put the cigarettes back in his pocket and took the chair by Stall's bed. "Allard called me from the Gulf station in Alachua, said he was afraid Tate would kill you and he'd get blamed."

"The milk of human kindness."

"Like I said when I gave you his number, the kind of trouble Allard can get into is bad."

"No, you said it was worse than the kind I could get into. You still think so?"

Silber shrugged. "Tate treated you pretty rough."

Stall had thought he understood what Allard Bryce might do to stay on the safe side of a man like Tate. Apparently, the list included pushing a chloroformed Tom Stall to the Thomas Hotel loading dock in a canvas laundry cart. "So you came to get me because Bryce asked you to? Or was it . . ." Stall rubbed his thumb and forefinger together. *Moulah, scratch, jack, money.*

Silber shook his head. "Neither.'

"What made you come?"

"I knew Tate would eventually figure out Bryce developed the film, and that wouldn't work out well for Bryce."

"So your loyalties are layered? You value Bryce's business more than you do Tate's?" *Or mine.*

"Well, I figure Bryce and me, we'll run our hotel business for as long as there's marriage. This thing with the Committee and chasing queers, it won't last."

"Let's hope not."

"I also knew Tate would figure out I helped you, and maybe he'd think I developed the film." Silber shrugged, leaving the rest to Stall's imagination. The shrug hurt his bandaged arm; he winced and adjusted the sling. "Actually, this'll surprise you. A cop I know called me. Buddy Carwin recanted his confession. Our Buddy says Tate killed Roney and delivered the body to him. Buddy only buried it under that beautiful driveway."

"You think it's true?"

"Why not? Tate had reasons as good as Carwin's to kill Roney. Roney knew what Tate was, and when things started to turn against the Committee, Tate figured he had to clean up his past. That included Roney and probably you too."

"And maybe Sarah Leaf."

"What?"

"Forget it. Just thinking."

"Saying what you think will get you in trouble." Silber sounded tired now.

Stall kept thinking. "So, they'll charge Tate with murder and kidnapping?"

"It looks that way. I can testify to the kidnapping."

"I didn't think Tate was that crazy." *Or that bad.*

"He probably figured he could confess it all to his Jesus and his soul would be clean."

"You don't believe in redemption, Rudy?"

Silber loosened his tie and pulled a gold Star of David amulet from under his shirt. "We don't believe you can kill one day and confess the next and you're okay. Tate should have paid more attention to the first five books."

Stall's eyes blurred. It hurt too much to lift a hand to wipe them. "You're a hero, Silber."

Rudy Silber shook his head again. He walked to the door, stopped, and turned. "Anybody you want me to call?"

Stall thought about it. "No, I guess not."

Silber's last words to Stall were, "This uses up your credit with me."

Stall would call Maureen tonight at seven as usual and hope she couldn't hear the incessant pinging of the elevator bell down the hall. It would worry her.

Stall called the university's personnel department and told them he was under the weather and would be out for a few days. He asked them to send a temporary clerical worker to his office to answer the phone. Later, he dictated to her research assignments for his classes. She was to type them up and hand them out to his students.

"If anyone asks, tell them I'm all right, just a touch of the flu or something." But who would ask? Stall was an exile from the fellowship of the English Department.

He hadn't counted on the *Gainesville Sun*. The newspaper led with, "Gruesome Discovery Under Driveway," followed this with, "Three in Custody Pending Murder Charges," then a day later, "Murder and Kidnapping of Professor Linked." And then Stall's hospital room was Grand Central Station. After the first reporter made it to Stall's bedside, notebook and camera in hand, hospital administrators did their best to keep the floor from being overrun. Stall, who was feeling worse on his second day in bed than he had on his first, told reporters as little as possible. Yes, he knew Cyrus Tate, knew that Tate was the Committee's chief investigator. Yes, he had been interviewed by Tate on behalf of the Committee. When reporters asked why the Committee had summoned Stall, his answer was only, "University business." When asked to elaborate, he refused and pleaded his pain and doctors' orders.

"Why did Cyrus Tate take you to that cabin in the woods?"

"I don't know. You'll have to ask him."

Stall's sketchy answers only whetted the paper's appetite. Scandal must be here somewhere. If it wasn't in Stall's testimony to the Committee, then it was somewhere else. Stall would never mention the photos to anyone. As far as he was concerned, they were Connor's to use as he thought best. He doubted that Rudy Silber would talk about them. Humdrum hotel transom photography was one thing; Silber's work for the Committee, men's room photography, was another thing altogether. That left Vane and Tate. The big blond killer was somewhere in this hospital. Was he talking? If so, what was he saying?

A detective named Harlan Morrison appeared at Stall's bedside. Morrison was about forty, painfully thin, and wore a brown suit that had fit him when he was twenty pounds heavier. He examined Stall through small pale-blue eyes.

"Silber says you're not a bad guy for an egghead."

"Right now I'd trade this head for an egg."

"Yeah, looks like he worked you over pretty good. The question is, why?"

"Didn't Silber tell you?"

"Some of it. Let's see what you have to say."

Stall had thought it through. "Roney Tyler told me he thought Tate might kill him. Tate knew that. He killed Roney, and he figured he had to get rid of me too."

"So, why'd he bother to beat the hell out of you like that?"

"I don't know. Maybe he liked it."

"Why do you think Tate killed Roney?"

"Because they worked together for the Committee. Roney knew things about Tate. Tate didn't want those things to come out."

"Things?"

Stall waited in silence. They both knew what interested the Committee. The detective shook his head in disgust—at what thing or things, Stall was not entirely sure.

"So, your story is that Tate invited you to the Thomas Hotel—"

"Subpoenaed me. That's public record."

"So, you went to the Thomas Hotel, then he drugged you and took you to the cabin in the woods west of Alachua?"

"If chloroform is a drug, then he drugged me, yes. The rest of what you said is true."

"Then he beat you, and then Rudy Silber intervened?"

"That's right."

"How did Silber know where you were?"

"He told me someone called him."

"Who?"

"That I don't know. I assume someone who worked with Tate. Someone who got cold feet about what Tate was doing, someone who didn't want me dead."

"And this someone, you don't know this person?"

"I do not."

"You never saw this person?"

"I was drugged. Then I was tied to a chair and beaten."

"All right, Professor Stall. I'll check this with Rudy Silber and with Mr. Tate when I can. I hope you feel better soon."

"Thank you, Detective Morrison."

* * *

Cyrus Tate died the next day of a raging sepsis. One of Rudy Silber's bullets had nicked a bowel, and the doctors had missed the leak. Fecal matter had polluted Tate's system so quickly that penicillin and the big man's vitality could not conquer the poison.

FIFTY-EIGHT

Sarah Leaf came, held Stall's hand briefly, and encouraged him to stay in the hospital until he was completely healed. "You're quite the subject of conversation around town, as far as this bookkeeper can tell. Of course, I don't travel in university circles anymore."

"What are people saying?"

"It's more about what they're asking. The big question seems to be, what the hell were you doing in a cabin in the woods with that goon Cyrus Tate?"

"Isn't it clear in university circles that I wasn't there because I wanted to be?"

"He kidnapped you, Tom. That's not the sort of thing that happens to your average English professor. University circles can think of a million reasons he did it, and none of them reflect well on you."

To hell with them. "Maybe I'll write a book about it. True crime. I can't seem to get anything else done."

By the third day, Stall was well enough to talk his way out of the hospital. He signed papers stating that he had been advised to stay longer.

At home, he iced his face, drank water to flush his kidneys, and typed his résumé, adding to it his recent promotion to chairman. Pecking carefully at the battered old Royal, he remembered Maureen using it for her application to teach at Kirby Smith Elementary School. He remembered the glow in her skin and spark in her eyes as she had pulled the completed application from the typewriter and brought it to him. It seemed a long time ago.

Stall mailed the article on Graham Greene's conversion that Martha Kenny had typed for him to *Modern Fiction Studies*. Then he walked all the way from the downtown post office to Anderson Hall, preparing his mind for his meeting with Fred Parsons and Ted Baldwin. He had told them to meet him in an empty classroom on the fourth floor where he was pretty sure there would be no interruption. When each had asked in his own way why Stall wanted this meeting, Stall's answer was, "To plan the future of the department."

Stall and Parsons had not spoken since their last meeting in Stall's office when Parsons had offered his deal—Sophie Green's tenure for Stall's silence about the letter.

Stall arrived early and arranged four chairs in a circle where they could not be seen from the doorway. Baldwin came breezing in a minute later wearing his best Oxford don outfit, a sea-green Harris Tweed coat, knitted black tie, and gray flannel "bags." His expensive brogues were in high shine. Seeing Stall already seated, he called, "Ahoy, Cap'n Stall. About time we got around to putting the old spyglass to the future."

Stall nodded. "Hello, Ted. Didn't bring my spyglass, but I've got some important things to say to you and Fred."

"Ah, well, I suppose you'll give me no hint? We'll wait for our dear Frederick to—"

And there was Fred Parsons, putting his head warily through the door as though some missile might fly at him.

"Come in, Fred, and join us." Stall gestured to the chair next to Baldwin.

When Parsons was seated, his wide hips snug in the chair built for youth, he, and then Ted Baldwin, looked at the empty chair in the circle, and then at Stall, who stood as Sophie Green entered carrying a manila folder.

The double takes Sophie Green received would have been the stuff of high comedy had it not been for the atmosphere of malice and dread that filled the room. Stall wondered what the two men were thinking. That this gathering had something to do with Professor Green's prospects for tenure? A satisfied expression had settled on Parsons's upturned face. Ted Baldwin, in keeping with his nautical metaphors, was completely at sea. He looked from face to face to face with exaggerated confusion. When Sophie Green was settled, serene and grave in a black pre-Raphaelite dress, the folder centered on the small desk in front of her, Stall sat and said what he'd planned on his long walk from the post office.

"We're here to talk about the letter that was sent to President Connor denouncing Roland Gilson and about another matter. Professor Green?"

Without a word, Sophie Green passed the file to Ted Baldwin. When Baldwin opened it, Fred Parsons groaned like a man who had been knifed in the belly. A man who knew he had only seconds to live. Parsons recognized Gilson's article. Baldwin did not.

Keeping his voice low and even, Stall said, "Fred, I take it this is the thing you would not tell me at your party. Your second reason for writing that letter."

Parsons nodded, groaned again, and sank in his chair. Stall had reasoned that Parsons probably would have tried to brazen it out, if Sophie Green had not been present. But the fact that she, Baldwin's colleague in the medieval period, had brought the article with her made lying futile.

Baldwin still seemed confused, though now not comically. Sophie Green had surmised that when Baldwin had supported Gilson for the job at Florida, he had forgotten the name of the obscure scholar whose work he had stolen. Three people watched as Baldwin leafed through the folder, found the passages he had stolen underlined, and then moved on to the appearance of those same passages in an article that bore his name. He shoved himself up out of the chair. "I don't have to sit here and—"

"Sit *down*, Ted!"

Baldwin fell back, shocked at Stall's merciless tone.

Quietly, Stall went on: "Professor Green discovered this. She wasn't looking for it. She was doing research, and as luck or fate would have it, she found Gilson's article, and Ted, she had read yours as a matter of courtesy to a senior colleague." He let this sink in.

Parsons and Baldwin did not look at each other.

"So now, Fred, tell us why you wrote the letter."

"I wrote it to protect a friend."

Baldwin's eyes rolled at the sad sweetness of the misbegotten motive, at the always-possible prospect of things going terribly wrong. He huffed out a miserable chuckle.

"Anything else, Fred?"

"I wanted to protect the department. We'd lost Jack. We would have lost Ted. And adding this charge to Ted's book, well, that would have been too much. We would have looked like a bunch of . . ."

"So the practical thing was to sacrifice Gilson?"

"I suppose so."

Stall nodded grimly and let the silence stretch on. "All right," he finally said, "Fred, you're guilty of forgery, and Ted, you signed your name to another man's work. Professor Green and I have decided to let you two resign at the end of the term rather than make this public. Fred, if you truly do care about the reputation of the department, you'll acknowledge the *practicality* of this offer."

"*You* have decided? You and *this girl* have decided?" Baldwin's face had recovered an angry red.

"That's right, Ted, and don't try our patience. You know very well that worse things than resignation can happen to you now. And I'll add this condition to our offer: if either of you ever tries to teach again anywhere, this *woman* and I will bring all of this to light. Is that understood? You're finished in this profession."

After another silence, Parsons and Baldwin looked at each other like two men waiting for the rope. Their expressions were weariness and resignation but Stall did not see blame. They were in this together, friends, he supposed, to the end.

"Understood." It was Baldwin.

"Yes." Parsons.

Stall stood and looked at the door. Parsons and Baldwin walked out. After a space, the fire door at the end of the hallway opened and shut. Stall sat again with Sophie Green and the silence grew.

"Stephen told me about California."

"Yes, lovely Berkeley."

"Ever been there?"

"Not yet. I'm a New Yorker, through and through."

"Will you follow him?"

"Not sure. He hasn't asked me yet." Voluntarily or otherwise, her right hand caressed the empty third finger of her left. "Anyway, I have to stay here at least until June to . . . see this through."

She meant this mess with the medieval period. Baldwin leaving in a few weeks and Gilson's replacement still not chosen. Maybe Stall could persuade Eugen Brugge to stay on through the spring and teach Ted Baldwin's classes.

She looked at Stall with a new speculation. "What about you? Will you stay or is this place poisoned for you now?"

Stall shrugged. Time did its work. Things changed. "I don't know either. There are good reasons to stay and good ones to leave."

"You could have made it a condition of Parsons's removal that he admit he wrote that letter. Wouldn't that have removed the poison from the well?"

"Maybe, and of course I thought about that, and at one time I wanted it, but it would put Jim Connor in a bad place at a time when he may be trying to do some good." *Using those photos to beat back the Committee.*

"So you're willing to stay here with people believing you're a rat?"

"For the greater good, maybe so. And, of course, you've unfinked me. That matters a lot."

"I'll tell people what I know."

"I'd rather you didn't. It's just a roundabout way of muddying the waters for Connor."

As she thought about this, Stall looked up at the sagging beams in the ceiling, the dusty lights, imagining the ancient wiring and plumbing hidden by the plaster and acoustic tile. The building seemed to know his thoughts, to sigh and shift in its old age. Someday a spark or a careless cigarette would burn this pile of linseed-soaked timber and brick to the ground.

Sophie Green stood and together she and Stall removed the chairs from their circle and put them back into the classroom's orderly rows. They parted in the hallway, she to her enviable office and Stall to the chairman's redoubt where he worked through his days as the servant of his faculty, their students, and the ideal of a university.

FIFTY-NINE

In late November, in what any scholar knew was record time, Stall's Graham Greene article was rejected by *Modern Fiction Studies*. That a series of so-called referees, scholars versed in Greene's work or at least in modern British fiction, should agree so quickly that the piece was unworthy of publication was a shock. The usual mildly apologetic and formally emphatic reports came with the rejection letter. All of the readers' reports used the word *derivative*. Stall's article did not break new ground. Seeing this, he allowed himself an extra martini before dinner and the vivid fantasy of hunting down and murdering his anonymous detractors. The worst of it: this had been exactly Fred Parsons's prediction after he had read only the title of the article.

Alight with the possibilities of the third martini, Stall set the rejected article aside and removed from his old briefcase the various drafts of other studies for which he had hopes. He promised himself that he would pick one and get to work on it with fresh energy. He'd taken his updated résumé to a local print shop and fifty copies rested on the dining room table beside the briefcase smelling pleasantly of printer's ink and possibility. He hadn't mailed one yet.

In their nightly conversation, Maureen made up his mind.

"Corey needs her father. I can't in good conscience keep you away from her any longer. I don't want to come back to Gainesville. Ever. I want you to come here, or we'll live somewhere else not too far from my parents." Was she keeping her parents in reserve for the news of any other children Stall might have lurking about?

Stall's voice had been reduced, for days it seemed, to the dull repetition of brief affirmatives—"Uh-huh," "I see," "Sure," "Mmm." He'd long ago used up all of the seductive poetry that was in him to woo his woman back, and anyway, Maureen's susceptibility to wooing was near its end. Stall told himself that this was not entirely his fault. She'd been sick so long that only practicalities mattered to her.

"Tom, I can never feel the same way about you as I once did. But I love you. I've asked myself a hundred times if I do, and the answer is always yes, damn it. I love you, and Corey needs you, so we have to get back together. I don't know what will happen after that. We'll just have to see."

Was this a ray of light? The words were given in the same dull monotone that for many days had been the sound of their seven o'clock calls. Sometimes after they hung up Stall was angry. *Shouldn't I have something to say about our distance from your parents? Must I always beg?* She might be surprised to hear his reservations about the future. The anger didn't last. The word *duty* drove it from his mind.

Finally, she said, "And I want to see that little girl in France and her mother too, I think. It's just not right that you're not doing something to care for that child."

In a wave of misery, Stall saw himself working two jobs, night and day, to support two establishments, American and French. But hadn't this been inevitable since a part of Stall had met a part of Brigitte in a narrow Paris bed? Frank Vane wouldn't or couldn't keep sending money. His money was as poisoned as his thinking.

Stall had imagined someday taking Maureen to Paris. Most couples dreamed of such a trip, but certainly not this way. Not to seek out a love child and her mother.

"Good night, Tom. You think about things."

What did she think he had been doing? "Good night, Maureen. All I can say is that I love you."

Stall made good on his resolve to talk with Martin Levy.

When the young man sat across the desk from him, Stall opened with, "Mr. Levy, I've felt that I owe you an apology for being a little harsh with you at the beginning of this term. I regret that and want you to know it." He waited.

Levy didn't seem surprised. "So I should thank you? Be humble?"

Stall smiled at the honesty, couldn't help shaking his head at the brass. "I'll take whatever's in there, Mr. Levy."

Levy looked up at the ceiling as if taking inventory of his feelings.

"Here's something. You think I need your apology, and you need to give it to me. I don't question your need, but I'm fine without it."

Vistas of what might be said now opened before Stall, including the very practical, *What if you need something from me later, a recommendation, a favor? Wouldn't common politeness serve you better?* "I guess you're right. I needed to apologize. It's how I was brought up. And I'm fine with your response, even though I'm sure you don't need me to be fine with it."

Martin Levy stood. "Are we finished?"

"Yes, Mr. Levy, we are."

Levy went to the door, turned back. "You can do one thing for me, Professor Stall. Tell me the truth: did you fink on Dr. Gilson for being a homosexual?"

Stall shook his head.

Levy examined Stall's face for a few seconds. "I believe you. It's odd, but I do."

Jesus, Stall thought, *too much Nietzsche? Fatal at an early age*. "Your belief cheers me, Mr. Levy. And here's something for you: I'm the underdog now." He had scars on his face to prove it. "You should go forth and defend me."

"I'll think about that one."

On a whim, Stall picked up a copy of the *Independent Alligator*. He didn't recognize the name of the kid who was now its managing editor. The lead story was about Tom Stall resigning his post in the English Department and leaving Gainesville for parts unknown. It was a long story whose main purpose was to regurgitate the seamy details of Stall's kidnapping and the killing of the Committee's investigator, Cyrus Tate, by local private investigator Rudolph Silber. The story quoted several people who had been interrogated by Tate at the Thomas Hotel. To a person, they described Tate as unrelenting, sadistic, and salacious. One victim told that for hours she had been moved back and forth between the interrogation table and the lie detector machine and threatened with the disclosure of her secrets to her family until she was a sweat-sodden wreck, arms raw from repeated applications of the machine's wires and cuff. She had given up names, she said, and for this she was eternally shamed.

For balance, the story quoted supporters of the Committee who said that Tate had been an upstanding public servant, or at least a man who had done an unpleasant duty for his state and nation. The article closed with speculation about Tom Stall. Stall, it said, was the mystery man of the Tate affair. The true nature of his involvement in the Committee's activities either as victim or as clandestine agent, or possibly even some kind of hero, had not yet come to light. But it would, the *Independent Alligator* promised, in a prophetic closing paragraph. The newspaper had asked Stall for his version of the story of that day in the cabin in the woods with Tate and Rudy Silber. He had declined to give it. They had followed with a request for his final thoughts on the Committee. He knew they wanted his ringing denunciation of Charley Johns and all of his minions. He was sorely tempted. In the end he decided that his trip to the Thomas Hotel, his climb up that ladder with the camera in his hand, his theft of the images of two men who quite possibly loved each other—this had disqualified him from any public statements about the Committee. He had done some dirty work. He had given the photographs to Connor and it was the president's job now to deliver a death blow to the Committee, if such were his desire or his expediency. Stall believed that Connor would handle things quietly. Frank Vane's admission that his wealthy father had seen the photographs was as good an indication as any that Connor would work that way. Connor had said nothing to Stall about who else had seen the photographs or who else, if anyone, had used them and to what end.

Stall had found that as he walked the streets of Gainesville, people sometimes stopped to watch him pass. He was never sure if they looked at him with eyes of malice or admiration or just simple curiosity. He was sure of one thing: the newspaper photos of him lying in a hospital bed, IV-punctured and half-witted with pain, had made a lasting impression on his fellow Gainesvillians. He longed to have his privacy back. Privacy was from the beginning what he had most fervently wished for everyone. For Jack Leaf and Roney, for Sarah Leaf and her boys, for Eugen Brugge, and even for Frank Vane and Cyrus Tate, though fate had made it Stall's grim duty to expose them.

After sustaining its first wounds in Miami, the Johns Committee, like its predecessor, the House Un-American Activities Committee, died a rather quick death of its own ineptitude, vice, and crime. And the episode of Tom Stall and Cyrus Tate had played a part in the final act of the sordid drama. HUAC had died when the lawyer Joseph Welch had asked Joe McCarthy, "Have you no sense of decency?" And when Edward R. Murrow had exposed McCarthy for a drunken fool on national television. The two men were heroes. As far as Stall knew, Florida had no heroes, unless they were the Committee's victims, whose courage was to protest or simply to endure. For Stall, Jack Leaf was a hero.

From the moment of Leaf's walk in the air, Gainesville had wondered why. Tom Stall knew more of the answer than anyone else alive. Surely it was the common fear of exposure that had caused Jack Leaf to walk. Simple logic gave that answer. But Stall knew that the larger part of the answer could be summed in two words, *Roney Tyler*. Jack Leaf had died for love. As Jack had seen it, it was only a matter of time before Cyrus Tate, who had used Roney to expose Jack, would turn on the instrument of his persecution. Roney had seen that Tate enjoyed his work a little too much, and in a way that his fellow Committee members would have considered unhealthy. Jack knew that eventually Roney would have to go. Jack could not have known that his suicide would bring the machinery to life that led to the end of the Committee, and of Cyrus Tate, but he could have hoped it. Stall believed he'd gone out that window with this hope in his heart. And Jack had provided Roney with the money he'd need to make his run for freedom. Some said there had been less kindness in Jack's heart for Sarah and their boys than for a garage mechanic named Roney. Stall's thinking was that twenty thousand dollars was a lot but it was neither the end nor the beginning of the world for Sarah. It could have meant life for Roney if the mechanic had better calculated the evil that surrounded him.

Stall and Sophie Green had a farewell lunch at the Primrose Inn. They ate and drank well—fried chicken, Stall his martini, and Green her wine—and found that there was not much left to say. Politically, they were still far apart. She was a true believer in historical inevitability, and Stall believed in the soul, either Emerson's and Whitman's, or his Presbyterian father's, or both. It would be the work of a lifetime to decide which it was or if in some grand convolution it could be both. In either case, history for him was not determined, it was a man's choice, and a soul could be lost in an instant. The soul of Whitman's creed, the one to which all men furnished their parts, was still, he told Sophie Green, despite all that had happened, his own best hope. Her response was this: "The only difference I see between Whitman's crowd on the ferry and Marx's masses is that all the poet's talk of souls conceals from the common man his main problem, which is economic." They were stuck. After their second drink and some thoughtful silences, Tom Stall and Sophie Green agreed that one thing would always bind them: their determination to make good their promise to Fred Parsons and Ted Baldwin. If either man ever tried to teach again, there would be hell to pay. This bond had been forged in their shared reverence for the creed of scholarly honesty.

Stall had sent his résumé to every college and university within a hundred miles of Oberlin. So far, there had been only tentative or contingent expressions of interest, though all of his fellow chairmen had thanked him sincerely for his interest and many had praised his credentials, especially his doctorate from the University of Virginia. If it was necessary, he had resolved to drive those hundreds of miles to show his honest American face to these chairmen and hope that his goodness and his love of the world, sorely tested but whole, would persuade them in his favor

Early one morning, Stall locked the front door of the house up the hill from the new law school. He stood on the front porch looking at the yard, and both ways up and down the street. More than once he had thought that he might live in this house to the end of his days. Indeed might die in it. He pocketed the key. A duplicate was in the purse of the real estate agent who had promised to sell the place quickly and at a fair price.

As Stall drove north out of Gainesville on US 441, the wind blew pleasantly through the little Ford coupe's vents, just as it had in his fantasy of flight. The air was fragrant with the spring that Florida's February promised. Winter waited in Ohio, but he hoped not in his wife's heart. At least not forever.

Acknowledgments

Once again, I am indebted to Jamie Gill for her resourceful and insightful library research. Thanks also to the University of Florida, and especially to the late Smith Kirkpatrick, for my seven years of apprenticeship in the English language, to the Pretenders (Dean Jollay, Gale Massey, and Louise Weaver) for helpful criticism and commentary, to Jack Vanek, MD, for vital medical information, to Norm Barker for some good catches, and to John Phelps for his deep knowledge of Florida statutes.

Thanks to Johnny Temple and his crew at Akashic Books for another wonderful journey to publication, and to my literary agent Ann Rittenberg for many years of thoughtful and patient guidance.

And, as always, a loving thanks to Kathy, my ideal reader and editor of first and last resort who grows in art and grace as my poor skills decline.